WHISPERS AMONG THE RUINS

Lori B Hines

ISBN-13: 9781522826972
ISBN-10: 1522826971

1

The two-inch-long tarantula hawk wasp, blueblack metallic body with orange wings, grabbed a plate-sized tarantula by one of its hairy front legs, flipping it over in a split second. The large wasp carefully probed its victim's abdomen then crawled onto the spider's stomach. A few seconds later, the tarantula's legs stopped moving.

The wasp sat atop its victim, drinking the viscous fluid oozing from the spider's recent wound. A minute later, the tarantula hawk climbed back down onto the ground and began to drag the spider away by its abdomen from the location of the attack.

Lorelei Healy, psychic medium and paranormal investigator, watched within two feet of the surreal scene, her long blonde hair falling around her while she leaned in to observe.

"That's only the beginning," Joe said.

Lorelei jumped. Joe Luna, Native American shaman and FBI agent, approached from behind, intently watching the morbid play between insects unfold.

Ian's son Paul, a very grown up eleven year old, walked around inside a ceremonial kiva, part of Cutthroat Castle group of ruins. The four of them had escaped to the Four Corners from Phoenix, each running from their own monsters and memories.

"The female tarantula hawk stung and paralyzed the tarantula. But that's only the beginning. She's going to take her victim back into her own burrow to lay a single egg on the spider's body and seal her underground chamber. When the wasp larva hatches, it will rip a small hole in the spider's abdomen, then plunge into its belly, feeding voraciously, yet avoiding vital organs for as long as possible to keep it fresh. After several weeks, the larva pupates. Finally, the wasp becomes an adult, and tears open the spider's belly to get out."

Joe looked over at Lorelei. His dark facial features serious, eyes fervid. "All while the tarantula is alive."

She shuddered.

The tarantula hawk continued to drag its victim toward a circular, partially collapsed stone tower, part of the Cutthroat Castle unit of ruins at Hovenweep National Monument in Colorado; one of six prehistoric Puebloan-era villages spread over a twenty-mile expanse of mesa tops and canyons along the Utah-Colorado border on a portion of the Great Sage Plain known as Cajon Mesa.

Lorelei thought of Shannon, who would have run screaming from the encounter with the arachnid. Shannon, Joe's ex-girlfriend, had turned out to be a goddess of the Universe named Galiena. Shannon had forgotten her true identity on her many years on earth, until Mattie, Annie and Dagon had returned for her the same day of Lorelei and Ian's wedding six months ago. None of them had gotten over losing her, especially Joe. He had planned on proposing to Shannon the very night Dagon returned for her.

Joe's gaze became solemn as it diverted from pinion-juniper forest scattered throughout the ancestral Puebloan towers and kivas to the blue sky and cotton ball-like cumulus clouds. He must have been thinking about Shannon again. Perhaps hoping she might return.

Her husband Ian Healy, Wiccan, healer and paranormal investigator, placed his hand on Joe's shoulder.

Joe turned and smiled. A half-hearted, forced smile.

Joe and Ian followed Lorelei from a partially collapsed round tower to Cutthroat Castle, a unit of ruins built on top of a boulder, with a circular tower in the center and two square buildings on either side. Smaller pueblos had been built underneath the shade of the massive boulder, surrounded by pinion, juniper and prehistoric rubble.

She knew most of these structures were built between A.D. 1200 and 1300. There were many theories regarding the use of the striking towers at Hovenweep, which archaeologists thought to be associated with kivas. Or they might have been celestial observatories, defensive structures, storage facilities, civil buildings, homes or any combination of the above.

Lorelei noticed Paul approach a two-foot-wide crack between two boulders on which Cutthroat Castle had been built. He stepped closer, staring down into the darkness. His gaze transfixed, Paul leaned forward, inch-by-inch.

Misty tendrils reached up from the darkness. The dark grey shape moved carefully, deliberately in the direction of Paul.

"Paul, be careful." Ian raced out of one of the Cutthroat Castle structures to catch Paul before he could fall in.

The mass had formed fingers, grabbing for Paul's arm. "Ian, hurry."

The three of them were tied together in ways most people couldn't imagine, each having their own distinct abilities. Paul had been trying to deny his dream reality and bizarre ties to Lorelei and Ian, but unfortunately, spirits didn't care. This could be an attempt from the afterlife to connect with Paul.

Seeing through Paul's eyes, Lorelei observed the rubble of remains below the boulder where Cutthroat Castle had been built. A three-inch piece of pottery lay just outside the air intake. Dark orange lines extended the length of the potsherd. She recognized the object as a brilliant three-inch piece of Tsegi Orange-Ware pottery created by the Anasazi around A.D. 1050.

Breathless, Lorelei stood in front of the circular tower, opposite the crevasse where Paul stood. He stared intently into the dark aperture, trembling violently.

Paul wouldn't move. Lorelei realized it wasn't that he didn't *want* to. He *couldn't* move.

Ian approached him from behind and pulled him back to safety. "Hey, buddy. You need to be more careful. What are you picking up on?"

Lorelei threw her backpack on the ground and jumped across the split in the rock.

"Ian, something has a hold of him." She tried to shake him out of his possessed state, but his body was stiff and unresponsive.

Paul's eyes were wide, his body shook and his face was ghostly pale. Lorelei gazed into Paul's eyes. They weren't his usual brown. They were a dark green. And his eyes weren't as round and bold as they should be.

"Oh, Paul," she whispered. She gently took his hand in hers. A few seconds after she touched him, a brief but fierce breeze blew through her. She gasped. The force threw her toward the chasm where Paul had been staring.

Ian grabbed for her. She desperately reached out, but something pulled her backward. She could feel arms around her waist as she slid through the mysterious aperture of Cutthroat Castle.

The last thing Lorelei noticed before she lost sight of Paul, Ian and the ruins of Cutthroat Castle was Paul's eyes had transformed back to beautiful, big and brown.

"Dad!" Paul screamed, as Lorelei vanished from his view.

"I saw! Get away from here!"

Paul ran past the round tower and another small pueblo next to it. His father took a big leap off the Cutthroat Castle boulder.

Ian and Paul raced around the bottom of the boulder where Lorelei had fallen, but she wasn't there. They both looked around frantically.

Joe quickly ran into the remnants of a tiny pueblo under Cutthroat Castle. He came out a few seconds later, throwing his hands in the air. "Where the hell could she be?" Sweat accumulated on Ian's forehead. His shaky right hand wiped it off in frustration as he slipped between the two boulders. "She fell right here."

Ian hugged Paul fiercely and placed firm hands on either side of Paul's shoulders. "I'm so glad you're all right. But I need to know. What did you see down in the crevice?"

Paul could see the tendrils reaching for him and hear the whispers emanating from the opening between boulders. Yet he couldn't react or move away.

"I didn't see anything. One minute I was looking around, and the next I felt totally different, like someone else. Dad, I'm sorry!"

Paul knew Lorelei attracted many spirits, both bad and good. He wondered if a spirit from the other side wanted to lure him to get to Lorelei. Or if it could have something to do with Peter and his mother. Even though they were no longer of this world, could they somehow be trying to obtain revenge because Lorelei had a big part in ending Peter and Emily's plan to steal Lorelei's powers?

Paul glanced up at his father. He couldn't bear the thought of Lorelei disappearing again and he knew his dad wouldn't be able to either. And it would be Paul's fault.

Joe shook his head and placed his hand around Ian's arm. Joe slipped through the opening that had transfixed Paul and taken Lorelei.

Paul knew Joe was using his shaman abilities to try to get a sense of what might have happened to Lorelei. His father held Paul close to him; so close Paul could feel his father's frenzied heartbeat.

A few minutes later, Joe re-emerged, brushing dirt and debris off his jeans. He slowly stood up and turned to face them.

"I'm picking up on a rather strong sense of desperation. Someone wanted attention and if they couldn't get it from Paul, they were going to steal Lorelei. I have no idea where she's gone though."

"What?" Ian yelled. "She has to be somewhere."

"I don't know." Joe removed his cowboy hat with a turquoise bolo tie on the front. "Someone, or something, has taken her on a journey to another plane."

2

Lorelei clawed helplessly against a dirt wall. She couldn't see who or what had abducted her. She tried to look behind to see the arms that held her firmly around her waist.

"You don't have to do this," she screamed. "I can help you without all this." The pressure from the strong hands eased up for a few seconds. She stopped moving. Lorelei could feel some sort of barrier behind her. Then the invisible arms grabbed her again.

Suddenly, she couldn't breathe. No light. No sound. Dirt collapsed in around her.

I'm being buried alive.

Just when she thought her lungs would collapse, she was pulled into the open and another small passage. Lorelei glanced up to see a wall of dirt and rock. She realized she had been dragged through a solid obstacle. Yet it still remained intact.

How can this be happening?

Whatever took her didn't feel malicious. It seemed desperate and scared. She wondered if it was the same entity that had taken over Paul. If so, had the spirit used Paul to lure Lorelei in?

She thought of Paul and Ian. *How long is this adventure going to last? Does this have anything to do with the ancient race I first encountered in Dragoon, Arizona, who gave me my astral and teleportation abilities?*

The spirit yanked her into an open, circular room thirty feet by twenty—a chamber with a lit fire and a roof of solid wooden beams corbelled into each other, which formed a dome held up by four massive pine tree pillars. Smoothly plastered walls covered the stones that shaped the structure.

I'm in a kiva.

"Where am I?" Lorelei asked. "Is this still Cutthroat Castle?"

No response. The fire crackled and popped repeatedly, throwing flame shadows across the perimeter of the kiva. Lorelei could see other shapes and figures moving about within the dimly lit building.

Her abductor had released her from its grip. Standing up cautiously, Lorelei felt drawn toward the blaze. Writhing, licking flames transformed into fiery, flowing red hair. Then a familiar face appeared. Someone she hadn't seen in six months.

A sob escaped from her throat. *I'm delirious. I must be seeing things.* Lorelei wiped her eyes, but Galiena still stared back through the pyre.

"Am I still at Hovenweep?" Lorelei asked.

Galiena nodded her head slowly, embers dripping from her bangs to land silently in the pit below.

This was no vision. Shannon, who had been Lorelei's best friend, had somehow appeared before her in a way she could never have imagined. Though she couldn't possibly understand Galiena's place in the universe and her relation to Dagon, Lorelei knew it was something big.

Lorelei glanced up at the perfectly round walls. Dark, enigmatic silhouettes danced around the room, some hopping on one foot with elaborate headdresses. They surrounded her. Her friend's face faded along with the fire. Then the ceremonial images disappeared.

Blood-curdling screams stifled the air and shadows of phantoms bearing axes and arrows pursued spirits of innocent women and children. A woman with long flowing hair knelt on the ground, holding a baby. Her shadow cringed and trembled against the side of the kiva while a tall man brought an axe-like weapon down upon the infant's and mother's heads.

Lorelei placed her hand over her mouth. Vomit started to arise in her throat, her whole body shook. She wondered if he would come after her.

Blood splattered everywhere among the subterranean past. The murderer looked down upon the body parts of the mutilated mother and baby one last time—a grin slowly crossing his face.

Lorelei backed away slowly, afraid she might generate attention from the evil specter. Shouting and movement continued.

Something horrible happened in this place. An ancient residual haunting surrounded her. One she knew would cause nightmares for months, maybe even years. She had been brought into a scene of extreme violence from the prehistoric past.

A breeze blew by her from behind and she turned to see an elderly, hunched figure attempting to escape from another warrior with a large stone in his hand. He yanked his prisoner by her hair, held her against his chest and bashed her skull in.

Chaos ensued everywhere. She glanced from one terrifying scene to another. Each piercing scream from a victim stopped her heart and brought her one step closer to madness.

She placed her hands over her ears and closed her eyes, breathing deeply. Clearing her mind from the ongoing horror in her midst, she imagined Ian and Paul—the three of them facing each other and holding hands. When Lorelei opened her eyes, she still stood in the kiva, ensconced in silence. The vision only took a minute to remove her from the bestiality and bloodshed.

She waited. Lorelei couldn't see the spirit, but she knew another presence remained; the same spirit who had lured and dragged her into another realm under the kiva at Cutthroat Castle.

"You brought me here to show me. You were murdered here."

A warm orange glow emanated from the bottom of the fire pit. The strange light changed from an amoeba-like form to a semi-solid human shape. Handsome with shoulder length black hair, her captor reminded her of Joe Luna, only six inches shorter without Joe's broad nose. And this man was physically fit with broad shoulders and stout legs.

No wonder you were able to drag me here so easily.

As she stared at the presence before her, Lorelei realized the woman and infant who were so callously murdered had been his family. He had been away on a hunt when the massacre of his village occurred, unable to defend his wife and child.

For some reason, she couldn't pick up on the identities of his family. She stood there, shaking uncontrollably. She picked up on the man's helplessness and sense of loss. The loneliness and need for revenge. He stepped back, away from the empty fire pit, observing Lorelei. Then he faded away.

An object sat in the center of the brick enclosed pit. Lorelei approached the place where the male spirit had been standing only seconds before. A human skull with wide empty sockets lured Lorelei into their mysterious past with teeth and an open mouth that seemed to belie some sort of suffering, and an empty naval cavity. Yet this skull bone wasn't from A.D. 1200, unlike the activities that had unfolded before her in the last few minutes. Her clairsentience told her the remains might be from a much more recent murder.

3

Ian stared intently, helplessly, at the foot wide crack formed on the round rock base of Cutthroat Castle. He couldn't wait anymore. Lorelei had been gone for twenty minutes.

"Paul, stay here with Joe. I'm going to take a look around again."

Joe gulped water from his bottle and looked out over the expanse of brush and ruins. "I told you. There's nothing down there. Someone or something wanted to communicate with her. This entity probably knew about her teleportation abilities, so she couldn't be harmed passing through solid objects. Paul might have been the lure."

"Maybe so. But I can't stand here and do nothing." Ian jumped five feet off the boulder. He hit the ground hard. "Shit!" Gasping and choking, he rolled around trying to catch his breath. Joe slid down after him.

Ian sat up, while Joe knelt next to him. "Are you all right?"

Nodding his head, Ian glanced up at Paul, gave a weak smile and waved. "Yeah, guess I was in too much of a hurry."

Ian cautiously approached the crevasse where Lorelei had disappeared. "Are you telling me my wife was taken to another world?"

"Not sure. But something managed to drag her through dirt and stone. I wonder if it took her further below ground. There are many kivas buried out here. Perhaps an ancient spirit took her to where a significant event occurred."

"She was grabbed so violently." Ian stared intently into the darkness of the air intake. A cool breeze blew his wavy bangs back. "Hard to believe its sole purpose was communication." He pounded his fist against the boulder wall.

Paul worked his way along the top of the Cutthroat Castle ruin and underneath the boulder where Lorelei had vanished and Ian now stood, glancing around in confusion and horror.

"Dad, when the entity took over my body, I was overcome with fear, disbelief, anger and sorrow. I couldn't move. But when Lore took my hand, I felt relief. Or the thing inside me did. It knew about her talents." Paul touched Ian's forearm. "She'll be okay. The spirit wanted to tell her something."

Ian hugged Paul tightly. "You'd think I would be used to this by now considering her dangerous encounter with Vince Joiner in southeast, Arizona. Not to mention her escape from Peter a few different times at Sunset Wupatki and Bryce Canyon in Utah." He pulled away and ruffled Paul's hair. "Yet she seems to come out of all of her adventures as strong as ever."

"We all know Lore's fine," Joe said. "It's another waiting game."

Ian held up his hand and glanced around excitedly. "I just heard what sounded like footsteps nearby, in the dirt." He prayed it would be Lorelei returning.

Lorelei walked toward them, stumbling out of a partially collapsed square tower incorporated into the Cutthroat Castle ruin. He wasn't sure if it was a trick of light or his excitement at seeing her again, but Ian thought he saw a large shadow cross under the boulder and in front of the small rooms built below.

Her jeans were dirty with a rip in the right leg and her long blonde hair was coated with dust—but what scared him the most were the cuts on her arms and face.

Ian, Paul and Joe raced up a string of boulders and through brush to get to her.

"Lore, what the hell happened?" Ian grabbed her and kissed her dirt-covered face repeatedly before looking her up and down. "Jesus, we need to get you cleaned up and checked out."

Ian gently wiped the dirt off her lips with his thumb.

"Honey, I'm fine." She placed her head against his chest and her arms around his waist. "I don't know where to begin. I went to help Paul, but when I touched him, it must have sensed my ability to communicate with spirits. That's when it pulled me inside."

Paul ran up and gave her a hug. "I'm so sorry. I tried to help you up, but it grabbed you before I could do anything."

She kissed Paul on the top of his head. "Sweetie, it's not your fault. It was a very determined man who lived over a thousand years ago." Lorelei gazed around at the buildings that made up the Cutthroat Castle village. "He lived here with his family. His wife and child died a very tragic death."

Ian placed his hands on either side of her face. Her eyes held the sorrow from her encounter with the ancestral spirit. "I think you should get medical attention."

"There's a hospital in Cortez," Joe said.

"No, I'm okay. Just a few minor scratches. Peroxide and antibiotics are fine. Let's head back to town so I can get cleaned up and get some rest."

While Paul and Joe turned away, Ian lifted her chin so her eyes met his and removed his sunglasses. He imagined his bluish-grey irises changing to royal purple, the specks colliding, floating—and healing.

Lorelei leaned in closer, her hand on his chest. She kissed him lightly on the side of his mouth, then more firmly on his lips. He gasped as a tingling sensation started from his lips and worked its way throughout his body.

Lorelei pulled away, breathless. "I'm sorry. It's just seeing what happened to that man's family. I love you so much. I can't even imagine…"

He caressed her cheek. "Let's talk about this later. I want to take care of you." Ian led her by the hand back to the car where Paul and Joe waited.

As Lorelei and Ian sat huddled next to each other in the backseat of the rental car, Ian could feel her trembling. "Are you cold?"

"No. Guess I'm still in shock from what happened. The things I saw. And I'm not sure how I ended up where I did."

Ian didn't want to ask what she had seen. He knew he would hear everything when she was ready.

Lorelei fell asleep in Ian's arms. At first her breathing was deep and her body relaxed. But after ten minutes, her respirations became shallower, she started quaking and moaning, and her eyelids seemed to develop an incessant tick.

He stroked her hair, but it didn't make a difference.

Paul turned his head to look at her from the front seat.

"It's okay," Ian said. "She's having a nightmare."

Joe slowed the car.

Just then, Lorelei twitched so hard her head hit the passenger window. Ian thought that would wake her up, but it didn't. Instead, she gasped and began to yell. "Noooooo!" A high pitched scream he had never heard come from her.

Joe quickly pulled off to the side of the road, almost causing a collision with the pickup tailgating from behind.

"Lore, baby. Wake up!" Ian grabbed her shoulders, shaking her. Twenty seconds later, her eyes opened wide. "You scared us all to death. You were screaming."

She looked over at Paul, Joe and back at Ian. "I'm sorry. That was the worst nightmare I've ever had. I think I better stay awake for now. Don't want to cause a car accident." Lorelei forced an embarrassed, weak laugh.

Ian placed his forehead against hers. "I love you so much. Most people can only dream of having your strength and patience."

14

"You're the reason I'm capable of such strength. I don't think I could get through any of these adventures without you." Lorelei placed her arm around his waist and rested with her head against his shoulder.

Forty minutes later, Paul, Joe, Ian and Lorelei arrived back at the Holiday Inn Express in Cortez, Colorado.

"Joe, why don't you take Paul out to dinner." After Lorelei entered the room, Ian started to give him fifty dollars.

"Hey no, man. I can handle it. Take good care of her." Joe winked at Lorelei. "I'll bring you both back something to eat."

"Thanks."

Paul gave Lorelei a big hug before leaving with Joe.

The turquoise carpet with black starburst patterns, matching curtains, lamps with metal Kokopelli bases, abstract turquoise, red and yellow paintings and canyon-themed wallpaper border drew upon the western feel of Cortez. The room had a mini log cabin with a bunk bed for Paul, brightly-colored southwest style linens and a wooden sign engraved in black at the entrance: FORT ADVENTURE.

As he shut the door, Ian heard the water running in the bathroom. He walked in to see her undressing, her dirty clothes dropping onto the carpet. She winced in pain as her top and jeans brushed past the scratches and bruises on her skin. He helped her take her bra and underwear off, then quickly undressed himself.

"Honey, you don't have to do this."

"Hey, you should know me by now," he said. "Any chance to get naked with you." They stepped into the shower. Ian took the washcloth with a small amount of soap and gently rubbed the wounds on her arms. "Am I doing all right? I'm not hurting you, am I?"

"You're doing fantastic. Not quite as painful as I thought it would be. Though maybe that's the effect you have on me."

He didn't know if it was her soft, sensual voice, her supple breasts, fair skin or beautiful face, Ian wanted to make love to her. Lorelei moved in to kiss him and started grinding her body against him.

"Lore, no," he said breathlessly. "This isn't the time. We need to get you cleaned up and get those scratches taken care of."

She smiled up at him. "I think this is the first time I've ever been rejected by you. But it's okay. You're right and I am pretty tired."

Ian finished washing her and carried her out of the shower to the bed. When he returned from retrieving the peroxide and bandages, Lorelei's eyes were half closed.

"I want to sleep but I'm so afraid of seeing it all again," she whispered.

He gently dabbed the peroxide soaked cotton balls on her scratches and bruises. "I'll help you with that, baby. You need to rest."

Ian walked around to the other side of the bed and scrounged through the clothes and toiletries in his luggage. Ian found what he was looking for—passion flower capsules. He handed one to her with a cup of water. "This will help you sleep. And I'll put a lavender scented sachet under your pillow to help relax you."

By the time he could find the sachet, she had fallen asleep. Ian went to pick up her backpack from the chair by the window. It seemed a little heavier than usual, so he unzipped the main compartment.

As he looked around in the bag, he came across a large white object. Ian could only see the top, so he pulled it out, his finger finding a large hole. "Son of a—" Ian dropped the skull on the floor. He glanced over at Lorelei to see if she had stirred.

He bent over to look closer. The skulls empty sockets glowed a fiery red.

4

Lorelei awoke to whispers outside her and Ian's hotel room. The smell of fresh coffee lured her from the comfort of her pillow. She turned to see the turquoise and red bedspread thrown back on Ian's side of the bed. The crack in the doorway revealed Ian talking with Joe outside. While she slipped on a pair of jeans, a short sleeved shirt and a sweatshirt, Ian came back into the room.

"Hey, beautiful."

She could tell he hugged her lightly so as not to bother her wounds, then looked her arms over to check out the scratches.

"Looking good." He stared into her eyes as he said it. "How did you sleep?"

"Great. What are you hiding from me?"

Ian stared at the brightly colored carpet. "I don't know how you do that."

She placed her hands on either side of his face. "Easy. When you attempt to keep things from me, your eyes transform to a dark grey."

"I'm afraid to tell you. Or rather show you." Ian took her backpack from its place on the chair by the window. He dropped it gently on the bed. "This could bring back bad memories of what happened at Hovenweep."

Lorelei opened the bag. She took two quick steps back when she saw the skull. The whiteness of the bone contrasted sharply with the black lining. Her suntan lotion, hat and snacks had fallen to the bottom, giving the skull center stage. "What is that doing here?" She continued to stare at the outside of the bag.

"So you have seen this?"

She could only nod. "I think you should get Joe and Paul in here. They're going to want to know what happened as well."

While Ian went a few doors down to get Joe and Paul, Lorelei lifted the skull from her bag. The arcane object had reappeared for a reason. And the entities at Cutthroat Castle wanted her to help solve another mystery. A murder mystery.

While turning the skull carefully between her hands, a two-inch wasp with orange wings crawled out of the gaping nasal cavity, resting halfway between the darkness and the light. She dropped the skull on the bed. It gazed up at her with intensity and secret knowledge. The wasp stared assiduously at another guest inside the empty sockets. Something with long furry black legs hid in the skull. Lorelei peeked closer. Its eight eyes peered back at her, legs splayed out from its body. She watched as an adult wasp tore open the spider's belly from the inside out. And thought she saw a glint of something in the spider's myriad of eyes.

Lorelei screamed and covered her mouth with her hand, recalling Joe's morbid story about the developing wasp larvae feeding on the paralyzed tarantula.

Ian burst into the room and grabbed her by the shoulders.

"Lore, honey. It's Ian!"

She looked around the room—at Ian, Joe and Paul, then down at the skull, which sat on the bed. No insects. No spiders.

"I saw a tarantula inside that thing. And a wasp ate through its stomach, like Joe mentioned would happen when I watched the wasp drag the spider away at the Cutthroat Castle. But I don't get what that has to do with what me being dragged under the earth—if anything."

Lorelei sat on the bed. Paul sat on one side with his arm around her and Ian sat on the other side of her. "Wait. Torture and suffering. That's what they both have in common," she whispered.

Ian stroked her arm. "Are you ready to talk about what happened?"

"As ready as I'll ever be. The phantom pulled me into the gap between the broken boulder and through a dirt wall. I thought I would suffocate. I ended up inside a fully-constructed kiva with roof beams and mortar."

Lorelei looked up at Ian. She took his hand in hers, hoping to draw strength. "That's when the horror began. A fire lit up the kiva."

She glanced at Joe. *Should I tell him I saw Shannon's face in the flames?*

Averting her gaze back to Ian, she could feel Joe staring at her intently. He knew she left something out.

"A woman and her child were hacked to death." Lorelei held Paul's hand. "My clairsentience told me they were the family of the entity who brought me there. The coldness, the hatred of the murderer." She shivered. "He killed them both so swiftly. So heartlessly."

Ian pulled her close.

"There has been evidence discovered of extreme violence, even cannibalism during the time when the ancestral Puebloans lived," Joe said. "There are hundreds of archaeological sites, especially in the Four Corners, with evidence of such violence. One crew of surveyors discovered human bones scattered all over in tight spaces, as if the people had been trying to hide. Catacombs stocked with food have been discovered, along with human skeletons. And these weren't burial locations, but sites of murders. Also, piles of burned remains and skeletons have been found in numerous sites, indicating mass destruction."

Joe got down on his knees in front of Lorelei. "I'm sorry you witnessed such violence. Obviously, as in all the other instances, there is a reason the spirit wanted you to see all of that. And to find the skull." He took her hands in his. "Yet there's something else you're hiding from me."

Lorelei couldn't answer. At least not right away. She focused her attention on the crème-colored walls and scenic western border of deserts and canyons surrounding the interior of the room.

"I saw Shannon, or Galiena."

Ian gasped. Paul fidgeted with his hands. Joe's shoulders hunched forward, his hands going to his head.

"Not in full human form. She showed herself in the flames, or rather her face. I thought I was seeing things. But the fire pit is the location where I found the skull."

Lorelei took Joe's hands in hers. "I'm sorry."

"You have nothing to apologize for." Joe's voice choked. "I've been hoping and praying I could see her again, in some form or another. Guess I'm a little jealous, not only of the fact you saw a vision of Shannon, but of your relationship with Ian. I thought I had a similar love. But turns out Shannon, or Galiena, is literally Miss Universe. Whatever we both had was lost the moment they returned for her."

Lorelei didn't understand how Shannon could have seemed so real to everyone, or how such a strong being could have forgotten her true identity. She also didn't understand who Galiena, Mattie and Dagon really were—even after everything that had happened at Vulture Mine. But one thing she did know. When she touched Joe's hand a few minutes ago, she clearly sensed an upcoming intimate relationship with another woman. And fairly soon, possibly within the next six months. She couldn't see the face, merely a feminine silhouette. She knew Joe wouldn't be ready for such a relationship now, but he would find someone else. Lorelei hoped this person would be his true love. Or had that already happened with Shannon?

"Enough about me." Joe smiled at her. A half smile that told her he was reliving his loss. "Are you picking anything else up about the skull? Other than the tarantula wasp and spider?"

"No. I only detected it might be a fairly recent remain—perhaps in the past few years."

Joe glanced up at the ceiling. "I think Shannon's still using her detective skills to show you the clues. But it might not be so easy putting the pieces together."

"Is it ever?" Lorelei smiled.

"Our fingerprints are all over the skull," Ian said. "I had no idea what it was. And Lorelei's prints are on it as well."

"It's okay." Lorelei stared at the object that had followed her from the ruins.

"What do you mean? Honey, that's evidence."

"No." She glanced up at Ian. "The real clues are at Cutthroat Castle."

"Whoa," Joe said. "The National Park Service isn't going to like the idea of us digging up their land very much."

Ian got up and poured cups of coffee for himself, Joe and Lorelei, and removed a carton of orange juice for Paul from the refrigerator. "What if we show them the skull?"

"The same skull that mysteriously appeared in my backpack? We could get in big trouble for walking off with an object on their land. Not to mention the park service will wonder where and how the hell we found it."

Joe removed his cell phone from its leather holder attached to his belt and made a call. "Alan, hey, it's Joe. Listen, looks like we've got a mystery in the Four Corners. This case is at Hovenweep National Monument. Need your support to do a little digging near Cutthroat Castle—literal digging that is."

Joe glanced up at Lorelei. "Yes. The one and only. And you know if she's seeing something out there, it must be true. She had a rather terrifying experience under the Cutthroat Castle ruins and thinks there could be proof of a murder."

Joe took a sip of his coffee. A few drops plopped over the edge and onto the turquoise and black carpet. He bent over and dabbed at the spots.

"Thanks, man. We'll see you out at the Cutthroat Castle site after the park closes at 5:00 p.m. Ian, Lore and I will be out there earlier. "

Ian smoothed her hair away from her face. "Are you going to be ready to go back out there so soon?"

She kissed him lightly on the lips. "With you by my side, I'm ready for anything."

He smiled at her. A warm, inviting smile that made her forget what had happened, if only for a second.

"So you're not getting any vibes as to what's going on?" Joe asked. He touched her arm. "Earth to Lore."

"Sorry." She looked away from Ian and up at Joe. "Not yet. Only that it's probably a fairly recent case. For some reason, I'm not seeing any faces or getting any names—things that usually come to me pretty quickly."

"One of your out-of-body experiences will more than likely open your mind and senses up," Ian said.

"I'll have to do that when we get out there. Probably in the very same location where the ancient spirit dragged me down."

Joe collapsed on his knees on the carpet. He stared at his phone in disbelief.

Lorelei and Ian leaned in next to Joe to look at his cell phone. One image appeared on the cell phone screen. A perfect triangle inside a perfect circle—made out of coffee grounds.

"That's what Shannon drew with her fingers before your wedding," Joe whispered. "It was one of the last times we were together."

"I think you got your sign, my friend." Ian patted Joe's back. "You were saying a minute ago how much you missed her and needed to hear from her."

Lorelei watched the ceiling as if observing the stars. "She's listening."

5

*L*orelei *rose into the early evening air, her silver cord from her astral form trailing behind her like glitter. Visitors from Hovenweep, miniatures from a hundred feet above, scurried to and fro. From their cars to the ruins. Driving from one prehistoric site to another. Or hiking the myriad of trails among the canyons and mesas.*

Sleeping Ute Mountain drew her in—a collective profile of peaks resembling a Ute Chief lying on his back with arms folded across his chest. In awe, Lorelei noticed the head and headdress, the crossed arms, ribcage, knees and even small, prominent igneous protrusions, which formed the great warrior god's toes.

Seeing how realistic the mountain peaks formed a human shape, she wondered if the legend could be true. In the very old days, the Sleeping Ute Mountain was a Great Warrior God who came to help fight against the Evil Ones. A tremendous battle between the Great Warrior God and the Evil Ones followed. As they stepped hard upon the earth and braced themselves to fight, their feet pushed the land into mountains and valleys, forming the country of this region. The Great Warrior God was hurt, so he lay down to rest and fell into a deep sleep. The blood from his wound turned into living water for all creatures to drink.

The Ute believe when the fog or clouds settle over the Sleeping Warrior God, it is a sign that he is changing his blankets for the four seasons. When the Indians see the light green blanket over the earthly representation of their god, they know it is spring. The dark green blanket is summer, the yellow and red one is fall, and the white one is winter. The Indians believe when the clouds gather on the highest peak, the Warrior God is pleased with his people and is letting rain clouds slip from his pockets. They also believe that the Great Warrior God will rise again to help them in the fight against their enemies.

Tearing her eyes away from Ute Mountain, she could see ancient ruins to the north in Colorado scattered over a massive range of land among mesas, canyon and rimrocks. Standing stone walls, square rooms, circular kivas, great kivas, and square towers were everywhere —part of Canyons of the Ancients National Monument and Hovenweep. She could also distinguish Painted Hand Tower, a partially collapsed circular structure she had visited two days earlier with Ian and Paul.

Directly east was San Juan National Forest and south of there, Mesa Verde National Park.

Her astral journeys were her second home. More than travels, they embodied peace, security and knowledge. But today, as she was getting ready to reunite with her physical form, Lorelei felt different. She was not alone. A non-threatening presence remained at a safe distance. Could it be Galiena?

Ian stared up at the sky, anxiously waiting for her return. She become one with her body and opened her eyes.

Ian and Paul were still staring up from inside the square pueblo at Cutthroat Castle, where she had started her journey.

She sat up on the pile of blankets next to them, her backpack and jacket by her side. "Honey, Paul, I'm back. I thought you had seen my astral form returning."

Ian and Paul exchanged worried glances.

Ian helped her up and gave her a kiss on the lips. "Didn't you see?"

"What are you talking about? See what?"

"Paul noticed it first. Two outlines following you."

"I felt something different right before I descended. Though nothing malicious. What did the shapes look like?"

"They were too far away," Ian said. "We could only detect two silvery-blue forms about ten feet away on either side of you."

"I wonder what they are and if they've been with me on other journeys."

"Not sure." Ian observed the darkening sky for another few seconds. "For awhile, I thought Peter and Emily might be back."

"I don't think we have to worry about them anymore," Paul said. "When Shiprock transformed back into a volcano temporarily, it destroyed much more than their physical bodies."

Lorelei stared nervously at the ground, knowing she was partly responsible for their harrowing end.

Joe entered the ruin carrying two shovels. Alan, the FBI agent from Utah, followed behind Joe.

Whitish, uneven patches of burn scars covered part of the left side of Alan's face, neck and left arm. The stocky man had slightly spiky pitch black hair with the tattoo of a woman's face on his right arm.

"So you're back for more fun." Alan gave her a hug. "Good to see you again. Are you getting any more detail about this new mystery?"

"Not yet. Maybe once we start digging."

"Well, let's get to it," Joe said. "Alan and I will start. We don't want to make too big of a hole if we can help it." He glanced around nervously. "I don't like the idea of doing damage to such an ancient structure."

Ian looked around inside the kiva. "Give me a shout if one of you gets tired. Where the hell did Paul go? He was here a few seconds ago."

"I'll find him," Lorelei said.

Joe grunted as he broke the surface of the earth with the shovel. "I think you need to stay here to see if you get any visions or sense anything about this murder."

"He's right." Ian stroked her arm. "I'll see where he went to."

A yell sliced through the solitude.

Lorelei jumped. "That sounds like Paul." She panicked, running in the direction of the yell. Had he fallen off a boulder, come across a mountain lion, or had the same prehistoric phantom that lured Lorelei into the past come back for Paul?

Please be okay!

Lorelei followed Ian with Joe and Alan behind her.

"Paul, where are you?" Ian screamed.

"Dad, help!"

"He's in that round tower in the distance," Joe said. He pointed to the remains of a partially collapsed circular structure.

Paul sat on the ground with his right pant leg pulled up, holding his ankle. Tears rolled down his face.

"Dad, a rattlesnake bit me."

Lorelei looked around to see if she could find the culprit, but it had already vanished. They all kneeled down to observe the wound. No marks were on his skin.

Ian panicked, pulling Paul's pants up a little higher. "Are you sure this is where it bit you? We need to get you to a hospital."

"A warning," Alan said. "It happened when Joe hit ground with the shovel a minute ago."

Lorelei placed her hand on Paul's shoulder. "How are you feeling?"

"I'm fine. I couldn't even see what kind of snake. I heard the rattle and felt the bite."

"There is no puncture mark on his skin." Joe said.

Paul stood up, walking around reluctantly. "I wouldn't make this up. I felt its fangs."

Ian sighed and gave Paul a hug. "It's okay. Are you feeling all right?"

Paul nodded adamantly.

Alan glanced back at the kiva. "Where do we go from here? Should we give it another try?"

"Maybe the skull *was* the only evidence," Lorelei ran her hands through her hair in frustration. "Or maybe it is from the days of the ancestral Puebloans. My senses told me otherwise, but perhaps my psychic and medium abilities are dimming."

Ian stood behind her, rubbing her shoulders. "This is your call, beautiful."

"I don't want to endanger anyone else. Especially since I'm not getting anything at all—no visions, no sensing, and no verbal clues." She looked at Joe and Alan. "I am so sorry."

"No worries," Alan said. "Something obviously happened to you out here. I know what you've been through, what you're capable of. Might just be a waiting game."

Lorelei walked over to where Paul had been bitten. She closed her eyes and concentrated. Imagined her historic surroundings and relived in her mind her experience in the kiva. Her feet vibrated slightly. The sensation crept into her legs, her stomach and chest, and finally, her arms and face.

She couldn't move, frozen in place and time. Something waited underneath. And that something was willing to scare a child to get her attention.

"Here," she whispered.

Ian grabbed her face with his hands. "Lore, are you all right? You were shaking to death."

Joe and Alan approached with the shovels.

"I'm fine." She forced a weak smile. "Get Paul away from here. Take him to one of the other sites, go for a drive—just get him out of the area."

Paul stepped in front of her, pleading with his eyes. "Lore, I want to stay here."

She turned to face him, speaking in a tone of voice she had never used with either Ian or Paul. "No!"

Everyone looked at her in shock.

She hugged Paul tightly. "Sweetie, I'm sorry. But what I'm sensing is not pleasant. It got my attention by attempting to injure you. I need to know you'll be safe."

Ian kissed her on the forehead. "Lore, I can't leave you."

"You have to. Joe and Alan are here. And we all know Galiena is watching over us. Please, Ian. I'll keep in touch by cell." Lorelei kissed him on his cheek, on the side of his mouth, running her hand down his chest. His breathing increased and he stood there, transfixed.

"I love you so much," Ian said.

Ian walked away with his arm around Paul's shoulder. Neither looked back. She knew Ian wouldn't be able to leave if he did.

"Are you ready?" Joe asked.

She looked up at him. "Are you?"

Joe and Alan slammed their shovels into the ground at the same time. The ringing echoed throughout the small room, half of which was open to the elements.

Lorelei removed her jacket from her bag to alleviate the continuously dropping temperatures. She realized an object was missing from her backpack. The skull.

"That's strange," she said. "Maybe I left it at the hotel."

"What?" Joe stopped digging. "Did you say something?"

"The skull is missing. I thought I put it back in here."

"You did. I saw you."

Lorelei opened the bag wide to show him the contents. "It's gone. And I know Ian didn't take it because I've been with him on the ride here." She threw up her hands. "What the hell is happening? I literally get dragged into the prehistoric past. I find a skull that follows me home. I have a vision of a tarantula wasp and its victim inside it. Finally, I come back out here and am led to a different section of ruins only to find the evidence is missing."

"That could be a sign you're in the right place." Alan forced his shovel into the ground.

She watched them dig for an hour. It was almost 7:00 p.m, minutes from complete darkness. She glanced at her phone. Ian had called three times, but her phone hadn't rung. Listening to her voice mail, Ian told her he and Paul were waiting in the parking lot of Cutthroat Castle.

"Lore, you know I love ya." Joe leaned on his shovel, taking a deep breath. "But whatever's out here has to wait. It's only going to get colder and it will be harder to find our way back in the dark."

"I understand."

"Sssh," Alan said. "Thought I heard footsteps."

"Probably Ian and Paul," Joe said.

Lorelei put her backpack on. "It can't be. Ian left a message saying they were waiting in the car for us."

The footsteps grew louder. She pulled her flashlight out of her bag and used it to peer into the direction of the parking lot.

"Let's get out of here." Joe nervously looked around, taking Lorelei by the arm. They stepped outside the tower. Footsteps approached from the north and the east.

"Stay calm," Joe said.

Lorelei felt he was saying that more for his own benefit.

Lorelei, Joe and Alan slipped though two pinion trees along the perimeter of the round structure to avoid the covert entities surrounding them.

She saw the hole, but it was too late. Lorelei lost Joe's grip and fell—ten feet to the bottom.

6

J oe watched helplessly as Lorelei fell into the three-foot wide hole. The ancestors who once lived in these ruins had planned for this.

"Lore, can you hear me?" No answer.

Joe tried calling Lore's cell phone with no results, though chances were slim it would work underground. His own phone started ringing. Ian was calling because he knew something had happened to her.

Handing Alan his phone to talk to Ian, Joe continued to yell for Lorelei. "Lore, are you there?"

No moans or movement.

"We're trying to see if she's hurt," Alan said into the phone. "But we can't see into the hole. Ian, calm down. Listen, I have some rope in the back of my truck. There are also a few extra flashlights. Get that stuff and be very careful getting back out here."

Joe peered down into the hole. "Lore!"

Mumbling came from the subterranean darkness. Not Lorelei's voice, these were sounds that sent shivers down his spine.

"Shit. Please be all right," Joe whispered. "If you can hear me, remember you can teleport out of there!" But she couldn't achieve that feat unconscious.

Joe could see pinpricks of light in the distance. Ian and Paul. Shadowy specters darted in between him and Alan and Ian and Paul.

Lying down on the ground to try and get a better view, Joe stuck his head into the void. Scraping and scuffling echoed underground.

"Lore," Joe yelled.

Ian and Paul's footsteps approached rapidly from behind.

Alan tried to take the rope from Ian, but Ian tied it to the thick trunk of a juniper tree.

"Paul, don't go anywhere," Ian said. "Stay here with Joe and Alan."

Joe watched as Ian completed the knot. "I'm going down with you. It might take the both of us to help her get out of there."

Ian threw his legs over the edge and was at the bottom in two quick pushes against the wall.

"Wait for me!" Joe shouted. He placed a flashlight in his back pocket, grabbed the rope and jumped to the floor of the passage in seconds.

"Here's another flashlight for Ian." Alan tossed the light to Joe. But Ian had already raced down one of the underground corridors.

Catching up with Ian, oppressiveness settled around him. The beams of light reflected off the stone walls. Rustling came from above. Joe glanced up to see bats swaying back and forth upside down on their rock perches. One of them crawled from the wall, wings extended, to the ceiling. In a few seconds, it had settled in among the colony.

"Don't yell," Joe said. "You'll disturb them."

"I know. I saw."

Something was really wrong. Lorelei had felt it in the circular tower where Paul had encountered a rattlesnake. Had she been lured here by the same entity who took her into the past of the ancestral Puebloans the day before?

Joe wiped beads of sweat from his forehead with his sleeve. He glanced over to see Ian doing the same thing.

"Strange," Ian said. "Why's it so warm underground? I would think it would be cooler."

The temperature rose rapidly. Joe watched Ian bend over, attempting to catch his breath in the oppressive heat.

Steps echoed from behind them. Joe and Ian turned. Their lights revealed a petite woman with long, blonde hair wearing jeans, sweatshirt and a jacket.

"Lore." Ian ran toward her.

The Lorelei look-alike stared coldly back. Then she took three steps backwards and vanished.

"What the hell?" Ian asked.

"Something is messing with us." Joe turned to face Ian. "Mocking us. And whatever this thing is could have Lore."

Ian didn't wait for Joe to finish his sentence. He raced into the darkness to find Lorelei.

7

When she fell, Lorelei expected her body to slam into the floor of the passage, either breaking a leg, arm or sustaining multiple injuries. Instead she went right through. Her body somehow merged with hard rock like at Cutthroat Castle. Yet she felt nothing.

Seconds later, she emerged in the midst of more Indian ruins. Ominous thunderstorm clouds were over Sleeping Ute Mountain to the east. But they moved rapidly in her direction. Lightning pierced the darkness and descended down upon the headdress of the stone warrior—forever in the form of a series of mountains.

Ruins stood on either side of her. She recognized the stone walls of Hovenweep Castle, part of the Square Tower Group in Hovenweep National Monument. Another bolt of lightning revealed Hovenweep House nearby, which was the center of one of the largest Pueblo villages in Little Ruins Canyon.

Eyes watched her. Two large ravens, perched on the highest wall of the castle, observed her in an almost human-like manner. The birds didn't preen themselves or make any noise. They merely sat atop the ancient structure, unmoving, and stared.

"Well, hello." Lorelei took a few steps toward the wall where they were sitting. The stately ravens didn't fly away or move to another spot. They vanished into thin air.

Lorelei thought back to the two silvery blue outlines Ian and Paul had witnessed while she returned from her astral journey. Could they have taken another form? And did her enigmatic guardians have anything to do with the missing skull and murder mystery? Or with her being here?

A clap of thunder hit with a force that made Lorelei jump. Drops began to pelt her body as she stood up. Glancing around, she could see nothing but pinyon, juniper and more ruins. Two dark shapes glided over her head; the ravens. They kept looking at her, then toward the center of the canyon. They wanted her to follow.

The ravens flew over Hovenweep Castle. Within seconds, the rain came down full force while she raced down a narrow dirt path, following the birds. Another clap of thunder echoed across the torturous heavens. Lorelei nearly slipped on a pile of rocks as a brilliant flash of light surrounded her. Gasping for breath from the force of the rain, Lorelei found herself at the eroded boulder house ruin—about half a mile away. Unlike Hovenweep Castle, Hovenweep House and the Twin Towers, which were off the main trail, the Boulder House was deeper in the canyon. She ran into one of the small rooms built into the massive boulder. Her winged guardians had again disappeared.

Faint whispers surrounded her—desperate ancient voices that became louder with each second. Brief cool breezes flew through and around her. She couldn't see the Native American spirits, yet they were everywhere. She wondered if they even knew she existed, or if they were expecting her. She thought she heard her name a few times among the murmurs and hushed tones.

An invisible hand placed itself gently on her stomach. She gasped and looked around. A pale brown mist rolled along the back wall, only ten feet away. It started to approach her, paused for five seconds then continued through a doorway and into another room.

Lorelei followed cautiously, only five feet behind the entity. The rain shower had stopped. She was being guided into another section of the ruins.

She walked for ten minutes in the darkness, grasping at walls for support, stumbling over occasional obstacles she assumed were stones from the ruins.

Scuffling and scraping noises came from somewhere ahead.

"Is someone there?" Lorelei didn't expect a response.

"Who is it? What do you want?" A woman's panicked voice spat into the unknown.

Lorelei still couldn't see anything. She didn't know what she had walked into.

"My name is Lorelei Lanier. Are you okay?"

No response. Sshe imagined a soft glow, like the light of a hundred candles throughout the chamberso she could see her surroundings.

A dim translucence began in the center and spread outward; gradually revealing an athletic looking woman with extremely short dark hair. Her wrists and ankles were bound together.

"I don't know how the hell you did that." The stranger glanced around the newly lit cave. "But I'm really glad I can see. Or at least from my left eye."

Was that me? Or is there a higher power at work here? Lorelei wondered if Galiena had helped her brighten up the environment.

The woman's right eye had been swollen shut with dark bruising and inflammation surrounding the eye. She was covered in dust from head to toe. Scratch marks were all over her body and she had bruises on her neck.

"What's your name?" Lorelei noticed she looked several months pregnant. The victim glanced down at her swollen belly.

"I'm Mandy." She tried to stand up. "Listen, we have to get the hell out of here. He's coming back soon. I don't know how you got here at night with the park closed, but we need to leave."

Lorelei didn't ask Mandy who she was talking about. She had been led here for a reason. To get this woman out of a dangerous situation.

Lorelei knelt down and began to loosen the knots on her bound wrists. She had only untied them halfway when footsteps echoed from another room.

"Mandyyyyyy!" a man's voice yelled. "Did you miss meeeeee?"

"Oh, God! He's coming." Mandy trembled violently, grabbing onto Lore's arm so hard she winced in pain.

Lorelei knew she wouldn't get them off in time. She took a deep breath and imagined the ropes dropping to the ground.

She was just as surprised as Mandy when her wrists and ankles were freed.

Lighting the cavern, freeing Mandy. These abilities are a first. Dagon freed me from my ties at the ranch in Utah by simply using his mind. Am I starting to obtain talents from Dagon and Galiena?

A figure over six feet in height charged into the small cave. He had come through a hidden hole in the darkest recesses.

Mandy stood up quickly, grabbing Lorelei's arm in terror.

Mandy's captor had straight, shoulder-length shaggy brown hair, burn scars covering his face and neck and a slight limp in his left leg. His eyes scared Lorelei the most—they had the same shape, dark color and inanimate feel as those of the Native American man who had murdered the young family in the kiva.

"Who are *you*? How did you find us?" His voice boomed throughout the chamber.

Lorelei stepped in front of Mandy, facing her, and took Mandy's hands in hers. She remembered the warmth of the pillars underneath Shiprock, thought of the safety of Ian's arms, the familiarity of the Caves of the Watchers and the comfort of Galiena's presence.

He ran at them with an unusual five-inch black curved hunting knife in an effort to prevent their escape. Lorelei saw herself and Mandy fading quickly, being teleported away as the lethal weapon sliced through the subterranean darkness where Lorelei and Mandy had been standing.

8

A few bats flew over Ian. He ducked down with his hands over his head to avoid contact. His heart stopped when he heard Lorelei's voice.

"Joe, did you hear that?"

Lorelei's voice reverberated throughout the stone walls. The sound emanated from where she had fallen in. "Ian, Joe, Alan. Can anyone hear me?"

"Lore, I'm here. We're coming!" Ian raced the quarter mile back to the entrance with Joe running behind him.

Ian pointed his flashlight toward the direction of the opening. Two figures stood directly under the aperture where Lorelei had fallen.

"Ian." Lorelei jumped into his arms.

"Are you all right?" Ian stroked her damp hair, which still clung to her face. "You must have been caught in that storm that came in so suddenly. For some reason, we missed it here at Cutthroat."

She stared at her wet clothes, peeling her sweatshirt away from her body. "I'm fine. When I fell into this tunnel, I ended up falling through the ground and transporting myself to another part of the Hovenweep Monument."

Ian looked at the disheveled, dirty woman standing next to his wife with a nasty-looking black eye. She trembled violently and stared at her surroundings in confusion.

"I don't get what just happened." The woman watched Lorelei. "He was coming at us with a knife. How did we get away? Where are we now?"

"What?" Ian glanced from the stranger to Lorelei. "Who attacked you?"

"A man. He seemed rather enamored with Mandy here." Lorelei turned to face her. "It's okay. I promise. This is my husband, Ian Healy."

Alan peered ten feet down. "Lore, can you teleport everyone out of there?"

"I just tried to get myself and Mandy up, but it's not working. Guess I can only do one trip at a time. Or maybe I expended extra energy getting us both here."

Alan threw a thick rope down tied with knots every foot. "Try and get at least halfway up. I can pull you out the remainder of the way."

"Wait." Joe stepped in front of Lorelei and climbed up the rope within seconds. "Ian, you next. Between the three of us men, we can get Lore and her friend out of there in no time."

Ian kissed Lorelei on the cheek and touched Mandy on the shoulder reassuringly before climbing up the rope.

"Mandy, you first," Lorelei said. "I'll explain everything once we're both out of this place."

Ian stood behind Alan and Joe. They pulled Mandy and Lorelei out of the passage. Mandy stood there shivering and in shock.

Joe took off his leather jacket and placed it around Mandy's shoulders. "We all need to get the hell out of here and back to the hotel. It's freezing and Lorelei is soaking wet. Not to mention our new friend might need some medical help."

"I'm fine." Mandy pulled the coat tighter around her. "I don't understand how the hell I got away from that insane man." She looked around in confusion.

Mandy walked up to within an inch of Lorelei's face. "Who *are* you? How did you get me here?"

Lorelei sighed. "Not sure you'll believe what I'm about to tell you."

Paul took Lorelei's hand in his.

"I was kidnapped by a crazy psycho while hiking and kept in a dark cave for over twelve hours. Try me."

"Teleportation. I got you to safety through teleportation, or traveling from one place to another instantaneously. I merely think about where I want to go—and I'm there. Let's say it's a gift. Though sometimes it happens without me trying."

"Sometimes, it doesn't happen at all. Remember when you sent Paul to southeast, Arizona and me to old Vulture City near Wickenburg. But you didn't go anywhere. I remember a few other instances also."

Joe quickly gathered the rope. "Abilities such as Lorelei's aren't always so cut and dried. My shaman skills don't necessarily yield the results I expect them to at times. We're not talking science here, intuition and psychic senses play into such unusual talents."

Ian couldn't explain it. But Mandy seemed very familiar.

"So we're talking time travel?" Mandy asked.

"Not quite." Lorelei glanced at Ian. "It's the ability to move from one place to another. A method of travel that takes only seconds. I haven't been able to travel into the past or future. At least not yet."

Footsteps came from the ruins. Shadow figures darted among pinion junipers. And twinkles of light appeared in the distance.

Joe grabbed Mandy's arm. "We can work this stuff out later. It isn't exactly safe here either."

Ian guided Lorelei and Paul back to the car. Whispers and unexplained flashes of radiance came from behind. Lorelei held his hand tighter.

"Do you think any of this noise and other phenomena is from the ancient astral race you've communicated with from Arizona?" Ian whispered. "After all, you did travel to the heavens and worked with them to stop Vincent Joiner from unleashing his monsters on southeast, Arizona. Not to mention the stone beds you found underground in the Caves of the Watchers. Maybe they are here to help you figure out what's going on."

Lorelei shook her head adamantly. "These spirits are from here. Both prehistoric and historic cultures. I'm also sensing excitement about something."

"It's probably you. The Native American spirits know who you are. They must have been responsible for Mandy's safety."

"Perhaps," Lorelei said. "I literally slipped and fell through the ground, similar to my experience at Cutthroat Castle. And I had two bird guides that made sure I found Mandy. Maybe the same guides you and Paul saw when I was in astral form."

"She's obviously pretty important. Perhaps the ancient ones, or maybe Galiena, chose Mandy for some purpose we don't know yet."

"That's possible. The ravens that led me to Mandy could have represented the ancient ones. Consider the eagle I traveled with to visit Joe at Shiprock, and the hawk you saw with Mattie, the deceased shaman who used to be the caretaker of Vulture Mine and the creator of the youth formula. She's now with Galiena and Dagon."

Ian glanced behind him but couldn't see or hear anything. "Don't forget the hawk we saw with Galiena before she left."

When they got back to Ian's car, Mandy sat in the backseat next to Paul. Every time Ian looked, Mandy was staring out the window.

Forty-five minutes later, Joe pulled into the hospital parking lot in Cortez.

"No!" Mandy said. "I'm okay. A few scratches, but he didn't get a chance to do any harm. All my injured eye needs is ice. I'm really tired and would like to get cleaned up."

"If you're sure," Joe said. "We'll take you back to the hotel with us."

Ten minutes later, Joe pulled into the parking lot of the Holiday Inn. In a daze, Mandy followed Lorelei, Ian, Joe and Paul up to Lorelei and Ian's room. Lorelei escorted Mandy to the bathroom. "You're welcome to get cleaned up. Take as long as you like."

Mandy turned on the water, watching it flow into the sink for thirty seconds before splashing water on her face. She dabbed gently at her swollen, injured eye. "Am I in some sort of dream?" she muttered.

When Mandy turned around after cleaning her face and arms, the can of soda Joe held slipped through his hands. Lorelei collapsed onto her knees.

Ian suddenly realized who she reminded him of. Mandy's black eye had prevented him from seeing it right away. Mandy's athletic frame, her dark red hair and her demeanor—the woman Lorelei had just saved had become the spitting image of Shannon Flynn—who had turned out to be Galiena.

9

Mandy couldn't understand why everyone stared at her with their mouths open, including her new friend Lorelei, who had dropped to her knees after seeing Mandy's face more clearly. Nor could she understand how the hell she had gotten from the cave in the boulder house to the Cutthroat Castle ruins. Lorelei mentioned teleportation. But wasn't that merely science fiction?

"You all don't have the right to be looking at me that way," Mandy said. "After all, I'm the one that appeared out of nowhere from one part of Hovenweep to another." She glanced at Lorelei, still on her knees. "Thanks to you. I appreciate you saving my life. Really I do. It's just that I'm having trouble absorbing all this."

Joe walked up to Mandy, gazing at her in astonishment. He turned her head to the left and then the right, studying her profile. "Amazing."

Mandy quickly stepped away from him. "You know what? I'll figure this out on my own." She slowly backed toward the door. "I'll go to the cops and tell them what happened and where my kidnapper is hiding out."

"Wait," Lorelei stood up. "Mandy, I'm sorry. *We're* sorry. You're the spitting image of someone we know. Or used to. It's hard to explain. And you don't need to go to the cops. Joe here is with the FBI. He can help. We all can."

Joe continued to watch Mandy with disbelief. After thirty seconds, he gently guided her to the bed and sat her down. "When and how were you abducted? You mentioned you were trapped for twelve hours?"

"Yes. I started hiking about 6:00 a.m. He approached me at 7:00 a.m. At first he seemed rather friendly, telling me about the history of Hovenweep and the ancestral Puebloans." She stared at the carpet and placed her hand on her protruding stomach. "We hiked together for a couple of hours, looking around at the ruins in the canyon. Then his personality completely switched while we took a break outside those ruins an hour later. He dragged me through the pueblos and into the cave where Lorelei found me."

"We've all been spending the past few days at Hovenweep," Lorelei said. "Why wouldn't I have picked up on the incident with Mandy when it occurred? Or for that matter, before Mandy was kidnapped so that I could have prevented her from going through that?"

"It wasn't exactly your decision," Ian said. "Remember, there were a series of events that led us back to Cutthroat Castle. We were dealing with an entirely different mystery."

Lorelei ran her hand through her hair and smiled at Mandy. "Guess we're all in a state of confusion." She sighed.

"Paul, go get some ice for Mandy," Ian said.

Joe stared out the hotel window. "As usual, we're left with more questions than answers."

A minute later, Paul entered the hotel room with a full bucket. He slipped a hand towel off the rack in the bathroom, ran water over it and handed the ice and cloth to Joe, who reached for them.

Joe tightly wrapped a few cubes in the wet towel, placing it gently over her eye.

In a split second, Mandy had a strong sense of déjà vu. She gazed into the intense brown eyes of the extremely handsome Native American man with long dark hair before her.

She gasped and jumped away from the bed. As far as she could remember, she had never met Joe. Yet, reflected within his eyes, Mandy had witnessed herself making love to him.

10

Joe couldn't believe the sight before him. Except for her short, straight hair, Mandy looked exactly like Shannon, even down to her athletic body.

How can this be happening? I'm having a hard enough time dealing with Shannon's truth. Is she trying to torture me, or is this some sort of sign?

Mandy had jumped away from him, as if seeing something she couldn't comprehend. When Dagon and Mattie had returned for Shannon in Dragoon, Lorelei, Ian and Joe assumed Shannon, or rather Galiena, took on the same human form for her universal role as she had been on earth.

Now Joe didn't understand who, or what, Galiena really represented. Had Galiena brought Mandy to them on purpose? Even stranger, was it possible she had taken over Mandy's body while on earth?

Joe couldn't show Mandy the picture in his pocket. It would be too much of a shock. Even for him.

"Tell me, Mandy." Joe held the ice pack over her bruised eye. "Have you always had short hair?"

Mandy stood between Ian and Lorelei. She stared at Joe with her mouth agape. She was trembling. "I had it cut a few months ago. It was longer, past shoulder length, and much wavier."

He barely heard Lorelei as she asked the same question on his mind.

"What do you do for a living?" Lorelei asked.

47

"I'm an emergency room nurse."

Frustration, anger and confusion overwhelmed Joe. How could Shannon have done this to him? Why did the ancients allow him to be a victim of false love—of someone that might not even be human? Had Galiena used this woman's body to achieve her mission to bring Ian and Lorelei together? Did Mandy back away so quickly because she had been linked to Shannon at one time?

"I need to go." Joe removed the ice pack from her face, handed it to Ian and ran out the hotel room door without saying goodbye to his friends. He didn't want to ask any more questions. He didn't want to think. He only wanted to distance himself from the torture.

11

Lorelei's heart went out to Joe because of his agony and persecution pertaining to Shannon and Mandy. Since Shannon returned to her place among Dagon, Annie and the others, he hadn't been the same. She had been the love of his life. And like Joe, Lorelei and Ian also wondered why the romance had happened. This couldn't be coincidence. Was Mandy part of Galiena's plan? Or were they one and the same? Even her personality seemed similar.

Lorelei and Ian glanced at each other, then Mandy.

"Sorry about that." Ian held the ice pack against her eye. "Joe was very close to this woman you resemble."

Mandy stared at a light-colored stain on the carpet. Lorelei saw her blush.

"He somehow seems familiar to me."

Lorelei touched Mandy gently on her arm. "Is there someone I can contact for you? I'm sure your family would want to know you're okay. Or maybe you want to let them know what happened."

Mandy let out a big sigh. "I have acquaintances through work, but no family."

"What about your husband?" Ian's eyes rose from her protruding stomach to her face. She looked to be at least five months pregnant.

Mandy's green eyes began to well up.

They aren't just green. They are emerald green, like Shannon's.

"There is no husband." Mandy spat the words out with venomous hatred. "I was engaged, but when the bastard found out I was pregnant, he left me. Says he left because he didn't want kids, but there are times when I wonder if there was someone else."

Lorelei sat down next to her. "I am so sorry. That must have been awful."

"Still is." Mandy rubbed her stomach. "I'm constantly worried about how I'm going to take care of this baby on my own. I'm thirty-eight years old and this is my first child. It's no problem financially." Her voice waivered. "But emotionally, I'm scared to death."

"Where are you from?" Ian asked.

"Flagstaff. I came here to get my mind off my troubles."

"Joe already contacted park law enforcement," Ian said. "It might only be a matter of time before that sicko tries to kidnap someone else." Ian took Mandy's hand in his. "Unfortunately, you'll need to tell them what happened."

"Should I also inform them about my escape?"

Lorelei noticed Paul in the miniature log cabin in the corner of the room, reading on his bunk bed.

"I think Joe and Alan need to deal with this," Lorelei said. "They are both strongly connected to the FBI and can handle it better than we could. There is a division dealing with the types of crimes I've been involved with. And the agents are very aware of my talents."

Ian put his arm around Mandy's shoulder. "I'm not so sure Joe is able to help with this case, considering the circumstances. Maybe Alan can take over."

A pounding on the door startled them.

Lorelei opened the door, glanced to either side the hallway, but saw no one. She noticed a slip of paper on the floor with the words facing up. She bent over to read it.

"Honey, what is it?" Ian stepped outside into the hallway.

She glanced back at Mandy, not wanting her to see the note.

Ian leaned in to read it.

HOW DARE YOU INVADE MY CHAMBER AND TAKE WHAT'S MINE! DON'T KNOW HOW YOU FOUND US, BUT YOU'RE ABOUT TO SUFFER FOR STEALING MY PREY. LOOK CLOSELY INSIDE YOURSELF—FOR WHAT YOU'RE YET TO DISCOVER, WILL MAKE YOU SUFFER!

Lorelei started to shake. She looked up at Ian in disbelief. "How could he have found us?"

"Let me get something to pick this up with." Ian removed a plastic bag from his backpack and used his fingers to wrap it around the note. "This is evidence."

Mandy glanced over Ian's shoulder in the hallway to read the words on the paper. "Could he have somehow come back with us through…" She cleared her throat and glanced nervously at Lorelei. "Teleportation?"

"He wasn't inside the tunnel when you both arrived," Ian said. "At least Joe and I didn't see anyone else. But maybe he could have been hiding."

Lorelei stared at Ian. "What are the chances of her abductor being able to teleport?"

"I would think slim to none. But now we can have this note checked for prints."

"I was going to have you both take me back to my car at Hovenweep so that I can go my own way. But after seeing that gift he left, I'm a little hesitant."

"You can't get rid of us that easily," Ian said. "You're associated with some amazing people who can help answer questions and keep you safe, including Joe. He'll help you get through this."

"We can get an extra room. Paul and Ian can stay here and you and I can bunk together," Lorelei said.

Mandy threw her hands up. "You're in as much danger as I am. After all, he threatened *you*. That jackass referred to me as his prey. What the hell did that mean?"

"No more sense than what he said about me. 'For what you're yet to discover will make you suffer.' "

Ian pulled her close. He trembled as much as she did. "I'll put together a protection spell." He winked at Mandy. "For all of us."

Mandy stared at Ian with a combination of curiosity, fear and uncertainty.

"So you're a witch?" Mandy asked.

"Yes, though some of us don't like to be called that. I'm Wiccan, which is a religion. We perform rituals and practice spells to enhance our lives or for protection. Unfortunately, there are others who misuse the craft for their own power and monetary gains. Or to obtain the love of a person they've been yearning for."

Mandy looked at Lorelei. "So is that how I escaped?"

"Lorelei has her own unique talents, such as astral projection and teleportation. Neither of which are associated with the craft. She's also a psychic medium."

"Did you have a vision about what would happen to me?"

"No. Like I mentioned in the tunnel, we were checking out the ruins and I fell into that passage. Only I didn't hit the ground. I fell through and found myself at the Square Towers."

Lorelei thought back to the harsh words written on the note that Mandy's torturer had left on their hotel door. "LOOK CLOSELY INSIDE YOURSELF—FOR WHAT YOU'RE YET TO DISCOVER, WILL MAKE YOU SUFFER!"

What could this complete stranger possibly know that she didn't? In what way would she suffer?

Ian placed his hand on her shoulders and pulled her to him.

Lorelei's heart stopped when Ian's phone rang.

Ian took his cell phone out of his back pocket and answered it. "Hey, Joe." Ian glanced up at Mandy and turned away. "No, it's okay. I understand. Lorelei, Paul and I are still in shock regarding her looks as well. Listen, Mandy's abductor just left a note on our door. He couldn't have hiked out of Little Ruin Canyon in the dark that quickly, gotten to his vehicle, somehow found us in our car and followed us back to the hotel."

Lorelei watched Ian's handsome face as he listened to Joe. She wondered if Joe would be able to help with the case considering his feelings.

"Sounds good. We'll see you soon." Ian disconnected the call. "Joe and Alan are looking into any previous abduction cases in the Four Corners area. They said they would meet us all at eight tomorrow morning at the diner next door. Joe wanted us to get some rest and insisted Mandy stay with us. He's going to stand guard outside our room the whole night."

Lorelei removed a bottle of aspirin from her purse on the round table next to the window, opened it and handed Mandy a few capsules and a bottle of water from the mini-frig. She noticed her new friend had been rubbing her temples. "I know this might be a little uncomfortable. But it's better to be safe. Paul can squeeze in with us and we'll give you his bed. I'm sure you'd rather have your own room, but we have no idea what we're dealing with, and considering his recent threat."

"No worries." Mandy popped both pills and downed them with a single gulp. "I completely agree. I'd be willing to sleep on the floor at this point."

Lorelei riffled through her suitcase and found a navy pair of workout shorts and an oversized t-shirt. "You'll be more comfortable in these."

Mandy tentatively took the clothes from Lorelei. "Thanks." After walking toward the bathroom, she turned back to Lorelei and Ian. "For everything."

Less than fifteen minutes later, Lorelei, Mandy, Paul, and Ian were in bed.

Paul lay in between Lorelei and Ian. She could hear them both breathing soundly, but she couldn't sleep. She wondered if Mandy were also awake.

Ian stirred, reached over and stroked her hair.

As he ran his fingers down her long blonde locks, something felt like it had moved in her stomach. Thinking it was gas, she ignored it. It became stronger and more painful. Sitting quickly up in bed, Lorelei grabbed her belly, yelling out in agony.

Ian and Paul woke up. "Honey, what's going on?" Ian sat up and turned the lamp on next to the bed.

"Something's really wrong. Ian, get help." Lorelei screamed and doubled over. A vision of the tarantula wasp laying its eggs inside its victim came clearly into view. Unable to move, the tarantula was aware of everything.

Joe pounded on the door. "What's going on?" he yelled.

Ian threw open the door. "We've got to get Lore to a hospital."

Mandy sat in front of Lorelei. Her green eyes reflected worry and fright. Right before Lorelei passed out, she saw Mandy's captor within her eyes. He stared back at Lorelei with contempt, revenge and a nefarious grin.

12

Ian had never seen Lorelei look so helpless. He had carried her to the car and rushed her to Southwest Memorial Hospital in Cortez, only minutes away. The room was small with stark white walls, mobile supply cabinets and harsh lighting. He shivered, though unsure if it was from the temperature or the sterile, austere environment. She had been hooked up to a blood pressure monitor and electrocardiogram machine with an oxygen mask, her hair splayed out across the pillow. Not moving. He sat next to her, holding her hand tightly. Hoping to bring her back.

What is that bastard doing to her?

Paul stood next to Ian. His eyes were wide with fright, staring at Lorelei in disbelief. Mandy sat in a chair across the bed from Ian, holding Lorelei's hand.

Joe stood behind Ian, his hand on Ian's shoulder. "It's a little strange she gets that threatening note right before this happens. Did Lorelei have any idea what he was talking about when he said 'for what you're yet to discover will make you suffer?' "

Ian glanced up at Mandy. She shook her head.

"I never experienced anything like what Lorelei's going through during my captivity. But maybe my kidnapper just didn't get the time. I don't understand how he's doing this. I mean, he's nowhere around to harm her."

Ian and Joe looked at each other.

"You'd be amazed at what some people are capable of," Joe said. "Consider how Lorelei saved you. Only she would never use such powers to harm others."

"Look closely inside yourself," Mandy muttered. For what you're yet to discover will make you suffer."

A gray-haired doctor in a white lab coat sat behind the nurses' desk reviewing a patient's chart. The man in the next room screamed for a nurse. And a group of ten interns followed a dark-haired physician on rounds.

"Does Lorelei have any health issues this guy could be exacerbating?" Joe asked.

Ian gazed intently at Lorelei, stroking her hair repeatedly. "Not that I'm aware of."

Mandy hovered her hands over Lorelei's stomach, four inches above her skin.

Ian stared in shock. It seemed as if Mandy were performing a Reiki session.

Joe stood on the opposite side of Lorelei, observing Mandy.

Mandy gasped and pulled back quickly. "Why didn't she mention she was pregnant?"

For the first time since entering the hospital, Ian let go of Lorelei's hand. He stared at Mandy. "What are you talking about? We've been trying to get pregnant."

Mandy became nervous, fidgeting with a lock of hair. "I'm not sure. I saw this weird energy above her stomach. So I felt compelled to find out more. Then I saw the fetus and had a vision of her having the baby." She glanced up at Ian. "You were right next to her. Both of you were crying tears of joy."

Lorelei stirred and Ian looked down at her in anticipation. He hoped and prayed Mandy's vision was correct. He squeezed Lore's hand even tighter thinking about her potential pregnancy. Yet he also wanted her to be safe and healthy.

What did Mandy's abductor do to Lorelei, if anything? Was it mere coincidence?

Joe walked over to Mandy and stood within inches of her face. "So you do have talents?"

Mandy looked at him as if he were nuts. "No. This is the first time something like this has happened. What if the teleportation experience brought this on?"

Ian held Lorelei's hand as she gained consciousness. Joe would not look away from Mandy. Ian knew Joe was trying to see if she was lying about her skills. Mandy diverted her gaze to Lorelei.

Lorelei moaned loudly as a nurse paged a doctor over the public address system.

Ian kissed her face, his head resting against hers. "You're going to be fine, baby. I just know it." *I hope you are pregnant. Because then I could see us together, even when you're not around. No telling what our child would be capable of.*

13

*W*eightlessness and darkness overcame Lorelei. She no longer felt the pain.
Am I in my astral form?

Lights began to twinkle around her. Some she recognized as stars; other spots of radiance were doing more than shining in place. These lights were moving toward her. They grew while approaching her. She could feel herself moving, but not nearly as fast as the strange objects.

She became frightened and thought of Ian. Lorelei stared down at the massive round shape far, far below her. Deep blue rivers, tall, craggy brown mountains and green oceans dotted the landscape.

The last thing she remembered was being taken into an emergency room, screaming in agony with the worst pain she had ever felt.

The brilliant white lights approaching her reminded her of the near-death experience in the Caves of the Watchers tunnel system.

Oh, God! I can't be dying or dead. Please! I have a family. I can't leave them alone.

The heavenly beacons found her and swirled around her; ghost-like specters among the cosmos.

They weren't solid figures. No eyes to see with, yet the silhouettes danced, twisted and melded together. No ears to hear with, yet they stopped for a few seconds when she gasped in wonder. The top of their "heads" glanced directly at her.

The brilliant organisms formed themselves into a sun spiral—a shape Lorelei had seen on many rock art panels throughout Arizona. They seemed to solidify for a few seconds, molding themselves into the design. The spiral collapsed in on itself. They swirled around her some more and created snake-like shimmering forms. One of the beings flew over her and hesitated directly above Lorelei. She reached into the enigmatic cloud. A slight static charge emanated from its core, but it didn't seem to notice her touch. Rather it joined up with the other three and they formed a circle, which spun so rapidly Lorelei couldn't distinguish one creature from the other. The spinning began to slow. Within what seemed like minutes, the living circle had nearly ceased.

An orange-red ethereal glow appeared in the center of the circle that the beings had formed. Sparks transformed into flames. Flames morphed into a molten mountain shaped like Shiprock. Rivers of lava formed and collided, as had the bright entities that greeted her only minutes before. But the winding rivers became thick dark red waves flowing downward. Shiprock transformed into Shannon's face with a hint of her once earthly emerald eyes.

"Shannon. I mean, Galiena. Is this who you really are in the universe? A fiery goddess?" Lorelei suddenly realized who had been responsible for Emily and Peter's punishment for stealing artifacts from Sunset Crater Wupatki National Monument, kidnapping and torturing Lorelei, and murdering Alicia Atwell, a young woman who made the fatal mistake of stealing from Peter's stash of valuable ancient artifacts. "It was you. You made Shiprock come alive. You encouraged the minions to drop Emily and Peter into the volcano."

Galiena nodded her head—twice.

"Only you didn't know what you were capable of as Shannon."

Lorelei could feel herself floating backward through time and space, away from Galiena. A willowy voice that sounded as if it were echoing from far away implanted three words clearly in Lorelei's. "No more guilt."

Her burden had been heavy, thinking she had been responsible for killing Emily and Peter by somehow dropping them into the volcanic pinnacle that had come back to life. She even had nightmares about it from time to time. Ian knew it, but he kept reassuring her that their deaths somehow served a purpose. And that perhaps she hadn't been the one who murdered them. He had been right. Galiena had just admitted it.

Galiena had brought her here to let Lorelei know the truth. "What about Mandy?"

There were no more answers. The face transformed back into a mixture of flame, lava and rock.

Lorelei then found herself inside a dark spinning tunnel. A black hole with a comforting presence awaiting her on the other side.

14

Bright hospital lights replaced the darkness of space. Whispers replaced the all encompassing silence from the cosmos. And Ian's firm hand held hers to replace the emptiness of the heavens.

A doctor in a white lab coat and a nurse stood at her bedside. They gaped at her with their mouths open. The nurse, whose badge read Alice said, "Uh, I'll be right back." She motioned for the doctor to follow her.

Joe and Mandy stood together on one side of the bed with Ian on the opposite side.

"Honey, they both saw you come back into your physical form. I didn't even know you had left."

"I didn't either," Lorelei said. "Galiena had an important message to give me. She murdered Emily and Peter by throwing them into the revitalized volcano." She reached for Joe's hand. "Her true form up there is as a fiery, lava-like goddess. But not human."

Ian kissed her forehead, his lips lingering on her skin. "Amazing. Galiena might also have been trying to help you. Speaking of which, how are you feeling?"

"I feel fine now."

"You were in such pain when we arrived. The nurse gave you something to help. Maybe that induced your journey."

Lorelei could see the nurse and doctor whispering between themselves in the hallway and glancing in her direction. They seemed afraid of what they had witnessed.

After a few minutes, the doctor came back into the room. "I was just about to tell your husband when..." He sighed deeply. "Never mind. We did some blood work on you. Mrs. Healy, you're six weeks pregnant. I've arranged for an ultrasound to make sure everything is okay with the baby. And we'll keep you overnight to monitor the situation."

Lorelei couldn't believe her ears. She looked at Ian. He kissed her hand, a tear rolling down his face.

"You mean I'm going to have a brother or sister?" Paul stood up from his chair next to Ian's and took Lorelei's other hand.

The doctor left the room quickly, as if expecting her to perform another strange feat.

Lorelei gazed up at Ian. "I hope you're happy about this."

"Are you kidding? This is the best news I've had since you told me you'd marry me. I'm looking forward to this." He stroked her hair and kissed her forehead. "You've mentioned a few times you wanted a child of your own."

Lorelei glanced over at Paul and squeezed his hand.

"I understand," Paul said excitedly. "Mom and dad raised me. You want a baby to raise from birth."

"Paul, sometimes I wonder how you can be so mature. Your father and I will always love you very much."

He beamed at her and stared at the sterile floor.

Ian rubbed her hand against his face. "I don't think any other man can love a woman as much as I love you."

Joe kissed Lorelei lightly on her cheek. "Congratulations." He smiled up at Ian. "To both of you. But I believe Lorelei should know what happened while she was on her journey." Joe stared at Mandy.

Mandy threw up her hands. "I can't explain anything that's happened in the past twelve hours."

"Okay, okay. I saw this weird energy above your stomach, and for some reason I felt compelled to place my hand there. Then I got this strong vision of a fetus inside you. Plus I saw you and Ian together right after you delivered."

Lorelei tried to sit up, but Ian gently pushed her shoulders back down.

"What? Have you had this ability to predict pregnancies for long? What if you healed me when you did that? Maybe you're a medical empath."

"It did seem as if she were performing a Reiki session," Joe said. "We'll have to wait and see if everything is okay as far as the ultrasound. But I'm sure you'll be out of here tomorrow."

"I'm telling you the same thing I told Ian, Joe and Paul. I have *never* had any abilities at all. Until this teleportation thing and meeting all of you." Mandy shook her head in frustration and walked out of the room.

Joe ran out after her.

Lorelei noticed two nurses outside her room; a taller, thinner woman with long dark hair tied in a ponytail and a heavier set nurse with short light brown hair and a flower tattoo on her ankle. They both checked Joe out from the bottom up. The taller nurse with dark hair muttered something to the heavyset nurse. They both started giggling.

"Lore, is Mandy the woman you saw with Joe in your vision you had at the hotel?" Ian asked.

"Not sure. I couldn't tell—I only saw a silhouette. There was definitely some serious intimacy going on." She looked at Ian and Paul. "I tried to ask Galiena about Mandy, but she sent me back to earth too quickly."

Paul pulled a candy bar out of his pocket. "Do you think Shannon, or Galiena, took over Mandy's body while she was here on earth?"

"Sweetie, I don't think so. Their looks are strikingly similar, but Mandy has had a totally different life than who we knew as Shannon."

Ian placed his hand gently on Lorelei's stomach. "What if Galiena modeled or cloned herself after Mandy as far as the appearance?"

"Makes you wonder if there are any others like Galiena on Earth. Are Dagon, Annie and Mattie assuming other forms?"

"I don't think so. The difference is they *were* human prior to their deaths. Galiena never was. Looks like she might have modeled herself after Mandy."

Ian traced his finger over her lips and down her chin. It made her want to be away from the hospital and alone with him.

"Ian, what if he tries this again? The note mentioned 'what you are yet to discover will make you suffer.' Sounds like Mandy's kidnapper knew of my condition and possibly did something to cause my pain. Unless this is all coincidence."

"Her abductor could have meant something entirely different. Or maybe he's just messing with your head. But I am concerned about it. I feel this is partly my fault. I meant to do a protection spell, but discovered I didn't have all the items I needed. Not to mention Mandy didn't seem too comfortable with that topic."

"Honey, you have nothing to feel bad about. This isn't an evil spirit we're dealing with. I know he didn't teleport with Mandy and me, so how the hell did he get to the hotel? Even if he were trying to pursue Mandy, how could he have found us so quickly?"

Lorelei started to shiver, though it wasn't from the temperature in the room. "I really hope we're not talking about another dark arts case."

Ian gave her a sexy smile. "You do have a way of attracting the nefarious types."

She smiled at him tiredly, barely able to keep her eyes open.

"Why don't you get some sleep?" Ian asked. "I'm not going anywhere."

Right before Lorelei closed her eyes, she observed someone watching her from outside another patient's room—a man with straight, shoulder length shaggy brown hair, and burn scars covering his face and neck. And as he took a few steps down the hall, Lorelei noticed a slight limp in his left leg. Just like Mandy's abductor.

She grabbed onto Ian's arm in panic, forcing her eyes open one last time. When she looked up again, Mandy's kidnapper was gone.

15

The clicking of the knob from the outside the door of the two-story home in Florence, Arizona, surprised Brandon Winn, network engineer and paranormal investigator. It seemed as if someone were about to welcome him and his girlfriend Jacenda inside—only this house was empty.

They stood at the front door, peeking into the window for a few minutes. He and Jacenda had come to check out the abandoned home to verify the reports of unexplained activity for the bank that owned the property.

"What the heck? There shouldn't be anybody in there." Brandon picked up his equipment case with two voice recorders and flashlights, night vision cameras, Tri-Field Meter, KII Meter, camcorder, and thermal imaging camera.

"Based on the experience with the door, I would say the action is starting. Are you ready for this? The previous homeowner abandoned this place due to some pretty extreme paranormal activity. The neighbor on a nearby lot said whatever spirit inhabited this house caused the roommate to go insane."

"I'll be fine." Jacenda winked. "You'll protect me if anything happens."

He couldn't understand why someone so stunning would be attracted to him. She had long, dark black hair and the brightest green eyes he had ever seen. Before he met her, Brandon thought there was no such thing as a fairy tale—at least for him. The most amazing thing, he knew she felt the same way. He could see it when she looked at him. "Who knows, you might end up having to catch my back."

She slipped his wire-framed glasses off his face and kissed him fiercely. "I have no idea what I would do without you."

Brandon pulled her close and looked at her quizzically. "What makes you think you would have to do without me?"

The knob rotated of its own accord, admitting the way into a place void of harmony, family and care. It had not only become an eyesore with the overgrown weeds, pigeon-packed roof and ledges, and driveway cluttered with flyers and newspapers, it had also become a symbol of its neighbor's worst fears.

They glanced at each other.

Brandon opened and closed the door a few times to see if it was loose. "Seems pretty secure."

"I guess we've been officially invited in," Jacenda said.

"Hello?" Brandon called out. He waited a few seconds then followed Jacenda into the home.

"What did you expect, honey? For the house to answer, 'Yeah, I'm here. Make yourself at home. And by the way, watch out for those mischievous spirits.' "

He laughed nervously. That was one of the things he really loved about Jacenda. She found humor in everything.

Brandon set his equipment on the aging brown cloth couch; the only piece of furniture in the room. He opened the equipment case and handed a larger flashlight to Jacenda. A stairway with wooden banister led from the great room they were in to the upstairs. As he stared into the darkness, he thought he saw a shadow appear out of nowhere in the living room before walking upstairs. The shape couldn't have been more than four feet tall.

Jacenda glanced out the window. "Dale just pulled into the driveway."

Dale, fellow computer geek, sandy-haired ex-football player and paranormal investigator, unloaded his equipment from his car.

Brandon opened the door to let him in. "Interesting stuff happening already. The doorknob moved before Jace and I entered and I might have seen a child's shadow."

Dale placed his equipment case next to Brandon's on the couch and waved to Jacenda. "Wow. Let's hope the action continues."

"Let's do a walkthrough before we establish the baseline readings," Brandon said. He glanced upstairs but didn't see any sign of the small shadow.

Walking further into the house, Brandon looked closer at the empty surroundings. Putrescence throttled his senses while he stood in the kitchen. Death and decay infiltrated his nostrils and even worked their way into his taste buds.

"Are either of you smelling what I am?"

Jacenda used her flashlight to scan the room. "No."

Brandon felt as if he were being asphyxiated by the Grim Reaper. He wretched and gagged, frantically trying to find a bathroom, with one hand on his stomach and flashlight in the other. "I'm going to lose my dinner."

The beam of light hit an open door with a glimpse of a white toilet. He shot in and prayed to the porcelain gods. "Shit!" He had thrown up the spaghetti and meatballs from a few hours ago. The smell of rotting flesh kept him captive to the tiny bathroom. Jacenda and Dale watched him from the doorway.

"Brandon, are you okay?" Jacenda entered the bathroom, removed a washcloth from the rack, ran it under cold water and handed it to him. She rubbed his back while he wiped his face and mouth.

"I feel better now. Didn't either of you smell that? Like I walked into a room full of dead animals."

Dale shook his head. "Are you sure you're feeling up to this investigation?"

"I'm fine now. The scent has completely dissipated." He headed back to the front of the house with Jacenda and Dale behind him.

Dale started to set up his night vision camera facing the living room. "Don't kiss Jacenda with that mouth."

She looked at him with concern. "We can do this another time."

"I told you, I'm better." He caressed her arm. "I think it's something in this house. Get some baseline temperature readings and photos."

Jacenda started to go upstairs.

"No!" Brandon said.

She turned and looked at him in surprise.

"I'm sorry. I didn't mean to yell. I want you to stay down here with Dale and me for now. I want to make sure you're safe. This is an extreme case and considering what's happened already."

She smiled. "Of course. I'll start in the kitchen."

He grabbed her arm as she passed by. "I love you."

Jacenda kissed him on the cheek, blowing briefly into his ear. "I love you, too."

Brandon began to mount his own digital camera onto a tripod to catch the childlike shadow he had seen when entering the house. He noticed Dale staring at something between the great room and the kitchen.

Brandon followed his gaze and saw an opaque mist. Human in form at first, it transformed into an amoeba shape. In a split second, the vapor became a baseball-sized, pulsating light that glowed golden, blue and pale pink. Brandon and Dale watched, mesmerized, as it zipped in between them and paused, hanging in mid-air. The light hesitated, checking them both out before vanishing through the dining room wall.

Brandon and Dale stared at the spot where the mysterious orb had appeared.

"Oh, man," Dale finally said. "That was intense."

"Yeah, so intense, neither of us caught it on camera. The damn thing went behind the night vision camera, not in front of it. I'd say that thing had some intelligence."

Brandon ran into the kitchen where Jacenda was taking pictures. "Are you all right?"

"Sure, why?"

"Dale and I saw a rather large, colorful orb. It headed in this direction."

"How come you two are having all the fun? I haven't heard or seen anything. I've been taking pictures, so maybe I caught something on camera."

"Why don't you come into the living room with Dale and me?"

"I'll be in there in a minute. I'm going to do some EMF readings and check the dining room out."

Brandon sighed and left the kitchen. "Shout if you experience anything."

Brandon walked into the living room to see Dale checking the camera.

"You need to stop worrying about her," Dale said. "Jacenda really enjoys doing this sort of work. And she knows what she's doing."

"I can't bear the thought of her getting hurt, especially considering all the stuff that's happening. And we haven't even been here fifteen minutes."

Dale removed a KII meter and a voice recorder and set them between him and Brandon. "How about we do an EVP session down here?"

"Fine by me. Maybe we'll catch the voice of that four-foot shadow I saw when I came into the house. Or that unbelievable orb." Brandon could see the flashes from the dining room where Jacenda was taking pictures.

"Maybe they are one and the same," Dale said.

"Is there a child here with us?" Brandon asked. The Tri-Field Meter he held spiked to fifteen milliGauss, indicating a spirit could be present.

"Holy shit!" Dale said. That's a large spike. My KII also lit up all the way to red.

"If there is a child talking here, how old are you?" Brandon walked slowly around the living room. "You can talk to us and we will hear you through this small device I'm holding."

"I could have sworn I heard a giggle." Dale pointed to the dining room. "From where Jacenda is."

Brandon and Dale ran into the kitchen.

Jacenda was on both knees on the hardwood floor, talking to someone Brandon couldn't see. "It's okay, honey. They won't hurt you. We're here to see what's going on."

Brandon couldn't believe his eyes. In the six months they had been dating, she had never mentioned she could talk to ghosts. That would explain her interest in the paranormal.

Jacenda looked at the floor rather than Brandon. "Guess you had to find out sooner or later. I can communicate with spirits. At least with children." She stood up. "The little boy ran upstairs."

"Did he tell you anything?" Dale asked.

"He's five years old and used to live here. I'm not picking up on any other spirits. For some reason, I've only been able to detect young children."

Brandon didn't want to mention it in front of Dale, but he wondered why she hadn't brought her ability up before. She should have known he would be accepting of it.

A noise from upstairs startled Brandon. "Did you both hear that?"

Dale and Jacenda nodded.

"Sounded like a shower curtain sliding on its rod," Dale said.

Jacenda ran upstairs with Brandon and Dale behind her. She entered the guest bathroom at the top of the stairs. She gasped and jumped backwards into Brandon.

Brandon pushed past her and slowly opened the maroon shower curtain. "What's the matter? Did you see something?"

She stared into the shower. "Yes. A large, heavyset man was standing in there. I only saw him for a few seconds."

"That must have had something to do with the sound we heard downstairs."

Brandon laughed and rubbed her shoulders. "What exactly did you see? Are we talking specific body parts or a shadow?"

"A solid outline—looked like he had clothes on." Jacenda slid open the shower curtain slowly. "His presence didn't feel very threatening."

Brandon focused the thermal imaging camera inside the bathtub. No heat image. "I thought you could only talk to children."

"That's right. I just happened upon this spirit at the right time. I think one of you would have seen him had you entered the room first."

Dale lifted his shirt away from his skin repeatedly. "Has anyone noticed that it's becoming increasingly warm in here?"

Jacenda removed her temperature probe from her back jean pocket. "Wow. This thing is showing eighty-four degrees and climbing."

Beads of sweat rolled down the side of Brandon's face. He removed his handkerchief from his pocket and wiped the moisture away. They began to form immediately on his skin again.

The bathroom turned into a sauna. Jacenda became faint with the overwhelming heat and nearly collapsed on the floor.

"Whoa." Brandon caught her from behind. "Let's get out of here." Dale supported her other side as they moved downstairs.

On the stairs, Brandon thought he heard crackling and popping. At the bottom, massive, orange-red flames suddenly popped up from the floor. They licked hungrily at the vaulted ceiling. Thick, swirling gray smoke engulfed them. Screams of agony emanated from everywhere.

"Follow me," Brandon yelled, racing to the front door.

Brandon, Dale and Jacenda dashed directly through the fire. Yet none of them were getting burned.

Brandon attempted to open the front door, but quickly pulled his hand away as the metal knob melted. Agonizing screams and uncontrollable coughs continued to come from behind them. In the midst of the smoke, he saw an unrecognizable human form disintegrate into a skeleton and drop into a pile of ashes on the floor.

Dale pushed Brandon aside and kicked the front door open. They helped Jacenda outside and watched the terror unfold.

Then it all stopped. The smoke dissipated. The fire disappeared. The horrifying screams ceased. Chaos turned into quiet.

"Are you both all right?" Brandon asked.

Jacenda and Dale nodded.

"No wonder the bank can't sell this place," Jacenda said.

Brandon placed his arm around her. She trembled uncontrollably.

"We at least have to go back in to get our equipment." Dale stared into the front window. "It looks okay in there now. I don't see any fires."

They looked at each other.

"If one of us goes in, we all go," Jacenda said.

"We need to finish this," Brandon said. "The Arizona-Irish is a professional paranormal group and we've been hired to provide answers."

Jacenda opened the door cautiously and stepped inside.

Brandon started to follow, but an invisible hand pushed him backward.

The door slammed behind Jacenda, trapping her inside.

16

Tony Zimmerman's heart beat furiously as he waited anxiously atop the solid black bull named "Force of Nature," infamous for bucking riders within three seconds. Tony had two goals in the Indian National Finals Rodeo—beat the previous buck-off rate and his previous score of 144.

His hands gripped the reigns tightly and he could feel the older bull shifting under his weight. Both were ready. Force of Nature stamped and snorted in anticipation within the pen. The bull was known to spin to the inside in an attempt to unseat the cowboy. But Tony had an uncanny ability for being able to determine the animal's movements and react accordingly.

The murmurs of the crowd died out and the last few seconds felt like hours. Finally, the gate opened and Force of Nature shot out, turning, kicking and bucking. Tony held on as tightly as he could while his opponent tried to repeatedly throw him off.

Each thrust into the air made Tony more determined. Each time the bull turned to the inside, Tony tuned into Force of Nature, becoming one with his angry, violent counterpart.

The hundreds of people in the stands hollered, cheered and waved their cowboy hats in excitement when he managed to stay on for four seconds.

"Unbelievable," the announcer yelled. "Tony Zimmerman does it again. FBI agent, hoop dancer and professional bull rider. This man is definitely in tune with this force of nature."

Four seconds turned into four and a half. He felt the muscles of the animal as it furiously attempted to buck him off. Five seconds. Tony could hear the heartbeat of Force of Nature. At the six second mark, the uncanny connection broken, Tony was thrown a foot into the air and hit the ground of the arena.

He lay on the hard dirt on his stomach, coughing and struggling to breathe, while the rodeo clown distracted Force of Nature.

The crowd roared when Tony slowly stood up and was led to safety by two other bull riders. Whistles and shouts of encouragement followed him out of the arena.

A younger cowboy, named Kirt, shook his head in amazement. "I don't know how you do it."

He glanced up toward the western half of the arena to see a man leaving the stands. For a brief second, the sixty-something Native American man with thick, long grey hair looked at Tony. The stranger had the same features as his biological father—who had given him up for adoption almost thirty years ago.

17

Joe hiked down to get to the Boulder House, part of the Square Tower Group at Hovenweep National Monument. Other federal agents were already at the location to find evidence. Or Mandy's abductor.

A white ceramic potsherd two feet off his path caught his attention. Joe leaned down and picked up the piece of pottery. He recognized it as Anasazi black-on-white with portions of an elaborate design detailed on the ceramic piece.

Mandy approached him from behind. "That's beautiful."

"Yes, it is." He handed her the sherd. "This is one of the styles distinctive to the ancestral Puebloans."

Joe turned to her so suddenly she stumbled back a step. Though not his intention, he could tell he made her nervous. Every time she looked at him, she seemed to be watching some sort of scene unfold.

Did Galiena find Mandy for me? Did Galiena create Shannon based on Mandy? Was the woman before him the one he had really fallen in love with?

"Are you sure you want to be out here? The man who kidnapped you could still be around."

"I feel safe. You and Alan are both here."

That was one difference between Mandy and Shannon. Being an FBI agent, Shannon never relied on anyone to rescue her. She didn't need to. Yet Joe sensed a quiet, internal strength about Mandy. A strength and determination that made him want to know more.

They carefully scrambled through pinyon and juniper to get to the ruins within the monumental boulder. Twenty minutes later, Joe and Mandy stood inside a ten-by-fifteen-foot pueblo, staring at the passage.

Mandy jumped when Joe touched her shoulder. "Is this the place?"

She shook her head adamantly. "Yes. This is where you enter to get to the cave."

"Alan." Joe waved his hand to get his friend's attention. "This is it. I thought there were other agents out here. We need two to enter and I want at least one agent out here with Mandy."

Alan ran up to Joe. "They are in the visitor center waiting for a National Park Service officer to lead them here."

"Mandy, could you tell if your kidnapper lived in the cave?" Alan asked. "NPS stated they haven't seen anyone in or around the Boulder House. Or the other ruins along the main trail. Tourists haven't reported anything either and this is a very popular place since it's so close to the visitor center."

"Trust me, he was here. You'll see this tunnel dips and leads to another cave or other ruins, though I didn't go into that part of the system. He tied me up in the first chamber."

Agent Tony Zimmerman jogged up to the ruins and shook hands with Joe. He was a handsome thirty-two year-old Native American of Navajo, Hopi and Apache descent, with long straight black hair tied in a ponytail, wearing a white polo shirt with navy pants and a navy jacket. A fairly new recruit with the FBI from the past year, Agent Zimmerman was considered one of the most intelligent on the force.

"Let's go," Joe said to Agent Zimmerman. "Alan, stay here with Mandy and keep an eye out. He could be watching us."

Mandy grabbed his arm. Her eyes pleaded with him. "Please, be careful. He might be expecting you."

Without thinking, Joe kissed her on top of her head. He thought he had been very intimate with Shannon. He had been wrong. The three seconds spent close to Mandy overwhelmed him.

She placed her arms around his waist for a second before stepping back.

Did she feel the same thing?

"Follow the short passage past the rooms. You'll find the cave," she said.

"How did you fare at the rodeo?" Joe led the way into the ruins, turning to look at the agent.

"Fantastic." Tony's eyes lit up. "I ended up with a score of 220, winning the adult division for bull riding."

He shook hands with Tony. "Congratulations." Joe had heard of Tony's strong connection to animals, especially to those that were wild and untamed.

"Well, Agent Zimmerman. Let's see if we can catch us a criminal."

Joe led the way, stepping over a stone wall and ancient fire pit. A T-shaped doorway opened up into a cave twenty feet by ten feet with a ten-foot tall ceiling. Joe motioned for Tony to stay inside the last pueblo. He listened for movement but didn't hear a thing. It could be an ambush.

Joe entered the chamber and waved Agent Zimmerman inside. He removed his flashlight from his back pocket and turned it on. Joe and Tony were the only ones in the cave.

Tony's head whipped to the right.

"What's wrong?" Joe asked.

"Felt like a hand wrapped around my arm."

Joe glanced around. "I'm sure there are Native American spirits here with us." He searched for the passage Mandy had mentioned.

"Over here," Tony whispered. He stared into a corner of the cave where the ground gradually dipped into a tighter tunnel three feet across.

"This must be the place Mandy mentioned. Let's found out where this goes."

Tony slipped and lost his footing, landing on his butt.

"Are you all right?" Joe asked.

He didn't answer.

Joe leaned down and noticed the younger agent had his fingers to his lips, instructing Joe to be quiet. Tony stood up slowly and pointed into a wide opening ten feet ahead.

They crept up to the entrance of the second chamber. Joe stared into the darkness for movement.

Scuffling emanated from the opposite side of what looked to be a six foot by five foot room. Joe and Tony pointed their guns where the sound had come from.

"FBI! Stop!" Joe yelled.

Joe turned his flashlight on. He saw a pair of legs step up from the top rungs of a wooden ladder and into a crawlspace about six feet above the cave floor. Joe quickly climbed the ladder and tried to grab the man's legs, but the stranger moved too fast.

"Jesus. That space is less than two feet wide," Tony said. "How the hell can he maneuver in there?"

Watching the person struggle to maneuver further into the above-ground space, Joe saw the torso and legs of a man transform into something much smaller. It scurried down the miniature passage. For a split second, the creature turned to look at him. Its eight, dark beady eyes taunted Joe.

Joe almost slipped and fell from the ladder, while he reached down for the radio Tony held. "Alan, we caught a man escaping from the ground of a very small chamber up into a crawlspace in the ceiling. We're on the opposite side of where you are. Keep a watch to see if he comes out anywhere in the vicinity."

Loud crackling burst from the radio. "We've got these pueblos and cliffs surrounded," Alan responded. "If or when he comes out, we'll find him."

Did I really see a man shapeshift into a tarantula? Could that be why no one sees this guy?

"From what Lorelei told me, can't miss him," Joe said into the radio. "He has serious burn scars on his face and neck. Wouldn't think he'd be able to get too far with that limp either."

"No. They haven't seen him. Bill, with park law enforcement, mentioned they would close the whole park until we catch him."

"Agent Zimmerman and I are going to check in the Boulder House more closely to see what we can find. Might want to send an evidence response team out here as well."

"Taken care of," Alan said. "See you soon."

Joe tossed the radio back to Tony. Joe wanted to mention the bizarre occurrence to Alan, but he wasn't sure what he had really seen.

Tony started swiping at his arms, neck and face. His fingers attempted to remove invisible threads from his body.

Joe smiled. "Something's taken a liking to you."

Tony rolled his eyes. "Why aren't you experiencing this?"

"Not sure. Maybe you have a ghostly girlfriend."

Tony suddenly stopped swiping at his body. He stared intently at something at his feet.

Joe shined the flashlight at the floor of the chamber and kneeled down to see a shiny black object. "It's an ancient serrated arrowhead made from obsidian or volcanic glass. Only what's on the end of this weapon isn't ancient."

Tony leaned over to take a closer look. "Blood."

Joe thought back to the piece of pottery used as a weapon by Ray, a man hired by Peter and Emily to help manage the Native American artifact theft ring in the unexcavated section of the Wupatki Ruin north of Flagstaff. Ray had used a large, sharp shard to kill Alicia Atwell, a student of Peter's also involved in the theft operation, for attempting to steal some of the artifacts. Now it appeared another handmade weapon of the ancestral Puebloans were being used for modern torture. Had the man who escaped their grasp used this arrowhead? If so, did he have another victim hidden away in another cave or ruin?

Tony removed a roll of blue tape from his back pocket, ripped off a piece and placed it next to the arrowhead. "For the evidence response team."

"Appears there's only a drop or two of blood on this tool," Joe said. "Looks recent, though Mandy didn't mention he had done any harm to her."

Tony placed a plastic evidence glove on his hand and turned the arrowhead carefully in his fingers. "The placement of this seems a little too convenient."

Joe remembered his vivid dream from the night before. A threatening shadow always in the darkness, darting from one collapsed pueblo to another, from a hole in the side of a cliff to a stone tower, and traveling from canyon bottoms to mesas. Women's screams penetrated the night repeatedly.

Only the shadow from his dream was no spirit. This man seemed to know Hovenweep National Monument better than any of the park rangers. He used that to his advantage. Like he had done with Mandy. There would be other victims, or were there already?

"You're right. Think we've got a major game player here. I have a feeling this man is also holding on to multiple women. Only this perp is going to do much more damage than breaking hearts."

Anger and confusion inundated Joe's mind. He wanted to concentrate on the case with Mandy's abductor. Yet he couldn't keep thinking about how much she looked like Shannon; another cruel hand dealt by fate. He had traveled to the Four Corners with Lorelei and Ian, hoping to escape her memory. Instead, Joe fell, trapped into a mirror of the past. Should he choose to play the game and help solve the crime

among the prehistoric Square Tower Group of ruins, would this looking glass reveal the relationship between Mandy and Shannon? Would
the perpetrator be leading him along blindly through an underworld
of ancient spirits rather than fairytale characters? And would he escape
the madness with his sanity?

18

Jacenda jumped when the door slammed behind her, trapping her in the haunted home. Brandon and Dale were outside, trying to get in. Brandon attempted to pull, push and open the door. In desperation, he started to pound on the wooden frame.

"Jacenda!"

"I'm okay, honey." She tried to open the knob. It wouldn't work. The house wanted only her.

Turning around to face the inside of the home, she shakily pointed her flashlight into the living room and dining room. The little boy spirit she had briefly talked with earlier stared at her from the bottom of the stairwell.

"Do you know what's going on? Why am I locked in?"

No answer. The blond-haired child dissipated.

Brandon kicked the door in frustration. Hard. "We're going to get you out of there."

A noise from behind her startled Jacenda. She quickly turned her head. Brandon glanced into the front bay window, his brown eyes wide with fear. The long beige curtains that revealed the street quickly closed, blocking him from view.

"Damn it," Brandon screamed.

"We're going to try and find another way in," Dale yelled. "You will be okay."

She heard their footsteps on gravel as they ran through the front yard, over the riverbed and into the side yard.

"Okay." Jacenda spoke into Dale's voice recorder that had been left on the table, still turned on. "If you're going to trap me in here, at least give me your story. Who is responsible? Why won't you let my friends in?"

She couldn't hear anything, but hoped the device would pick something up. Desperation filled the air. Jacenda had always had amazing intuitive abilities pertaining to the living and the dead. Perhaps that's why the house had taken her hostage.

The cameras were still recording.

Brandon and Dale's voices called from the backyard.

"Jace!" Brandon pounded so hard on the sliding glass door at the back of the house she thought he would break it.

"I'm fine," she yelled, running to greet him.

He placed his hand against the glass, as if trying to touch her. She had never seen such panic in his eyes.

Brandon started to talk to her, but his voice became drowned out by a humming noise. Low and steady for a few seconds, the sound rose to a level Jacenda couldn't bear. She dropped her audio recorder and placed her hands over her ears.

Looking up, she noticed Brandon and Dale's faces. They glanced around nervously. Brandon's hands dropped from the sliding glass doors to his side and he looked over at Dale quizzically, pale-faced. She remembered Brandon telling her about the adventure at Texas Canyon Ranch and how the team had encountered the very same phenomena under the ranch while trying to solve a murder mystery. Why would she be experiencing the same thing at a home in Florence? Could it be due to the unseen explosive energy around her?

Unhappiness and desperation resonated from everywhere inside the home. She should be focusing on *it*. Not her friends. As soon as the thought entered her mind, the humming ceased. That's when the cobweb-like sensation started. Invisible tendrils encircled her. Wispy fingers wrapped around her upper body, working their way down to her stomach and legs. A gentle finger stroked the side of her face.

When she looked up again, Jacenda found herself standing at the foot of the stairway. She gazed up in trepidation, hesitant because of the man she had encountered in the upstairs bathroom earlier in the evening.

I have to go up there. That's why they've locked me in here.

She could feel Brandon and Dale watching her helplessly from the backyard.

She tried not to focus on the open door of the guest bathroom; instead, Jacenda observed the hallway. A brilliant orb of light shot from the master bedroom toward one of the other two bedrooms.

Cautiously, Jacenda ascended the stairs, holding onto the banister tightly. The floor below her creaked. She took a deep breath and kept going until she reached the top floor.

Standing between the two bedrooms, Jacenda could feel a presence behind her. Had something followed her?

She turned to look back. Nothing.

The icy chill from the larger bedroom made her shiver. She pulled out her temperature probe from her back pocket. It read forty-five degrees.

"This can't be good," she whispered, slowly entering the bedroom.

Loud banging occurred downstairs. It sounded like the kitchen cabinets slamming shut repeatedly.

The carpet had a few stains. The dark red walls were covered in fist-sized holes. And the walk-in closet hid a strange glowing light source that emanated from under the closed door.

She breathed deeply, placing her hand on the brass knob. "Angels, give me your protection." Then she opened the closet door all the way.

A radiant cocoon overcame her and she shielded her eyes. She could no longer see the shelves, the ceiling, the floor or the closet.

I'm in a portal.

Warmth surrounded her. The same warmth and comfort she found in Brandon's arms. She wondered if he and Dale were still trying to get into the house.

Jacenda felt as if she were floating and glanced down. At first, she thought she could no longer see the carpet due to the bizarre, bright light. Then she realized the floor wasn't there. Her body hung freely.

Have I been consumed by the house? Turned into another of its spirits?

The vibrations she heard earlier returned. This time, her very being trembled from the movement they created.

The light intensified until she thought she would go blind.

The vibrations stopped. The brilliant ray of light vanished. The whole house relaxed and returned to normal. She could feel it breathe a sigh of relief as she stood in the middle of the closet.

"Jace," Brandon screamed from downstairs. "Jace! Where are you?"

He ran into the bedroom with Dale right behind him.

She turned and jumped into his arms. "I'm so happy to see you."

Brandon held her tightly, picking her up off the ground. "I felt so helpless not being able to get in. I could only imagine the worst."

"Wait." Dale looked around in the room. "I checked up here a minute ago looking for you."

"I was in the closet."

"No. I saw the clothes hanging in there, some boxes on the shelves and a few blankets. But you weren't in there."

Jacenda suddenly understood. The extraordinary home had taken her, enfolding her in its blanket of illumination.

19

Brandon reviewed the video footage of himself, Jacenda and Dale in the bathroom of the haunted home in Florence. He slid the shower curtain slowly to the right. Unseen to the naked eye, yet visible to the camcorder, the spirit of a stocky Native American man stood there; his dark skin stark against the white ceramic tiles. He stared back at the investigators with curiosity, confusion and a hint of fear.

Despite his size, something about this spirit didn't seem so threatening. He wore a buckskin leather top and matching pants and a wooden spear in his right hand rested against the tub floor. Black shoulder-length hair cascaded around his shoulders and his brown eyes glanced from Brandon, to Jacenda, to Dale, then back to Brandon. *Definitely an intelligent haunt.*

Having an interest in history and archaeology, Brandon knew the Hohokam had resided in the Phoenix and Tucson areas starting around A.D. 400 until A.D. 1300. Archaeologists had found evidence of ancient villages in north Phoenix, central Phoenix and the eastern suburbs of the Valley of the Sun, including Florence. Could the house they were asked to investigate be built where the Indians used to live? Many pithouses were burned prior to migrations or from violent invasions. Had the fire been the result of an event from the prehistoric past? Or was this particular phantom even related to the Hohokam?

Seeing the Native American apparition was minor compared to what had happened to Jacenda. The house, or something within it, had kidnapped her, lured her upstairs and absorbed her into some sort of portal.

She hadn't sensed any particular spirit that had caused the trouble. Rather, Jacenda told Brandon that she felt the house itself had wanted her.

All the doors on the Florence home opened once Jacenda had been overtaken by the strange energy. She insisted she felt fine, but Brandon was concerned about the trauma she might have experienced.

The night vision cameras had caught fiery flashes from the faux fire. But Brandon and Dale didn't come across any other evidence. Jacenda, however, still hadn't reviewed her audio from her lone vigil in the house. Brandon downloaded her audio file and listened to it. The first five minutes of her audio revealed a child's chilling laughter. Probably the little boy she had connected with.

Forty-five minutes later, there were a few loud bursts of static. Then various voices came through. Some were talking in another language—possibly Native American. Others were inaudible male and female whispers.

This has to be the closet. The portal.

The next voice he heard was Jacenda's.

"I will. I promise."

20

Lorelei got up from the couch and walked over to Ian, who prepared dinner in the kitchen of her Mediterranean-style home with hanging tapestries of cottages by the sea, paintings of stately homes overlooking vineyards, beige walls, and a large rug with warm tones of maroon, brown and green. Native American influences of a coffee table shaped like a drum along with a dream catcher, rattle and miniature drum hanging together in the hallway blended well with the soft colors and reflected Ian's tastes. A stunning picture in earth tones of American Indian elders telling stories sat next to a picture of a Mediterranean sun rising above cliff-side buildings by the sea. "Honey, I want to help. I'm not an invalid."

Ian put down the knife he was using to cut the chicken and kissed her softly on the lips. "I want you to relax. You've only been out of the hospital for two days."

"I'm going to rot away sitting here doing nothing. The doctor gave me the stamp of good health. So did Mandy."

"Mandy's not a doctor. But after predicting your pregnancy…."

"Do you think the teleportation really did cause her to develop the energy talent? I wonder if she can also determine other diseases and illnesses."

"Maybe it's been lying dormant. Her experience here might have somehow brought it out. She is five months pregnant herself, so that might have made her more sensitive."

"Is she coming to dinner tonight?"

"No. She's back in Flagstaff. The FBI has someone keeping a watch on her." Ian smiled and winked. "I think she's had enough of us for awhile."

"I suppose. I hoped she would be here."

Ian placed the raw cubes of chicken in a plate on the side and washed some whole mushrooms. "Lore, she isn't Shannon. And Joe isn't ready for a relationship right now. I know you miss the way things were."

"Ian, you spent enough time with Mandy. She is Shannon. I really think Galiena used her likeness to create Shannon."

"Even if that's the case, it doesn't mean she's going to end up with Joe. I know you want for him to have what we have, but maybe he's meant for someone entirely different. I don't see him getting together with Mandy under such harsh circumstances. She's five months pregnant, her boyfriend abandoned her, and she's had a rather bad experience with the kidnapping."

Lorelei sighed and picked up a paring knife to cut the red and green peppers on the counter. "Ian, do you think Mandy might have actually healed whatever damage her abductor did to me? After all, the threat he made in the note. That horrible pain can't be mere coincidence. I think he knew I was pregnant."

Ian put chicken and chunks of vegetables on skewers. He placed it on a plate and turned to her. "I was thinking about that in the hospital. Not sure how he would have picked up on that fact. But then again, we don't know how the hell he found us at the hotel so fast."

Someone knocked on the door.

Lorelei glanced at her watch. It read 5:30 p.m. "I thought we told Joe 6:00?"

Ian looked at the door hesitantly. "Joe said he might be here a little early."

Lorelei started to answer the door.

"No," Ian said. "Let me." He overtook Lorelei, beating her to the front door. He opened it cautiously.

She breathed a sigh of relief when she saw Joe.

Joe glanced from Ian to Lorelei and back to Ian. "I see you're both a little jumpy still." He handed Ian a gift basket with wine, cheeses and snacks.

"You could say that." Lorelei kissed Joe and hugged him before leading him to the couch. "Thanks so much for the nice gift."

"A congratulations gift. I know you're going to have a very healthy and *special* baby."

Joe glanced around. "Where is Paul?"

Ian took the basket from Joe, removed the bow and plastic and took out a bottle of red wine. "Over at a friend's house."

Ian retrieved a corkscrew from a draw in the kitchen and popped the cork on the wine. "So what's going on with the investigation at Hovenweep? You mentioned the FBI was out there to look around the ruins in the Square Tower Group."

"There's an evidence response team out there now. I saw a man disappearing into a small crawl space in the ceiling, or rather his legs. I couldn't see anything else. Between park law enforcement and the feds, we had the whole damn area covered. But we never found the guy. Must be holed up in the caves somewhere. We believe he's taunting us, treating this as a game."

Lorelei watched Ian remove three wine glasses from the cabinet. He poured a glass of red wine and handed it to Joe. Then he removed a pitcher of non-alcoholic margarita from the refrigerator and poured her a glass.

Joe stared down at the drink, swishing the liquid.

"Why would you think he's playing games?" Ian gave Lorelei the margarita.

"We found an ancient arrowhead with a few drops of blood on the tip. It's like he wanted us to see it."

"What if this man is merely careless?" Lorelei turned to face Joe. "Wait. You're hiding something."

Joe sighed heavily. "I climbed the ladder the man used to get into the crawlspace to escape. I aimed my flashlight to see and I could have sworn I saw his body change into…"

Lorelei placed her hand on his arm. "Into what, Joe?"

His beautiful brown eyes looked into hers. "A tarantula."

Ian had stopped in the middle of the living room, on his way to the grill. "That must be why Lore is seeing those visions. Perhaps the spirit or spirits who lured Lore underground know about the kidnapper."

"If Mandy's abductor *can* shapeshift, that would explain why no one is seeing him." Joe took a sip of his wine. "I've also had a few dreams. I'm seeing a man traveling around other sites of Hovenweep, including the Cutthroat Castle. He could have multiple victims hidden in different parts of the park. I believe he timed it for us to see him, yet so we couldn't see his face."

"Did you get specific visions of where the other victims might be?" Lorelei asked.

"No. Just images of the ruins. But if he tried to get to another location we'd spot him. FBI has that whole area surrounded. Plus there are copters covering the other sites in Hovenweep and Canyon of the Ancients."

Ian went outside to the patio and placed the chicken kabobs on the grill. He spoke loudly so Lorelei and Joe could hear in the living room. "Is anyone out there looking for the other victims? If there are any?"

"Unfortunately not. It's kind of a challenge telling the FBI to search for victims based on visions. I'll have to see whose blood shows up on that arrowhead. Mandy stated she never saw the arrow. Only a pocketknife and the hunting knife he pulled on her and Lorelei. Mandy claimed he didn't use either on her. So it can't be her blood."

"I hope it's not the blood of any other victims," Ian said.

"Perhaps he feels we won't be able to catch him. No matter whose blood it is. Agent Zimmerman is interviewing park rangers and other staff to see if they've spotted someone fitting this guy's description. Park law enforcement is putting up posters with his picture and will provide the FBI with the contact information of visitors who might have seen him.

Lorelei got up from the couch, took a plate of raw veggies, crackers and dip from the kitchen counter and placed it on the living room table. "Mandy said her abductor walked up and started a friendly conversation regarding the ruins and history of the area. Obviously, that's a ruse to lure victims."

"Yes, her kidnapper made sure there weren't any witnesses." Joe popped a wheat cracker in his mouth. "Some Hovenweep sites are much more remote, but the Boulder House ruins are pretty visible from the main trail. The Square Tower Group is the most popular site because of the accessibility. It stays pretty busy, so I would think someone would have seen him."

"Well, you can't miss him with those burn marks on his face," Lorelei said. "Definitely makes him an easier target. And he walked with a limp."

Lorelei and Joe joined Ian on the patio while he cooked dinner.

Ian turned the skewers. "Lore does have a tendency to come across the dark arts types. I'm wondering if this guy fits in that category, considering the unseen, unexpected encounter at the hotel and the way he's eluding the FBI and park officials."

Lorelei shivered when she thought of the possible transformation from human to arachnid. "The kidnapper's eyes looked familiar. Sort of like those of the warrior who murdered that poor family. Dark and malevolent."

Joe removed his smart phone from his back pocket and texted a message to someone.

Could this be news from Hovenweep?

"Shit," Joe blurted. "No luck. It's like the bastard completely disappeared." He looked at Lorelei and Ian.

Ian turned the kabobs on the grill. "Joe, you said he escaped into a rather small crawl space in the cave. If he is truly capable of changing into something smaller, then he could still be in there or might have escaped right before everyone's eyes."

Joe sighed and glanced at Lorelei. "I'm thinking we are dealing with another unorthodox mystery here. Perhaps the most challenging one yet."

Ian closed the top of the grill cover. He stared at the black cover as if seeing his own vision. "I still don't understand how he found us. Maybe he does have the ability to teleport. Or even out-of-body travel."

"That makes sense," Joe said. "He could have astral traveled or transported himself to a spot above ground while you, Alan and me were focused on getting Lore and Mandy out of the passage."

"You don't think he could be associated with the ancients?" Ian asked.

Lorelei looked up to see a shooting star. "I would hope not. Galiena, Dagon and the others usually aren't associated with people who would do such harm."

"Except for Scott, Mattie's son. Mattie was the caretaker of Vulture Mine and she cursed her son to a slow death of old age because of his attempt to steal her youth formula."

"True," Joe said. "But I'm not getting that impression this man's related to the ancients from my dream visions." He stepped out into the yard and stared up at the night sky. "What if we're not talking teleportation?"

"How else could the bastard find Lorelei and Mandy so quickly?" Ian walked over and stood next to Joe. "Even if he turned himself into a bird, he couldn't have followed us at 70 miles per hour."

Joe observed the stars intently for a minute. Lorelei wondered if he were trying to communicate with Galiena.

"Think about it," Joe said. "No one saw Mandy's kidnapper. Only the note on the door."

Lorelei traced her finger around the rim of her margarita glass. "Even if someone else left the note, her abductor would have had to communicate with this mystery person rather quickly. *I* didn't see anyone else in the caves and Mandy also confirmed she was alone with him. Not sure a cell phone would work in such a place."

Joe pulled the opposite patio chair next to hers and sat down. "You should understand better than anyone. I've dealt with my own share of bizarre, dangerous criminals specializing in magic and the supernatural." He moved his face within inches of hers. Joe's brown eyes were wide and she could see every tired crease-line. "How were you and Ian communicating during the mystery in Dragoon?"

"Telepathy."

Lorelei went inside to the kitchen and brought back cold salads and the veggies and crackers while Ian plated kabobs. "But who else could he be working with?"

Joe repeatedly turned a kabob over in his hand. "No way to know right now. We don't even know who the abductor is or where he's hiding. There's a manhunt for him. If he is indeed hiding other victims, hopefully the officers will find them as well."

Lorelei slid the green peppers, chunks of chicken, mushrooms and artichoke sections off the skewer. "I'm more than willing to go back to Hovenweep and help. I would like to figure out why I was dragged underneath the kiva and find out about the skull. Galiena appeared to me right before the recreation of that family's brutal murder. So it has to mean something."

Ian threw his head back in frustration. "Honey, you just got out of the hospital. I don't want you placing yourself in further danger." He knelt down, placed his hand on her stomach and looked her in the eyes. "Especially in your condition."

"We might not have a choice," Joe took a bite of chicken. "Her astral abilities or her nature talents could really help us."

Ian touched Lorelei on the shoulder and sat next to her. "Hey, man. You're my friend. You're supposed to support *me*."

"Sorry, not this time. We can do without her for another few days. But if we can't find him, Lore will have to be brought in. I know you and Paul will be able to help as well."

"What if she gets dragged into another tight passage, or ends up in the middle of another mystery? I'm worried about the stress and the potential for injury."

Lorelei placed her fork down. She took Ian's hand in hers. "Honey, as you've mentioned before, I didn't sign up for this. The ancients chose me to help others through my abilities. I can't walk away from women like Mandy who might be trapped in the middle of nowhere. Innocent victims who are suffering—wondering when, and if, help will come. You know very well what men like that are capable of. You stopped a very nefarious cult from sacrificing Abby, the young pregnant woman, years before you met me. Think of *her* out there alone."

"Okay, okay." Ian's chin fell to his chest. "You've convinced me. I know Galiena will protect you, and our baby, from harm."

As Ian mentioned Galiena, a radiant, snake-like formation shot across the moon. Lorelei stood up and followed the brick-lined cedar path to the edge of her property. Ian and Joe were right behind her.

They gasped. The quarter moon flashed a brilliant orange-red. Lava tendrils exploded around it. Invisible arms encompassed her own. Then warmth surrounded her lower stomach from the inside out.

21

Nicole never saw him coming. No cars were in the parking area of the remote Cajon Group at Hovenweep, a small group of ruins at the head of a canyon with views of Abajo peaks and the stone spires of Monument Valley. Nicole heard nothing except bird calls. No footsteps. No sense of dread or apprehension. He had grabbed her from behind. Nicole kicked and screamed, hoping someone would hear.

Her captor had punched her in the face, knocking her out. She woke up and found her tall frame had been callously crammed into a tight space. She couldn't see a thing in the impenetrable blackness and could only move two feet to either side. Her nose was swollen and throbbing and Nicole could taste blood.

Right before he grabbed her, her watch read 11:43 a.m.; fifteen minutes before her friend Matthew was supposed to call. Her watch had fallen off of her wrist when her abductor yanked her off of the trail. Now Nicole couldn't tell if it was day or night.

She gently ran her hand back and forth over her pregnant stomach. Nicole glanced up at the crags and crevices in the ceiling, praying to a god who could allow such injustice to happen.

Please don't let us die like this.

Something crawled over her right hand as it rested on the ground. Something with a light touch, yet with a feel of fur.

Nicole yanked her hand away and slid as far to the other side of the cave as possible.

She thought about her good friend, Matthew. He told her he would call her on her cell phone at noon, but she missed his call by fifteen minutes. Hopefully, he would keep trying to get hold of her, realize something was wrong and contact the authorities. Matt had been very concerned regarding her traveling alone.

When she had decided to have a baby through artificial insemination, Matt had proposed. He was in love with her, but she only thought of him as a brother. Now, she would give anything to see his smile again.

"Heeeelp!" Her voice hoarse, she yelled as loud as she could.

Panic started to set in again. She didn't want it to overtake her completely, or she might not make it out. Neither would her unborn child.

No! I'm going to fight to the end. I survived the plane crash my parents died in. I survived through the fire at my grandparents' house. So I can survive this.

Nicole stood up with the back of her head against the rock. She ran her hands along the sides of the cave a third time to find a possible entrance. He had to have gotten her in somehow.

Yet she could only feel damp stone and cracks. Nothing. Not even so much as a two-inch gap.

She kneeled on the ground, shuddering when she realized what might be down there with her. She covered every inch of the ground, but could not find a way to escape.

Leaning back against the wall, she began to kick to loosen chunks of rock. She kicked repeatedly on all of the walls for what seemed like hours.

"Damn it!" Nicole overextended her right leg in one last ditch effort to escape. She screamed in agony as the motion caused a leg cramp. But she couldn't walk it out. Crying and rubbing her calf, she began to sense this might be her tomb.

She suddenly became exhausted. Her eyes could no longer stay open, whether from lack of sleep, the recent strenuous activity, or both.

Nicole woke up, minutes or hours later, she wasn't sure. She gasped when hot breath touched her face. The cave walls were a blur and she could feel a stare penetrating through her.

A ring tone suddenly echoed throughout the chamber. Her cell phone. His breathing increased with every ring.

"Someone really misses you." His deep voice belied his calm demeanor. "He's been calling every few minutes."

He showed Nicole the lit display. Though she couldn't read it clearly, she knew he referred to Matt.

Nicole became more afraid the longer he sat in front of her. "People know where I am. Matt is going to get worried and call the cops."

A malevolent grin started at the corner of his mouth. For a second, his face seemed to turn sympathetic. Then he smiled— his face within an inch of hers. "I'm sure he will. And the police already are searching for me, but that doesn't mean they will find us. You see, I have all sorts of special hiding places in the park for my treasure."

She pulled her windbreaker around her tighter, shivering from the cold. It must have been getting dark outside. Closing her eyes, she willed him away. She didn't want to know why the police were searching for him.

"Please let me go," she begged. "I'm six months pregnant."

Nicole jumped when he slammed her phone onto the ground, smashing it with his hand.

"You're my prize now. You don't need that guy anymore." He made a fist with his right hand and a sudden, intense pain shot through her abdomen. The fist tightened even further. His hand shook and veins popped with the effort.

She screamed in agony, writhing in pain on the cold ground. Whether from the torture or fright, Nicole thought she saw her kidnapper's legs and torso vanish. A tarantula seemed to appear out of nowhere, right where he had been sitting. The plate-sized spider stared at her intently from two feet away with its eight beady eyes.

The tarantula moved closer. The pain intensified to a level she could no longer handle. At the last second of consciousness, she knew she would lose her baby and her life.

22

Joe stood by the bottom of the stairs in the haunted home in Florence. Bare, dirty walls, dull, light beige stained carpet and cobwebs in the corners of the ceiling told a tale of neglect and abandonment. Along with Lorelei and Ian, he had been asked to investigate the place that had terrorized Brandon, Dale and Jacenda. As a Native American and a shaman, he hoped he could help solve the paranormal puzzle. Joe closed his eyes. The house may have been abruptly forsaken by the living. But the dead had a very strong hold here.

"Are we ready?" Brandon brought Joe out of his reverie. Since the recent visit by Brandon, Dale and Jacenda two days before, the neighbors reported seeing flames erupting through the bay window, only to watch the fire dissipate seconds later. And they saw a group of three Native American men in the backyard.

Joe met Dale at the front door and took one of two cases of equipment from Dale's hands.

Brandon opened one of the cases and handed Joe a camcorder and audio recorder. "I appreciate you, Ian and Lore coming out to help. The bank and the neighbors need answers. I know you all will be able to help us figure this out."

"Glad to help," Joe said.

Lorelei stood inside the living room looking around. "I'll do what I can also. But Ian, Joe and I do have to leave for the Four Corners again tomorrow morning."

There had been a new victim in another part of Hovenweep National Monument. Yet the kidnapper remained undetected. Nicole Malloy had vanished four days prior—the same day Lorelei had been released from the hospital.

Her friend Matthew had talked to Nicole soon after she had arrived at the park and she had told him she was headed to the Cajon Group of ruins. Matthew attempted to contact her numerous times, but to no avail. And like Mandy, this victim was also pregnant; six months along. Joe hadn't wanted to return to the Four Corners. He had initially gone to the land of the ancients to escape from the pain. But found himself in the midst of two mysteries—and to solve one, he would have to rely on the one person he found so hard to be around. He wanted to abandon the case, just as the Florence home had been abandoned. Joe had told Alan he might have to take over. But the thought of numerous innocent women trapped in a subterranean hell made him realize he could never forgive himself.

"Dale, Brandon, you're both welcome to come to Hovenweep," Joe said. "The FBI is dealing with stuff way beyond the paranormal, but you might be able to add some perspective."

Dale placed batteries in two cameras. "Thanks for the invite, but it was all I could do to convince my wife to let me finish this investigation. Plus my son has a little league game this weekend."

"I think Jace and I will be relaxing around town." Brandon smiled at her. "Maybe do a day trip or head to the zoo."

Jacenda winked at Brandon.

Lorelei walked in a circle around the living room, staring down at the floor.

Jacenda began to take temperature and energy readings, watching Lorelei. "Are you detecting a presence?"

"Not in the house. I'm seeing a skeleton buried, placed in a sitting position underground."

Ian recorded the conversation. "Is the burial under the living room where you're focusing your attention?"

"I think so. At least the vision is the strongest in this spot. All I can detect is the skeleton though. No face. No voice. In other words, no communication."

"Dale and I did discover a conversation going on in here during the first investigation," Brandon said. "Not like the ancients' dialect, but we're thinking it could be Native American." He looked over at Joe. "I've got the audio file saved on my laptop if you want to take a listen."

"Sure, I'll see if I can help."

Brandon setup his computer on the dining room table and opened the file.

Placing Dale's headphones on, Joe noticed Lorelei's focus was still on the middle of the living room. Ian watched her closely.

Joe hit "play" on the software. There were a few seconds of silence then two voices. "Definitely sounds Native American. However, I don't think it's a present-day dialect. Could be prehistoric tongue, perhaps Hohokam. There have been excavations done in the 1970s in the Florence area. All sorts of villages have been found, many dating from the classic period, or A.D. 1100 to 1450."

Ian removed the thermal imager from its case. "There is no real way to verify if that language is Hohokam since no one today speaks with that dialect. Of course, Lore might be able to communicate with whoever it is to find out for sure."

"There is a conversation going on," Joe said. "I can hear two distinct voices. One is deeper than the other, but they are both male."

Dale placed a camera on a tripod. "The two men whose voices we caught sound sort of frantic. Maybe we'll be able to catch other evidence tonight to help us learn about the fire."

"What about the upstairs closet? Ian removed a recorder from his pocket and grabbed a tripod and camera from Dale's case. "You mentioned Jacenda had an intense experience up there."

"Yes, she did," Brandon said.

"Unfortunately, I don't remember much about it, other than a very bright light. Brandon noticed on audio that I responded to something because I said 'I will, I promise.' Only I don't remember that."

Dale started to hook cables to the video monitors. "Jacenda and Lore should do an EVP session in the closet once everything gets set up. Lore might be able to help Jacenda figure out what happened."

Brandon glanced from Jacenda to Dale. "I don't know if I want her going back up there. I'm worried about her being in this house at all considering what she went through."

Ian slapped Brandon on the back. "I know *exactly* how you feel. I worry about Lore constantly. Especially now that she's pregnant. But she's also a very independent woman who is going to do what she wants when she wants."

Brandon and Jacenda looked at each other and smiled.

Jacenda helped Dale with the monitors. "This place didn't do anything to harm me. Maybe it wanted me up there for a reason."

"Like it or not, Brandon," Lorelei said. "Jacenda might have talents the both of you aren't aware of."

"I can see and communicate with child spirits. But it doesn't happen too often."

A knock on the door interrupted the setup.

"Are you expecting anyone else on this investigation?" Joe asked.

Brandon shook his head and opened the front door. "I don't see anyone." He leaned his head out further. Joe saw him walk around in the front yard. "Maybe kids playing pranks, though it's pretty remote out here."

"And the fun begins," Dale said.

Joe walked up behind Brandon and glanced outside into the purplish, pink and orange tinges of sunset. A dilapidated, abandoned white trailer sat nearby amid barren desert interspersed with occasional prickly pear and palo verde trees. The ten-year-old ranch house they were investigating had been built on a three-acre lot with newer southwestern style homes on surrounding acreage, and another much older home a half mile to the south.

Stepping back inside the house, Joe suddenly had a clear vision of Mandy. She lay on her bed in a long pink night shirt. Her nipples shown through the cotton fabric and her well-toned legs drew him in further.

Mandy tossed and turned, muttering things he couldn't hear.

Am I daydreaming?

She continued to roll around in her sleep. Taking in a deep gasp, Mandy sat straight up in bed, rubbing her eyes. Then they widened in surprise. She seemed to be looking right at Joe.

Someone shook him repeatedly.

"Joe," Dale said. "What's up? It's getting dark and we're ready to get going."

Joe cleared his throat. "Uh, yeah. Sorry, thinking about the Hovenweep case." He didn't want to reveal the truth. Caught having an intimate vision of Shannon's double.

Ian handed Joe a camcorder, staring into Joe's eyes with mild humor.

"Are you sure there isn't something else you'd like to tell me?" Ian asked.

"No, why?"

"Because you're blushing. I've never seen your face that red before."

Joe turned away and began to film in the living room. He didn't understand why he had seen Mandy in such an intimate manner.

While Brandon and Dale were doing an EVP session in the dining room, Joe continued to film in the living room, occasionally requesting responses from whatever spirits might be present.

His cell phone rang and he removed it from its holder. The display read "Mandy."

Lorelei floated fifty feet above the earth. The Superstition Mountains towered to the northwest. Remnants of prehistoric walls a foot high were laid out along the desert ground below, scattered with pottery pieces, shell fragments, jewelry and malachite and quartz crystals.

Jacenda's shout caused Lorelei to crash back down to reality.

Lorelei's feet were six inches above the floor. Jacenda stared at her in horror.

A few seconds later Lorelei landed with a hard thump on her feet.

Ian came running from the hallway into the master bedroom. "What happened?"

Lorelei glanced from Jacenda to Ian. "I'm not sure. I had a strong vision of prehistoric ruins in this area. I floated above them. Then I heard Jacenda's cry and noticed my body was hovering inches above the floor."

Jacenda continued to stare at Lorelei with her mouth open. "I tried talking to her while we were going into the closet. We were getting ready to investigate. Then Lore's thoughts went elsewhere. I couldn't get her back. That's when she began to rise off the carpet."

Embarrassed, Lorelei felt her face flush. She glanced from Ian to Jacenda. "I'm so sorry. I didn't mean to startle you."

Ian gave Lorelei a hug.

"That's never happened before. I mean, I was out-of-body in the vision. I wonder why my physical body would react that way."

"It's possible," Ian said, "that being pregnant might be having some other metaphysical side effects."

Lorelei rolled her eyes, placing her head against his chest. "Great!"

Ian laughed. "Honey, you'll be fine. Jacenda, you can close your mouth now. If you're going to be around the team, you'll need to get used to strange things happening."

"Sorry. Considering what happened to me the other day, I guess I shouldn't be so shocked about *this*."

"I think we need to get going with that EVP session," Lorelei said. "There's a camera setup facing the closet, so hopefully we'll catch evidence pertaining to my visions and your experiences."

"I'll leave the two of you alone," Ian said. "I'll be checking out the other rooms and the hallway upstairs."

Jacenda touched Lorelei on her arm. "I'm sorry if I made you feel like a freak. I've never seen anyone do that before. It's almost like you were flying."

She hadn't thought of it. But Lorelei wondered if she were developing another talent.

Jacenda smiled. Brandon's girlfriend was one of the most stunning women she had ever seen. Long jet black hair, emerald eyes, tall and leggy, she had a figure that would make any man drool. Ian seemed to be the only one on the team that didn't take a sneak peak at Jacenda every now and then.

Lorelei followed her into the walk-in closet.

"Lore and Jacenda in the master bedroom at 7:10 p.m.," Lorelei said.

They sat across from each other.

"Are you sensing anything?" Jacenda asked.

"No. More importantly, are you? You were the one who communicated with something in here."

"Nothing. Not right now at least."

Lorelei observed the two lights on the ceiling. "Just how bright was this light you saw?"

"A hundred times brighter than the closet lights. What I experienced seemed to come from everywhere. The blinding light hid the floor and everything else in here."

Lorelei had sensed something about Jacenda, even in her initial vision of Brandon and Jacenda together during their adventure at Caves of the Watchers near Wickenburg. Jacenda admitted to being able to communicate with child spirits. But something else lay underneath that Lorelei couldn't detect, but maybe the spirit world could.

Jacenda stared at her in awe. "What's it like to teleport? Do you feel anything in between your journey from one place to another?"

"Not quite as exciting as it sounds. Things sort of fade out, like when I rescued Mandy from the cave at Hovenweep. Then I appear at my destination based on where I think about going. Sometimes I can't control it. I teleported Ian to me in Utah without being aware of it. And I teleported through the tunnel to get to Mandy at the Boulder House in the Four Corners."

"Brandon mentioned you only developed out-of-body and teleportation within the past year or so. Do you really think this unknown ancient race you're connected with has something to do with your skills? Or have these abilities been lying dormant until you figured out you were the reincarnation of Annie O'Shea, the owner of the Texas Canyon Ranch in Dragoon where your first mystery took place? I mean, Annie was also very tight with this race."

"That's a great question. One I've thought of many times. We did discover chambers in the Caves of the Watchers indicating the ancients connected with the universe through astral travel. Dragoon in southeast Arizona had strong evidence as such, including a brilliant triangle surrounding the ruins and pillars and a place on top of the pueblo, also marked with a triangle. Not to mention Annie was closely aligned to this race—in life and death."

"I can't imagine how I would handle such talents or the life threatening scenarios you've been through."

"I never imagined I'd be able to handle such abilities. Not to mention use them to help solve such extreme cases. But I have an amazing man by my side—my fairy tale. Some fantastic friends. And the ancients themselves have been a great support system."

"Who are the ancients? Are they a Native American tribe no one's identified yet? Brandon mentioned you've spoken a strange dialect without knowing. The Dragoon ruins and tunnels you all found with those petroglyphs of the solar system indicate a possible prehistoric presence. Yet Dagon, Mattie and Annie, who are so closely associated with the astral race, weren't Native American."

Lorelei thought back to the journey to the heavens with Galiena. "Many Native Americans believe they were derived from the stars, as indicated by a lot of UFO and alien rock art in places like Utah and Nevada. All over the world really. And since Shannon turned out to be a goddess of the Universe, I'm thinking they're more of an alien race that might have resided on earth at one time, though not the extraterrestrials or big-headed beings humans think of. Mattie, Annie and Dagon were humans who had a rather special connection with the ancients, like me. They were transformed after death to help others."

There were answers Lorelei would never obtain about the ancient astral race. Neither Dagon, Mattie nor Shannon had addressed the question of who, or what, they really were.

She heard someone on the stairs.

"Brandon, Dale?" Lorelei hollered.

"Lore, we're downstairs," Brandon shouted.

"Did you hear something?" Jacenda asked.

"Yeah, in the hall." Lorelei left the closet to see if she could detect the presence that made the noise. At the threshold between the bedroom and the hallway, the door to the walk-in closet slammed shut. With Jacenda inside.

"Damn it!"

Ian came running from one of the other bedrooms. "What's the matter?"

"Were you walking around a minute ago? I thought I heard footsteps."

"No. I was sitting on the bed doing an EVP session."

"Something lured me out of the closet. It wanted Jace in there alone."

"What's going on?" Brandon ran upstairs.

"Jacenda." Lore ran back into the bedroom and tried to open the door. "I came outside to check on something I heard. She's still in there."

"I can't believe this." Brandon pushed and pulled on the knob. "Jace, are you okay?"

No response.

Ian touched Lorelei on her arm and stared at the opening into the closet. A resplendent white light burst from underneath.

Brandon used his foot to attempt to knock down the door. It sounded as if he were kicking at a cement wall.

"Stop," Lorelei said. "You're going to injure yourself."

Dale and Joe had come upstairs.

Brandon turned to look at Lorelei. "You shouldn't have left her in there alone knowing what happened before.

"I'm sorry. I was tricked. But she came out of this fine the last time. I'm not feeling any ill will from this house. I think this place knows things about Jacenda."

"The strange light is gone. Let's see if we can get in." Joe motioned for everyone to get back. He cautiously turned the knob and opened the door.

Brandon pushed by him. He turned to stare back at them from the center of the closet. "She's not here."

"Let's search the rest of the house." Dale ran out into the hallway. "Jacenda," he yelled.

"Definitely a portal," Joe said. "Not sure why this place is so focused on your girlfriend."

Brandon raced out of the master bedroom and downstairs. "Jace, Jace, can you hear me?" He did numerous 360-degree turns in the living room.

"What have I done?" Lorelei looked from Ian to Joe.

Ian placed his hands on either side of her face. "I'm sure she's fine." He walked into the closet and inspected the ceiling, walls and floor closely.

"I know there's no evil here," Lorelei said. "But I can't sense anything else about the home, what's happening with Jacenda, or about the phantoms residing here."

Lorelei heard the front door open. Brandon and Dale shouted Jacenda's name repeatedly from the outside.

"Ian, we can't go to Hovenweep if we can't find Jacenda."

Dale yelled up from the bottom of the stairs. "I don't understand. We've looked everywhere. What the hell happened to her?"

Lorelei stood inside the walk-in closet, trying to get a feel for where Jacenda might be.

Brandon threw open the front door, charging back inside and halfway up the stairs. He glared at Lorelei. "This is your fault. You were supposed to stay in there with her! Do you at least know what's happened to her?"

Tears began to form at the corner of her eyes. She shook her head. "I'm sorry. I can't tell what's going on." A tiny river escaped from her right eye, traveling to intersect with the corner of her mouth.

"Stop," Ian said. "Brandon, we're going to find her. Let's give this a bit of time. If there's no sign of her within the next half hour, Joe and I will see what we can do to get her back. Perhaps Jace has her own lessons to learn. This house is obviously trying to tell her something."

Lorelei stepped back into the closet. "I'm going to spend the night up here if I have to. I'll be here when she returns." But Lorelei wondered when and where Jacenda would return. Of if she would come back.

Ian whispered in her ear. "She's coming back. Remember, you saw her and Brandon meeting and getting married right before Peter abducted you at Vulture Mine."

It didn't happen often, but every now and then Ian could read her thoughts, usually during periods of stress. The telepathic connection began during the murder case in Southeast Arizona. Intense at first, the mind-reading dissipated after they became a couple.

"I hope she's not suffering." Lorelei rubbed her hand over her abdomen, thinking of the unborn baby.

Brandon, Dale and Joe continued to roam through the house in the hopes of finding Jacenda.

Lorelei thought of her and Ian's infant still inside her. She grabbed Ian's arm. "I need for everyone to leave."

"Honey, what do you mean?"

"Everyone needs to leave the house. Go outside and wait until I tell you to. Trust me on this. I'll be fine."

Ian went downstairs and informed Brandon, Dale and Joe of her wishes.

Ian glanced up at her one last time. He mouthed the words, "I love you," before leaving the house with the others.

She went back into the closet. Gently running her fingers along the wall, Lorelei started to talk to the home. "You've taken someone very important to my friend Brandon, and to the rest of us. Can you please give me a vision, a sign, or communicate with me to let me know what she means to you." Lorelei watched the ceiling, the back of the closet and the walls. "Everyone else has left. It's just me and you now."

Suddenly, it hit Lorelei. Jacenda mentioned saying, "I will. I promise" when she had her first encounter in the closet. Could the house be holding her up to a promise Jacenda didn't understand or remember making?

"Is my friend safe?"

Writing began to form on the wall at the end of the closet. First a *y,* then an *e* and *s.*

"Is Jacenda coming back to us?"

No more scribbles on the white paint. But the *yes* remained on the wall.

"What did you make her promise you?"

The words *stop the burning* rapidly etched themselves onto the left wall. Each of the words formed a foot apart and about six inches high.

"The fire they experienced downstairs…," Lorelei whispered. "How can Jacenda help you stop a residual event?"

Lorelei heard pounding on the front door.

She ran to the top of the stairs. Flames emanated from the floor and licked the ceiling. Sparks flew everywhere. Thick, grey smoke made its way across the living room and kitchen.

Intense heat overcame her. She tried to make her way downstairs quickly to save herself and the baby. Her skin felt as if it were peeling. Her lungs were suffocating. She couldn't stop coughing.

Lorelei collapsed halfway down the stairs, barely able to breathe. Ian pounded on the door and called her name in desperation.

Taking one last deep breath, she thought of Ian and vanquished herself from the home.

A cool breeze hit her as she found herself outside the front door.

"Lore!" Ian ran to her as she collapsed to her knees outside the home. The second she teleported, the symptoms from the fire and smoke ceased.

Ian held her tightly by her arms, his smoky eyes wide with fright.

"Honey, I'm okay."

She looked up at Brandon. He stared at the deserted house in disbelief and terror.

"This place is somehow alive—whether through the prehistoric past that took place on this property, the people who resided here, or both. This home needs her help."

Brandon helped her stand up. "It told you that?"

"Yes. The home wrote a message on the back of the closet when I asked what it wanted with Jacenda. It said, 'stop the burning.' Your girlfriend is somehow supposed to stop this residual fire. Even though Jacenda didn't know of her abilities, this place did. It knew she could communicate and become one with its walls."

Brandon watched the fire, which burned as fiercely as ever. "So what happens now? Is Jace all right?"

"She's fine. At least that's what I was told. Now, we wait."

A figure appeared in the middle of the flames. Lorelei couldn't distinguish if it were male or female.

"That's her. It has to be." Brandon raced to the door and placed his hand on the knob.

He immediately jumped back, holding his wrist and bending over in pain. Lorelei, Joe and Ian approached Brandon to look at his hand.

Peeling, blistering red skin started to heal immediately. Within seconds, his hand returned to normal.

A minute later, Joe walked up to the house and looked inside the bay window. "Fire's gone." He touched the knob lightly before yanking open the door and running inside.

Lorelei, Brandon and Ian followed. Jacenda lay on the floor.

Brandon took her hand in his.

Joe placed his forefingers on her carotid artery. "She's got a strong pulse."

She rolled her head slightly and opened her eyes. "Where am I?"

Brandon smoothed her hair back. "You're at the house in Florence where we were all doing an investigation."

Jacenda sat up quickly, staring back at the home. She looked at Brandon imploringly. "I want to get away from here. Please take me home."

Brandon helped her up from the floor and helped her to a bench outside. "Stay out here. I'll go get the equipment. We'll leave in just a few."

Dale and Ian began to collect the cameras and equipment inside the home.

Lorelei sat down next to Jacenda, placing her arm around her shoulders. She didn't know what to say. Or if she should say anything. Jacenda rocked back and forth in shock.

Joe took Jacenda's arm and led her to Brandon's truck. He opened the passenger door and helped her inside.

A few minutes later, Brandon came out with two cases. "Ian and Dale are handling the rest. Let's get out of here. We'll go back to my place."

"No!" Jacenda yelled. "Take me back to my house."

A look of hurt crossed Brandon's face. "Okay." He closed the passenger door.

Lorelei realized whatever had happened to Jacenda, whatever talents she possessed, had left her terrified and confused. Brandon would have to learn his lesson in patience. Lorelei sensed Jacenda feared her new and unique abilities would drive Brandon away. Unfortunately, probably to avoid the pain, she was going to run away first.

23

Joe stared up into the partly cloudy skies, but couldn't see Lorelei. Her astral self traveled above the ancient Cajone ruins at Hovenweep, the place where Nicole Malloy was headed before her disappearance. He had asked her to take an out-of-body journey to see if she could find the man who had been abducting pregnant women. Or possibly to find his hideout for Nicole. How many other victims were hidden among the prehistoric dwellings?

Lorelei and Mandy had both given a description to have a forensic artist replicate the abductor. Still, no one working or living in the area recognized him or had seen him inside the park.

"What the heck is that?" Joe pointed to two blue-gray shapes floating fifty feet above the earth.

Ian shielded their eyes from the sun. "Those are the same figures Paul and I noticed with Lore the first time she did her out-of-body at the Square Tower ruins. She said she didn't see them or feel threatened, so I'm guessing they are guardians. I wonder if they've been escorting her on all her astral journeys."

Alan approached Joe and Ian after inspecting a round tower built into a boulder. "Maybe they were also the two ravens that led Lore to the Boulder House to save Mandy."

"Yeah, we thought about that." Ian continued to observe the bluish forms. "Speaking of keeping people safe, what about Mandy? Isn't the FBI worried this guy will go after her again? Or send someone else for her?"

Joe blushed remembering the inadvertent invasion of Mandy's privacy. She looked so beautiful and innocent, yet sexy at the same time. He hadn't been able to stop dreaming of her. He turned his face away. "I've got agents keeping an eye on her. She'll be fine. The suspect seems to be focusing his attention on sites in Hovenweep."

Ian turned Joe to face him. "Hey, my friend. What's going on? Your face turned beet red like that last night also." Ian's magical irises stared intently into Joe's. "You're not admitting it, but you're developing feelings for Mandy. Aren't you?"

"No. Of course not." Joe sighed. "Something really bizarre happened during the investigation. Out of nowhere, I got this strong vision of her. She lay in bed alone, wearing only a long nightshirt. Her body *is* very similar to Shannon's, only Mandy's legs are longer, more slender. Galiena might have developed her own earthly form based on Mandy, but not her exact proportions. Anyways, Mandy sat straight up. She seemed to look right at me."

"What if you and Mandy *are* meant to be? I know Lorelei really wants to see the two of you together. Perhaps it was all part of the bigger plan."

Joe laughed. "How well do any of us really know her? She's pregnant and was abandoned by her boyfriend when he found out. Not to mention what she went through with the kidnapping. I doubt her feelings about men are very positive right now."

"I don't know, man. It's rather strange that Lorelei ended up saving the very person Galiena modeled herself after."

"Not really when you consider the abilities of the ancients. I'm not so sure of anything anymore. How could such an amazing race of people allow a human man to fall in love with a fiery goddess from the stars?"

Ian started to speak, but Joe didn't want to hear it anymore. He turned away and waited anxiously for Lorelei to return from her out-of-body experience.

Five minutes later, Lorelei's essence joined back with her physical form. She stood up slowly and glanced from Ian and Paul to Joe.

Agent Tony Zimmerman approached Joe and Joe shook hands with him. "Agent, this is Lorelei Lanier, the amazing woman capable of astral and teleportation feats. This woman helped us solve the supernatural murder mystery in Southeast Arizona and shut down a Native American artifact theft operation at Sunset Crater Wupatki National Monument."

"Wow." Tony shook Lorelei's hand. "It's an honor to meet you. I've been hearing so much about you."

Joe noticed Lorelei watching Tony with curiosity. She had picked up on something special about the agent, as had Joe when he first met Tony. Tony had his own talents, whether he knew about them or not was yet to be determined.

Joe watched the sun as it went behind the clouds. "You see anything unusual from up there?"

"I'm sorry, no," Lorelei said. "Not the man who abducted Mandy. Or any sign of the victims. There are so many places he could be hiding, including ruins, caves, maybe hidden alcoves."

"Take a walk around for a more physical perspective," Joe said. "See if you can pick up on anything. Nicole's friend Matt mentioned the Cajon Group was her destination before he lost contact with her. I'll need you and Ian to check out all the other indigenous villages at Hovenweep, including Holly, Hackberry and Horseshoe. Agent Zimmerman will be going around with you. This bastard seems to be eluding those on foot. But I'm hoping your abilities can help us find him."

Joe and Tony were being waved over to a spot near a group of juniper bushes. Joe started to go with him.

"Joe, wait." Lorelei turned to face him. "There's something I haven't told you about an incident in the hospital. You were talking to Mandy outside of the room, and I thought I saw her abductor. Only a glimpse, but after the note he left I'm not so sure it wasn't him."

"Why didn't you mention this sooner?"

"I guess finding out I was pregnant made me forget. For a little while, at least. I didn't even mention it to Ian until yesterday."

"Not sure what's going on or how he can appear in two places at once. We have to find out who he is. No telling who he's kidnapped or what he's got planned."

Tony waved his hand frantically to get Joe's attention. Lorelei and Ian walked with Joe.

Ian put his arm around Lorelei's waist. "By the way, did you know you had two entities following you around up there again?"

"How come everyone else can see them but I can't?"

Lorelei stopped suddenly and placed her hands on her temples as Joe approached Tony. "I'm seeing it again. The wasp and tarantula vision from the hotel room. The wasps young were eating their way out of the spider."

The young Native American agent observed Lorelei intently. "Interesting considering what we just found." He glanced over at Joe. "I don't think you want them seeing what's inside this cave."

"What cave?" Joe asked.

A younger man with short dark hair wiggled out between two juniper bushes only a few feet above the ground. Joe looked closer and noticed an aperture in the rock approximately three feet wide by two foot tall. He couldn't believe the team found the opening. The man emerging from the hole was tall, thin, but athletic, with short blond hair and fair skin. He looked like he could be Prince Charming.

The prince, named Kevin, stood up, brushed himself off and stared at Joe. "The son-of-a-bitch killed Nicole Malloy. This has to be one of the strangest, most disturbing cases I've ever seen. I'll let Alan know and contact evidence response."

Lorelei had turned away and stood next to Ian with her arms crossed. Joe could tell Lorelei felt guilty for not being able to find Nicole in time. "Stay with Lore. I'll be out as soon as I can."

Joe stared at the tight confined space with trepidation. Beads of sweat began to form on his forehead. If he hesitated too long everyone would sense his fear.

"The cave is ten feet in," Tony said. "I'm coming behind you."

"Of course," Joe said. He bent down and squeezed the front of his body through the yard-wide opening. He wiggled quicker to reach the cave, pushing off on his forearms and toes.

The agent's flashlight beam illuminated from behind. Joe could see cave walls and a woman's body lying on the ground.

"How could Nicole's abductor have gotten her inside?" Tony grunted from the effort of maneuvering through the passage. "Unless he had a gun or other weapon threatening her."

Joe looked down to see drop of about four feet. "Be careful. There's a little bit of a distance to reach the ground. I'll help you."

Joe pulled himself out of the micro-tunnel before helping Tony out. The four-foot cave height made it impossible for him to stand. The length of the space couldn't be more than five feet.

"Shit!" Tony tried to stand up and hit his head on the ceiling.

Joe wiped his hands off with his handkerchief. "It's going to be very tight in here between the victim's body and the two of us." He bent on his knees and shined his flashlight on Nicole.

Joe wound loose strands of his thick long hair behind his ears. "Jesus. What the hell did he do to you?"

An attractive woman with light black skin, wavy dark hair and a barely protruding stomach, Nicole had to have been extremely uncomfortable in such tight confines due to her tall frame. Her petite, upturned nose had been broken. It had shifted to the right and blood had dried underneath. Her stomach and abdomen had received the worst damage.

Tony took one quick look at the body and turned away with his hand over his mouth. The agent started to get sick, but took a deep breath and regained his composure.

"Are you all right?" Joe asked.

Tony nodded. "Sliced clean open."

"Yeah." Joe glanced up at him. "The sick bastard removed the fetus."

A section of Nicole's large intestine began to move slightly. A bluish-black insect crawled out. Its wings matched its body. "A tarantula hawk wasp," Joe whispered. "They catch the spiders, paralyze them and bring them back to their nest to use as a live host for their eggs."

"I know." Tony looked closer at the insect. "The wasp is walking sort of strange, almost as if it's drunk."

"It is. These bugs have a tendency to become flight-challenged after consuming fermented fruit. I'm thinking her kidnapper found the tarantula hawk. Maybe this is the abductor's live calling card."

Joe and Tony watched while the wasp crawled, inebriated, out of the corpse.

"Grab it," Joe said. "The wasp could have the killer's DNA."

When the insect stumbled past Tony, he stopped it by placing an evidence bag over its body and scooping it up.

Had Nicole's kidnapper chose this location because it was the tarantula wasp's lair? He remembered the wasp they had watched at Cutthroat Castle. And that Lorelei had a vision of such a scene inside the mysterious skull found in her backpack. Not to mention the vision she had right before he entered the cave where Nicole had been murdered. Now he knew why. Could there also be a tarantula somewhere inside the cave, suffering a death worthy of the scariest horror story?

Slipping a glove on, Tony carefully picked up an object next to Nicole's head. "I found something else."

Joe had never seen a projectile point so beautiful. Two inches long, triangular, and burnt orange blended with streaks of off-white.

"I don't see any evidence of blood," Joe said. "That doesn't mean he didn't use it as a weapon. Though I don't think he could have used the arrow to do *this* job as the edges aren't sharp enough to have sliced

Nicole open like that. Bag it and we'll analyze it with the other arrowhead we found."

"Do you see another way in?" Joe looked around for a crevasse large enough to fit a human body.

"Other than the tunnel, no. Nicole was too far along to fit through there. I don't even know how the hell we're going to get her body out of here for the coroner."

Joe scooted along the length of the cave floor, pushing against the rock wall. "Damn. A mystery on top of a mystery." Panic began to set in. He had never handled tight confined spaces well. "Let's get out of here. I'll check for another way in from the outside."

Joe squeezed his way back through the passage. Each inch he moved seemed to take him further away from daylight. His breathing became shallower with every effort. He saw Lorelei and Ian on the other side waiting for him, which kept him going.

Ian helped pull Joe and Tony out of the tunnel.

"Think I found the answer for Lore's visions. This might be a tarantula hawk wasp's lair. The damn thing came out of Nicole's body. I believe this kidnapper is fascinated by the way the insect kills its prey, which might explain why he targets pregnant women. And why you're having visions of the wasp and tarantula. Maybe we can find this bastard based on his fascination with the relationship between the two."

Lorelei placed her hand on Joe's arm. "I did get a rather intense vision a few minutes ago."

Five seconds of silence ensued. Joe held his breath.

"I just told the park law enforcement. There's another woman who is eight months along. She's Hopi. But I can't figure out where she is. I only see her silhouetted in darkness, sitting in a scrunched position. Joe, the farther along these women are in their pregnancies, the tighter the confines he's placing them in."

"Damn it," he shouted. "Someone has to have seen this man."

"We have to find her," Lorelei continued.

Joe sighed heavily. "I know, I know."

Lorelei stepped up to Joe and took his hands in hers. "You have to call Mandy. Maybe she saw something—a tarantula or the wasp. That would be a much stronger indication that he's deliberately placing his victims into his own sick fascination."

"You act as if I would be afraid to contact her."

Lorelei stared back at him.

He removed his cell phone from his pocket. His hands began to sweat. His face felt flushed, and he started to tremble.

Lorelei and Ian smiled reassuringly.

Joe dialed Mandy's number. No answer. He started to leave a message, but decided he would call her back in a few minutes.

He immediately received a text message after hanging up. I DID SEE A TARANTULA. Three seconds passed. AND A WASP.

24

Mandy's thoughts of a relaxing evening, beginning with a steak dinner followed by a good novel, were interrupted by Joe's deep, sensual voice while she headed home a day of errands.

Mandy, is there something you haven't told me? Is there something else you've seen in that cave where you were being held?

She slammed on her brakes and heard screeching of tires then two extended honks from the blue pickup truck behind her.

"Okay, I'm sorry." She waved and continued to drive down South Milton Road to her house in Kinlani Estates in Flagstaff.

She waited. But his voice ended there. Then a distinct image slammed into her mind—a picture of a hairy black tarantula and a large wasp with a bluish-black body and matching wings. Joe wanted to know about her experience in the cave.

An hour before Lorelei found her in the cave, the insect world had unfolded a disturbing scene in front of her. A tarantula six inches across approached her, on the verge of her vision. A few minutes later, *he* stepped out from the darkness, holding something in his right hand. Her abductor knelt before her and opened his palm. Mandy slid back against the cave wall when she noticed the two-inch insect.

"Don't worry, Mandy," he had said in a chilling tone. "You're not what it's looking for."

She wondered why the wasp didn't fly away. It remained completely still in the middle of his hand.

"This will be my gift to you. After you're gone." He leered at her. His breathing became heavier the longer he watched her. She began to pray.

She shook her head to try and erase the image of her kidnapper.

Mandy didn't know if the weirdest part of the whole thing occurred during captivity. Or after. She had never had any special skills. But in the hospital she had predicted Lorelei's pregnancy. And last night, while she lay resting in bed, Joe's face came into her mind. Now she was hearing his thoughts.

Mandy didn't want to become attracted to anyone, didn't want to trust again. Trust equaled trouble. Yet her face flushed every time she thought of him. Her knees became weak. Fantasies started consuming her thoughts and not only at night. Though they had met briefly, he seemed so familiar.

If I stay away from Lorelei, Joe and Ian, perhaps all these bizarre occurrences will stop.

But even as the thought left her mind, Mandy knew she would be seeing them again, especially since she had been a surviving victim. She needed to help catch her abductor so he couldn't harm anyone else.

Mandy slowed the speed of her vehicle, pulled off the side of the road and texted Joe that she had seen a tarantula and a wasp.

Her phone rang again a minute later. Joe's number showed in the display.

She answered the phone, but didn't give him a chance to speak. If she heard his deep, sexy voice, she would weaken.

A sigh escaped her lips. "I'm sorry. I didn't think about the details with the spider until today, when you called me the first time. You all keep grilling me about these *things* that are happening to me. Talents, capabilities, whatever you call them. I never had psychic abilities, could never read people's minds and definitely never predicted pregnancies until I met you, Lorelei and Ian. I just want the nightmares, and all this other strange stuff, to go away."

"I can't imagine how hard this is on you. The abduction was bad enough. Then you get rescued by Lorelei in a very unorthodox manner, only to discover you've developed your own special abilities. Maybe they are temporary. But I…"

Five seconds of silence ensued.

"I mean, Lorelei, Ian and myself can help you through this."

Mandy remembered Joe's invasion in her bedroom last night. Though he wasn't there physically, he had looked so real.

She began to imagine his dark, naked body next to hers in bed.

"There's another victim that's been found dead," Joe continued. "Nicole Malloy. This guy has a rather morbid fascination with the tarantula wasp and what it does to its victim—the tarantula. We believe he's torturing his victims, all pregnant women. Lorelei thinks there might be a third victim out in Hovenweep National Park."

Mandy began to tremble. She realized she could have died. She teared up thinking of what the poor woman had been through. "Why didn't Lorelei find this recent murder victim before she died?"

"We don't know. Lore's extremely upset that she couldn't at least figure out the woman's location, which happened to be another cave. Much smaller than the one you were in. There was barely room to move. The further along the victim's are in their pregnancies, the tighter the hiding spot."

"Jesus," Mandy whispered. "A few hours before Lorelei found me, he came in holding something in his hand. He showed me a large blue wasp in his hand. Then he said, 'This will be my gift to you. After you're gone.' "

"What about the tarantula?"

"I saw one coming toward me from the darkness. A few minutes later, I started hearing strange noises. That's when my kidnapper appeared again—right where the tarantula had been."

"This man is very disturbed and is leaving a live calling card, which is the tarantula hawk wasp you saw. The tarantula is their main prey.

The wasp larvae eats its way into the paralyzed prey, then the adults get out the same way. I believe he's targeting pregnant women because of the idea of the fetus growing inside."

"He's comparing the birth of a baby to a morbid feeding frenzy?"

"Seems that way. I can't tell you everything we found. But it was heinous, to say the least. You're lucky, Mandy. Very lucky. I'm not sure why Lorelei found you and not this woman. I pray to God that we find this other victim soon. And any others before he can kill again. But I firmly believe there's a reason for everything. You may not want to hear this, but what if this all happened because you were meant to discover who you really are?"

25

Cool to the touch, the round, slightly pitted Moqui Marble vibrated in Joe's left hand. For centuries, Native American shamans had been using the sandstone rocks encased in iron oxide for out-of-body travel—and to interact with intelligent life forms from other planets.

Lorelei and Ian sat cross-legged under a full moon, across from Joe inside a ten by ten medicine wheel made of rocks found among the Cajone Group of ruins. Agent Zimmerman stood off to the side, outside of the circle, to film the ceremony. Alan stood by his side. Joe had never tried a ritual this extreme. But he was desperate to find out if Galiena could provide any clues pertaining to the abductor or his victims. Yet he had to admit, he also had a selfish motive. He hoped Galiena would tell him about Mandy.

"I'll be going into a meditative state, then a full trance." Joe glanced over at Tony. "Keep the camera on me throughout the event. I normally don't allow such rituals to be filmed. However, this is also an attempt to gather evidence for the Hovenweep case. Feel free to use any other equipment, including audio and thermal imaging."

"Joe, Galiena appeared to me as a fiery goddess," Lorelei said. "She formed herself from the image of Shiprock. And…"

Joe placed his hand up to stop her from talking. "You've mentioned it all before. I know about the weird light beings and Galiena's confession that Shannon was guilty of Peter and Emily's unorthodox murder by volcano. I doubt I'll have the same encounter. Perhaps she won't even show herself at all."

"What can we expect?" Tony balanced a tripod onto the hard desert ground, and then mounted the night vision camera on top. "I mean what will happen to you during this attempt to connect with Galiena?"

Joe picked up another Moqui Marble out of a small basket beside him and placed it in his right hand. "Not sure. I could get strong visions. Or I might end up doing an astral journey. Unlike Lorelei, it takes a deep meditative state for me to travel."

The scent of sage wavered heavily in the air. Ian had cleansed Joe, Lorelei and himself to prevent any negative energy from entering the circle. The full moon illuminated a tarantula climbing cautiously out of its burrow ten feet away.

Joe observed the creature, which stood completely still. "It's time."

He closed his eyes, focusing on the golf ball-sized stones in either hand. He imagined brilliant, healing golden light starting at the root chakra at his genitals and extending upwards to his heart chakra and eventually to his third eye and lastly, to his crown chakra.

The stone marbles vibrated intensely. Heat emanated from every pit and crack in the rock. And absorbed itself into Joe.

Time was an unwelcome visitor. Seconds could have been minutes. Minutes could have been hours. His soul exited his body. He noticed Lorelei pointing skyward to let Ian and Brandon know what had happened. The silver cord connected him to his physical form through his heart chakra.

He looked down. The tarantula now stood just outside the medicine wheel within two feet of Joe's physical form.

His soul shot up into the stars. Within what felt like seconds, Joe found himself in a massive cavern. This had never happened on previous out-of-body experiences. Divided into three large rooms, each beckoned with a different radiant color. A warm yellow lit up the chamber to his left, straight ahead was a soft purple. The fiery orange glow from the chamber to the right drew him in. *Flame-like tendrils beckoned. As he entered, the brilliance threatened to overtake him. Simultaneously, warmth began to spread throughout him.*

"*Galiena, I've made this journey to speak with you. Lives are at stake.*"

Shapes appeared out of the glow, now a deeper orange-red. Spirals of light danced, wrapping themselves around his astral form. Tingling sensations coursed through him. He attempted to touch one of the "light beings." It shot up further into the darkness above and stopped for a few seconds. The top of it curled downward, as if peeking down at him. Each particle of the being glistened and sparkled.

Mesmerized by the beauty before him, Joe had nearly forgotten the purpose of the journey until the mysterious forms darted toward each other and melded together into a massive light being in the shape of an eagle's head—His spirit animal.

The glow that had surrounded him when he entered the cave-like room had vanished. Only the darkness and millions of stars remained. The light beings stayed in the eagle formation for what seemed like a minute. Then they began to excitedly swirl, spiral and dance again. Sensing something behind him, Joe turned.

Shannon stared back at him.

The same warm, caring, yet sexy smile crossed her oval face, framed by a lava-type substance that cascaded down in waves. Her eyes, though merely dark orbs with occasional twinkles, cut right through him. Memories he had forced out of his mind came flooding back to the surface. All their passionate love-making sessions, working closely together on cases, their picnic lunches, hikes in the mountains and even their disagreements.

It was more than he could handle. Joe started to back away, thinking of his body on earth. Wanting nothing more to return to where he could forget.

Galiena wouldn't let him. His silver cord stiffened. He couldn't move. She wanted him to remember. But he wasn't sure why.

The light beings swirled briefly around him. They darted over to where her face hung among the Milky Way. Her eyes focused on them with love as she had once done with him. She seemed to hear his thoughts. For the being that looked like Shannon observed him with sympathy. She didn't speak, yet he heard her familiar voice all around him.

"I appear to you as Shannon. Yet I am no longer. The person you knew as Shannon is but a memory. You will soon have new memories with the Earth One called Mandy. Do not doubt what you know to be true. You belong together, as I foresaw long ago. Lorelei also knows this to be true."

"I don't know if I'm ready. I don't understand why your race would allow a simple earth man to fall in love with a goddess of the universe who appeared in human form. Only to have such love ripped away."

She didn't answer. Joe realized he would have to find the answer to that one on his own. Or could it be a mistake?

"What about Hovenweep? Why can't we find the abductor? Why was Lore able to find Mandy and not the unfortunate woman who was tortured and killed? And there's another woman Lore's picked up on. I thought you were supposed to help. You said you would be watching over us."

Of course it wasn't Galiena's responsibility to find the murderer. Joe had hoped she would be able to help the FBI. Or at least nudge him or Lorelei in the right direction.

No more words escaped the fiery lips. A distinct voice reverberated throughout his head. Two words took over every part of him—astral and physical form. Spoken together, yet separately. "Mandy. Knows."

A ten second pause ensued. The most intense silence Joe had ever experienced. A silence only the black void of the heavens could provide.

"We have to enable others like us to hone their talents. Help her, Joe. And Mandy will be able to answer your questions." Galiena smiled one last time. The three light beings shot fifty feet up, swirled together and created a large spiral.

Within seconds, Joe found himself traveling backwards through space. The face he had fallen in love with had disappeared. Yet he could still feel her presence. Joe watched as hundreds of light beings descended upon him. They created a swirling tunnel of sparkling radiance for him to pass through. Indistinguishable whispers followed him on his way back to earth. Were the radiant creatures of the universe attempting to communicate?

Back in his body, Joe took a deep breath. Tony stood at the camera. Lorelei and Ian remained in their places across from his physical form. And the tarantula had found its way into the center of the medicine wheel. It stared at Joe.

"Definitely a sign," Lorelei whispered. "That thing's been sitting there like that for the past two hours. It crawled into the middle of the ceremonial ground within minutes after you left."

Ian nodded. "Yeah. Considering Shannon was so damn afraid of those things, I'd say she's sort of watching out for you. Not to mention how fascinated the abductor is with tarantulas."

Joe stared into its eight eyes. "This arachnid is also a reminder of the work we have ahead of us." He looked from Ian and Lorelei to Brandon. "I found Galiena. Mandy *is* one of the chosen ones. And she's the one who will help solve the case, after we help her develop her abilities. Since she figured out Lorelei's pregnancy before any of us, I'm guessing she might have a connection to other pregnant women."

Tony placed the camera strap around his neck and collapsed the tripod. "Lore, since you found Mandy, did you consider you now have the ability to find other chosen ones, like yourself? I mean, you mentioned while Joe was gone on his astral journey that you felt helpless because you couldn't find the latest victim. But what if all the chosen ones are working together to find this guy?"

Lorelei stood up, stretched, and rubbed her stomach. "I hadn't thought of it that way." She walked up to Joe. "Mandy is so freaked out about everything. It's going to take time to work with her even if she's up for it. Meanwhile, this man is going to continue to abduct, torture and possibly murder other women."

Suddenly, Mandy stood in front of him, a vision so real he had to glance around to see if she were really there. In a split second, she had vanished.

"Joe, what's happening?" Ian asked.

Joe couldn't believe the timing. He had only returned from Galiena minutes before. He wasn't sure if he should tell Mandy what had happened.

"Mandy was here. I mean in my mind. I could see her so clearly." He grabbed his cell phone and called her. She answered on the second ring, without giving him a chance to speak.

"I don't understand what's happening. When I woke up this morning, I heard a woman crying. Only I live alone. This woman was hysterical. I heard her muttering things like, 'please, God, please get me out of this' and 'what are you going to do to me?'"

Joe closed his eyes. "Mandy, you have to calm down. I believe you're picking up on pleas from the third victim. This connection with pregnant women is a gift. You have the opportunity to save lives. Who knows? Maybe these talents will go away after this case is over. Lorelei rescued you for a reason. I really need you. I mean, we all need your help."

"I can't do this anymore."

"Please, wait," Joe said. "Did you have any other visions or experiences? Anything that would tell us who abducted you and these other women? Or where they might be located?"

"When I heard this woman crying, 'Canyons of the Ancients' popped into my mind. Not an image of any particular place, but the name itself. Then I saw her shadow. She looked to be pretty far along in her pregnancy, but that's not all. For a brief second, I heard *his* voice." Mandy shivered. "I could have sworn I heard him say, 'I know you're there.' I'm so terrified this man might be able to find me. The hospital is giving me two months off because of everything that's happened."

"Why don't you come to the Four Corners?" Joe asked. "I know it might be a little rough emotionally, but we really need the help. Maybe you'll pick up on something at the Canyons of the Ancients, if you're sure that's the location of the third victim."

"Hey, this stuff is new to me. But that name implanted itself pretty clearly in my mind. Just not sure I'm ready to go back up there so soon. And I don't want to think about these so-called talents anymore."

Joe sighed. Mandy reacted the same way anyone would to such newly discovered abilities. Unfortunately, he didn't have the time to work with her. She was about to get a crash course in dealing with her skills.

"I wonder if the woman you briefly saw is the same one Lorelei did in her vision."

Alan and Tony ran up to Joe.

"Mandy, hold a minute."

"I just received a message from the Colorado State Police," Alan said. "A thirty-two-year-old married woman by the name of Jan Stinson disappeared yesterday at 12:20 p.m. while visiting Lowry Pueblo. Her husband went to the car to get their picnic basket to have lunch. When he came back ten minutes later, she was gone. I contacted the Anasazi Heritage Center, which is the museum and visitor center for Canyons of the Ancients."

"I take it this latest victim was also pregnant."

Alan sighed. "Yes. Eight months."

"Did her husband see anyone before or after she disappeared?"

"No. Says he thought they were out there alone."

"Damn it! I don't get this. Why isn't anyone seeing this guy?" Based on what he had witnessed at Boulder House, Joe realized they had to be dealing with a modern-day shapeshifter.

Alan wiped his brow with the back of his hand. "No one at Hovenweep or the Anasazi Heritage Center seems to know who he is, according to the drawing the forensic artist did. And none of the visitors have seen him."

"Are there any footprints, or other evidence?"

"Not that we've come across. Her husband, Jonathan, said he didn't hear anything. The car was less than a quarter mile from where they were going to eat. There was very little wind yesterday, so seems like he would have heard *something*."

"Maybe the kidnapper is right in front of our eyes, but he's able to camouflage himself."

"How could he hide that limp and his burn scars?"

"Very easily," Joe muttered. "If he has the powers I think he does."

Tony glanced from Alan to Joe. "You're talking shapeshifting?"

"Yes. We need to find this guy before he kills again. I'll pay to have Mandy come up. Her first-hand encounter as a victim, plus her ability to connect with pregnant women could come in handy."

Tony seemed to be distracted by something in the night sky.

Joe touched Tony's arm. "I'll need you to meet, Alan, Lore, Ian and me at Lowry Pueblo at 6:00 a.m."

"Of course."

Joe got back on the phone with Mandy. "I'm going to contact the Phoenix office to have an agent bring you up here. I don't want you to come alone after what you've been through."

"I heard everything. But I don't know if I will be able to help solve this case."

"We're grasping at straws here with the abductor and we have to travel down any path possible."

A few seconds of silence.

"Okay. I guess."

"You won't be alone up here," Joe said. "Either myself or another agent will be with you at all times. Ian, Lore and I are at the same hotel in Cortez. Someone will drive you to Lowry Pueblo, where the latest victim has gone missing. You'll be contacted tonight about the time they will pick you up."

"That's fine. I guess I'll see you all again soon."

Joe hung up the phone. He didn't want to admit it, but he was excited at the prospect of seeing her again.

Tony zipped up his jacket. "This abduction was much more brazen with her husband nearby. Mandy and Nicole were alone, making it much easier for this guy. Could he have lured this married woman away with mind control?"

"Definite possibility," Joe said. "Not to mention the fact he's so elusive. Lore and Mandy have seen him, but no one else. We've got that sketch out everywhere, yet nobody's seen this man." He shook his head slowly. "After seeing what I did at the Boulder House with the abductor transforming into the tarantula."

Joe stared at the moon. "He could be taking on more than forms of animals and creatures. Objects, things in nature, people, and who knows what else. That would explain why we can't find him. Park law enforcement and the FBI have been scouring Hovenweep."

Ian helped Tony place the tripod and camera in its case. "What if he's living underground? You mentioned he escaped into a small passage inside the cave where he hid Mandy."

"We had an agent climb into that tunnel who is an expert at exploring caves. It only went twenty feet and ended at a rock wall. This agent also explored the other Hovenweep sites and anything resembling caves. He couldn't find proof of a tunnel system. Could he have missed something? Absolutely. It's a rather large area. We know the kidnapper is fascinated by the underground, so it makes sense. But there isn't an extensive tunnel system linking ruins."

Joe's phone buzzed with an incoming text message.

"When he first tied my wrists together, the ropes weren't tight enough. I maneuvered my right hand to work at the ropes. I heard a fluttering sound in the cave and looked up to see a bat directly above me. It hung on the ceiling, watching. Then it flew into the smaller cave. Within ten seconds, he came back in and immediately retied my wrists. I thought it strange, but I was too terrified to connect anything."

Ian checked his phone for messages. "Joe, what if the woman who vanished yesterday was lured away by something he changed into?"

"The big question is," Alan asked, "how could Jan have wandered off so quickly without a trace?"

Tony snapped the equipment case shut before standing up. He stared at one of the remaining walls of the prehistoric village. "Very easily. Especially if this guy is able to not only transform himself, but his victims."

26

Jacenda stood inside her house in Anthem at the sliding glass doors by the breakfast nook, a cup of coffee in her hand. She watched a pair of desert dwelling javelinas come in from the arroyo behind her yard. They were drinking out of a small pool of water that had collected in a shallow hole under a mesquite tree. A great horned owl perched on top of a Saguaro cactus on the other side of the arroyo.

She had woken up around 5:00 a.m. every morning for the past few days, since the terrifying incident at the house in Florence. Jacenda had forgotten what had happened. She only remembered the resplendent light right after Lorelei left the closet. The next thing she knew, Brandon, Lorelei, Ian and Joe had been looking down at her on the living room floor.

Jacenda stared at her cell phone, lying on the kitchen table. She had picked up her phone over twenty times since she got out of bed; had even started to dial Brandon's number a few times. But she couldn't get herself to call.

He's going to think I'm insane. Hell, I'm beginning to think I'm insane.

He had been calling her ten times a day at least. Telling her how much he loved her and that he would be there for her, no matter what. She wanted to believe him, just like her mother had wanted to believe her father. Then Jacenda noticed how her father reacted when her mom started seeing spirits. He kept telling her she needed to see a psychiatrist. When Jacenda was only ten years old, her father abandoned them. She saw it coming. At first, it was the late nights—until he wouldn't come home at all. A week before her tenth birthday, her father returned, only to announce he had met someone else. Someone sane.

Her phone rang. Brandon. Maybe he knew she would be up or maybe he wanted to leave another message. She couldn't think too much about him. It would be too hard to stay away from him.

She also had started to have dreams of a necklace made with olive shells interwoven with shell beads. An elaborate jade turtle pendant hung at the bottom. She couldn't explain it, but Jacenda realized the jewelry piece had been made by the Hohokam. Lorelei had seen the remains of the pithouses and other objects left behind on the property during her brief astral journey at the home. Could the ancient piece of artistry have been created by someone from the prehistoric past? Was the house somehow responsible for her visions of the necklace? Was that why its walls had absorbed her?

Frustration and confusion overwhelmed her and she began to cry. She had occasionally communicated with spirits. But not with homes. Jacenda slammed her cup on the glass-topped dining room table, spilling hot coffee over her hand. "What the hell are you trying to tell me? Why did you pick me?" She looked around, not really expecting anything to happen.

She went into the kitchen and ran her hand under cold water. The doorbell rang, but she attempted to ignore it. The ringing turned into pounding. Her nearest neighbor was a quarter mile away.

Nervously picking up her phone, she headed toward the door.

"Jace, honey, it's me Brandon. I know you're there. Please, I need to know you're okay."

His voice stopped her breath and her heart. She flung open the door.

"I'm sorry," he said. "I know you don't want to see me. I don't know what happened at that house, but I don't care. Baby, all I want is to be with you."

Torn, Jacenda stood at the threshold between the comfort of her home and the warmth of his arms amid the brisk temperature outside. Caught between safety and love.

He made the decision for her, taking her hand and pulling her into his arms. He trembled, though she wasn't sure whether it was from the cold or fear of how she might react.

She started to let herself go inside his embrace, started to place her arms around his waist. Began to remember how good it felt.

Jacenda pulled away. She looked into his eyes. "I can't do this." She found herself doing something she never thought she would. She shut the door without looking at his face, leaving him outside alone. For a second, she wondered if she had made a mistake. If perhaps Brandon could love her, no matter what.

A scuffling emanated from the backyard. She wiped her eyes and glanced up from the living room to see the pair of javelinas within three feet of her sliding glass doors, observing her intently. After watching her for thirty seconds, they slowly turned, walked back out of her yard, and disappeared into the arroyo beyond.

Brandon alternated between knocking on her door and ringing the doorbell, begging to see her.

After ten minutes, it stopped. A car door closed, an engine started and she heard him back out of the driveway.

Pressing her head and hands against the front door, she began to sob. Her shoulders wracked with grief as she dropped to the floor.

Jacenda turned and leaned her back against the door, watching two hummingbirds feeding on nectar in a hummingbird feeder on her patio. A brilliant streak of light bounced from where the javelinas had been only minutes before.

I'm going completely crazy.

Another white light circled the mesquite tree where the javelina had been drinking before shooting up into the hazy Arizona sky.

She stood up quickly and ran to look outside. The mysterious streaks were gone.

Jacenda turned her head to face the living room, which had inexplicably turned dark. An orange-reddish light hung in the center of the sudden blackness. Yet she didn't feel threatened. A face began to form among long, wavy locks. The intruder smiled at her.

She walked toward the hovering figure.

Jacenda had met Shannon and Brandon at the hotel in Wickenburg. Shannon had interviewed Jacenda briefly to see if she had seen Peter or Emily, after Lorelei had been abducted by Peter.

Now, Shannon's features were barely detectable.

Jacenda turned her head away for a split second as another light wrapped itself around her body, and then shot through the patio door and toward the sun.

When she looked back, Galiena stood before her. Or was it Shannon? For the person before her was the replica of the former FBI agent, Shannon Flynn.

She stepped forward and reached out a hand to Jacenda.

Jacenda didn't know what to expect when she touched the silent visitor. A subtle jolt of electricity ran through her. For a brief period, the haunted home from Florence slammed into her memory. Shannon held on firmly to Jacenda's right hand.

"It is not the house that contacted you for help," Shannon said. "It is you who absorbed your own human form into its walls. You have a rather amazing ability. You can connect not only with the spirits inhabiting a place, but the land or structure itself." Her dark orange orbs stared intently at Jacenda. "You cleared all entities, Native American and otherwise, from the space, releasing them out of their confines."

"I don't even know what happened! I only remember being shut in the closet. And why can't these spirits free themselves?"

"They were trapped. Like Lorelei, it's going to take you time to learn to control your abilities. The home screamed for help. You responded. It knew what you were capable of."

Shannon began to fade.

"Don't leave," Jacenda begged. "How do I deal with this?"

"You are watched. Always. Believe in your friends. They can help more than you realize."

Shannon released her hand from Jacenda's and disappeared. As she did, a group of twenty Native Americans revealed themselves in a shadowy form.

The tallest of the tribe stepped forward wearing a buckskin shirt and pants, sandals made from yucca fiber and a shell thunderbird necklace. Men, women and children wore buckskin or cotton garments. Some men wore only breechcloths. Some were highly adorned in shell, turquoise and stone jewelry and a few villagers' bodies were painted in brilliant colors.

"When I said, 'I will, I promise,' I was promising to help you escape the confines of the four walls and send you back to your land."

They smiled and nodded.

27

Brandon parked his car in the cul-de-sac near Jacenda's home. New homes and pristine desert landscapes painted in bright greens, yellows and pinks, and dotted with mesquite, palo verde and creosote, led up to a gently sloping hill with a hiking trail leading to the top. He debated whether to return to her and refuse to leave until she talked to him. Or to go home and suffer in silence.

Unbelievable heartache threatened to drive him insane. Brandon never imagined Jacenda would be able to physically and emotionally close the door on him. *Could I have been wrong about her? Could Lorelei, Ian and Joe all be wrong about Jacenda and our future together?*

He could no longer deal with the heartbreak. Brandon needed to escape and be with his friends. He dialed Joe's phone number to see if he could join them in the Four Corners to help solve the case.

"Brandon," Joe said. "Sort of early for you." A cross between a question and a statement. He wondered if the shaman already knew what had happened.

"Could I come up to the Four Corners?" Brandon desperately fought the tears and emotion. "I would like to see what I can do to help."

"Of course. Mandy's heading up here this morning as well. Or were you planning on coming at a later date?"

"I'm leaving in the next hour or two. I have to get home and get packed."

"Does she know?" Joe asked.

"What do you mean?"

"Does Jacenda know you're leaving town?"

"No. I don't think she cares."

"She cares much more than you think, my friend. That's the problem." Joe hung up, leaving Brandon staring at the numbers on his cell phone.

Speeding up to eighty miles an hour, he raced home, anxious to pack and leave town. He desperately wanted to help her, and if Jacenda called, he would be there for her. Short of breaking her door down, he could do no more. It hurt like hell that Jacenda didn't trust him. She knew the talents and capabilities of Lorelei, Ian and Joe. So why didn't she think Brandon would accept hers?

He arrived home a little after eight. While he folded shirts and placed them into his suitcase, the sound of chanting echoed faintly throughout the bedroom. Ten seconds later, the music became louder. Chanting mixed-in with drums and ceremonial music.

Brandon glanced around nervously. He checked every room in his house before throwing open his front door and listening. Nothing. The sound came from inside, from everywhere. He slowly turned around to look into the living room. The Native American music continued, gradually becoming softer.

"Who's here?" Had something had followed him home from the house in Florence? After all, Lorelei had mentioned the Hohokam had once resided on the land. Native Americans who had somehow managed to turn a stark and unforgiving desert landscape into thriving and fertile farmland by building an extensive irrigation canal system with primitive stone tools. He had heard of the Hohokam people. He just never knew how amazing they were.

Am I experiencing the sounds of the past? If so, why are they here with me?

Brandon finished packing. He set up a camera to record while away to see if he would be able to catch some activity.

Brandon went outside, placing his luggage and equipment case in the back of his car. He remembered Jacenda's face the last time he saw her, only a couple of hours ago. He remembered the feel of her arms around him. For a few seconds, she held on. Tightly.

He texted her mobile number. I WILL BE HERE WHEN YOU'RE READY.

28

Lorelei stood outside, among the thousand-year old Indian ruins at the Lowry Pueblo Great House within the Canyons of the Ancients National Monument. The ancestral Puebloan had constructed the village in the Great Sage Plain around A.D. 1060 and inhabited the area for 165 years.

Once a thriving, two-story village, the FBI roamed among brush, shrub, rubble and remains of the second floor and lower components, which had been reburied to protect them. Windows and doorways were visible among partially standing brick walls. She observed the south end of the structure, roofed to protect some of the oldest, most substantial areas of the pueblo, including a painted kiva.

Most visitors didn't know that many of the prehistoric villagers never left. Even after their death. Lorelei saw the spirit of a young woman working hard to grind corn with a large round stone inside the room next to her. Three children, approximately five to fifteen-years old, played near the Great Kiva. Two men flaked chips off stone to form tools. And a Native American man in his thirties, with an animal pelt over his shoulder, climbed a ladder to the third story; a level of the structure that no longer existed.

Were any of these phantoms aware of what happened here a few days ago to an innocent woman named Jan Stinson? Or were they blissfully unaware—going about their daily lives in another dimension from the past? A time without running water or electricity, grocery stores, computers and smart devices.

Watching the spirits of the children, the elderly and young families among the ruins, Lorelei understood such modern conveniences only get in the way. This prehistoric race had to work together to plant and gather food, build stone tools and elaborate structures, and trek long distances for water and resources to survive.

Galiena had brought the group together again for this morbid mystery among the ruins and relics of the Four Corners. It began with the connection of Lorelei to Ian, Paul and the members of the Arizona-Irish in Wickenburg. The bond further strengthened with the Caves of the Watchers mystery. Now the story continued with the abductions and murder mysteries in the Four Corners. With the new case came new talent.

Mandy had a special connection to pregnant women—a connection that *could* help to solve the kidnapping case. The raven-haired beauty named Jacenda had captured Brandon's heart. And apparently, had also managed to become one with a haunted home entwined with the prehistoric past.

No question about it. The ancients *had* chosen Mandy and Jacenda. Lorelei believed they both had their talents for a while, but were hidden away until the right time came.

From the beginning, Lore, Ian and Joe had been dealing with a highly intelligent race of individuals. Many of those who were once human, like Dagon, Mattie and Annie, had extremely high IQs. This seemed to be the reason the ancients endowed certain people with rather distinct abilities. Mandy and Jacenda were just as intelligent.

Lorelei still hadn't figured out why she had heard Native American tongue during their adventures in Southeast Arizona, and why she had been involuntarily speaking the language herself. Mattie, Annie and Dagon weren't Native American. Could Galiena and her people have their own tongue tied to the Native American races on earth?

Or were the spirits of the ancient prehistoric cultures aligned with Galiena's race, living among the stars and galaxies of the Milky Way? After all, many Native Americans believed they were descended from the stars—and many believed they would be going back some day.

Lorelei gently guided her hand across her stomach. Not quite two months pregnant, she wondered what talents her baby would possess.

Ian came up behind her and slid his arms around her. His hands encompassed her own as they rested over her stomach.

"How are you feeling?"

Lorelei rested the back of her head against his chest. "Amazing."

He kissed the top of her head. "I love you."

She turned around to kiss him. Just as their lips brushed together, a brilliant display streaked across the sky.

"Wonder if that could be Galiena?" Ian asked. "Perhaps reminding us of how Shannon would always manage to interrupt us at the most inopportune moments."

Lorelei stared up into the late afternoon sun and smiled dreamily. "I'm sure she is keeping a close watch. After all, I believe she did bring Mandy and Jacenda into our lives. Look at the talents they have."

"You still miss Shannon, don't you?"

"Every day. She was so easy to talk to and fun to be around. Definitely not the profile of a typical FBI agent."

Ian turned Lorelei to face him.

She found it hard to focus on the scenic desert surroundings and ancient spirit dwellers as she leaned in to kiss Ian.

A female voice shouted something, threatening to destroy the reverie with Ian. Lorelei glanced away from his face to see Mandy waving her hands.

"Ian, Lore," Mandy yelled. She motioned for them to join her, Joe and Agent Zimmerman nearby at the Great Kiva.

Ian looked at Lorelei and whispered in her ear. "I think someone's taking over for Shannon. In more ways than one."

Like Shannon, Mandy seemed to have perfect timing for interrupting her and Ian's romantic moments.

"Go ahead, honey. I want to stay here and see if I can communicate with any intelligent spirits. Maybe I can get a clue as to who the kidnapper is and what he's done with his latest victim. I'll catch up in a few minutes."

Ian kissed her firmly on the lips and leaned down to kiss her stomach. "Okay, but I'm keeping a very close watch on you." He headed toward the Great Kiva near the main ruins.

Lorelei bent down and entered a T-shaped doorway into another open room. Another mystery of the ancestral world, T-shaped entrances were believed to have functional uses, such as protection against the wind and insulation against heat and cold, as well as spiritual meaning. She could hear the woman still grinding corn two rooms away. Standing in the center of the dwelling, she glanced up to see the Native American man with the animal skin staring at her, standing on an invisible third story room.

"Can you understand me?"

Of course he can't, you idiot.

He continued staring at her. The man began to talk, but she couldn't make sense of the words. The grinding stopped. The children suddenly went quiet. Everyone looked up to watch and listen.

Lorelei glanced around nervously, wondering if they considered her a threat. She began to back slowly toward the doorway. But the shapely young woman with medium-length black hair and brown eyes who had been busy grinding corn blocked her exit.

"I'm not here to harm you. My friends and I are here to…" She didn't get to finish her sentence. The woman, dressed in a deerskin dress with fringes at the bottom, reached out to Lorelei with her hand.

More noticeable than the woman's beauty was her necklace. The artisan had interwoven olive shells with other types of stones, shell beads and turquoise chips. A jade turtle pendant, two inches across, hung at the bottom.

She reached out to meet the hand of the mysterious Anasazi woman.

"Lore!" Ian shouted excitedly for her. She looked above the walled remains to see him running in her direction. "Lore, where are you?"

When she glanced back, the woman had vanished. Along with the man who had stood above her on a balcony that no longer existed.

She left the pueblo. "Ian, I'm okay."

He took her hands in his. "Tony found something in the Great Kiva. We wanted to see if you could get any vibes from it."

Ian pulled her gently to the waiting group where Tony, Mandy and Joe stood. They had their backs to her with their heads down, observing an object the agent held. He must have heard Lorelei and Ian coming and held up the necklace for them.

Lorelei stopped in her tracks.

"Beautiful, huh?" Ian said.

She couldn't say a word. She stared at the shell necklace with the turtle pendant.

"I can't believe this."

Joe looked up at Lorelei. "It is rather a shock to find such a piece. Especially intact."

"No. That's not it. I mean, it is a surprise. But even more so because I just saw that exact piece on the spirit of an ancestral Puebloan woman."

"Did she tell you who she was?" Joe asked.

Lorelei shook her head. She reached out to me, but Ian scared her away when he came running up to me.

Ian hugged her. "Crap, I'm sorry."

"It's okay. You had no way of knowing."

"Maybe she was about to give you an important clue." Ian threw up his hands in frustration. "I should know better by now than to interrupt you like that."

"Or she might not have told me anything. I'll try and connect with her again. I also noticed a handsome Native American man. He spoke and captured the attention of the whole community. I'm thinking he might have been a shaman."

Lorelei noticed Tony staring at Julie, a petite blonde woman in her thirties with the evidence response team. She was photographing an area of ground near the picnic area from different angles.

Joe followed her gaze. "We found the footprints of the last victim, Jan Stinson. Hard to tell they were hers because her husband's shoes had occluded them in his attempt to find her. But what's really strange is her prints stop behind a boulder. They don't lead anywhere. It's like she vanished into thin air."

"Are you sure the prints are hers?" Ian asked.

"They were her shoe size and led from the picnic area to the place her husband last saw her."

"No other prints indicating her abductor?" Lorelei asked.

"There are multiple other impressions, more likely from a number of different individuals visiting the place. The FBI will have to rely on other types of evidence. But this will be a very challenging case considering the abilities of Nicole's murderer."

"What did Jan encounter that made her wander away?" Mandy asked. "If the kidnapper could perform such a feat as shapeshifting, he could have appeared to her as her husband."

Joe stared at Mandy in astonishment. "Her husband did mention she was out of sight for five minutes. So the abductor could have taken that opportunity."

Mandy looked up at three turkey vultures that were circling the sky. "I thought only books and movies portrayed stuff like that. How is it physically possible for someone to take on another human or animal form?"

"As a shaman, I perform what many consider shapeshifting through meditation and visualization. My favorite form is the eagle. I don't transform into the raptor, but I wear a mask created with eagle feathers. By performing such a ceremony, it helps me develop the abilities of the animal. In the case with my power animal, I gain strength, exceptional vision and solitude. Very important assets for a medicine man."

Joe and Mandy stared into each other's eyes. It reminded Lorelei of the way Ian looked at her. Even though Lorelei couldn't see clearly in the vision, Mandy had to be the woman she saw with Joe.

He looked away from Mandy and up at the vultures, now landing on the dirt road leading to Lowry. "Anyway, I've seen many unbelievable things in my lifetime. At least, what most people would have trouble understanding. However, because something is beyond the realm of science doesn't mean it can't happen."

Mandy looked around as if something might jump out at her at any second.

Ian glanced at Lorelei in amazement. He seemed to have caught it as well. The exact same look had crossed Mandy's face that had crossed Shannon's on numerous occasions.

"You should have this." Tony gave Lorelei the stunning shell necklace. "Not that it has anything to do with the case, but you might be able to get some clues pertaining to the woman who wore it."

"Tell her how you found it," Joe said.

"I saw a tarantula in the middle of the Great Kiva. It stared at me for a few seconds. When it moved, I saw part of the jade pendant."

Lorelei watched Tony suspiciously. She realized he had been present before Joe's journey to the stars—when another tarantula moved into the medicine wheel. Tony seemed to be attracting the very creature consuming her visions recently. Could it be coincidence?

She caressed the pearl-like turtle hanging from the bottom. Smooth, round olive shells had been cut on either end to fit onto the string. And flatter pieces of shell alternated with turquoise beads.

"Amazing." She held the necklace closer to her body.

Ian, Tony, Mandy and Joe watched her intently.

Ian put his arm around her. "Lore, what is it? What are you seeing?"

"The house in Florence where we investigated."

"Are you saying the necklace has something to do with that home?" Joe asked.

"Yes, or rather the property it's built on. My rather unorthodox vision upstairs in the haunted home briefly showed a young girl beading a piece of jewelry, though I couldn't really see the details of the necklace."

Joe walked to the edge of the Great Kiva. "You mean when Jacenda saw you floating above the floor?"

"Yes."

The pendant held memories, images of stories and lives, and reflections of extensive travel. "I believe this impressive piece might have been made by the very tribe that resided on the property in Florence."

"The Hohokam received shells as trade items from Mexico," Joe said. "And they had a rather extensive network, including the ancestral Puebloan people. The woman phantom you witnessed wearing the likeness of this could have received it through trade, if it's the same necklace."

Lorelei kept seeing flashes of Jacenda in between the images of the Native American woman making the necklace.

She glanced from Joe to Ian. "No wonder Jacenda had such a connection with that place." Lorelei held up the necklace. "I think Brandon's girlfriend is the reincarnation of the woman who made this. I'm also getting the impression the creator of this is rather important, possibly a shaman's daughter."

Tony's face reflected knowledge and understanding. "That house you all investigated, it's the living essence of the Hohokam. The home remembered. It wanted her back."

Tony observed the Great House where Lorelei had encountered the ancient ghosts. Rather than looking at Lowry Pueblo, he seemed to be staring *through* it. Like Joe, Tony had an arcane aura surrounding him. But unlike Joe, the energy from the striking young FBI agent seemed to extend to every pinion/juniper, sagebrush, rock, tree, ruin, and blade of grass within fifty feet.

Lorelei shivered. She glanced over at Joe and Ian. They seemed to have picked up on it as well and watched Tony intently. Tony wasn't merely a temporary part of the environment; a visitor as the rest of them. Rather an extension of the prehistoric villages, canyons, mesas and high, dry, rolling plateaus of the Great Sage Plain.

29

Joe's sharp eagle-like instincts told him the perpetrator hid in silence and solitude. The FBI and park law enforcement were being taunted by a highly elusive criminal who managed to get his victims into such tight confines and make them vanish without a trace.

Joe shivered amid the warmth of the afternoon rays. The bastard waited somewhere nearby. Watching.

Joe stood next to the Lowry Great Kiva, a circular stone structure thought to be a central gathering place for ancestral Puebloans from several hundred miles. The kiva was forty-seven feet in diameter, making it one of the largest in the area. Built underground, it had to be accessed either through a ladder through a central opening, or a series of steps through the rooms on the north. People gathered from all over the Great Sage Plain to trade, exchange information and conduct religious ceremonies.

Joe watched Lorelei and Mandy walk into another kiva inside the main remnants of the village about thirty feet away. Lorelei wanted to help Mandy develop her ability to connect with pregnant women. However, Joe knew if Mandy didn't believe, she wouldn't get any further. Mandy glanced back at him right before she stepped into the kiva, giving him a half smile. For a split second, she didn't seem real.

Her beauty undeniable. His desire no less so.

He closed his eyes. A majestic bald eagle swept into his inner vision, gliding gracefully on air. The raptor observed Joe with curiosity before diving out of his internal darkness, directly toward him.

This isn't right.

The two luminous beings connected to Galiena appeared alongside the giant raptor, though not dancing and twirling playfully as they had days before during his astral journey. Their radiant bodies formed a straight line and they seemed as intent as the eagle on a prey Joe could not see.

Within five feet of Joe, the eagle transformed. Molten lava burst into his inner vision, blinding him and sending orange-red flames across the stars.

A piercing scream entered his startling day vision. Joe opened his eyes to see Mandy running toward him with Lorelei a few feet behind.

Tony came running over to see what had happened.

"He knew we were out there." Lorelei put her arm around Ian. "The murderer. Mandy and I walked around in one of the village kivas to see if either of us could pick up on the victim. We heard breathing, only no one else was around."

Mandy placed her hands on Joe's waist. "At first, Lore and I thought we heard a spirit. Then he laughed. The same maniacal sound from my captivity."

"It's okay now." He stroked her face. She closed her eyes and tightened her grip on his body.

"I'm sorry." Mandy pulled away and stared at the ground. It felt like a piece of him had been ripped apart. An important piece.

"You both need to stay with me, Tony or one of the other agents. No more roaming alone." Joe glanced at Lorelei. "Did he say anything else or attempt to harm you?"

Mandy and Lorelei looked at each other for a few seconds.

Lorelei nervously pushed her hair behind her ear. "He said, 'I see you,' and the word *you* was drawn out."

Ian hugged her tightly. "I'm glad you're both all right. But you and Mandy are still in danger."

"Did either of you *see* anything at all when this happened?" Tony asked.

"Sorry," Mandy said. "Guess I was a little too freaked out."

"I didn't either. No other human, animal or otherwise nearby to indicate he had taken another form. And his voice was *very* close. Not sure if it's out-of-body as most people can't hear those who are in their astral form. I wonder if he can transform himself into a phantom."

"That would explain how he left that note at the hotel," Ian said. "After all, some spirits can manipulate objects."

Joe wondered why he had the stark vision right before Mandy and Lorelei's experience. The eagle turning into the flames had to be an urgent message from Galiena. But why now? Why didn't the eagle vision occur when the abductions started?

Joe waved for Tony to follow him into the kiva where Lorelei and Mandy had been. "Come on, you bastard," Joe said. "What's the matter? You only have the courage to torture pregnant women?"

Nothing. Except for Tony's footsteps as he roamed the area.

Joe closely observed the inside of the kiva to see if anything moved. Tony had closed his eyes, remaining completely still in the middle of the ceremonial structure. Tony hadn't mentioned that he had any abilities, but Joe detected something now. Tony's aura seemed to have invisible tendrils that reached out from every part of his body to pull on the lifeforce of objects within the vicinity.

Joe left the kiva and entered a nearby pueblo. He felt as if someone had walked directly behind him. He whipped his head around. No one.

"Joe, Tony." An older agent in his fifties named Don waved to them from near the Great Kiva. "Over here. We finally had a sighting of the abductor. Description is straight, shoulder-length shaggy brown hair, burn scars covering his face and neck. Walked with a limp in his left leg."

Something in the air changed. Tony seemed to notice it also, glancing around nervously.

"Where and when?" Joe asked.

"A park ranger in Canyon of the Ancients saw the guy at Painted Hand Pueblo ten minutes ago. I told the ranger to keep his distance and that we would be on the way."

Tony glanced up at the sky as the clouds passed over the sun. "Lorelei and Mandy heard his voice here only a few minutes ago. The Painted Hand ruin takes at least twenty minutes to get to from here."

"We're dealing with a highly unusual murder mystery. This guy has abilities keeping him well hidden, including shapeshifting. But he finally made a mistake by letting someone see him. Let's hope we can find him, Jan Stinson or any other victims."

"I don't want to think how many other women might be out there, frightened and alone," Tony said. "Or being tortured."

Joe didn't want to think about what other innocent women might be going through. He hoped Mandy and Lorelei would be able to help.

"This could be a trick," Tony said. "Maybe he wanted the ranger to see him to lure us away from Lowry."

"He does seem to like playing games. But we have to check out the lead."

On the way to the parking lot, Joe called Bureau of Land Management's law enforcement division. A deep voice answered.

"Sam, BLM law enforcement."

"Joe Luna with the FBI. The kidnapper's been sighted at Painted Hand. We'll need your assistance. When can someone meet me and another agent out there?"

"This guy really gets around," Sam said. "I just talked to an officer who was checking on one of the more remote sites within a half-hour of Painted Hand Pueblo. I'll call him back now and have him head that direction. I'll also contact Montezuma County Sheriff's office."

The murderer had a major advantage because of his unique abilities. If he could transform into animals or any objects in his environment, Joe realized he could probably use his talents to turn into a spirit. Out-of-body travel had not been ruled out either.

Jan Stinson could be anywhere. Canyons of the Ancients National Monument encompassed almost 164,000 acres of rugged high desert, including semiarid mesa and canyon country. The monument also had the highest known density of archaeological sites in the United States; more than one hundred sites per square mile in some spots. Nicole's murderer could be using many of the inaccessible ancient sites as hideaways.

"The road heading out to Painted Hand is rather rough, as all of the roads to the Hovenweep sites," Sam continued. "It's off of a high-clearance road, number 4531. There will be a small parking area off to the left a mile in. But the site itself requires a short, steep hike down to the ruins."

Joe drove down County Road CC—the dirt road leading away from Lowry Pueblo with Tony. Two large ravens flew alongside his truck before diving into the rolling farm fields on the side of the road.

The alcove dwellings, potsherds, remnants of stone tools, petroglyphs and other ancient landmarks offered clues about the lives of people who lived in the region over a span of many thousands of years. Joe wished such history could provide some detail as to how to catch this mad man.

"We're not sure if his latest victim is at Painted Hand," Joe spoke to Sam on his cell. "But if we can at least catch him, we might be able to save Jan. And whoever else he's holding captive."

Tony's phone rang as Joe was hanging hung up with BLM.

Tony grabbed onto the roof as the truck flew over a bump. "She found him. Your friend Mandy found Jan Stinson alive at Lowry Pueblo."

30

Mandy didn't understand how it happened. One minute she had been walking alongside the Pueblo Lowry Great House. The next minute, she had touched her stomach in response to what felt like the baby kicking. She could see a vision of Jan Stinson, the pregnant Hopi woman, in an underground prison outside the perimeter of the Great House.

Mandy raced away from the rectangular Anasazi structure and into the tall grass. She walked for half a mile, felt the kick again and stopped. Looking down, Mandy could detect slight movement through a small hole in the ground.

"Hello!" she yelled.

A slight moan rose to the surface.

Mandy bent over, peeking into the two-inch hole. A woman with long dark hair sat completely still on the ground, holding her stomach. Even if she wanted to move, she wouldn't be able to in a space with only a few feet.

"She's here," Mandy screamed. "I found Jan!"

At the mention of her name, Jan slowly glanced up.

Mandy bent down and spoke into the opening. "Don't worry. Help's here. We're going to get you out of there."

"Please." Jan begged. "I'm having contractions."

Lorelei, Ian, and an officer with BLM looked raced over to Mandy and looked down into Jan's tiny prison.

"She's having contractions." Mandy held her own stomach. She realized she had somehow experienced what Jan did, which helped to find her.

"I'll be right back." The officer ran to the parking lot.

Jan bent over, screaming in pain. "It's coming! The baby's coming."

"What the hell are we going to do?" Lorelei whispered. "It's going to take a while to get her out of there."

"Jan, watch out. I'm going to try to increase the size of the opening." Ian stomped on the ground. More dirt gave way, creating a bigger hole five inches across.

"Wait, that will work." Mandy lay on the ground and reached in. "Jan, grab my hand."

"I can't. It hurts too much."

Mandy desperately extended her hand to Jan. A rain of dirt fell into the hole. "Shit. I can't reach."

"I can't have my little girl here. Please. It's not supposed to be like this." She stretched her hand up to meet Mandy's.

"It won't be." Mandy stretched her arm as far as she could until she took Jan's hand in hers. Closing her eyes, she imagined warmth flowing from her body into Jan's. A calmness she had never experienced overcame her. As if she were enveloped in an angel's arms.

Jan suddenly seemed more tranquil as she loosened her grip on Mandy, glancing at her stomach in astonishment. Jan stared up at her in surprise. "The contractions have stopped."

Mandy and Ian moved aside while the FBI agents and park law enforcement worked to get her out.

Everyone kept glancing in Mandy's direction. She didn't want to acknowledge them or explain. And really, she didn't know how.

What's happening to me? I didn't ask to get kidnapped and be some sort of magic healer. I only want to forget about the past few days and go on with my life.

Jan held her hands over her head to avoid the dropping debris while the agents desperately pounded on the ground with shovels to widen the opening.

Mandy glanced toward the parking lot to see a truck pulling in.

"Ian called Joe and Tony," Lorelei said.

Two car doors slammed. Thirty seconds later, Mandy saw Joe come running up with Tony.

Joe looked at Mandy. Her heart pounded. She couldn't look back at him, lest he pick up on her impure thoughts. She thought the FBI agent and shaman was the hottest man she had ever seen. She kept picturing him on the cover of the sleazy romance novels, without a shirt, staring down at Mandy while slowly undressing her.

Come on, Mandy. Get it together!

Mandy averted her gaze to the ladder dropping down into the tight confines of the chamber. While the BLM officer climbed down and helped Jan up, she could still sense Joe's intense dark eyes upon her. She breathed a sigh of relief when Joe turned to help another agent pull Jan out of confinement.

Ian glanced back to County Road CC. "Damn it. Where is that ambulance?"

Jan reached out to grab Mandy's hand when Joe lifted her out of her prison. Mandy didn't know if it was for comfort, or to ensure her contractions would wait for the ambulance.

"It's almost a half-mile back to the Great House," Joe said. "Do you think you can walk back to the main trail?"

Jan nodded. "As long as I don't have any contractions."

Mandy took Jan's hand and held it tightly.

Fifteen minutes later, they arrived back at the Lowry ruins. Joe and Tony guided Jan to the Great House and sat her down on the remnants of a wall.

Mandy heard the siren of the ambulance coming down the dirt road.

Tony looked toward the parking lot. "I'm going to meet the paramedics to show them up here."

Joe knelt down and took Jan's hands in his. "I've contacted your husband. He's staying in Cortez and will meet you at the hospital there."

Jan's eyes lit up when she heard the news.

"I suppose you're going to question me."

"Later, after you've delivered." Joe gave her a gentle smile. "You won't get rid of me that easy."

Mandy turned to look as the ambulance pulled into the dirt parking lot.

Jan placed her hand on Joe's wrist. "I'm not the only one. I mean, there are other victims. At least that's what they said." She screamed and grabbed her stomach.

"You need to get to the hospital." Lorelei motioned to the two young paramedics, a man and a woman, who were quickly rolling in a gurney to help Jan.

"Wait," Jan shouted. She looked from Mandy to Joe. "I don't know how I ended up in that damn hole. One second I was following a collared lizard. Then I awoke to find myself in the dark. I could barely move."

The paramedics lifted and placed Jan down on the gurney.

"It's okay." Joe gently stroked her arm. "You're safe now. And you're going to have a very healthy baby."

"This man you saw," Mandy said. "Did he have scraggy brown hair with burn scars on his face and neck?"

Jan stared at her in confusion. "What man? I never saw anyone."

Mandy looked at Joe and Tony after Jan left. "The bastard is invisible."

"Not only that," Lorelei said. "How could he have gotten Jan into that space? It's the same scenario as with Nicole."

Joe turned to Mandy. He lifted her chin up to face him. "How did you find Jan? For someone who doesn't claim to understand her talents, you sure managed to accomplish quite a bit."

"I'm not sure how I found her. I got what felt like a minor contraction and received a vision while walking around the Great House. These false contractions led me to her. As far as the healing, I felt an inexplicable urge to reach out to her. Then a strange energy passed between her and me. Next thing I know, her contractions stopped."

Mandy placed her hand into her jeans' pocket. Lorelei had loaned her the jade pendant to test her skills. Mandy slowly removed the beautiful piece of shell jewelry now.

"I remember having my hand on this when I got the vision of Jan." Mandy looked at Lorelei, then Joe. "In the Great Kiva. Maybe the bastard wanted the necklace and that's why he tried to scare us."

Joe removed a handkerchief from his back pocket and wiped the sweat from his brow. "Not sure how we're going to catch someone who can transform himself into anything he chooses at will, including an invisible man, or spirit form. Thanks to Mandy, we managed to find Jan. But he's killed one woman. How many more will lose their lives until we can figure out how to stop him?"

31

*W*ithin five minutes of Lorelei starting her out-of-body journey, she found her astral soul inside a majestic Golden Eagle, diving out of the sky toward a jackrabbit with its sharp orbs focused on its prey. Twenty seconds. The rabbit glanced up, noticing its demise.

Ten seconds. The rabbit ran for its life. Not looking back.

For a split second, Lorelei wanted to feel her sharp talons embed themselves into warm flesh. To feel the weight of her prize. And to use her curved beak to tear apart tissue and muscle.

Her talons spread apart, she dove. The jackrabbit took a flying leap into a hole at the last second. The Golden Eagle let out a screech before flying back up into the sky, leaving Lorelei's astral soul next to the animal's escape route. A pile of stones that looked like building material for the prehistoric dwellings were next to the opening.

She had landed among gently rolling slopes of farmland with a modern two-story beige Victorian-style farmhouse a quarter mile away. Black cows grazed nearby and ravens flew overhead, searching for carrion.

The light beings associated with Galiena came out of nowhere. Lorelei almost didn't recognize them in the light of day. The playful, enigmatic beings shot in front of her. Ian had seen them as blue outlines against the sky, possibly because the creatures alternated between an angelic golden glow and a pulsating blue-green. The two of them took a place on either side of her. They danced and swirled around her like they had in space.

A few seconds later they vanished. Into the very hole the rabbit had gone down.

Am I supposed to follow? Are they guiding me to another victim? *She wouldn't be much good in her astral form if there were anyone who needed help. At least she could report back to Joe, so Lorelei followed after her faithful guides into the darkness. Cave, tunnel, or simply a hole—she couldn't tell.*

Though miles away, she could sense Ian's anticipation. He would be sitting anxiously next to her lifeless body, stroking her hair and whispering how much he loved her.

Apprehension followed her into the darkness, until two radiant flashes lit up her surroundings. Her astral guides were helping her to see.

Lorelei floated above a small kiva about twenty feet below the cave ceiling. Two rooms were on either side. The larger pueblo had a two-foot-high entrance with a window on either side of the door. Hovering over the ancient remains, she noticed a modern backpack, aquamarine with black trim. Mandy mentioned she had been carrying a backpack fitting that description before her abductor found her. She also saw a few cell phones, sleeping bag, small cooking stove and a lantern.

An intense image of the abductor forced itself into her mind as clearly as if he stood before her, followed by a vision of an ancient phantom who had callously murdered an innocent young family over a thousand years ago. Could the man guilty of kidnapping and murdering pregnant women be the reincarnation of the vicious Anasazi warrior from Cutthroat Castle? Perhaps that is why he chose caves and ruins for his hiding places—memories from the past.

She didn't see the man responsible for so much terror. Nor did she hear anything. That didn't mean he wasn't there, watching in another form. Jan mentioned she didn't see anyone before she ended up in her underground lair. Could he somehow make himself invisible? Or maybe use mind control to make his victims forget? Or even more frightening, somehow morph his victims into the virtually inaccessible spaces?

Her guides danced around the ruins, creating radiant spiral patterns like those found on many petroglyphs through the Southwest. At one point, the two beings joined together to form a horizontal double spiral, extending half the length of the cave. She felt relieved. If there were immediate danger, they would make sure to let her know.

How many other hiding places does he have?

The two light guardians ceased their play, stopping in an "S" shape. They seemed to be looking back at her. Then they both shot forward and vanished into a crevasse two feet across, barely big enough for her physical form to squeeze through. She followed them through a narrow slot that opened up into a larger cavern. A man sat completely still in the center of the chamber with shaggy brown hair and burn scars over his face and neck. It was him. Panic overcame her.

Lorelei began to escape back through the aperture. The light beings blocked her path. She heard two distinct whispers in unison, the first time she had heard them speak. Their voices had an electric tone to match their lustrous appearance.

"Stay. He does not know you're here."

Two slivers of daylight forced themselves through cracks in the ceiling. The man who had managed to elude law enforcement positioned himself between both sun beams. He chanted quietly and swayed, his motions became quicker and more intense. A woman's straw sunhat rested on his lap.

In desperation, Lorelei waved her hand through the energy of one of her guides. She pulled her hand back when she received a slight shock. He's luring another woman to her demise. I'm seeing the word *Cody* in my mind for a first name.

A strange force pulled her backward. Out of the cave, through his living space and out into the open.

She could not see the two light beings, but felt their presence. "You knew. You guided me here to find him."

"No!" The word came from all around her. "You did. You led us here."

"We have to stop him. He's taking another victim and I have no idea where this person is."

Lorelei heard footsteps. A diminutive woman with fair skin and brown hair approached the entrance to the cave from the direction of the farmhouse. She appeared to be in a trance. An older man waved frantically at the woman, calling a name Lorelei couldn't understand.

This woman didn't look pregnant. But she could have been in the initial stages. Lorelei wanted to stop her from getting near Cody's lair, but didn't know if she would be heard without her physical form.

"*Stop!*" *Lorelei attempted to grab her arm. No reaction.*

A brilliant flash of light crossed through the stranger. Then the young woman screamed in pain.

Lorelei's astral guardians had awoken the woman from her hypnotic state by shocking her. She glanced around in confusion. The man from the farmhouse had pulled a brown horse out of the corral, jumped on its back and started racing toward the woman. The wind began to pick up as she turned and ran to meet him. The older man asked her why she took off, but she merely threw her hands in the air and glanced back at the entrance to the cave.

The horse stomped its feet and shook its head from side-to-side before rearing up, almost knocking its rider off.

"*Whoa,*" *the man said. He gently stroked the horse's neck.*

"*Let's get out of here.*" *The petite woman glanced nervously around and jumped on the back of the animal.*

Movement from the ruins below. Cody was restless. The shuffling became louder and more frenzied.

How can I tell Joe how to find this place? Of course—the farmhouse.

Cody worked his way through the narrow passage. He came out head first, looking from side-to-side. He slid out of his subterranean lair, stood up, and stared intently at the couple getting off the horse a quarter mile away.

The woman had escaped once. Would she be safe after Lorelei left? Lorelei had no choice. She had to get back to Joe to let him know about Cody's hiding spot, or rather one of his many traps. Lorelei left the solidness of the earth and floated into the atmosphere.

When she glanced back down, Cody had vanished. A massive raven, almost two feet tall, stood in his place. The bird ruffled its feathers before flying back up into the sky and toward the farmhouse.

Lorelei quickly headed back to Lowry Pueblo, five miles south of Cody's hideout.

Within minutes, she was back in her physical form at Lowry; Ian's warm hand a pleasant shock.

"Lore." Ian helped her sit up. "I thought you would never get back. I think this is the longest journey you've taken."

"How long was I gone?"

"Over half an hour."

Lorelei glanced around and slowly stood up. "Where's Joe? I have so much to tell him."

Ian turned her to face him. "Honey, Joe's gone. He went to find your location."

"What? But I haven't told him anything yet."

"Joe somehow picked up on your experiences, perhaps because you've both recently visited Galiena. He described your surroundings and Tony recognized the farmhouse. He knows the people who live there."

"Ian, I believe the kidnapper's name is Cody. My guides managed to stop a woman he attempted to lure into his lair, more unexcavated Indian ruins, before she could get close enough. Within a few seconds, he managed to transform himself from a man into a raven. His raven form flew to the farmhouse, probably to get his victim back."

"Joe told us everything. That's why he rushed to get out there. We can only hope Joe gets to her first."

Lorelei gazed into Ian's eyes. "How can we stop such a powerful person?"

"We have to prevent him from using his abilities."

Lorelei put her arms around his neck. "First of all, who is 'we?' And how are you going to accomplish that task?"

"Since you did such an amazing job of finding Cody's hideout, Joe should be able to pick up some trace evidence. Maybe enough to figure out exactly who Cody is. I think this man's powers are beyond any of my Pagan rituals."

Brandon waved and ran up to Lorelei and Ian. Tony followed him with the ancient necklace in his hand.

She gave him a hug. "Joe told us you'd be coming. I hope things are okay with Jacenda."

He smiled. "Yes. She called right before I got to Lowry. She's pretty freaked out with everything that's happened, which is why she tried to shut me out of her life, but she's willing to let us all help her through it."

Brandon took the necklace from Tony. "Listen, you all need to know that Jacenda described this necklace to me on the phone. I couldn't believe it when I saw it. She mentioned the type of beadwork, the length and the jade turtle pendant. She's been having recurring visions about it, starting with the investigation at the Florence house."

Lorelei placed her hand on Brandon's shoulder. "I saw alternating visions of Jacenda and another Native American woman. I believe she could be the reincarnation of the person who made this. I also saw this piece of jewelry on the spirit of an ancestral Puebloan woman at the Lowry Great House, meaning the ancient ghost could have been wearing another exactly like this one. Or the necklace could have made its way to the Four Corners through trade. I personally think Jacenda made this artifact in her past life as a Hohokam and it ended up here."

Tony held the precious strand of stones, beads and shell tightly, his right hand on the turtle pendant. "Mandy mentioned she thought her kidnapper wanted this because it hid his secrets." Tony glanced up at the darkening clouds approaching from Cortez. "If that is the case, what if those secrets involve Jacenda?"

32

J acenda watched a family of quail walking around in her backyard. An orange glow highlighted the horizon as the sun slowly set to the west. And children on the street shouted excitedly when an ice cream truck drove by, playing the "Mister Softee" tune repeatedly.

The peacefulness and normalcy of her neighborhood seemed in stark contrast to the surprises in Jacenda's life. She had found out through Brandon that an FBI agent had found the very necklace she had been dreaming of at Lowry Pueblo. He also mentioned Lorelei had a vision of Jacenda being the possible reincarnation of a Hohokam woman who had created it. She had been through a gamut of emotions with the discovery of her bizarre ability: confusion, anger, terror and disbelief. Now she just felt drained and exhausted. She didn't know what to believe. She felt as if she should be checking herself in to the nearest hospital or mental institution.

Excuse me, Doctor, can you give me a prescription for the rather close connection I have to haunted houses?

The night before, Jacenda had dreamt of a man with scraggly brown hair and burn scars on his face and neck. He transformed into a prehistoric Native American warrior wearing only a deer-hide apron, bearing an axe and a spear, who sat in the center of a large cavern, the warm glow from a fire behind him. Silent words spilled forth from his lips. Images of deer, snakes, spirals and other abstract images revealed themselves as flame light flickered on the stone walls. A panel showed stick figures lying below a blanket of stars and a petroglyph in the shape of the Milky Way above. Right before she awoke, Jacenda's subconscious zoomed in on the tall, intimidating man. Around his neck he wore the turtle pendant.

Both men she dreamt of had the same dark, malevolent stare.

Maybe she *was* the reincarnation of the Native American woman who created the pendant. The theory would explain Jacenda's frequent visions.

She saw an incoming text message. HEY BEAUTIFUL. Those two words made Jacenda feel even more guilty and embarrassed for shutting the door in Brandon's face. She knew she had to face up to the cards she was being dealt. COMING HOME.

NO, she texted back immediately. COMING TO SEE YOU.

Brandon called her within thirty seconds. "Jace, it's an eight-hour drive. I would worry about you the whole way up here."

"I'll be fine. Considering everything that's happened—my visions, my possible connection to the woman who created the necklace, the crazy experience I had in Florence. I have to do this."

"Okay, okay. You're right. I'm sure the rest of the team would agree." Brandon sighed. "I can always come get you."

"Brandon, no! That's way too much driving. I'll pack tonight and leave early tomorrow morning around six. I should be in Colorado before six in the evening."

"That works. But I'm going to be calling you frequently."

Jacenda laughed. "I wouldn't expect you to call any less than every ten minutes."

"I might have to take you up on that."

She heard car doors open and close in the background, somewhere in Colorado.

"Seriously, Jace. I don't have the talents that you or Lore do. But you could end up as a key player in solving this case."

She laughed. "That's a scary thought."

"Talk to Lore when you get here, spend more time with her. Trust me, Jace. I know what she went through in Southeast Arizona with the Vincent Joiner case and when she was kidnapped by Peter and Emily. She can help you learn to deal with your talents."

Brandon became quiet for a few seconds. She wondered if the line had disconnected.

"Ian has always been there for Lorelei. I kept thinking during that case how wonderful it would be to have someone to love and support. I have that now. You may be different. But among the Arizona-Irish, that's perfectly normal. Baby, I would love you if I found out you were a Reptoid from the Taurus Constellation."

Jacenda pulled a suitcase from her closet while talking on the phone. "I know, I mean I should have known that, but with what I watched my mother go through. My dad had her thinking she was crazy." She sighed. "Anyway, you have no idea how much that means. I can't wait to see you."

"I'll be thinking about you all night," Brandon said softly. "Call me in the morning after you've left. Get a good night's sleep—don't want you falling asleep on the road. But if you do feel tired, pull off and get something to eat. That always helps me. Or…"

"I'll be fine. I've driven from Arizona to Oregon before."

"I'm sorry."

"That's okay. It's nice to have someone who cares." Jacenda glanced at her watch. 7:10 p.m. "As much as I want to stay on the phone with you, I should go. I need to do some laundry and packing."

"I understand. I'll call you in the morning. I love you so much."

"I love you, too. As I mentioned earlier on the phone, this isn't easy. What with my past and the way my father treated my mom when her skills started developing. But with you by my side, I know I'll make it through."

"You might not believe me. I can't look you in the eyes right now so you know how serious I am. But I will *never* abandon you. *Never.*"

Jacenda didn't have to look into his eyes. She knew he wouldn't leave her. "Well, you'll have plenty of time to tell me when I see you tomorrow."

"Hopefully, for much, much longer." It sounded distant. As if Brandon had turned away from the phone.

Her suitcase lay sprawled open on the bed, waiting to be filled with more memories, more visions. Jacenda somehow understood that this trip would define the rest of her life.

33

Ravens were everywhere. Two flew overhead, watching the rolling hills below. Another sat on the top of a red windmill next to the Victorian two-story beige farmhouse. And a stately, two-foot tall black beauty rested on the roof peak of the home. It observed Joe with piercing dark orbs as he stared up from the front of the house next to a vegetable garden.

Two dark orange streaks dotted with specks of yellow decorated the evening sky, forming a v-shape, with blue sky remaining in the center. The bird's dark form stood proudly in the between the brilliants rays of sunset.

It had to be Cody, teasing Joe.

An older man approached Joe. He had salt and pepper hair, about 5'8 in height, wearing jeans, a denim jacket and a navy shirt underneath. Worry lines crossed his forehead and dark circles made him appear gaunt and sickly.

Joe reached out to shake his hand. "Joe Luna. FBI." He showed the man his credentials.

"James Calder."

A weak handshake, considering the man's stocky build. A woman came out of the house and James waved her over.

When she climbed off the wraparound porch and out into the open, the largest raven from the roof ruffled its feathers and bent over, as if it were trying to get a closer look.

"This is my wife, Aubrey."

The same brown-haired, petite woman Joe had seen through Lorelei's astral journey looked much younger than her husband.

Aubrey gave him a weak smile. "Nice to meet you."

"Joe Luna. I'll try not to keep you long. As Agent Zimmerman mentioned to you on the phone, we're dealing with a murder mystery. This man has killed one victim and kidnapped others. We have reason to believe he might be in the area."

Joe glanced from Aubrey to James. He showed them a forensic drawing of Cody based on Lorelei and Mandy's sighting. "Have you seen this man?"

They both shook their heads adamantly.

Two FBI agents were inspecting the area where Lorelei had seen Cody. The raven's gaze went from Joe, Aubrey and James, to the men a quarter-mile away.

Joe tried desperately to focus on the couple. "Have either of you seen anything unusual?"

Aubrey glanced at her husband nervously. "Should I tell him?"

"My wife wandered off earlier today." James placed his arm around Aubrey's shoulder. "We were outside doing some work in the vegetable garden. I turned around to see her walking toward where your men are now."

"I have no idea what came over me. I was pulling some weeds out of the ground. All of a sudden, I felt I had to head in that direction. I didn't see or hear anything to distract me. My body seemed to go of its own accord."

The large raven left its perch. It let out an ear-piercing screech, and circled ten feet above them before flying toward Cody's hideout.

Joe hit speed dial for Tony. "High alert. The abductor's coming in raven form and I don't think he's happy."

Aubrey and James exchanged confused glances.

"I'm sorry," Joe said. "I'll be right back. Get in your home and stay there." He jumped in his truck. His vehicle flew over hills and sagebrush. With his window rolled down, he could hear the loud cawing noise. The raven continued to circle the area where the underground ruins were located, swooping repeatedly at Tony's head.

Until now, Cody had been doing everything to elude law enforcement. Braver in his animal form, he brazenly attacked the FBI in a desperate attempt to keep his property and his secrets.

Joe got out of his truck and noticed Tony climbing into the hole leading to the subterranean Anasazi pueblos. Even though the agent was tall with an athletic build, he seemed to slip into the confined space effortlessly.

Cody angrily attacked Tony as he attempted to make his way further inside the passage. In his raven form, he pecked at Tony's legs and butt. The raven's wings repeatedly hit against the dirt walls in an effort to keep the agent away.

Tony kicked again and again to try to get the raven off of him. "This has to be the kidnapper. He kept circling above my head before you got here!"

Joe looked around for something to distract the raven. He grabbed a rock near the opening and threw it.

"He's trying to protect his territory," Joe shouted to Tony.

Joe crawled inside the three-foot-high opening. "Are you okay?"

"He started attacking my head, but I managed to pull a knife. I must have wounded it because I've got blood on my right hand where I used the blade. The raven flew further in."

Joe hoped Tony didn't kill Cody. If so, they might never find his other victims.

"Can you get turned around?" Joe asked. "We need to get you out to see your injuries."

"No. I'm going all the way in. I want to see this through."

Joe sighed. "If we get into this cave and I find you're seriously hurt, you're coming back out."

As he got closer to Tony, Joe could see blood from scratches, pecks and claw marks from the repeated attacks.

Grunting and holding his breath, Joe struggled to maneuver through the tight confines. His arms scraped against the walls and he sweated from the effort of pushing. He used a final burst of energy to propel himself to the end.

Tony helped Joe out of the narrow tunnel and onto the floor of the cave, a drop of around four feet.

No sounds. No movement.

What if Cody had escaped?

Joe removed his gun from his holster and pointed it into the darkness. His breathing increased thinking about where Cody might be. What he could be changing into. His right hand started to tremble. Tony had been viciously attacked by a raven. What could Cody do in much larger animal form?

A small kiva with two rooms on either side opened up before them with a larger circular brick tower, about ten feet across, directly behind the kiva. A tunnel led from inside the ceremonial kiva into the round tower. Joe knew many kivas connected to towers included small passages for sudden, dramatic entrances for shamans.

A mano and metate, used for grinding corn, were in a narrow five-foot by one-foot section of the cave floor. A constant chore for the prehistoric culture, dried or parched corn would be stored in pottery vessels for years in the dry, Southwestern climate.

The backpack, lantern and camping equipment that were there earlier had disappeared.

Darkness had descended and they were in the territory of a madman. The breeze gone. The air stagnant.

"Something's not right," Tony whispered.

What if the bastard had eluded them, gotten back outside and trapped them? Joe could feel sweat forming on his brow as his adrenaline increased. He glanced from one end of the cave to the other.

He passed his flashlight across the partially fire-blackened walls. A shadow darted from behind the ceremonial tower and through a vertical slot less than two-feet-wide, toward the larger cavern where Lorelei had found Cody sitting in a trance—trying to entice Aubrey into his lair.

He and Tony would not be able to make it through to pursue Cody.

The gun, solid in Joe's strong hands, would be defenseless against something he couldn't see. Cody might have transformed back into human form, or something worse. They crept through the small pueblos, tripping over remaining wall rubble. Joe turned the light back on to find the location of the crevasse where he had last seen Cody. But the gap no longer existed.

"What the hell?" Joe whispered. "I saw a shadow walk through here."

Tony ran his hand over the cave wall and quickly pulled his hand back.

Joe placed his hand where Tony's had been. The spot was warm to the touch, but with cool, rough rock on either side. He took Tony's arm and pulled him away. Pointing his pistol at the wall, he watched while bits of stone collapsed around their feet.

"Cody," Tony whispered.

The man had shapeshifted into the cave wall, preventing them from intruding.

Tony slowly bent to the ground, picking up a small stick. The dark mass conformed even tighter into the crevasse. He quickly poked it into the warm, slowly shifting substance. A thick, sap-like liquid dripped off the stick.

Evidence. Joe prayed the FBI would be able to get human DNA from the inhuman mass.

The viscous substance rapidly retreated into the narrow fissure.

"FBI!" Joe yelled. "Cody, you're under arrest for murder and kidnapping!"

The mass stopped, hanging in mid-air. Eyes formed. A human nose came into view. Within seconds, a nefarious face had formed along with the rest of his body.

How can he be doing this?

Cody's voice boomed from the opposite side of the chasm. "How did you find out?"

Tony glanced at Joe.

Was Cody asking how they knew his name, how they found out about his hiding place, or his shapeshifting ability?

"It doesn't matter. Give yourself up!" Joe kept his eyes on Cody.

Cody stepped back into the recesses of the other cavern. "She's coming."

"Who's coming? What are you talking about?" Tony asked.

"The one who created the pendant. She's on her way."

Is he talking about Jacenda?

"Hands up or I shoot," Joe shouted.

Cody turned away from Joe and Tony. He kept walking.

Joe squeezed his body between the walls of the fissure, slicing and scraping skin. The jeans on his right thigh ripped from a sharp protrusion.

Tony slid through the crack sideways. "You realize we can't shoot. It could collapse the whole place or it might ricochet."

Bursting into the massive cavern, Joe could see a circle, approximately three by two feet, in the center of the room where Lorelei mentioned Cody had been practicing his magic to lure Aubrey.

The hues of the chamber were light orange, dark red, rust, tan and off-white. Round, smooth formations covered the ceiling. Smaller holes and mini caves lined the perimeter.

No movement or sound. Joe scanned the cave floor with the flashlight. Maybe Cody had turned himself into something much smaller. Like a tarantula.

A keyhole-shaped pocket, seven feet tall, in the back of the chamber contained a smooth, bulbous cave formation, four-feet-tall . Joe carefully approached the grotto. Rocks fell from somewhere inside.

Tony stood a few feet behind Joe.

"Back away, Tony. Something's coming."

Slow, deliberate steps tiptoed inside. Lighter, sure-footed movement made little noise.

Chills went up his spine.

A foot-tall, reddish-brown, hairy leg poked out behind the bulbous formation.

"Shit." Joe leapt backwards, tripped over a rock and fell on his butt.

Two long spider longs felt their way around the mound. Its eight beady eyes focused on Joe and Tony. And its fangs lifted slightly.

Joe quickly got on his feet and aimed the gun at the tarantula. Its jaws moved and it hissed.

Whispers echoed throughout the chamber, bits and pieces of an unfamiliar language. Brilliant, baseball-sized orbs flew across in front of the arachnid.

The tarantula backed up slowly.

The whispers and dialect became louder. Shadows frantically darted around the cavern.

The hairy beast continued to retreat.

Holy crap! Was I just rescued by the ancient ones?

34

Highly-colored sedimentary rock of soft fine-grained mudstone and claystone, along with harder beds of somber-colored siltstone, sandstone and conglomerate, created a stunning palette of tie-dyed, corrugated hills. Mesas, buttes and badlands were painted in Mother Nature's hues of pearl as well as light and dark pink.

Jacenda stood before a sign at one of the scenic pullouts along Painted Desert Drive, which read:

GIANT REPTILES AND AMPHIBIANS RULED THE TROPICAL WATERWAYS THAT EXISTED HERE OVER 200 MILLION YEARS AGO DURING THE LATE TRIASSIC PERIOD. THEN, NEW AND VERY DIFFERENT ANIMALS ARRIVED ON THE SCENE TO SHARE THE ENVIRONMENT—SMALL DINOSAURS.

FOSSIL BONES OF AN EARLY DINOSAUR, CHINDESAURUS BRYANSMALLI, WERE DISCOVERED NEAR HERE IN 1984, AND THE PARK IMMEDIATELY RECEIVED WORLDWIDE ATTENTION. THE FOSSIL FIND WAS AFFECTIONATELY NAMED "GERTIE" AFTER AN EARLY CARTOON DINOSAUR. THE APPEARANCE OF THIS SMALL CREATURE IN THE FOSSIL RECORD MAY BE A KEY TO UNDERSTANDING THE ORIGIN, EVOLUTIONARY RISE, AND SUCCESS OF THE DINOSAURS THAT FOLLOWED.

Another sign along the scenic drive had mentioned the air quality in and around Petrified National Forest was among the purest in the Continental United States. Taking in a deep breath of the clean air, Jacenda imagined dinosaurs roaming among the expansive, beautiful badlands.

She wished Brandon were here to see it with her.

She had hoped the further away from Phoenix she got, the fewer visions she would have about the necklace. And about the Hohokam culture, which was such an integral part of her past. If anything, though, the visions were getting stronger as she drove closer to New Mexico and the Four Corners. Along with her anxiety. Even scientifically-minded Brandon admitted Jacenda served a purpose in the murder case.

The surreal landscape spread out far and wide before her helped her relax and put things into perspective. She smiled thinking of Brandon. His dark-haired good looks, his gentle demeanor, confidence and sex appeal. But his patience and understanding were his most valuable assets. She feared he would be tested to the limit with her newfound abilities.

Who was the scraggly-haired man Jacenda had seen turn into the prehistoric warrior? And what relationship did he have with the necklace? The last vision hit with frightening clarity as she passed the exit for Meteor Crater. His black evil gaze preceded a metamorphosis from human to thunderbird.

The illusion happened quickly. Was it a glimpse into the future? Or a view of the past?

Jacenda got back in her car and traveled the stretch of National Park between Interstate 40 and Highway 180. Heading south to look at the scenic section of Petrified Forest, she noticed a road stop for the Puerco Ruin.

She drove into the parking lot and disturbed a flock of ravens scavenging for food among two middle-aged women. The woman with long blonde hair tossed a piece of lunchmeat at the bird and the woman with red hair threw another raven a chunk of bread. One of the ravens hopped alongside the blonde woman as she walked to the other side of her blue CRV.

"Sorry, sweetie," the blonde said. "I only have enough left for me and my friend."

Jacenda got of her vehicle and smiled at the two tourists. At the beginning of the paved trail, she came across an information sign with a solid orange image of what looked like a heron holding up a frog with its long, sharp beak:

THE PAVED PUERCO RUIN TRAIL WINDS AMONG THE RUINS OF PUERCO PUEBLO. OVERLOOKS PROVIDE VIEWS OF PETROGLYPHS THAT THE PUEBLO'S INHABITANTS INSCRIBED ON SURROUNDING STONES.

OVERLOOKING THE FLOODPLAIN OF THE PUERCO RIVER, PUERCO RUIN IS A PARTIALLY EXCAVATED RECTANGULAR PUEBLO OF APPROXIMATELY 100 ROOMS BUILT AROUD A LARGE PLAZA. HERE, AT THE LARGEST OF PETRIFIED FOREST NATIONAL PARK'S ARCHAEOLOGICAL SITES, RESEARCHERS HAVE FOUND EVIDENCE OF HUMAN OCCUPATION FROM ABOUT A.D. 1250 TO A.D. 1380.

PUERCO PUEBLO STRADDLED THE CULTURAL FRONTIER BETWEEN THE MOGOLLON ZUNI PEOPLE OF THE MOUNTAINS TO THE SOUTH AND THE ANASAZI HOPI PEOPLE OF THE MESAS AND CANYONS TO THE NORTH. ARTIFACTS FOUND DURING EXCAVATIONS REVEAL THE INHABITANTS OF PUERCO PUEBLO HAD CONTACT WITH BOTH GROUPS.

Wandering among the remains of a once thriving community, Jacenda listened for the language of a long-ago culture, children's laughter, stone tools being chipped into shape, or chants and songs.

No such sounds came to her. Perhaps the Native American spirits who resided at Puerco Ruin were unaware of who she had once been.

She arrived at the end of the paved trail, where a pile of massive stones had been decorated with ancient drawings of stick figures, human feet, four-legged shapes, horned toads, spirals, geometrics and the heron with the frog that she had seen on the informational trail sign.

A group of twenty elderly tourists gradually filtered their way back toward the parking lot. Standing alone, she gazed across an open valley dotted with sagebrush and toward a mesa.

A light breeze blew a few strands of her long black hair into her face. With the draft came an uncontrollable feeling of anxiety. She tightly gripped the railing that protected tourists from a potential fall into the rocks decorated with prehistoric art.

"Come on, Jace," she whispered to herself. "You're just tired and hungry."

She walked back down the paved trail, got into her car and drove through hill-like, white, pale blue and maroon layered formations called teepees. The vibrant, awe-inspiring terrain lightened her anxiety.

Jacenda made her last stop in the Petrified National Forest at the Blue Mesa overlook. Petrified logs of quartz wood were scattered on hilltops and permanently stuck between layers of stone.

The monochromatic landscape spread out before her used to be a large basin with numerous rivers and streams. According to the brochure she had picked up at the visitor center, the abundance of water supported coniferous trees up to ten feet in diameter and two hundred feet high. Galleries of trees, ferns and giant horsetails grew abundantly along the waterway, providing food and shelter for many insects, reptiles, amphibians and other creatures.

As trees died or were knocked down by wind or the action of water, rivers and streams carried them downstream, breaking off branches and roots along the way, so only the trunks remained. Many tree trunks came to rest on the banks of the rivers while others were buried in the stream channels. Most of the trees decomposed and disappeared, but some were petrified, becoming the beautiful fossilized logs.

Standing near the edge of a drop-off, Jacenda began to feel apprehension again. An eight on a scale of one-to-ten. Her breathing came in short spurts. Her body felt ten degrees hotter than the outside temperature.

She removed her cell phone to call Brandon, hoping it would calm her down. Before she could hit *dial* for his number, Jacenda was pushed forward, closer to the edge of the cliff.

She whipped her head around, but saw no one behind her. She tried to back away, but felt something pushing her forward. Her phone slid out of her hands, bounced off a fossilized trunk and slid down with small rocks and broken bits of petrified wood to the bottom.

Losing her balance, Jacenda fell face forward down a badland hill of bluish bentonite clay. Her body rolled over twice on her way down the hill. Her head slammed into a chunk of petrified log and excruciating pain overcame her. Her head begin to spin. The partly cloudy afternoon skies started to turn pitch black. Within seconds, a figure appeared before her. Jacenda tried to lift her head, but couldn't. Tried to speak, but couldn't.

Please don't let it end like this. I need to see Brandon again. And I need to find out who I really am.

35

Lorelei heard Irish music emanating from the hole where Mandy had found Jan Stinson. Julie, the crime scene investigator with the Evidence Response Team worked diligently to find any evidence of Cody. The woman didn't know it, but she wasn't alone. Three spirits were with her. Only these particular spirits weren't prehistoric Indians from the Four Corners.

Lorelei grinned, watching a short, spriteful, youthful looking man named Seamus with light red hair dance around the attractive investigator named Julie. He desperately played an upbeat Irish tune Julie couldn't hear. Slender, with short red hair, fair complexion and freckles, the impish, bright blue-eyed being wore jeans rolled up to mid-calf and a dark green cotton shirt. His bare feet jumped around the rocky ground in rhythm with his own beat.

A tall, thin man with wavy blond hair stood on her other side, staring at Julie with adoring eyes. He stroked the woman's hair and attempted to hold her hand. The name *Lars* came to mind. A third Native American spirit guide wearing khaki pants and khaki shirt with long dark hair stood behind her, rolling his eyes at the Irishman's antics. He looked up at Lorelei and smiled. Though slimmer and shorter than Joe, this man was no less attractive.

Julie glanced up at Lorelei. "Hi, Lore. Did you need something?"

Lorelei observed the feisty Irishman in surprise. Within seconds, he had transformed into a cute, four-foot tall child-like leprechaun with long pointed ears.

"Uh, no." *Should I tell Julie about her guides?*

"There's something in here with me? Isn't there?"

Lorelei sighed heavily. "Yes, but nothing bad. And these aren't Native American. Well, one is, but he's not from the Four Corners and not prehistoric. I'm picking up early 1900s."

"What, or who are they then?"

"You have three spirit guides. One of them is rather enamored with you."

Julie shaded her eyes from the morning sun as she looked up at Lorelei from the small hole where Jan had been hidden. "You know, if anybody else told me this, I wouldn't believe them."

Lorelei glanced over at Ian and Brandon, who stood inside a small pueblo at the Lowry Great House. It seemed they were involved in a serious discussion. "Something tells me you've experienced unusual things, but you're not admitting to it."

"Sometimes, I think I hear whispers at night. A few times, right before I awoke, I saw clear faces. One of which was a nice looking younger man with long, wavy blond hair. He bent over, smiling at me."

"You described Lars. I'm seeing you with him in a past life."

Julie wiped her brow with her forearm. "Wow. I'm trying to absorb all this."

"Don't worry. They are around to protect you and guide you on your life's path. I don't usually see people's spirit guides. Not sure why I'm seeing yours."

"Too bad Lars isn't real. I would love to meet someone who is so devoted to me for a change."

"He's desperately trying to make himself real. Unfortunately for him, there will be a few other men coming into the picture rather soon."

Julie looked up at Lorelei as if she were insane. "Now that's even harder to imagine."

Lorelei laughed. "I understand. I felt the same way before I met Ian."

Julie climbed out of the hole. "I can only dream of having the same kind of relationship you and Ian have."

Lorelei gave her a brief hug and whispered in her ear, "You won't have to dream for much longer."

Ian and Brandon came over and waved to Julie.

"Lore, I don't normally ask you to do readings." Brandon glanced at Ian and looked at his smartphone. "But I can't get a hold of Jacenda. I'm getting really worried."

"How long has it been? She's probably traveling through an area without reception."

Ian took Lorelei aside and handed her the turtle pendant. "Honey, I saw something when I held that, about Jacenda—probably because of her past life and association with it."

Lorelei took the pendant, rubbing her fingers over the smooth shell. Soft pinks, purples, blues, mauve and earthen colors gradually separated and formed into the landscape of the Painted Desert.

She glanced up at Brandon, who watched her anxiously. His gaze pleaded for hope.

Petrified brown logs lay stuck in stone, scattered on mesas and hilltops.

"Blue Mesa," she whispered. "Something happened at Blue Mesa in the Petrified Forest."

Ian nodded. "I saw the same location. Though not Blue Mesa in particular."

Brandon glanced from Ian to Lorelei. "Did either of you see her? Is she all right?"

"No. I mean, I didn't see her," Lorelei said. "I could see Jacenda driving through the Painted Desert and into the Petrified Forest. I think Blue Mesa was her last stopping point."

Lorelei held the pendant tightly in her right hand.

Brandon placed his hands on her shoulders. "Lore, what do you see?"

"Sweetie, not sure what's going on. Something did happen, something bad. But I just saw her arriving here tonight."

Brandon tried to call Jacenda on his cell phone again with no answer.

Throwing his hands up, Brandon paced up and down. "Jacenda could be hurt and there's nothing I can do."

"If she is hurt, it can't be that bad. Like I said, she is going to make it here tonight. On her own."

"I'll call the Petrified Forest National Park," Ian said. "Find out if anyone's seen her."

As soon as Ian turned around to call, Brandon's phone rang. His jaw dropped when he heard the voice on the other end of the phone. "Jacenda, thank God! Are you okay? I've been trying to call."

Lorelei waited anxiously for a few minutes.

"What? Maybe you should hang out at the park office and I will come get you. We'll head back to Phoenix."

Brandon paced up and down while listening. "Jace, I don't know about that. You still have quite a drive and after what happened…" Brandon sighed. "Okay. Please be careful. If you start feeling bad, pull over and get a hotel. I love you, too. Call me in an hour." He hung up the phone.

"What happened?" Ian asked.

"She fell off a cliff at Blue Mesa. Said she got lucky and didn't hurt herself. Managed to find her way back up to the parking lot. Says she's fine and is insistent on coming up here."

Lorelei feared the fall off the cliff was no accident. Could Tony be correct about the necklace and its connection between Cody and Jacenda? If so, Jacenda could be in grave danger herself. But would Jacenda's tight bond with her past help solve the impossible?

36

Joe glanced toward Ute Mountain and Mesa Verde National Park to the south, the Abajo and La Sal Mountains to the Northwest in Utah and then to the east, the location of Lone Cone and San Juan Mountains. He knew the landscape of the Great Sage Plain contained the highest recorded density of prehistoric and historic sites in North America. And Cody had managed to find yet another ancient, unrecorded site to use as his lair.

The Bureau of Land Management had contacted a local archaeologist to survey and document the site near the farmhouse. Within two hours of investigating the ruins, Gary Gentry, a tall lanky man with white hair and dark, leathery skin, had discovered broken pottery pieces of a black-on-white shallow bowl and a Mancos black-on-white dipper. He had also found dried corn stalks and other artifacts, including stone axes, weaving tools, two bone pins and an end scraper made from the humerus of a mule deer. Gary mentioned the scraper may have been used to prepare hides or to remove the pulp enclosing the fibers in yucca leaves.

Joe flipped a shiny, obsidian projectile point over in his fingers.

"Obsidian, or volcanic glass, used to make that came from deposits near Jemez, New Mexico or Flagstaff, Arizona. Evidence we've found so far indicates occupation of this site during the Pueblo II period from A.D. 900 – 1150."

The FBI and local law enforcement surrounded the area, inside and out. Since Joe had encountered Cody as the tarantula, there had been no other sign of his presence. But it didn't matter. Cody had been careless. Joe had received DNA from the gooey shapeshifting substance and human prints near the prayer circle. Whether human, spider or something in between, the proof should still point to the same person.

Joe watched Mandy walk a two mile perimeter with Tony to detect any other victims. Lorelei, Ian, the FBI and law enforcement had been amazed at how easily she had located Jan Stinson.

FBI and law enforcement had no idea how many more victims could be out among the wide open spaces of the Four Corners. There had been no additional reports of missing women. But Mandy herself had been a victim. And she had no friends or family who knew of her location.

Cody had also been careless by attempting to lure Aubrey from her home. Only Aubrey said she couldn't get pregnant since her husband had had a vasectomy. So why did he attempt to lure her into his cave? Were his pregnant victims somehow keeping his shapeshifting abilities alive?

The husky, sandy-haired college intern working with the archaeology professor squeezed through the passage, looked around and waved to get Joe's attention.

Joe blushed. He had been staring intently at Mandy. She caught him watching her and smiled shyly. She threw her hands up and shook her head to indicate she hadn't come across anything.

"Hey," said the intern. He wiped his forehead with his arm to reveal sweat stains on his armpit. "Professor Gentry found some human remains."

Joe crawled through the tunnel with the twenty something archaeology student and into the prehistoric village.

"Over here," the professor called.

Following the sound of Gary's voice, Joe carefully stepped over fallen ruins and intact pueblo walls to get to the dark corner. He hadn't noticed it before, but a recess in the back right section of the ancient ruins hid another small room containing a massive cooking pot.

Gary pointed at the vessel. "We've discovered the remains of one child and two infants. Judging by the size of the bones, the child was eight and the babies between one and three years old."

Joe glanced inside the receptacle. Two nearly complete infant bodies rested against each other. On one body, one of the arms had detached, and the other infant was missing a leg. The bones of the eight-year old rested in a pile. "Are you saying this site is evidence of cannibalism?"

"Not necessarily. Cannibalism is rather hard to prove. Many sites have similar evidence and some consider it a normal burial practice, especially for infants."

"Is this particular room a burial site?" Joe asked. "I've visited many ruins that reserve blocks for the dead."

Gary nodded emphatically. "Yes. My intern, John," the professor pointed to his student, "also found one adult male dumped, mostly intact so far, into the kiva." He pointed to the center of the village."

"Was he dead before being thrown in?"

"Yes. It was a violent attack—he had an arrow through his heart."

Joe glanced at the row of two-story room blocks. "What would you recommend doing with this site once we are finished with the investigation?"

"This place is part of BLM land. So these ruins could be opened up to the public. Or backfilled to protect the structures, pottery and lithics."

"I appreciate you coming out at the last minute to check this place out," Joe said. "I feel bad for the rather unorthodox method of getting in here."

"Not to worry. As an archaeologist, I'm used to tight, inaccessible spaces and rough trails. I sometimes think it's better to leave ancient sites as is. There are too many people who lack respect."

Joe noticed John, the intern, attempt to squeeze his bulky form through the narrow crack leading into the cave.

He hurried over and placed his hand on John's shoulder. "Sorry. That's off limits. Do you see something in there?"

John backed out of the tight fissure, handing his flashlight to Joe. "Yeah, focus my light on the far wall—almost straight across from this fissure."

"I can't believe this," Joe muttered. He hadn't had time to spot the artwork before because of the terrifying incident with Cody. Petroglyphs similar to the ones in the tunnels in Southeast Arizona were etched onto the rock wall, including an image of the solar system with hundreds of twinkling stars. On the top of the panel, a drawing with four spiral arms surrounded by a central bulge, seemed to represent the Milky Way with a myriad of horizontal stick figures below.

Loud, muffled voices echoed from above ground. It sounded like Mandy and Tony.

"Excuse me. I need to find out what's going on." Joe raced to the tunnel and crawled back out.

Mandy held her stomach and bent over, trying to catch her breath. "You need to call Lorelei. She's in trouble. Cody is really pissed off about you finding this place. He knows how. Plus the fact that she took *me* from him isn't helping the situation."

Joe took her hands in his. "Did you run across him? Did he hurt you?"

"I'm fine. Tony stayed by my side while I looked around. We did see a turkey vulture. There was some sort of dead animal nearby, but it didn't pay any attention to the carrion. It just watched Tony and me. The damn thing actually held us in a trance for a whole minute."

"Sounds like it could be Cody."

"The vulture flew off in the direction of Lowry. That's when I developed overwhelming abdominal pains, like the ones that put Lorelei in the hospital. They stopped when the bird got out of range."

Mandy glanced at Tony, who stood next to her.

"I already contacted the special agent at Lowry," Tony said. "Told them to get Lore out of there and back into Cortez."

Joe called Ian. No answer.

He dialed Brandon who picked up the phone on the first ring.

"Hey, Joe, Lore's really sick."

Piercing screams came through the phone.

"Get her away from there," Joe said. "Cody's out for revenge."

"We're trying." Brandon's voice sounded shaky and scared. "None of us can start our cars. I've called the ambulance, but I can't get through."

"I'm coming." Joe nodded toward Mandy. She jumped in the truck with him and they drove to Lowry. "You helped Jan Stinson," Joe said.

"She was in labor. The situation with Lorelei is different. I'll try, but I don't know if I can help."

Fifteen minutes later, Joe slid his truck into the dirt parking lot at Lowry Pueblo and threw open his door. He could hear Lorelei's screams coming from the paved trail. He took Mandy's face in his hands. "Tell them to get her to my car. I'll drive her to the hospital."

Before Mandy could jump out, his vehicle died. He tried the ignition a few more times. Cody wanted to make sure she had no escape.

"Damn it!" Joe slammed his hand on the steering wheel.

Mandy and Joe met Lorelei and the rest of the group on the paved walking trail, close to the parking lot.

Ian glanced up at Joe. "She's vomiting and can barely breathe." Ian held her from behind. "We can't get her out of here and can't get an ambulance. She won't be able to take this much longer."

Mandy quickly bent down and took Lorelei's hand. She placed her other hand on Lorelei's stomach.

Joe could see Brandon trying to get through to the emergency service. Tony and Julie also tried on their cell phones. They threw their hands up in frustration.

Lorelei bent over to throw up but nothing would come out. She placed her hand on top of Mandy's, which rested on her stomach. "Please." Lorelei's head leaned back against Ian. "I can't lose the baby."

Ian held Lorelei and kissed her on the top of her head. He trembled from the effort of holding back his tears.

"Not happening on my watch," Mandy said. "You saved me. Now I'm going to try and help you."

Tony and Julie approached from the main pueblo. "She's calmed down since you placed your hand on her," Julie said. "I can't believe this happened. We were talking only an hour ago about my guardian spirits."

"Thanks." Lorelei glanced up at Mandy. "I feel a little better."

"Has anyone been able to get an ambulance?" Joe glanced around. No wildlife. No sounds. The air seemed to be thickening—Cody watched and waited. He wanted to make Lorelei suffer, or perhaps worse. Joe hoped Mandy could alleviate the pain until they could get Lorelei to safety.

Brandon ran back from the parking lot. Ian looked at him pleadingly.

"Sorry. There are five different vehicles. None of them are working."

Joe leaned down and placed his hands on her face. "Lore, what about your astral guides? Can you call on them to help you?"

Ian held her limp body while Lorelei's eyes remained half shut. Lorelei stared at Julie, who had been there to help.

Lore touched Ian's arm. "They're gone."

"Who's gone, honey?"

"Julie's spirit guides." Lorelei rolled her head from side-to-side. "They are always around her. Lars is in love with her."

"Don't worry about me, Lore," Julie said. "I'm sure they'll be back."

"But they were there a few seconds ago," Lorelei said.

Ian stroked her hair. "It's okay, baby." He looked up at Joe. "I'm carrying her toward the road. Maybe if I can get her away from the ruins…"

Ian started to pick Lorelei up.

"Wait!" Joe said. He pointed to two lights ten times brighter than the sun that appeared out of nowhere. They all had to shield their eyes. The radiant objects turned from an angelic white to blue; the same blue he had seen when Galiena's beings escorted Lorelei during her out-of-body journeys.

Joe gasped. These beings were the ones he had seen during his vision quest. Only they weren't playful. They were on a mission.

"Stand back," Joe said.

The brilliant lights shot straight toward earth at a speed he had never seen. He heard strange electronic type chattering. They were talking among themselves.

The beings combined themselves into one. A soft blue light pulsated. Ian held onto Lorelei while the enigmatic energy being gently stepped into her body. Her eyes morphed from hazel to blue. Within thirty seconds, Lorelei sat up straighter. She turned to look at Ian, then Mandy and Joe who were both at her side.

"Please tell me you're feeling better." Ian kissed her softly on the lips.

The lights had entered her body theatrically as effulgent beings, but exited as grapefruit-sized orbs.

"Much better."

Lorelei glanced from Julie, to the retreating lights, playfully dancing and pirouetting in the sky. "They're back. Lars, Seamus and your Native American guide are back."

37

*L*orelei's astral journey took her to an enormous section of sandstone cliff, one hundred feet tall, that leaned precariously toward the thirty rooms of the Anasazi Great House directly underneath. A supporting masonry terrace had been built at the base of the towering rock.

A D-shaped structure with hundreds of rooms, some four and five stories high, sprawled out across the valley floor. The half-circular portion of the D was up against the towering orange sandstone cliffs. Two main interior plazas, divided by a central wall along a north-south axis, held twenty or so people. Three pillars of smoke rose into the sunset, one from the very back near the canyon wall, and the two others from rooms on the westernmost edge of the structure.

A woman sat on the ground cross-legged playing a flute in the romantic, early evening glow. The instruments' soft, luring melody drew Lorelei down among the village life.

Two giggling children raced each other between a large kiva and a smaller kiva. They ran past a single ponderosa pine, through a doorway of the exterior wall and out into the open landscape. An elderly man, five feet tall, raced after them as quickly as he could, cane in hand, muttering under his breath.

The larger kiva contained a square sub-floor vault, a ventilation system, a firepit, a low masonry bench encircling the base of the kiva, and pilasters built on the benches to support the massive log and earthen style roof.

Lorelei was drawn to a man in his thirties handing a necklace to a young woman. Her eyes were big and bright. She held the piece of jewelry as if it were glass, her hand trembling in excitement. The beautiful woman nodded her head *and handed the man a copper bell and a small, brilliant blue-green turquoise effigy shaped like a bird.*

The man left and the woman placed the necklace on. The others in the plaza turned to admire her trade, which was adorned with obsidian, turquoise and shell beads with a black frog hanging at the bottom.

Startled by a loud squawking sound, Lorelei saw a man reaching into a pen. Vivid red, yellow and blue feathers of a Scarlet Macaw, transported hundreds of miles from MesoAmerica, were pulled out of the cage.

As the colors of dusk faded, apprehension came over the village. A baby cried from somewhere nearby. Overwhelming silence settled over everyone and everything. The woman with the frog pendant glanced around nervously and left through a doorway at the back of the D-shaped Great House near the canyon cliff face.

The flute music began again. Drums soon accompanied the rhythm. Lorelei almost forgot where she was. Her astral form swayed to the relaxing, spiritual tune.

The gentle sounds of the flute lured Lorelei toward a second Great House against the wall of the canyon. An extensive network of rooms, kivas and other foundations connected this D-shaped structure to the other multi-storied Great House a quarter mile away where she had witnessed trading and daily life of the Anasazi culture.

The straight back wall of the main structure had a sort of balcony with ponderosa pine extending out of the walls and planks across the tree trunks. A woman stepped out of a second story door and onto the balcony to get a blanket, glanced into a pueblo next to the one Lorelei was in and quickly went back inside her own home.

Lorelei peeked inside the low, open doorway to see a man with his back to her. He was average height and muscular with shoulder length, tangled dark hair. A large brown corrugated cooking pot rested on a fire. The man standing next to the pot quickly turned his head and glanced in her direction. He looked right through her. For a second, Lorelei wondered if he had seen her. But a few seconds later, he went back to what he had been doing.

Lorelei's astral form watched from the doorway connecting the two pueblos. He poured water into a gigantic cooking pot before stepping outside. She stumbled back in surprise when she saw the body he dragged behind him.

Oh, God, no!

It was the young girl who had traded the copper bell and turquoise effigy for the necklace. Her lifeless body lay on the hard ground, next to the cooking pot. Her head slumped to the left with large brown eyes staring right at Lorelei. Blood slowly escaped from the back of her skull and a hatchet was buried in the woman's stomach. He had also hit her in various other places on her body, including both arms and her right leg. The man moved a few feet to the other side of the cooking pot. That was when Lorelei saw he wore the woman's turquoise necklace.

He positioned the woman's body so her head rested on a metate, or large flat stone used for grinding corn. Lorelei quickly turned her head when he used the ax to dismember the head from the body. Though she could no longer look, she heard bones breaking and water boiling. He began to hum while dropping the remains into the pot.

I've had enough. Get me away from this place. *She ran out of the room, but remained at the prehistoric site. She observed the box canyon enclosing the second Great House and the towering orange cliff with the 30,000 ton leaning rock.*

I can't believe this. That's threatening rock, before part of it collapsed. Why didn't I see this at first? I'm at Chaco Canyon in New Mexico.

An excruciating scream came from the area where the man had been working with the girl's body. He stumbled out of the pueblo holding his face and neck. He removed his hands from his face and she noticed his skin was bright red with blisters.

Lorelei awoke with a start, her heart pounding and her breath coming in short spurts. She jumped out of bed and stomped her feet on the carpet to ground herself.

She glanced over at Ian as he slept soundly. His blond locks covered his face. He stirred slightly and reached for her. When he realized she wasn't in bed, he sat up and looked around.

"I'm right here."

"Are you all right? You're not sick again, are you?"

"No, I'm fine. I think what my astral guides did will prevent Cody from doing anymore harm."

Ian had taken her to the hospital after Cody's curse had been misplaced by the mischievous light beings. Both she and the baby had made it through the ordeal.

"Did you have a nightmare?" He kissed her neck after she climbed back into bed.

"Sort of."

She looked in his eyes. "I journeyed into the prehistoric past, at Chaco Canyon."

"Are you sure?"

"Yes. The colorful canyons, threatening rock before it collapsed, and Pueblo Bonito and Chetro Ketl in their full glory. Those two communities were connected by another set of room blocks, so it didn't look anything like the ruins of today. Amazing to get a glimpse of life back then."

Lorelei's excitement turned to sadness. She hugged Ian tightly, hoping it would alleviate the memory.

"You're trembling." He pulled away and placed his hands on her face. "What did you see?"

"Cody, I believe, or rather his Native American past self. He had the same dark eyes and looked very similar to the warrior who murdered that family in the kiva. I saw him drag a woman's body into a room. Ian, he used an axe and had split the back of her head, cut her arms and legs. Then he laid her head on a metate and cut her head off. I heard him snapping bones and throwing them into a large cooking pot."

Ian sighed and placed his forehead against hers. "Damn it. And right after your experience at Lowry. Sometimes, I wish I could take away your talents."

"Sometimes, I wish I didn't have these abilities. But then I wouldn't be able to save lives or help people." She glanced away from Ian.

"Lore, what else happened?"

"The woman who was murdered traded a copper bell and a turquoise effigy for a necklace with a black frog pendant. I saw Cody wearing it after he killed her. But that's not all. Ian, right before my journey ended, I heard Cody scream. He stumbled out of the pueblo with serious burn marks on his face and neck."

"Amazing. I've heard it is possible for people to carry forward marks from their pasts, but usually not so prominent. His past is catching up with him physically as well as mentally." Ian placed her head on his chest. "Are you sure that necklace you saw wasn't the one Tony found? The one Jacenda's been seeing in her visions?"

"I'm positive. The pendant was black and in the shape of a frog and there was obsidian beads in the string."

"Jesus. Do you think Jacenda's past self knew Cody's? Perhaps she traveled to the Four Corners from Phoenix."

"Definite possibility, especially considering what happened to her at Petrified Forest. Joe mentioned Cody made a comment saying, 'She's coming. The one who created the pendant.' "

Lorelei sat up and stared into Ian's eyes. "He remembers and knows who she is."

"What does that mean?" Ian asked. "Who was she and why would Cody want revenge?"

38

Jacenda lay close to Brandon's naked body, her hand on his chest. She hadn't told him the truth about what happened at Petrified Forest. She didn't know the truth herself. She was not only confused about how the fall happened, but how she survived and made it back to her car.

When she first met Brandon at the hotel in Cortez, he had been hysterical about Lorelei's experience at Lowry Pueblo. He begged Jacenda to leave town with him. "If he is doing this to Lorelei, what will he do to you? Cody knows you're coming and has already threatened you!"

Brandon woke up, turned over in bed to face her and stroked her hair. Neither of them had been sleeping well, only getting intermittent periods of slumber.

He pulled her closer. "So, are you going to tell me what happened to you?"

"If I had told you someone tried to kill me, you wouldn't have wanted me to come up here. And to be honest, I didn't know *what* happened. One minute I was looking out over the Blue Mesa overlook, the next minute I lay on the ground."

Brandon lifted her chin so she looked into his eyes. "What else, Jace? I heard you mutter in your sleep. You said, 'It's you. Shannon, can you help me?' "

"I don't remember."

"When we talked on the phone before you decided to come, you told me you wouldn't keep anymore secrets. Galiena showed herself to you in the form of Shannon, didn't she? She saved your life."

"Yes," she whispered. "I'm sorry, Brandon. This is all so overwhelming. I guess part of me feels that everything is okay if I don't talk about the strange things happening." Jacenda kissed his cheek. "I don't remember anything after I saw Shannon standing there, staring at me as I lay on the ground. I remember hitting my head against a rock, or perhaps a piece of petrified wood. But I didn't even have a headache afterwards. I've heard all the stories from you about how close she and Lorelei were, so I'm not sure why she's been showing herself to me."

Brandon sat up on his elbow. "How many other times has Galiena visited you?"

"One other time, at my place right after you showed up at my door. She told me about my connection to the land and the Hohokam people. That I somehow deliberately absorbed my own human form into its walls to release the Native Americans."

"We all figured you had some sort of connection to the house itself. What if the spirits in the house knew who you were? Maybe subconsciously, you heard them calling for help."

"I'm starting to realize anything is possible."

"Do you remember any details about what happened inside the house?"

Jacenda snuggled closer to Brandon, placing her arms around him. "No. But I'm not sure I want to."

"Eventually, you're going to remember and I doubt it's as bad as you think it is. Lorelei said she wants to help you through this." Brandon softly ran his fingers down her stomach, stopping just above her pubic area.

"I'll talk to her tomorrow." Jacenda rolled on top of him, her legs straddling either side of his lower body. "Since neither of us can sleep, there is something much, much better we can do."

Jacenda watched the faces of Brandon, Ian, Lorelei and Joe at the table in the hotel restaurant as she held the artifact made by her prehistoric self. The large, brightly-colored room was busy with tourists eating a hot breakfast. Glasses clinked, the smell of eggs and bacon permeated the room, and a tall, thin woman grabbed a yogurt and a banana before running out of the hotel.

Jacenda had envisioned the necklace so many times. Olive shells interwoven with shell beads, and an elaborate jade turtle pendant hung at the bottom. Her hand trembled as she held the ancient artifact in her palm. The prehistoric trinket caught the attention of women from nearby tables at the hotel restaurant.

"Take a few minutes," Joe said. "Let me know if you get anything about Cody or his victims."

Brandon put his arm around Jacenda. "Come on, man. This isn't that easy for her."

"From what Lore's telling me and from what I've been through in the past few days, I'm supposed to be the reincarnation of the Hohokam woman who made this. But I'm not getting any visions associated with my past, or with Cody."

Joe placed a gentle hand on her shoulder. "Galiena came to you, didn't she?"

Lorelei gasped.

Jacenda glanced at Lorelei and Brandon. "Yes, a few times. She's the one who saved me at Blue Mesa in the Petrified Forest. How did you know? Did Brandon tell you?"

"He didn't have to. When I look at you, I see Galiena in my mind."

"I'm not sure what Galiena really looks like, but she appears to me as Shannon."

"You have to understand," Joe said. "Galiena doesn't visit us on Earth. Lore and I were both drawn to her in the stars. But for her to come down and see you, to save your life, tells me you might have a stronger connection," Joe glanced at Lorelei and Ian, "than any of us."

"I don't understand how." Jacenda grasped the turtle pendant firmly. "I didn't know her, Shannon, I mean."

"It could be your Native American past," Lorelei said.

"Galiena is sort of the queen of the universe," Joe said. "I believe she and her counterparts have ties to Native American cultures. And many prehistoric races built their structures to align with the stars or the solstices. Most of the public buildings in Chaco Canyon were purposely situated to integrate with other great houses, with the movement of the sun, moon, planets and stars and with places in the surrounding landscape."

Lorelei reached across the table and took Jacenda's hands in hers. "It's interesting Joe brought up Chaco because I ended up taking an astral journey into the past last night. I'm thinking A.D. 1050 or 1100. I saw Cody's past self. He murdered a young woman and stole her pendant, though it didn't look like the one you're holding. The most disturbing part of the journey was discovering that he was into cannibalism."

"Did you see me?"

"No. Your past self lived in Arizona, as you know. But you could have traveled to or resided in the Four Corners at some point in time. That young woman traded a copper bell, probably from Mexico, and a turquoise effigy for the necklace Cody took from her after he killed her. Not sure if he killed her for the necklace, but I saw him wearing it. The interesting thing is that people reincarnate to pay off karmic debts, meaning if he were a heartless warrior from the past, he should be making up for those sins in this, or other lives."

"But you didn't see this?" Brandon took the necklace from Jacenda. "Or Jacenda for that matter."

Lorelei shook her head. "No. But I wouldn't have recognized her anyways as a Native American woman."

"I'm sorry. I wish I could tell you all what my past Native American self was thinking. But I can't. At least not right now."

Lorelei gave her a big hug. "Nothing to apologize for, and Brandon's very lucky to have you."

Joe glanced from Brandon to Jacenda. "I have a feeling you already know what you're getting yourself into. But when we confronted Cody at the Indian ruins that were just discovered, he referred to you as 'the woman who created the pendant.' The Petrified Forest experience could have been a botched attempt."

Brandon's grip on her waist tightened as he pulled her closer. Jacenda knew he desperately wanted to take her away from the danger. Yet they both realized she could help solve the case due to her past.

"How can Cody possibly remember Jacenda?" Brandon asked.

"Somehow, he's still living in the ancient past," Joe said. "Both mentally and literally, which would explain why he's living in caves and near ruins."

Jacenda sighed and closed her eyes. Her right temple began to throb. "What happens now?"

"Lore and I will take you to Lowry Pueblo, the ruins and cave where he was hiding, and Painted Hand. Places he's been seen. Keep the necklace with you and we'll see if we can draw him out, or at least see if we can stir some memories."

Jacenda glanced over at two maids who were giggling and pointing in Joe's direction. A happy couple held hands at the next table and gazed into each other's eyes. "I had a vision recently of Cody being associated with a warrior, but nothing about what might have occurred between us."

"Are we ready?" Lorelei stood up and walked to the breakfast bar. She grabbed a few apples and granola bars before coming back to the table. "This is going to be a long day."

Joe started to stand up, but Jacenda grabbed his arm. "Wait. That vision I just mentioned. I can't believe I didn't make a connection earlier."

Joe sat back down and looked at Jacenda anxiously.

"I watched as the man you've all described as Cody seemed to turn into a warrior sitting in the center of a cave. The Native American man was chanting to himself and the light of the fire in the chamber revealed a petroglyph."

Joe leaned forward. "Did you see a large panel of rock with horizontal figures, stars and an image of the Milky Way?"

She nodded. "I remember Brandon telling me a few times about the petroglyphs you all saw underground in Southeast Arizona."

Lorelei dropped two of the apples, grabbing the attention of a few passersby. "Joe, you noticed the drawings also?"

"Yes, when I went back to Cody's hiding spot with the archaeologist. Actually, his intern found the rock art."

Ian took Lorelei's hand in his. "Looks like we might have discovered another of the ancient ones' sites. It makes me wonder what else could be hidden down there."

"When Cody shapeshifted into the tarantula, he came out of what looked to be a rather tight passage. Perhaps there are more tunnels and undiscovered places that could be associated with Galiena and the ancient race."

Ian helped Lorelei put her jacket on.

Joe tossed his empty plate in the trash next to the table. "The FBI is trying to find out who Cody is. Hopefully, we can find out *why* he's so enamored with his murderous past."

Jacenda stood up. "Should Brandon and I follow the rest of you to the ruins?"

He took her hand in his. "Jace, Joe asked me and Ian to stay here. Cody might not appear with us there."

"Oh, okay." Jacenda felt disappointed. She had wanted to spend time with Brandon and needed his support.

He stood up and kissed her with a passion that caught the attention of everyone in the room. She wanted to take his hand and run.

"I love you, Jace. I have since we met. I know you'll be fine because Joe, Lorelei and Galiena have your back."

"I love you, too. I'm really going to miss you." She kissed him lightly on the lips.

Brandon pulled her close. "I'll be waiting. When you get back, I'll take you out to dinner then we'll go for a moonlit drive."

A few minutes later, Joe was driving Lorelei and Jacenda away from the pleasant western town of Cortez on Highway 491. Jacenda placed the pendant around her neck, feeling the cool jade against her skin. Staring out at the passing farms, she wondered what the immediate future held.

Neither Joe nor Lorelei asked her about visions or memories.

Jacenda turned to Lorelei. "Listen, I appreciate you doing this. Especially considering what happened to you yesterday."

Lorelei grabbed Jacenda's hand. "I'll be fine, and so will you." She stared at Jacenda's neck. "You know, that looks amazing on you, like you were born for it."

Less than an hour after leaving the hotel, they turned west onto County Road BB, traveling six miles to County Road 10. The scenic road wound its way through farms and canyons for what seemed like an eternity.

Joe turned onto a primitive dirt road. "Painted Hand Pueblo is a mile down. These roads are a bit bumpy, so hold on."

The tree-lined dirt road occasionally revealed glimpses of the canyon beyond.

"How often has Cody been seen at this site?" Jacenda asked.

"Once, as far as we know and he could have many more victims scattered throughout this area. Since Lorelei mentioned running across Cody's past self in Chaco during her last astral journey, makes me wonder if he has victims scattered across a much wider area."

"With the exception of Aubrey, his latest attempted abduction who lived near his hideout, his victims have all been pregnant," Lorelei said. "Mandy was the first victim we found."

Joe cleared his throat.

Lorelei sighed. "Okay. The first victim *I* found. We believe Cody was just about to kill her. He murdered the second victim, Nicole Malloy, at the Cajone Group of ruins. Mandy found the third, Jan Stinson, at Lowry Pueblo, in the nick of time. She was about to deliver her baby."

Jacenda watched out the window. A sick feeling started in the pit of her stomach and became progressively worse with each jarring bounce of the truck.

Joe pulled his truck off to the left in a small parking area.

Though Jacenda wanted to find out more about her abilities, she didn't want to have another experience like the one at Petrified Forest. She hesitated a few seconds and took a deep breath before getting out of the car.

Joe smiled and showed Jacenda the trail leading through the forest. "There's a short hike. Then the trail descends sharply through the cliff face to the pueblo."

They walked a quarter mile through the forest to a cairn where a sign with an arrow pointed to Painted Hand and a drop-off. Large stone steps led to the ruins below.

"Give me a few minutes to make sure we're alone."

Joe disappeared and came back up the trail five minutes later to wave them on. "Okay. It's safe. Watch you're footing. I want you both to go first and I'll follow."

Jacenda headed down the steep trail first with Lorelei and Joe behind.

The trail opened up to reveal a single standing tower perched on a flat boulder. Collapsed ancient stone littered the ground. Jacenda walked around the structure. A pueblo had been built underneath the Painted Hand tower.

Lorelei placed her hand on the main tower, closed her eyes and remained completely still.

"She's trying to get vibes," Joe said. "See if there might be any victims nearby."

Jacenda placed her own hand against the one of the stones. A jolt of electricity shot up her right arm.

"Damn!" She shook her arm to get the feeling back. "That hurt."

"What happened?" Joe gently lifted Jacenda's arm to look it over. Lorelei came running over.

"She's okay," Joe said. "She touched the ruins and received a shock." Joe turned to Lorelei. "What about you? Did you get any visions?"

"No." Lorelei looked at Jacenda. "Which stone did you touch?"

Jacenda pointed to the stones in the center of the hidden ruin cautiously. "This place must be helping me with my experience in Florence."

Lorelei removed a bottle of water from her backpack and took a drink. She put her palm flat against the same stone as Jacenda. "What are you remembering?"

"When I got that jolt, I had a strong recall of being absorbed into the Florence home—vanishing from the closet and feeling strong panic with nothing but light. I don't remember any physical sensations."

Lorelei stepped away from the ruins and stood directly in front of Jacenda. "Whatever happened to you during the investigation has probably strengthened your ability to connect to other ancient sites. Maybe the spirits here know who you are."

Something moved in the trees at the top of the cliff where the trail descended. "What do you mean?"

"Jacenda, I placed my hand in the exact spot of the ruin you did. It showed me what happened to you in that house."

Joe followed Jacenda's gaze to the top of the cliff. "I wonder if the necklace is causing the connection." He removed his gun from its holster.

"Only one way to find out." Jacenda took off the pendant, handed it to Lorelei, and reached for another stone with her left hand. She jumped back as another volt of electricity, more intense than the first, raced up her arm.

"Brandon never told me you were into pain." He grinned, but his eyes didn't leave the top of the cliff where they had descended.

"Probably hikers," Jacenda said nervously. She placed the necklace back on.

A piercing scream came from the parking lot above them.

"Let's go," Joe said. "Stick close."

Jacenda motioned for Lorelei to go behind Joe. She followed last on the trail.

No footsteps or noise. Her senses didn't warn her. An unidentifiable shadow came out of nowhere from above. She started to shout out, but didn't have time.

39

For Brandon, time had ceased to exist after Lorelei and Joe returned to the hotel without Jacenda. Lorelei, Mandy and Joe continued to talk, but he could hear nothing. Ian placed his arm around Brandon, but he couldn't feel it after finding out about Jacenda's disappearance at Painted Hand Pueblo.

Joe and Ian guided Brandon to a chair by his hotel room window. He watched cars drive by on Main Street and heard children running in the hallway—normal sights and sounds that were a shock considering the circumstances.

"I don't want to sit. I want to find Jacenda."

"I'm getting ready to go back out and do a search," Joe said. "The FBI and law enforcement is out at Painted Hand, Lowry and Cody's hideout. We'll get her back."

Brandon looked from Lorelei to Joe. "How did this happen?"

"We all heard a woman scream. I ran back up the trail toward the sound and called for Lorelei and Jacenda to follow."

"I should have made her go first." Lorelei paced back and forth. "She was right behind me."

"The son-of-a-bitch created a distraction." Brandon stood up and glared at Joe. "And you fell for it. Damn it! He tried to kill her once. You delivered her into his path again."

Ian stepped in between Brandon and Joe. "I know how hard this is. I've been right where you are. Remember when Lorelei was abducted at Vulture Mine? And you were there to help me through it. Now I'm here to help you."

Brandon remembered how upset Ian had been when Shannon had delivered the news about Lorelei—frustrated, scared and angry. And Ian had wanted to do anything he could to help.

"This situation is very similar," Ian said. "Like Lorelei, Jacenda has a lesson to learn, a role to fulfill. She knew it coming here and so did you."

"Are you saying I have to stand back and do nothing? Like you did when Lore was kidnapped?"

Joe flipped his long, thick dark hair back. "I'm going back out there now. Ian, Lore and Mandy are coming out very early tomorrow. I know it would only be torture for you to sit here alone. So you're welcome to come."

Brandon nodded his head. He stared out the hotel room window. Children's excited laughter echoed from the parking lot. A faint drumming emanated from nearby and he began to hear chanting. Within seconds, the sounds of a Native American ceremony drowned out the outside noises.

Brandon glanced from Joe to Lorelei, Ian and Mandy. "I'm hearing it again."

Ian faced Brandon and placed a gentle hand his shoulder. "What?"

"The music and chanting. I heard it in my house right before I left."

"You didn't mention it before," Lorelei said.

"I was more focused on Jacenda, I guess, what with her rejection. I never saw anything, only heard drums and voices." Brandon did a 360-degree turn. "I'm experiencing the same thing here, but I can't tell where it's coming from."

"So now Brandon is developing skills?" Mandy asked.

Lorelei smiled. "Not quite. These ceremonies, if that's what they are, seem to be associated with his separations from Jacenda."

She touched Brandon's arm. "Maybe she's reaching out to you without knowing it. Through her past."

Brandon hugged Lorelei. "So she's okay?"

She pulled away, placing her hand on his face. "I'm not seeing what's happening to her, but she's a strong person."

Brandon approached Joe. "I have to go out there with you now. Maybe Jace is using her past to guide us."

Joe threw his hands up. "There's nothing you can do. Just like Lorelei, your girlfriend has her lessons to learn. But maybe having you out there will inspire her to make it through."

"I'll go with you two." Ian turned to Lorelei. "I want you to stay here with Mandy. You'll be coming out tomorrow morning and I don't want you getting too tired." He placed his hand on her stomach and kissed her on the lips.

Brandon could see Lorelei tremble. It made him long for Jacenda that much more. He headed to the door. "Let's go."

"Whoa," Joe said. "We're heading out on some hiking trails to get to the location Cody was last seen. It's only 9:00 a.m., but pack plenty of water and food as we could be out there a while." He glanced at Ian. "Same for you. I'll meet you both down at my truck in half an hour."

"Mandy and I will see what we can do from here. I can always try another astral journey," Lorelei said.

Lorelei and Mandy stayed with Brandon while Ian and Joe went to pack supplies.

"Are you still hearing the drums?" Lorelei asked.

Brandon pulled a few bottles of water from his mini-refrigerator along with some dried snacks and a turkey and Swiss sandwich. He didn't know if he would be able to eat anything until he found Jacenda. "Yeah. But it's fading now."

Thirty minutes later, Lorelei and Mandy walked Brandon to Joe's truck. Brandon got into the front seat next to Joe and waited for Lorelei and Ian to say goodbye.

"I figured the drums and chanting I heard in my home were Hohokam. I thought I had brought something home from the investigation. What if the ancient spirits in Phoenix and the Four Corners are aware of Cody's past? The ceremony I've been hearing could also be in honor of Jacenda's potential ability to help solve this case and stop Cody's violent rampage."

Joe smiled at Brandon while they sat inside the truck.

Brandon sighed. "By that shit eating grin on your face, I'd say you obviously determined that before I did."

"I think that's an important part of it. I'm amazed at how well you're dealing with this."

"It helps to have someone like Lorelei to tell me Jace *is* coming back." Brandon glanced out the passenger window as Ian climbed into the truck and Joe pulled out of the parking lot. "I'm trying so hard not to think about what Cody's putting her through. I can't guarantee how well I'll be handling this in another hour, or in five minutes."

Joe's phone rang. "Tony. Have you come across anything at Painted Hand?"

Brandon closed his eyes tightly. He could still see Jacenda's voluptuous naked body lying next to his from their last moments together.

Joe continued to talk with Tony on the phone. "Has anyone else come up missing, either at Painted Hand or anywhere else?"

Brandon waited while Joe listened to Tony. He hoped there were no more victims. But he also hoped Jacenda wouldn't become one.

"I'm on my way now. Should be there within half an hour." He disconnected the call.

Joe picked up speed on Highway 160. He looked over at Brandon. "A couple of hikers spotted Cody."

Brandon's heart pounded. "Where?"

"Sand Canyon, which is also part of Canyon of the Ancients. There are trails starting off of County Road G that lead to a bunch of ruins. Sand Canyon Pueblo itself is off of County Roads P and N."

"There are all sorts of hiking trails through there," Ian said. "Where did they see him?"

"Rock Creek Canyon near North Sand Canyon Pueblo. Neither hiker saw anyone else. The two friends were on a horse trail and saw Cody wandering around near the cliffs. They estimate a distance of a quarter mile away."

"What caught their attention?" Ian asked.

"They heard a woman scream. When the two men looked in that direction, they noticed a man fitting Cody's description. One of the hikers used his binoculars to get a closer look."

Brandon's head began to spin. The look on Joe's face told Brandon he had left an important detail out. "What else?"

Joe glanced back at Ian.

"What else?" Brandon yelled.

"Cody had splotches of red on his clothes. The hikers called it blood." Joe sped along the windy, scenic highway to Sand Canyon. "We don't know that for sure. Cody noticed them and stared them down. That's when the wind began. From a gentle breeze to what they claim was a hurricane force wind within five seconds."

Brandon watched side roads pass by that descended into valleys with ranches and wineries, which were overseen by towering canyon walls. His whole body shook, though he didn't know if it was from anger, trepidation or both. He was angry at Joe for not keeping a watchful on Jacenda and upset with himself for not being there to help prevent it.

"Did they get hurt?" Ian asked.

"No. When they started to run away from the area the wind stopped. The officer interviewing the two men said they were rather athletic. The hikers are good friends and have been backpacking in the Grand Canyon and other remote areas. These men have been in some tough situations during their adventures, including being attacked by a mountain lion. This encounter left them with a whole new fear."

Was Jacenda the one who had screamed? Or did Cody have yet another victim?
Brandon closed his eyes and prayed for her safety.

Ian leaned forward. "Joe, how the hell are you going to get this
guy? His powers are keeping him well hidden. And he could have
another victim, or victims, who we don't know about."

Joe swerved to the right to avoid another car in the opposite
direction coming into his lane. "Cody has us all over Canyon of the
Ancients right now. And Jan Stinson mentioned during the interview
with Tony in the hospital that she started hearing whispers right before
we found her. The spirits wanted Jan to know about the other victims.
She couldn't understand the language, but she was getting very brief
images of caves and underground spaces. Of course there is no way
to verify the locations."

"What if Cody is playing games?" Brandon asked. "He could be
luring us away from his victims. And from Jacenda. Consider what he
did at Painted Hand to separate Jacenda."

Joe pulled into a parking lot with slickrock and a castle-like rock
formation. BLM officers and FBI agents were turning disappointed
mountain bikers away.

"Cody's been playing games since this began," Joe said. "He really
enjoys the fact that he has all the power."

Brandon opened his car door. "Someone has to be able to do
something. You're a Native American shaman. Lorelei is a psychic
who can perform out-of-body and Ian is a witch. Considering
Cody's abilities, there isn't enough evidence to catch him the traditional way."

Joe put his denim jacket on over a long-sleeved shirt and nodded
to Tony, who headed toward the truck. "How many agents and officers
are out there?"

Tony glanced past the large formation called Castle Rock where
the trail started. "None yet. We have a helicopter patrolling this part of
the trail system as well as Sand Canyon Pueblo off of County Road P

and N. There are other teams patrolling Painted Hand, Lowry Pueblo and surrounding BLM and national park land."

"Great. I'm going to head in on foot with Brandon and Ian. I'll need you to follow us in for extra backup."

Joe, Ian and Brandon grabbed their backpacks out of the pickup. They waited for Tony to get his supplies.

Tony slung his backpack over his shoulder. "We're on a wild goose chase with this bastard. FBI, BLM and local law enforcement have exhausted their troops trying to catch Cody. What makes you think the four of us can accomplish anything?"

Joe didn't answer. He headed past the Sand Canyon sign and visitor log and onto the open slickrock.

"If the FBI can't catch this guy, or anyone on this team with astral travel, teleportation and warlock abilities, who can?" Brandon muttered. Even as he asked himself the question, he knew the answer had lain in his arms that very morning.

40

Well-preserved prehistoric walls hid among Pinion Pine and Utah Juniper behind Castle Rock. An estimated forty to sixty rooms once provided shelter for seventy-five to a hundred residents.

Joe glanced up to see an oddly placed ancient wall nestled between two boulders. Perhaps it had been a lookout tower. Unfortunately, they didn't have time to dwell on the surroundings. A madman was on the loose; a criminal virtually impossible to catch.

At Painted Hand Pueblo, Jacenda had received a painful shock from the ruins. Her talents from the home in Florence could be extending to the Four Corners and Canyon of the Ancients. The structures of the ancestral Puebloan were more than a reminder of the past. They could be the resolution to a thousand year old mystery involving Cody.

Joe ran his hand over a pile of ancient tumbled brick. He nodded for Ian to join him. "Let me know if you pick anything up."

Ian placed his hand where Joe's had been. "That's weird. I'm getting an image of a Native American woman. But I don't normally get visions."

Brandon approached and stood between Joe and Ian. "What's going on? Shouldn't we be continuing on the trail to where the hikers saw Cody?"

Joe placed Brandon's hand on the stones. "Stand here for a minute and concentrate."

Brandon looked at Joe, then Ian.

"Close your eyes."

Joe held Brandon's arm while it rested on the ruins. Ian continued to hold on to the structure.

"What's happening? I'm seeing a woman wearing the turtle pendant."

"Keep focusing," Joe said. "There's more."

"Jace," Brandon shouted. "Can you hear me? We're here. At Sand Canyon!" He pulled his arm away, staring at the ruins in shock. "The Native American woman transformed into Jacenda. She looked right at me."

"Your girlfriend is tied to more than the land in Florence. She's connected to many ancient sites. I suspect she's originally from the Four Corners and migrated to Phoenix, like thousands of others when their resources were depleted. Jacenda received quite a shock when she touched the Painted Hand Pueblo this morning. Those ruins might have been trying to communicate with her."

"I don't get it. Why don't the spirits themselves talk with her?"

"There are so many primitive phantoms here. The easiest way to connect with her and remind her of what she is capable of is through the structures and land."

Brandon sighed heavily. "Damn it. This isn't going to be over that quickly, is it?"

"No. Cody has a personal vendetta against Jacenda. He's a strong opponent."

A helicopter came into view. It hovered over a spot in the canyon. A few minutes later, Tony received a phone call. He didn't say a word and his mouth hung open while he listened.

"Thanks," Tony whispered. "Keep a close watch. We'll head that way." He turned to face Joe. "The copter pilot saw a woman off the East Rock Creek Loop trail with long dark hair, about 5'7, wearing jeans and a dark green shirt with a denim jacket."

Joe grabbed Brandon's shoulder. Tony had described Jacenda.

"Shit." Brandon grabbed his backpack off the ground. "We have to find her."

"I'm not sure how easy that's going to be," Tony said. "She was also seen at Sand Canyon Pueblo two minutes before. There's no exposed walls there, but the copter pilot saw her walk into the middle of the site and disappear. She reappeared out of nowhere in another small ruin off of East Rock Creek Loop miles away, less than ten minutes later."

Brandon collapsed on his knees.

"Did they say anything about Cody?" Joe asked.

"No sign of him."

"We can't track Cody or Jacenda," Tony said. "And we have no way of knowing if, or where, any other victims might be."

"We'll hike in to where Cody was spotted." Joe glanced up at the early afternoon sun. "We have to make sure it's not another hiding spot for victims."

Joe heard the sound of footsteps in rock. He turned to see Jacenda standing in a collapsed pueblo. Her long, silky black hair was messed up, her face had superficial scratches and her clothes were dusty and disheveled. But she still looked amazing.

Brandon leapt the twenty-foot distance in a few bounds, taking her into his arms. "You're okay."

Jacenda held on tightly as tears rolled down her dirt-smudged face. "Brandon, is it really you?"

"Yes, I've been so worried."

She kissed Brandon gently on his lips. Then their passion intensified. Jacenda couldn't seem to get enough of Brandon, pulling his body closer to hers.

Seeing Brandon and Jacenda together made Joe think of Mandy. He imagined kissing Mandy as intensely, feeling her hands around her waist. Within seconds, Mandy's face intruded into his mind. A stunning, close-up vision, she watched Joe with desire. Her eyes half-closed, leaning in with lips parted.

He shook his head and placed his hands on his temples. Somehow, Mandy had picked up on his emotions.

"Oh, come on." Joe muttered to himself, blushing profusely. "I don't need this right now."

Ian smiled mischievously.

Joe, Tony and Ian walked over to Brandon and Jacenda.

Joe noticed she looked dazed and confused, looking around at her environment and back at Brandon.

"Jace, we're here to follow a lead on Cody," Joe said. "Two hikers spotted him. They said he was covered in blood."

Brandon took her head in his hands. "Are you all right? Did Cody hurt you?"

She shook her head no. "He tried to. I barely escaped the talons of a massive bird by being absorbed into the ruins, but I don't think Cody expected it. He watched with his feathered head cocked to the side as I vanished."

Jacenda glanced up at Joe. "I don't know what's happening. I guess it's similar to the house in Florence. This is all too much. I start out at one place and within minutes end up at a totally different location."

Joe placed his hand on her shoulder and pointed up to a black copter flying overhead. "The men in the helicopters witnessed you at Sand Canyon Pueblo and at East Rock Creek minutes later."

Brandon stroked her hair. "We'll take you back to the hotel."

Joe didn't want to burst Brandon's bubble, but he knew Jacenda wouldn't be returning with them.

Tears rolled out of Jacenda's eyes. She pleaded to Brandon. "I'm sorry for my disappearances. For scaring you. What if you get tired of all this?"

Brandon held her tightly. "I'm not going anywhere. I told you before, I don't care what abilities you have."

Jacenda pulled away and wiped her eyes. "Listen, you all have to leave." She looked at Joe. "Cody is not happy about his plans being ruined. He wanted to draw you all out here to punish you."

"How do you know that if you escaped from him?" Ian asked.

"They told me. Spirits, I guess. Voices communicating with me while I was traveling between sites."

"Lore. She can journey out-of-body," Ian said. "Has she been helping you?"

"No. I don't think so. Nor should she be out here."

"Let's get back to the parking lot," Tony said.

Jacenda grabbed Tony's wrist. "Get rid of the copters. Tell the agents and officers to leave. Go back to town." She glanced up at the afternoon sky.

A low humming filled the silence, causing the hairs on Joe's arms to stand up.

Brandon took Jacenda's hand and started to lead her away from the ruins. Brandon turned back in shock when she vanished from his grip.

Joe, Tony and Brandon stared at the spot where she had disappeared.

Joe expected Brandon to yell Jacenda's name or collapse on his knees. He didn't have time to react. Soft-spoken Tony yelled in a tone Joe had never heard. "Sister, where are you?"

Joe turned Tony to face him. His eyes were wide with terror, his whole body trembled and any sign of the sensible, intelligent FBI agent had gone. To Joe, it seemed Tony was in the midst of a nightmare.

41

Lorelei walked with Mandy down the rustic, western streets of Cortez. They were getting ready to go into Homesteaders Restaurant for lunch when Mandy suddenly stopped in the middle of the sidewalk. Her fair facial features turned to a dark blush. Lorelei knew her friend had seen something pertaining to Joe.

Lorelei gently placed her hand on Mandy's arm. "Tell me what you saw."

"Joe. Well, first I saw Brandon kissing Jacenda. Then I noticed Joe. He blushed as he watched them and he was thinking of me." Mandy took Lorelei's hand. "Lore, he looked right at me. And this has happened before."

"Like it or not, sweetie, you and Joe have quite a connection."

Mandy turned to go into the restaurant. She didn't want to hear the facts.

"Mandy, wait. You're here because you wanted to help and you have by finding Jan Stinson. You're learning to accept what you can do. Unfortunately, part of that ability involves connecting with a very handsome Native American FBI agent—being able to see him and pick up on his emotions when you're apart."

"I can deal with these abilities more than I can the damn emotions. Everything used to be so normal, so safe. Now I'm part of a murder mystery and my mind is being romantically invaded."

"Joe's not doing it on purpose, the same thing is happening to him. Neither of you wants to want the other, you've both been through too much. I know exactly how you feel because I was the same way with Ian. Unfortunately, the universe has other plans."

Lorelei's smartphone rang. "It's Ian." She placed the phone to her ear. "We're coming back," Ian said.

"What? You've only been gone a few hours. I thought you all were going to stay out there for the night."

"That was the plan. Jacenda found us. Honey, she's traveling through the Indian ruins out here, using them as a portal. It's unbelievable. She was pretty adamant that we leave the area and I believe she has help. Not just the ancient spirits either."

"Galiena?"

"Joe and I think so because of how well she's dealing with everything."

"Oh, my God. Did she look okay when you saw her?"

"Other than a little dirty and disheveled, yes. There's definitely a war going on with her and Cody, but she did manage to escape from his grasp. She seems to be accepting her talents rather well, but didn't give us any details. Jace insisted we get the hell out of Sand Canyon."

"I hate to say this. I'm rather ashamed of how I feel. Ian, I'm jealous. I'm very happy Jacenda is okay, but I wonder why Galiena is helping Jacenda so much. I thought she wanted *me* to help others with their talents."

"Lore, you are helping. Look at Mandy. And I'm sure Jacenda will need your support going forward. You've played a very important role. You found Mandy, Cody's first victim, who then found Jan. And you used your astral abilities to discover one of Cody's hideouts. Not to mention, you have a constant connection to Galiena through those two light beings."

"Thanks, Ian. Maybe I should go back to the hotel and journey to help her."

Lore, Jacenda was very insistent that no one be out there. Law enforcement, tourists, and even you. It could jeopardize everything.

Brandon tried to bring her back with us, but she dissipated in the midst of his grip. I saw her vanish."

"So we're all supposed to stand back and let Jacenda handle Cody alone?"

"We don't have a choice."

Lorelei remembered how Ian, Shannon and Joe had to stand by while she single-handedly dealt with Peter and Emily at the ranch house in Utah. "How is Brandon handling this?"

"Rather well. He misses her and is worried sick about what she's going through. But the fact that you're seeing them together in the future, and with Galiena on her side…"

Mandy leaned against the window of an antique store. She bent over, staring at the ground.

"Are you all right?"

"I don't know. Feeling a little strange."

"Ian, I've got to go. Mandy's not looking too well."

Mandy slid down to the ground on the sidewalk. A couple in their fifties stopped to help.

"My friend's sick," Lorelei said. "I need to get her to the hospital."

"No." Mandy touched Lorelei's arm. "I'll be fine. Just get me back to my room."

"You're five months pregnant." Lorelei called 911. "We need to get you checked out."

Lorelei spoke into her phone. "Yes. My friend needs help. We're off of Main Street in front of Homesteaders Restaurant."

Mandy threw her head back against the cement. "Lore, I don't feel so well."

The wail of the ambulance siren sounded in the distance a few minutes later.

Lorelei held her hand and stroked her hair. "Help's coming."

The ambulance pulled up and the two paramedics jumped out, pulling out a gurney from the back of the vehicle. The men placed her on the gurney and into the ambulance. Lorelei climbed in with them.

Her phone rang as the ambulance left Main Street.

"How is Mandy?" Joe blurted out before Lorelei could say hello.

"Not well. The paramedics are taking us to the hospital."

"Ian, Brandon and I will meet you there."

As the ambulance raced to Southwest Memorial Hospital, Lorelei kept getting clear visions of Mandy's hand on her stomach during her own hospital stay. Mandy had taken the sickness Cody had given Lorelei. What if she absorbed it into her own body during the healing?

The wailing of the ambulance's siren became a last desperate groan as it pulled in front of the emergency room entrance. Lorelei jumped out and stood aside while the paramedics rushed Mandy into the hospital.

The sliding doors opened to reveal an open reception area with rows of chairs, tables littered with magazines, soda and snack machines and colorful scenic photos of streams, Mesa Verde Cliff Dwellings and Ute Mountain to take away from the drabness of the beige walls. In the ER waiting room, a young couple with an infant waited patiently at the main desk. The woman had her head on the man's shoulder. Were they waiting for help themselves? Or anxiously awaiting news of a loved one? The bright-eyed baby quietly watched Lorelei. She couldn't wait to hold her own.

Mandy lost consciousness as she was wheeled into an emergency room. Lorelei held her hand tightly. "Come on. You have to make it out of this. You didn't survive Cody to let this beat you." Yet Lorelei realized Mandy could still be trying to survive Cody.

She watched a male nurse named Jason with shoulder length dark hair follow the paramedics with the gurney, directing them to room ten. She stayed in the cramped room bathed in stark white light, while a female nurse hooked Mandy up to a blood pressure machine. Fifteen minutes later, Lorelei went out to the waiting room to wait for Joe, Ian and Brandon. Joe ran into the hospital, followed by Ian and Brandon. She waved to them.

"Mandy's in room ten."

Joe entered the cramped room in two large strides with Lorelei and Ian behind him. He sat in the chair next to Mandy's bed while Jason took Mandy's blood pressure.

Lorelei observed Mandy from the opposite side of the bed. "I've been talking to her, but she's not responding."

Ian hugged Lorelei. "Has anyone said what might be wrong with her?"

The blood pressure machine read 158 systolic over 90 diastolic. Jason left the room.

She shook her head. "This is my fault. When she used her healing abilities on me she must have taken his curse onto herself."

"This could be something different." Joe took Mandy's hand.

"I saw it in the ambulance on the way here, the past vision of Mandy with her hand on my stomach."

"You can't blame yourself," Ian said. "She wanted to help. You weren't even aware of what she had done until afterwards."

Joe placed the back of his hand on Mandy's cheek, his other palm against her heart. His voice choked. "She's really sick."

Lorelei tried to see the future. She desperately wanted Mandy to be okay. And so did Joe. But she could see nothing.

Joe looked up at Ian. "Take Lore home. There's nothing she can do here but worry."

Ian kissed her on her forehead. "He's right. Let's go back to the hotel. You need some rest."

"No," Joe said firmly. "You both should get home to Cottonwood, to Paul. Leave in the morning. The FBI will pay for the rental car back. I will stay here with Brandon and make sure Jacenda and Mandy make it through their journeys."

Lorelei sighed. She could not argue with Joe. She and Ian did miss Paul and she was beginning to worry about the safety of her own unborn baby.

"I'll update you both regarding Mandy and Jacenda."

The dark circles under Joe's eyes told of his long hours pursuing Cody and tracking down his victims.

Lorelei walked around the other side of Mandy's bed and gave him a hug. He stood up, placed his arms around her waist and pulled her close. She could feel him tremble.

"I can't lose her." Joe whispered in her ear. "Not again."

42

When the shadow loomed over her, Jacenda had no time to react. She glanced up to see a massive bald eagle with a wingspan of forty feet, a beak that could remove limbs with one bite and talons that could rip flesh and lift her off the ground. She had managed to grab onto the wall of the Painted Hand Pueblo. Her hand dissipated into the structure followed by her arm. She remembered the intense shock that her whole body had experienced followed by peace. The bird of prey soared away from the ancient site and up into the air.

The massive eagle had hung in the air before diving back down. She wanted to run but couldn't; afraid, yet transfixed as it dove in her direction.

As the rest of her body was pulled away into the prehistoric structure, the deadly bird swooped up and glided over the area and surrounding cliffs.

The bird of prey had looked right at her after the ruin had consumed her, but it didn't seem to see her. Eagles were known for their sharp vision, being able to see four times that of a person with perfect vision, not to mention the ability to look forward and to the side at the same time. That was probably the reason Cody had taken the form of such a magnificent creature.

She hadn't been transported. The structures of the ancestral Puebloan people merely hid her from view of the giant bird. The pinion juniper forest and cliffs above were still visible and the breeze gently rustled her hair.

She had heard Lorelei and Joe call her name repeatedly. They climbed back down the steep steps to the pueblo.

Jacenda waved and screamed. "I'm here!"

She recalled Joe's intense, steely gaze as he looked right at her for a split second. But then he looked away and continued calling her name. She didn't understand how Lore and Joe could have missed the giant eagle—unless it had something to do with mind control.

Jacenda had jumped out of the Painted Hand Pueblo to get the attention of her friends after the eagle left. She waved her hands frantically and ran up to Joe. No acknowledgement or response. Except from the ruins. A tenebrous grasp seemed to be pulling her back. She forced herself away from its grip and ran up to Lorelei.

Jacenda grabbed Lorelei by her shoulders. For a second, it seemed as if Lorelei had felt Jacenda's touch, for she looked directly at her.

"I'm right here. Why can't you see me?"

A low humming sound emanated from the pueblo. Jacenda approached the circular structure cautiously.

The ruins somehow saved me from Cody, but now no one can see me. Is this similar to what happened in Florence?

Until now, Jacenda had no memory of what occurred upstairs during the paranormal investigation, other than Lorelei leaving the closet. But the low frequency vibrations from the ruin brought a distinct flashback of a blinding white light and a sensation of walking through a wall of liquid.

She closed her eyes and took a deep breath. "Calm down, Jacenda. You have to face facts, you have unusual abilities. And you also have an important role to play here. Don't let yourself down. Or anyone else."

The humming intensified. The prehistoric pueblo called to her. She stepped back inside the ancient tower from the 1200s. A resplendent light encompassed Jacenda. Within seconds, she had been transported to Lowry Pueblo. She stood in the middle of the Great Kiva between the winter and summer figures made of stone.

This is where Tony found the turtle pendant.

Jacenda touched the smooth shell turtle and collapsed on her knees. Vision slammed into reality as she found herself in the midst of the prehistoric past.

Wisps of dark clouds passed over the sun and a strong wind whipped through the village. Jacenda pulled her wrap tighter around her as she stood in an open plaza in front of a series of rooms, where other ancient villagers were milling about.

The men and women of the village wore buckskin wraparounds fastened at the chest by elaborate coverings of rabbit fur, yucca cords, bird skins and feathers. Their laced yucca sandals covered the foot and wrapped around the ankle.

The main building faced east toward a Great Kiva where a young man used a ladder to access a second story pueblo. The quiet, remote ruins of Lowry Pueblo had become a thriving community.

A man with short dark hair approached her—she got the impression he was her husband. In an unfamiliar dialect, yet one she somehow understood, he said, "I'm going hunting, should be back before dark." He pulled her close and kissed her hard on the lips. She felt nothing. His dark eyes put her on edge.

Based on the activity of her surroundings and the dress of the people, she assumed he spoke to her in an ancient dialect—ancestral Puebloan.

Piles of seeds, bones, a variety of stones, and olive, abalone and snail shells were laid out on the ground. On her knees, she sorted through the pile of stones, selecting a variety of turquoise to be shaped for the bracelet. A tall figure blocked out the sun. Taller than the rest of the men at an average height of five feet, this handsome stranger had a presence that made everyone stare.

He looked down at her and his hand reached for hers. She didn't think twice. Jacenda took his hand and he pulled her up. His fingers stroked a massive bruise on her upper arm. She inhaled sharply as his touch made her head spin.

"Let me take you away from this, Tiponi," he whispered in a deep and sensuous voice. "You are true beauty. The daughter of a shaman. And I've been in love with you…forever."

He leaned in to kiss her. The warmth of his breath lured her closer. He placed something in her hand, forcing her fingers closed around it. "A gift for you." Her admirer was forcibly pulled back.

Jacenda gasped. Her husband turned the man around, punching him in the face. The punch seemed to fuel more rage, which is when her lover was stabbed in the shoulder with a sharp bone pin.

"What are you doing with my wife?"

"Stop!" she screamed. "You're hurting him."

Her husband turned on Jacenda. He slapped her in the face. Hard. Blood trickled from her nose. Her cheek stung from the blow.

"She deserves better than you." The taller man pulled the bone pin from his shoulder, knocked her husband to the ground and stabbed him in his side and leg.

He extended his hand to Jacenda. "Let's go. I'm not leaving you here with him."

"You're hurt." She grabbed a fistful of cotton from her blanket and tried to stop the bleeding in his shoulder.

"I'll be fine." He kissed her with a passion that threatened to bring other memories to the surface. She put her arms around his waist, responding to his love. Being in his arms felt right.

A shadow sprung out from nowhere.

Jacenda screamed. One of her husband's friends attacked her lover from behind; a hatchet raised high to split his head in half. Her husband yanked her from behind to get her out of the way. She tried to fight his grip, but he was too strong. She cried and screamed in horror as the weapon came down on her lover.

"Save his head." Her husband glared at Jacenda. "As a reminder."

He limped away on his left leg. The bone pin stuck firmly in his flesh.

The prehistoric memories vanished. Lowry Pueblo was quiet again, but Jacenda's mind reeled from the events of her past life. "Cody," she whispered. "I can't believe it. I was married to Cody."

Footsteps crunched through the grass and shrub behind her and above the kiva. She turned her head to see a man standing on the north rim of the kiva where the remains of a three-room antechamber were located.

He had straight, shaggy brown hair and burn scars covering his face and neck. A shiver went down her spine. Jacenda backed up to the edge of the kiva. His dark eyes cut through her like knives and she couldn't speak. An intense pain spread from her chest to her leg.

"How's it feel, bitch? You thought your lover would get rid of me. I knew he would come to see you when I left. So I planned the whole thing." He kept staring at the pendant around her neck.

Had Cody just experienced the same vision? Or had he initiated it?

"You're not getting this." Jacenda gripped the necklace tightly in both hands. Her past life experience hadn't revealed anything about the pendant.

"I'm not asking." He extended his arm, making a "come to me" motion. The necklace lifted harshly up her neck, face and over her head.

She screamed in pain as it tore past her ears.

Cody laughed. A laugh full of anger and satisfaction. "I knew it would be easy. Even as a shaman's daughter, you were useless. You have no idea how to use your abilities. It would be more of a challenge for me to kill Joe, the FBI agent." Cody leered at her. "Or even your boyfriend. Thanks to me, they'll be out here soon."

"Leave them out of this. I may not know how to deal with my talents. But I do know that you are threatened by me, or you wouldn't have tried to kill me at Petrified Forest."

Cody stroked the turtle pendant. "Not sure how you made it out alive after that fall. No matter. It gives me the satisfaction of killing you." He vanished into thin air. She stumbled backwards when he reappeared in front of her. "Face-to-face."

Jacenda had relived but a tidbit of her past as a younger woman. *I'm going to have to journey through my past. To learn about myself and the necklace to stop Cody.*

"What do you want with the pendant?"

Cody changed from a lizard to a rabbit within seconds. Jacenda watched in shock, her mouth open and eyes wide. The jackrabbit changed into a coyote with teeth barred. The animal leapt at her, knocking her to the ground, its teeth against her throat.

Is it going to be over this quickly?

Jacenda waited for the coyote to crush her throat with its jaws. Instead, it glanced up, looked warily around and ran away.

Cody toyed with her, making her feel insecure.

Jacenda stood up and looked around. *Even if I can stop him, how am I supposed to find his victims?* She wondered if Galiena, or any Puebloan spirits were around that might provide an answer.

Deafening silence.

She noticed a two-inch long brown rock at her feet.

Leaning over for a closer look, she noticed dark brown and tan striations through the stone.

Petrified wood. How the hell did it get here?

She picked it up, running her forefinger along the darker lines. Intense heat radiated from her fingers throughout her body. For a split second, Jacenda was at the ruins of Chaco Canyon, at the once D-shaped structure of Pueblo Bonito.

"What is going on?" Jacenda rested the fossilized piece of wood in her palm. She glanced up at the afternoon sky. When she looked down, a Native American woman stood before her with slightly wavy, shoulder-length raven hair, a petite frame and an ample bosom peeking through the top of a moccasin dress as she bent over. Two men walking by nearly tripped over a large rock, too focused on watching the alluring woman. The stunning spirit looked to be in her thirties.

Is this yours?" Jacenda tried to give the rare object to the attractive entity. The spirit smiled and nodded, closing Jacenda's fingers around the piece of wood. When Jacenda looked up again, the woman had vanished.

She heard a low humming, but it didn't emanate from the Great Kiva. She held the colorful stone to her ear. The familiar sound came from the gift she had just been given.

Who was the mysterious woman who had just appeared before her? Did the gift she had been given have anything to do with Cody? And how could she possibly use her abilities traveling through ancient ruins to stop a seemingly all-powerful shapeshifter?

43

Still angry with Galiena for putting him through a relationship never meant to be, Joe desperately wanted to fight his feelings for Mandy, to ignore their ability to see each other miles apart. He wanted to be able to walk away, even when her beauty and innocence pulled him closer.

Brandon sat next to Joe on a bench outside the emergency room. The dark gray storm clouds gathering in the sky above the hospital only cemented the ominous occurrences: Mandy's sudden illness, Jacenda single-handedly fighting Cody with only her newfound abilities and the possibility of multiple pregnant victims out there alone.

Brandon was handling the dangerous situation between Jacenda and Cody well. But time would be the real test. How long would she have to be in the wilderness alone? Would she really be able to stop Cody?

Joe called Tony. "Are the parking lots to Sand Canyon Pueblo and the south trail off of County Road G secured?"

"Yes, but it's interesting. No one is even pulling into those places. Sand Canyon is usually such a popular spot for hikers and bikers. People are driving right by without taking a second glance at Castle Rock and the slickrock formation. It's like it's not there."

"Let's just say there is a higher power helping to ensure no one else is put in danger."

"Galiena, I assume. How come she isn't preventing these poor women from being abducted?"

Tony asked a great question. Galiena may be the goddess of the heavens, but she wasn't God. Perhaps she could only help those with special talents, such as Lorelei, Jacenda or Mandy.

"Let me know if anything changes." Joe disconnected the call.

Joe wondered why Tony had blurted out 'where are you' after Jacenda had vanished. According to Tony, nothing like that had happened before. It had taken Joe five minutes to shake him out of his reverie.

"Joe, maybe you should go get some rest," Brandon said. "I can stay at the hospital with Mandy."

As soon as Brandon mentioned her name, she appeared in his mind as clearly as ever. She smiled at him and started talking. But he couldn't hear her.

Joe ran into the hospital, pressing the up arrow repeatedly to the elevator. "Damn it." When the doors didn't open, he sprinted up the stairs, nearly knocking over a male doctor headed the other way.

"Joe, wait." Brandon struggled to keep up.

Joe bumped into Mandy's nurse, whose name was Carrie, on the way to her room.

"We've been looking for you." Carrie glanced around frantically, pushing her hand through her thick blonde hair. "Your friend is missing. I left her room for a few minutes and when I got back, she was gone."

Joe anxiously glanced around. Two paramedics wheeled a bloody child in, a twenty-something man burst through the swinging doors, and a plump woman with short dark hair, who looked exhausted, sat by a sick man's bedside. Typical hospital despair and chaos.

Brandon looked at Joe. "You don't think Cody had anything to do with it?"

"I have no idea who Cody is," Carrie said. "The only people who've been in to see her are the two of you and the blonde woman who came in with her."

"Did you bother to find out if any of the other staff saw her leave?"

"Of course. Right away. But there was a serious car crash and we've all been tending to the victims. I heard the blood pressure machine go off. When I went in to check, her personal belongings were there, but she wasn't. I thought maybe she had gone to find you."

"Neither of us has seen her." Joe raced down the hallways, peeking in and out of rooms.

Brandon caught up with him. "She couldn't have gone too far. Maybe she took her cell phone."

Brandon followed Joe ran into Mandy's room.

Joe removed her purse from underneath the bed and opened it. "Her phone is here."

"Wait," Brandon said. "Why did you go running inside the hospital? Did you get a vision of something happening to her?"

"Mandy somehow connected with me visually. We've been able to see each other when we're apart and I saw her smile at me. I knew something was going on."

"Where would she go?" Brandon asked. "She doesn't know anyone here. If she's walking around alone out there…"

"She tried to tell me something. I couldn't hear what." Joe grabbed Brandon's arm. "She hasn't had time to go far."

"What if Cody is playing with us again?" Brandon ran his hand through his thick black hair.

Ten minutes later, Joe found Mandy's nurse only two rooms away from Mandy's room. "Any sign of her?"

"No. But I have an alert out to the stations on all the floors and to security."

Joe's phone rang. Lorelei and Ian's number showed on the display.

"Mandy's gone," Joe blurted. "Looks like she left her room when the staff was busy with another emergency. The nurses and doctors are looking for her now."

"They're not going to find her at the hospital," Lorelei said. "Joe, Galiena has her." Lorelei started to cry. "I believe she's in danger of losing her baby. Galiena called on me while Ian and I were eating in the middle of a busy place. A woman looking exactly like Shannon walked by, staring at me. That's when I heard Galiena's voice. She said, 'I've got Mandy. She needs help beyond that of traditional medicine. The sickness Cody placed into you was transferred into Mandy when she healed you, but do not burden yourself. Mandy felt the need to test her abilities and help you in return for saving her life.' This is proof that Galiena, Dagon—all of them. They can't control everything that happens."

"When Brandon and I were downstairs for a few minutes to get some air, I saw Mandy for a few seconds. She appeared in my mind. She smiled and said something, but I couldn't understand her."

"Probably trying to tell you she was safe. "

Joe had glanced at his watch right before he saw Mandy. It said 4:08 p.m. "It must be serious if they took her whole body. God, I hope she's going to be okay."

"You know the answer, Joe. Galiena wouldn't have told you that you and Mandy were meant to be together otherwise. Though I can't get a future vision of Mandy or her baby."

"Don't blame yourself. Maybe Mandy would have had problems no matter if she healed you or not."

Silence on the other end of the phone. It didn't matter what anyone told Lorelei. Joe knew she would continue to feel guilty for Mandy's plight.

He placed his hand on Brandon's shoulder. "Lore, are you seeing anything about Jacenda?"

"No. Not sure if I will either. You and Brandon should continue to support each other right now."

"How is Paul?"

"Physically, he's fine. Ian and I know things are happening with him, but he doesn't want to admit he's different. Ian walked into Paul's room to get him up for school and saw Dagon standing next to his bed and he told me Dagon had a very sad look on his face. He got the impression Dagon wanted to let Paul know just how special he is. I don't think it worked."

"I'll be more than happy to work with him. I could lead him through a shamanic journey."

"Ian and I mentioned that to Paul. Even though he really admires you, he's just not open to what he can do." Lorelei sighed. "That's not what's important. Keep thinking about Mandy. It will mean more to her than either of you realize."

"Be careful driving back to Phoenix." Joe disconnected the call and turned to Brandon. "Galiena has Mandy. She and her baby are in danger since Mandy took the negative energy from Lorelei and into herself."

"At least we know she's safe." Brandon watched the passing doctors and nurses. "What do we tell these guys?"

44

A warm amber glow encompassed Mandy. She lay on a soft cushiony surface conforming to her body. A trickling stream and waterfall resounded somewhere nearby and sweet, flowery scents flooded her senses as gentle breezes wafted over her.

Mandy sat up. Her eyes opened wide when she saw the lush tropical paradise surrounding her. The temperate, scenic environment was a shock to that of the hospital.

Oh, no. I'm hallucinating.

Palm trees, ferns, bamboo and vibrant bird of paradise reminded her of her trip to Hawaii; a trip she and James had taken before she became pregnant.

Two women approached her bed. One of them gently pushed Mandy back against a pillow of dreams and the softest cotton she had ever felt.

"Where am I? The last I remember, I was in the hospital in Colorado."

A tall, elegant woman with light strawberry-blonde hair stood on the right side of her bed. Her facial features were strikingly similar to Lorelei's. "They can't help you."

"I'm Annie." She pointed to a stately, gray-haired woman on the other side of the bed. "That's my sister Mattie. We're friends of Lorelei and Ian."

Mattie's deeper, reassuring voice took over. "You are in this place of beauty to be healed. You were dreaming of such a serene environment in the hospital, so we recreated it especially for you."

"I don't understand."

"Don't be frightened," Annie said. "You will feel so much better when you leave here."

Mandy felt curious and full of awe. But not scared. She had never felt so comforted and welcome in her entire life.

"What's wrong with me? Will my baby be all right?"

"That's why you're here. When you healed Lorelei during her hospital stay, you absorbed the sickness Cody gave her into your fetus."

Mandy started to cry. "Please. Don't let anything happen to my baby."

Mattie and Annie took her hands in theirs. "We won't. But this will take a little time, even for us."

"The healing has begun," Mattie said. "We don't rely on what you would consider modern medical technology. Like you, we use our hands and our hearts."

Another person approached from behind where she lay.

"What about my friends? Joe, Lore, Ian and Brandon. They were all there with me."

"They know you're safe now and that you will return." Annie looked up at the person standing behind Mandy. "You're better now. But you and your unborn still need time."

A young man stepped from behind her head and stood next to Mattie. He had long dark hair on one side. The other side of his head had been shaved. "Joe has been by your bedside most of the time. Talking to you, praying for you. He cares for you very deeply."

"As do you for him." Annie smiled.

Mandy looked from the dark haired man to Mattie and Annie. "I don't understand what's happening between Joe and me. We can see each other miles away sometimes. And Lorelei, Ian and Joe keep telling me of this person named Galiena. That she took my identity to create a person named Shannon, an FBI agent who helped solve cases with Joe and the team. He was so in love with her. I see such hurt."

"As does Joe with you," Mattie said. "That's part of what is stopping the both of you."

For some reason, Mandy kept seeing the word "Dagon" when she looked at the youthful looking, enigmatic man next to her.

Dagon spoke in a deep, yet soft, tone. "What happened with Joe and Shannon shouldn't have. Galiena, or Shannon, had a mission on Earth to help Lorelei and Ian get together as a couple; a very special couple. And to help Lore understand her powers, a mission which has been accomplished. Unfortunately, her lengthy period of time on Earth left her confused and conflicted. She felt highly attracted to Joe due to his spiritual nature. Now there are two others who are meant to develop their unique talents."

"I am aware of what Lorelei can do. She somehow managed to save me from Cody by transporting me to safety with her friends. But what do you mean by 'two others'?"

Dagon knelt at her bed with his face very close. "You are one. Jacenda, Brandon's girlfriend, is the other. You have a gift—the ability to determine who needs healing, and when. Right now, the focus seems to be on pregnant women, including Lorelei and Jan Stinson. Possibly because of your own pregnancy. But that will change and expand to include others who need you."

Dagon stroked her hair. "You will have plenty of help. Lorelei, Ian and Joe will be there. Joe is a shaman and a healer himself. Being reassigned to the FBI has taken away some of his concentration. But he is realizing how much he loves you. For you *are* Shannon."

"This relationship was meant to be," Annie said. "The proof is with the connection between the two of you. Even as you left the hospital, you sent Joe a message. This bond is going to rival that of Lorelei and Ian."

"Relax," Mattie said. "You are among friends and family. If this," the woman swept her hand across the expanse of tropical wilderness, "isn't what you desire, merely think of what you do. And it will be."

"This is perfect." Mandy observed the brilliant pinks, oranges and greens of the foliage.

"Rest now," Dagon said. "We will be here by your side until you leave."

"Galiena." Mandy could barely hold her eyes open. The figures before her became blurry and distorted. "I want to meet her."

"You will." Annie placed her hand over Mandy's stomach. "Sleep and you will."

Mandy looked out over a series of waterfalls flowing through a canyon amid palm trees and lush green foliage. She closed her eyes, breathing in the scent of Heaven. When she opened them, a beautiful woman appeared, standing in the midst of the pool below. She saw a tall Hawaiian woman with a string of flowers in her long, flowing dark hair, a bare midriff, and a long grass skirt.

Mandy followed a narrow trail, pushing through colorful violet and yellow orchids, bright red anthurium and shiny, waxy leaves of ti plants that seemed to grow out of nowhere. She peeked through thick foliage to see the native woman wading through the pool below the falls.

Mandy raced around a bend in the trail to try and catch up with the stunning stranger, and ran right into her.

"I've been looking for you," Mandy said breathlessly. "I don't understand why but I'm drawn to you."

The woman took Mandy's hands in hers. A warmth spread from Mandy's arms, to her chest and stomach.

"For you, I am the Hawaiian Goddess, Haumea. The goddess of fertility and childbirth. In preparation for the beginning of civilization, I gave form to all star children who first walked on the Holy Land of Mu as goddesses and gods. My mortal name was La'ila'i.

"Are you going to help me and my baby?"

The warmth in Mandy's stomach intensified. As if a ball of heat floated around inside her.

"I already am."

Mandy awoke among the breathtaking beauty of the heavenly version of Hawaii. Mattie, Dagon and Annie were gone. She didn't know how long she had been asleep.

Where is this Galiena? They told me I would be seeing her.

A woman's voice answered her thoughts.

"You met her. In your dream."

Mandy glanced over to see Mattie standing under a palm tree.

"The woman from my dream said she was a Hawaiian goddess.

Galiena is not just one, she can be many. For you, she revealed herself in a form to help you—the goddess of fertility and childbirth. You will be returned to your home soon," Mattie said. "But not to the hospital, to Joe. The doctors are no longer looking for you as we have taken care of that. The time you will have been missing is a few hours."

"What if I forget all this?"

"You won't. You will remember every detail for eternity."

Mandy's eyes became heavy. She tried to take in the beauty around her before falling asleep again. For she knew when she awoke, it would all be gone.

45

A brilliant streak raced across the quarter moon. Jacenda wished upon the falling star, shivering in the crisp winter air. Darkness fell quickly. Thoughts of Brandon warmed her a little, but not enough to survive the chilly night.

Heat began to radiate from the chunk of petrified wood in her front jean pocket. The warmth spread to her upper body and down her left leg. She cautiously removed the object from its hiding place, holding it in her right hand. The fossilized wood increased its temperature gradually. Within thirty seconds, Jacenda stopped shivering and her body relaxed. She stared at the fossil in astonishment, realizing it would help her survive.

She leaned up against the wall of a small ruin tucked beneath a rock overhang, staring into the thick blanket of night. Jacenda could only imagine what waited for her, out there among canyons, mesas and archaic deserted villages. Rocks fell from the cliff above, an eerie howl sounded in the distance, shadows chased each other in the darkness, and the ruins she rested against began to vibrate. The past called to her. Again.

Smoke from a fire in the center of the Great Kiva rose to the pine roof beams above. A crowd of thirty people were sitting on the bench encircling the interior of the ceremonial structure. Jacenda began to speak, using the same language she had

spoken at Lowry Pueblo. She held the turtle pendant with her right hand. Chanting and drumming started softly, accompanying her. The crowd watched the stone steps leading into the underground chamber. Two stout men dragged a prisoner down the stairs.

"You have killed for the last time," Jacenda shouted.

The man, his hands bound together with yucca cord, glowered at her.

"Your inhumane punishment will fit your past crimes of murder, sorcery and cannibalism. You will become the beast you truly are."

She nodded at the two guards holding him. "After I give him the potion, take him away from the village. The transformation will not be safe here. This change will take at least five minutes, in which time he will not be able to do harm. He will receive the pain and suffering he has placed on others."

The guards glanced nervously at each other. The man they held who had callously killed numerous people showed emotion for the first time—fright.

The audience was wide-eyed and in awe. They knew what she could do. "You will all be safe inside the walls. He cannot get within fifty feet of another village or person. If he does, he will be stopped by the same excruciating torture from his initial transformation."

An elderly woman stood up. "Why not just be rid of him now?"

"A quick punishment would be too kind."

Jacenda nodded to bring the prisoner to her. She dipped a ladle into a wooden bowl, placing the spoon up to his mouth. One of the guards forced his mouth open and she poured the concoction in. He tried to spit it out, but the guard prevented him by forcing his jaw shut.

The prisoner swallowed. He choked and spit on the ground.

"You are banned from this place and from life as you have known it. Your survival from now on will depend upon being alone."

He trembled in the guards' arms. "Get him out of here."

Jacenda picked up a chunk of petrified wood from a stone altar next to her and raised her hands to the heavens. The drummers in the center of the kiva pounded fast and furious. "This fossil is a symbol of growth, of time and of the Earth itself. Like many of us, it has been on a long, arduous journey to find its true home. Breaking into pieces on the way, yet not being destroyed. And it will help cleanse this place of evil, now and forever!"

The smoke from the fire went out with a magical breeze. Jacenda ran up the stairs and into the night air, taking a deep breath.

Towering cliffs rose above the village and a massive rock threatened to collapse onto thirty pueblos below, but the villagers had rested a prayer stick between the cliff and the leaning boulder to prevent the potential loss of life.

Agonizing screams echoed from outside the walled village. The change had begun. She didn't know what form her ex-husband would take. But she wanted him to suffer for taking away the loved ones from her village—as well as the love of her life over ten years ago.

46

The placid water of Narraguinnep Reservoir off of Highway 184 near Cortez held no answers about Mandy. Joe knew Galiena would take care of her. But he didn't know how well Mandy would handle the concept of what Galiena, Annie, Mattie and Dagon represented.

He never thought he would fall in love with a pregnant woman. But then he never expected to be an FBI agent, or to be chasing the supernatural. His father had drunk himself to death on the reservation when Joe was only ten and his mother had been killed by a drunk driver near Flagstaff a week after his sixteenth birthday. Two years before her death, Joe had become close with her boyfriend, a Navajo shaman and healer. His name was Cheveyo, meaning spirit warrior. Joe had watched Cheveyo's astral self project out-of-body, call upon spirits to create rain and use a mixture of saliva, soil and plants to stop a tornado.

Cheveyo had told Joe he would be a powerful shaman some day. He had lived with Cheveyo until age eighteen, studying, researching and practicing. He never dated or went out with friends. He knew those things would only interrupt his focus. At the age of twenty-five, Joe had earned a reputation as the youngest, most gifted shaman in Arizona. By the time he turned thirty-six, he was being considered the most well-known shaman in the Four Corners.

Joe zipped up his jacket as he sat with Brandon in the flatbed of Joe's truck. Restlessness and worry had overcome Brandon. Though

Jacenda enjoyed day hikes, she wasn't a camper, and had no idea how to survive in the wilderness. The highs during the day were near fifty degrees. The nights would be in the twenties or below. Brandon trembled uncontrollably while watching the moon. Joe knew Brandon wanted to place himself through the same torture as Jacenda.

Joe and Brandon jumped when Joe's cell phone rang.

"Hey, Tony. Any news?"

"We know who he is," Tony said.

"What are you talking about?"

"Cody," Tony said excitedly. "We managed to obtain a DNA sample from the ruins near Lowry and that blob of goo from the cave near the farmhouse. His last name is Burgess. He was a transportation inspector and mechanic at the airport. Laid off six months ago because of behavioral and attitude changes."

"That might explain why he's living in the wilderness." Joe observed a shooting star streaking across the sky.

"He lost his home and doesn't have too many friends, no family. Believe it or not, Cody has never had a prior arrest or conviction. He's clean. At first, I thought the bad luck got to him. His shapeshifting abilities could be the cause of his life changing so drastically from an everyday working guy to a madman. His co-workers said Cody began acting strange prior to the layoff, calling in sick pretty frequently and avoiding people. And they heard strange noises coming from his office. Two people, at different times, saw Cody walk into his office. One of his co-workers went into Cody's office within a minute of Cody entering, only to find a bat."

"How can this person be sure Cody didn't leave the office?"

"The woman had been following behind him. She went to get help to remove the bat. When she came back a minute later, Cody had returned. Another time, someone saw him go in to his office and heard what sounded like grunting and growling. The co-worker went to check on him, but he had vanished."

Tony was silent for a few seconds. "Makes me wonder if Cody found some object enabling him with these powers."

"Or, he could have had these shapeshifting abilities all along and they just came to the surface. Lorelei has the gift of astral projection, but didn't know it until the mystery in southeast Arizona," Joe said.

"You think Cody's extreme abilities are from a past life?" Tony asked.

Joe looked over at Brandon, who hadn't said a word in half an hour. "That's what I'm thinking. Lore had a strong dream about Cody in Chaco Canyon. She saw him drag a woman's body into a room. Then he took a hatchet and cut her into pieces. Lore didn't witness any shapeshifting, but murder is a commonality."

Brandon paced alongside Joe's truck. Then he picked up a large rock and threw it angrily into the water of the reservoir.

"Maybe there was an incident in Cody's life that set this in motion. We know he lost his job and home due to his change in behavior at work. But what if a relationship ended, he experienced the death of a loved one, or had a string of bad luck—something that might have set off Cody's murderous mindset."

"We're still interviewing co-workers. Like I said before, he didn't have too many friends. And there is no family."

"At least we have an identity," Joe said. "It's a start. Do you have some better photos other than the forensic sketch based on Lorelei and Mandy's testimony?"

"Yes. It's no wonder no one recognized him from the community. The pictures of him before he turned show him with shorter hair, clean cut. Even stranger, Cody didn't have the burn marks on his face and neck or the limp."

Brandon had walked down a small trail. Joe knew he didn't want to hear any more about Cody. "Interesting. The limp could be from an injury in the wilderness. But Lorelei mentioned those burn marks looked as if they had been there for years."

A sneeze and muffled voices came from the background.

"That sort of disfiguration could cause a person to retreat from society," Tony said. "But no one mentioned Cody being in a tragic accident as far as the limp."

Had Cody been pulled physically and mentally into his past self? "I need to go. Send copies of those photos of Cody over."

"Brandon!" Joe followed the path he had taken. "Brandon, where did you go?"

"I'm right here."

Joe turned around. He couldn't believe his eyes. Mandy stepped out from behind Brandon.

"I went for a little walk and found this beautiful lady."

Joe ran over to her. He stroked her face. "Are you all right?"

"Yes." Mandy looked around at her surroundings. "How did I get here?"

"Do you remember being in the hospital?"

"Of course."

"Let's get you into the truck. It's cold out here." Joe removed his leather jacket and placed it over her shoulders. He helped her into his truck and slid in next to her. Brandon got in on the passenger side.

Mandy looked amazing. Her eyes sparkled, her skin glowed and he saw a strong blue aura, meaning calm, collected, caring, and intuitive. She was more beautiful than he had ever seen her. Galiena had done more than heal Mandy's body, she had helped her come to terms with her abilities.

Joe and Brandon glanced nervously at each other during a moment of silence.

"So, I suppose it wasn't a dream," Mandy said. "Mattie, Annie and Dagon. They told me the people at the hospital couldn't save my baby in time."

"Wow," Brandon said. "You were definitely in great hands. Mattie was a powerful shaman. She lived at Vulture Mine as the caretaker for awhile and Annie is her sister."

"What do you mean, 'was a powerful shaman' "? Mandy asked.

Joe took her hand in his. "They are spirits. And you must be very, very special for them to care for you personally." Joe pulled onto the highway. "We'll get you back to the hotel so you can get some rest."

"I feel terrific," Mandy said. "The best I've ever felt." Mandy didn't let go of Joe's hand. She squeezed tighter and slid a little closer. He had almost forgotten what it felt like to have a woman respond to warmly to him.

Could Mandy be in shock? Had she seen Galiena in the same form he and Lorelei had, as a fiery figure? For someone who had taken a journey to the stars, she seemed rather calm.

Why had Galiena, Mattie and Annie returned Mandy to the reservoir rather than the hospital? As soon as the thought passed through his mind, Galiena's voice answered his question.

We returned her to you, where she belongs.

He supposed he had already known the answer, but hearing it made him his heart explode with joy. A smile started at the corner of his mouth and gradually spread until he noticed Mandy watching him in curiosity.

Joe cleared his throat and blushed.

None of them said a word on the way back to the hotel. Mandy had fallen asleep as Joe drove closer to Cortez. She awoke when Joe parked his truck.

"We're at the hotel." Joe stepped out of the truck, taking her hand to help her slide out.

"I'm going to head to my room." Brandon yawned. "Let me know if you hear anything. I don't plan on sleeping, so give me a call or knock on my door."

"At least lay your head down," Mandy said. "Jacenda would want you to."

Joe and Brandon glanced at each other. Joe didn't understand where her comment had come from.

Joe walked Mandy to her room. "Are you sure you're all right?" He placed his hand on her stomach. Mandy laid her own hand over his. He saw a brief vision of Mandy on a bed with Mattie, Annie and Dagon surrounding her. But Mandy wasn't seeing the stars or anything related to the Universe. They had placed her in a lush, tropical paradise.

Joe slid Mandy's key card into her door. "Here you are. It's been a long day, so I'll leave you alone. I'll make sure there's an agent outside."

Mandy grabbed his arm. "Please stay. I'm feeling great. But after all that's happened, I won't be able to sleep." She opened the door and took a step into the room, looking back at him. "If you want to."

Joe took her face in his hands. "You have no idea how much I want to stay with you, but both of us know it would not be safe. The passion that's been ignited, the visions we have of each other. This isn't the time. At least not until this mystery gets solved."

Mandy diverted her eyes to the television screen sitting inside a black entertainment center in the middle of the room. Joe took her chin and moved it so she looked into his eyes. "We both know this is going to be an unusual, hot and intense relationship to rival that of Ian and Lorelei."

Mandy walked into the room and dropped her purse on the queen-sized bed. "That's what Mattie and Annie said."

Joe followed behind her. He placed his hand behind her head and kissed her lightly on the lips. She put her arms around his waist and pressed herself against him.

Her supple skin and the feel of her body put him on the verge of losing control. Joe pulled away. "I'd better go. If you need me at any time, call. Or I'm only two doors down in room 252." He started to turn away.

"Joe, what happened when I disappeared from the hospital? How is it possible that I'm in a hospital in Cortez, Colorado one minute and in Hawaii the next?" Mandy sat on the corner of the bed. "Mattie and

Annie told me they created that environment to make me comfortable because they knew I loved that place so much."

He leaned down in front of her. "I want to tell you. Just not sure you're ready."

"Joe, please." Mandy placed her hand on his chest. "I need to know."

He wanted nothing more than to lay her gently on the bed, take her clothes off and make love to her. She blushed. Had she picked up on his vision? Her hand never left his body. It traced softly down his shirt.

He removed her hand and kissed it. "You were with Galiena." He walked her out to the balcony and pointed to the stars. "Up there." He stood behind her and whispered in her ear. "But I think you knew that."

A streak of light raced across the heavens. The thunder of waterfalls interrupted the calm Cortez evening. And a scent of the tropics permeated the atmosphere. Mandy hadn't left the peaceful, lush setting among the stars. She had brought a taste of it with her.

47

Lorelei smiled, watching Ian and Paul play football in the backyard, from inside her home. Ian tagged Paul and the two of them rolled around on the ground.

She slid open the patio door and set two glasses of lemonade on the table outside. "Looks like you both are working up a thirst."

Ian smiled, waved and ran over to her. "Hey, gorgeous."

She put her arms around his neck.

Ian rubbed her stomach gently. "How are you and the baby doing?"

"We're both great." She handed the drinks to Paul and Ian. She couldn't look at either of them because of the news she had to deliver.

"Lore, what's the matter?"

Paul ran off to play in the backyard, kicking the football around.

"Did you see something pertaining to the case in the Four Corners?"

"Turns out Jacenda won't have to confront Cody. She is traveling through the Indian ruins up there, into her own past and Cody's, at Lowry Pueblo, Sand Canyon and even Chaco. The same places Cody is associated with. Every time she does, it weakens him. I saw Cody and he's not the same. He attempted to shapeshift, but couldn't. The look in his eyes...Ian, the man was terrified."

"How do you know Jacenda's responsible? Maybe his talents are just weakening."

She pulled a patio chair away from the table and sat down. "The vision went back and forth between Jacenda and Cody. She would melt into a prehistoric ruin and I would get an image of Cody. The last two scenes involving Cody showed him barely able to walk, let alone shapeshift."

"That's fantastic. She'll be safe if she doesn't have to confront him, which is probably why you saw her making it through this."-

Lorelei nodded. "I think so. Unfortunately, Jacenda doesn't know her talent is helping to trap Cody. She thinks she has to find him and somehow stop him." Lorelei waved to the next door neighbor. "Honey, Jacenda needs to know she is already helping to stop him, or she could be out there for much longer than she needs to."

"I don't want you involved in this anymore, using astral travel or teleportation." Ian sat down on the couch and pulled her onto his lap. "I don't need you getting hurt or risking our baby."

"I don't need to go anywhere, physically or otherwise. Ian, Paul can get through to Jacenda with his dream reality."

Ian kissed her on the neck. "Lore, you know how Paul feels about that lately. He's hesitant about using his abilities. We've tried talking about this with him before and it only makes things worse. And besides, Paul's only connected with *you* through his dreams. I'm not sure it would work with someone he doesn't know."

Lorelei stood up and walked back in the house. "I don't think we have any other options. Perhaps talk it out with Paul. We'll both be there to help him through it."

Ian placed his hands on her arms. You've already attempted astral travel and teleportation. Didn't you? That's why you need Paul to try using his dream reality to contact Jacenda."

"Ian, I had to try. But it doesn't matter because neither ability worked."

"I'm not the only one who thinks you shouldn't be placing yourself in such a dangerous situation. Galiena might be the reason for your failed attempt."

Lorelei sighed. "I don't know, maybe."

Ian placed board game pieces from the kitchen table back in the Monopoly box. "What if you and I lie down with Paul to help him focus and give him courage?"

"Courage for what?" Paul had just come in the open sliding glass door, carrying his lemonade, without them knowing.

Lorelei looked at Ian.

"Come sit down. Lore and I need to talk to you."

"Dad, I told you both I don't want to deal with dream reality or any other ability. If I ignore it, it will go away. Just because the two of you choose to use your talents doesn't mean that's what I want out of my life."

Lorelei led Paul to the couch. She was afraid to broach the subject, but she wanted him to understand that his gifts made him unique. "First of all your talents won't disappear because you decide to ignore them. I've tried that tactic myself during the investigation in Southeast Arizona. Second, I wouldn't be asking for your help if I didn't need it."

Paul took a few gulps of his lemonade. "Does this have something to do with what's going on in the Four Corners?"

"Yes. There's a very special woman who has placed herself in danger to help catch the murder suspect. Like you, she has abilities. Hers are traveling through Indian ruins, the ancestral Puebloan right now, to understand her own ancient past in relation to Cody's and to help solve the case. But Jacenda isn't aware her journey through these prehistoric villages is helping. I know because my vision switched between the two of them."

Paul sighed. He looked from Lorelei to Ian and back to Lorelei. "Jacenda has a stronger bond with Cody than you think."

Lorelei watched Paul, anxiously waiting for him to continue. Had he somehow fed off of her recent vision off of Jacenda?

Ian put his hand on Paul's shoulder. "What do you know?"

"Jacenda and Cody were married in a past life. But she has figured that out."

Lorelei glanced from Ian to Paul. "How long have you known this?"

"A vision suddenly popped into my mind while watching the stars a few minutes ago. No voices. It showed a woman with long dark hair, a Native American woman, with a man in the prehistoric past. As soon as I saw them, an internal voice said 'Jacenda and Cody.' I put two and two together when I heard you and Dad talking."

"Paul." Ian kneeled down in front of him. "Can't you see? Nothing is going away. You had a message—an important one. Perhaps Dagon is encouraging this somehow or it could be you. But it's a sign you are meant to help."

"Dagon was here a few weeks ago, wasn't he? In my room."

"Yes, and he didn't look happy. He knows how remarkable you are but he wants *you* to know that."

"Did Dagon talk to you?" Lorelei asked.

"No. Right before I woke up, I saw him standing there, watching me." Paul stood up and headed toward his room. He turned around to look at Ian and Lore. "What if I can't find Jacenda? Or what if I locate her, but she can't hear me talking to her? Lore, you're the only one I've visited in my dreams. How can I find someone I haven't met?"

Ian glanced from Paul to Lorelei. "You saw Paul in your vision a little while ago. You witnessed him connecting with Jacenda."

She nodded. "I didn't want to say anything because I don't want him to feel pressured."

Ian walked over to Paul. "How about I do a formal ritual before you go to bed? Place some candles out, do a chant and protection ceremony? I have a feeling you don't need it. There are much higher powers watching over you. But if it makes you feel better."

"I guess." Paul stared at Lorelei. "I don't have a choice, do I? I mean, my talents are going to happen whether I want them to or not."

Lorelei nodded. "I'm sorry."

❖

The scent of lavender and vanilla filled the air. Candles in every corner and by the bed created a soft glow, throwing flickering shadows against the warm beige, faux-colored walls with Navajo tapestries. Soft Native American flute music started to calm Paul. His father folded his fingers and palm around a stone.

"This is obsidian," Ian said. "It is a natural glass created by volcanic activity and is very powerful when used for grounding. I've placed some rose quartz around you and by your bed to attract positive energy. There are also a variety of black stones, as well as a turtle and an eagle to represent animal totems. I've used a turtle because it is armored and also a rather respected creature to the Native Americans. The eagle sees all and will also overlook you on your journey."

His father stroked his hair gently back on his head. "Begin by drawing energy into your body. Feel it building here." His father laid his hand gently on his stomach. "In your Chi, or abdominal area. Imagine a ball of pure light, energy and strength at the core of your body."

Ian gave him a few seconds. "Can you see this sphere?"

Paul nodded.

"Slowly let the ball expand, with your Chi at its center. Begin to see it as a bubble or hollow sphere with you on the inside. Let the earth's energy and vibrations flow through you and into the shield."

A moment of silence gave Paul time to comprehend and imagine. Warmth and peace encompassed him inside his protective environment. Gold light rays spread outward, pushing the walls of the bubble with them.

"Let the sphere penetrate the ground beneath you, cover the air above and to all sides. You are well-protected and have nothing to fear."

The flutes began to fade, along with his dad's touch. Sleep brought on obscure images in greens and tans, which gradually morphed into scrub brush and ancient structures spread out over an arid landscape. A two-story, tall square structure stood out among the rest. It had been built atop a boulder. Yet Paul could see no easy access to the tower. Another structure stood nearby on top of a mesa: the Holly Group of ruins at Hovenweep National Monument.

A tall woman with long, straight dark hair stood alone behind a massive rectangular boulder with the remains of a pueblo, which leaned precariously into the canyon. A soft white light surrounded her and radiant tendrils extended to the nearby structures.

Jacenda.

He focused on her and managed to get within five feet of her. Paul called her name but she didn't respond, so he yelled louder. He didn't understand how or why he could clearly see people from the earthly plane and talk to them while sleeping, but he did notice a pattern—the dream reality only happened during cases his father and Lorelei were involved in.

Jacenda glanced up. Her eyes darted back and forth. "Who's there?" She backed away from his voice.

"It's okay. I'm not Cody and this isn't a trick."

"Then why can't I see you?"

"My name is Paul Healy, Ian's son. This sounds strange, but I've reached you through my dreams. I have to make this quick since I can't communicate for long periods of time this way."

Jacenda stepped toward him. "I've heard so much about you. But dreams are hard to control. How can you so easily find me and talk to me?"

"I— I don't know. But I'm here to tell you that you don't have to confront Cody to stop him. You're weakening him by traveling through the ruins and going into your past."

"What? How can you be so sure?"

"Lore saw Cody in a vision. He tried to shapeshift, but wasn't able to."

"I hope she's right. That might explain why I haven't seen him. But I had hoped I could find out if there are more victims."

Jacenda started to fade. Paul would either be waking up in bed or transitioning into another dream. "I've got to go."

Her lips moved, but he couldn't hear her. The ruins of Hovenweep rapidly faded. Paul awoke to see his father and Lorelei sitting on either side of his bed, holding his hands.

"Hey, buddy," Ian said. "Are you all right?"

Paul nodded. "I found Jacenda at The Holly Group of ruins at Hovenweep."

Lorelei stroked his hair. "Were you able to talk to her?"

"Yeah. She couldn't see me, though. Sort of freaked her out at first. But I had just enough time to tell her that her travels through the ruins were destroying Cody."

"Great job," Lorelei said. "We both knew you could do it."

Ian leaned over Paul. "You were muttering in your sleep."

"You heard me talking to Jacenda."

"No, sweetie," Lorelei said. "You said, 'Stephanie is here. But nobody knows.' "

Paul sat up. "What? I don't remember saying such a thing. I only talked to Jacenda and came right back."

Lorelei glanced up at Paul's wall clock. "You fell asleep at 10:00 p.m. It's after midnight. That's a long period of time considering your short meeting with Jacenda."

"I think you might have found another of Cody's victims," Ian said. "Lore called Joe when she heard you mention Stephanie."

Paul shouted in frustration. "I don't get it. I didn't see anyone else besides Jacenda."

Lorelei placed her hands on either side of Paul's face. "You also mentioned a last name. Maxwell. Stephanie Maxwell. Joe sent a text to your dad's phone and mine right before you woke up. Honey, a woman with that name went missing. Stephanie traveled to Cortez for an overnight stay to explore the area—that was five days ago. Her friend never heard from her, though Stephanie was supposed to have contacted her when she arrived."

Ian placed his arm around Paul. "I guess we've discovered your dream reality can help in ways *you* weren't even aware."

48

Jacenda waited inside the Holly House, staring through an ancient window to a tower in the canyon beyond. The unusual contact with Paul had given Jacenda hope. She felt relieved when Paul mentioned her enigmatic method of travel placed Cody at a disadvantage, especially since she had no idea how she would be able to stop him physically.

Frigid air should have made the nights long and unbearable. She should have been dead by now. She found if she remained within twenty feet of any prehistoric remains with the chunk of petrified wood in her pocket, she would be able to survive the winter nights. Every journey through a different set of ruins left Jacenda feeling safer and stronger than ever.

She only wished she could let Brandon know she was safe. It didn't matter whether Lorelei told him Jacenda would make it out alive. Brandon would be terrified for her.

In a weak moment before Paul had made his appearance, she had focused on Brandon and imagined being in his arms, but nothing had happened. Unlike Lorelei, who could teleport at will anywhere, Jacenda's abilities were linked to the ruins. Perhaps it was for the best, for neither would want to let go.

Spirits surrounded her inside and outside of the ancient buildings. Some of them traveled with her. She knew many of them were a part of her journey and possibly, a part of her past.

The air began to change. The temperature increased by ten degrees inside her haven. She stood up when a gray mist appeared in front of her. This particular entity seemed special, though she didn't understand why. A tall, Native American man with dark skin and muscular arms slowly appeared in front of her. He had a well-toned torso, legs and a face with smooth skin, high cheekbones and a penetrating gaze that brought her back to prehistoric Lowry Pueblo.

Jacenda collapsed on her knees. The man standing before her had been her lover, callously murdered by Cody's past self.

He walked over and held his hand out to Jacenda. She couldn't believe how solid, how real he felt. As she stood back up, the word "Tawa" came into her head.

"Tawa. Is that your name?"

He nodded.

"What was my name?" she asked.

In one long stride, Tawa stood within two inches of her. His dark, alluring eyes never left hers. "Tiponi, meaning 'child of importance.' "

Tawa stroked her face. His touch felt light and airy, like Brandon's. The way he looked at her made her feel loved, wanted and secure.

"I can't believe this. My boyfriend, Brandon, was *you*."

Tawa smiled and nodded. "Everything now is as it should be. I have never stopped loving you. Neither will he."

Tawa smiled at her as he faded into the darkness, but with Brandon by her side, he would never be gone.

A faint cry came from the same location where she had encountered Paul; the boulder that leaned precariously into the canyon. It sounded like a woman. A brilliant white light emanated from the walls of Holly House. Jacenda would be making a shorter trip to find another of Cody's captives.

Jacenda found herself next to the gigantic leaning boulder, not far from the house she had taken shelter in. She stood on top of a round layer of rock next to the boulder.

A fit of coughing interrupted the last cry.

"Hello," Jacenda shouted. Early morning rays peeked into the cracks. Shuffling and scraping came from below her.

A woman's weak voice called out. "Is someone there?"

The footing underneath where she stood was treacherous. There didn't seem to be a way to get to the victim safely.

Another faint call. "Help me."

"I'm trying. I have to figure out where you are and how to get there. My name is Jacenda." She stepped carefully off the flat rock surface and into a crevasse next to the time-shifted boulder. "What's yours?"

"Stephanie Maxwell. How did you find me? Are you a hiker?"

"Not quite. Stephanie, I'm looking for a way to get to you."

Jacenda used her hands to guide her safely along the length of the slab of stone toward the upper part where she heard Stephanie's yells. A bolt of energy raced down both arms, through her torso and into her legs and feet, throwing her backwards.

What the hell? I've never experienced anything that strong.

Hearing moaning, she glanced up to see a woman lying in the ruins and rubble on top of the leaning boulder.

"Stephanie?" Jacenda climbed up and approached a tall woman with wavy, dark blonde hair. She was covered in dirt and her arm bent awkwardly behind her.

Stephanie moaned and looked up at Jacenda.

"How did I get out of there?"

"It doesn't matter. We need to get you to the hospital."

The FBI had established barriers at both parking lots, and she knew a much higher power worked to keep others out of the area. She had somehow managed to move Stephanie out of her underground prison, but Jacenda wouldn't be able to get her to civilization.

Within minutes, Jacenda started to hear helicopter blades. A solid black copter came into view. Had the FBI known about Stephanie?

Joe leaned out one of the passenger side windows, his long black hair blowing in the man-made breeze of the rotor. It landed in a spot bare of ruins and brush. Joe leapt out of the copter and ran over to Jacenda and Stephanie.

Jacenda stood up and hugged Joe tightly.

"Getting a little lonely out here?" He grabbed her hand and held it tightly.

"I guess so. Did Lorelei have a vision about Stephanie? Is that why you're here?"

The other FBI agent who had landed the copter jumped out along with a paramedic. Stephanie screamed in agony as they gently placed her on a gurney removed from the helicopter.

"No. Ian's son Paul has some rather unusual abilities."

"I know. He came to me a while ago through dream reality. He told me that my travels through these ruins were weakening Cody, but I didn't talk to him for long. I couldn't even see him."

"He's an amazing young man." Joe glanced over at the helicopter. "Apparently, he somehow detected Stephanie was here." He looked back at Jacenda with his mysterious smirk. "Tell me, how did *you* find her?"

"I heard her yelling for help. She was under that square boulder. When I scrambled along the side to try and find where Cody hid her, I received a terrible shock. That's when Stephanie appeared at the top." Jacenda giggled nervously. "Guess I also have the ability to transfer others through ruins."

The pilot and FBI agent who had landed the copter waved to Joe that they were ready to leave.

"I've got to go. We need to get Stephanie medical attention."

A tear rolled down Jacenda's face. Joe wiped it away with his finger. "You will be seeing Brandon *very* soon. I performed a ceremony last night and took on the form of my eagle. Cody's still out here," Joe glanced around at the canyon, brush and ruins, "somewhere. Staying hidden, though not for long."

"What?" But Joe turned and entered the copter, leaning over next to Stephanie. When it took off, Jacenda's heart sank. Along with her hope.

"Hey, beautiful."

Jacenda turned her head. Brandon stood there with a picnic basket, a leather jacket, blanket and a bag of clothes.

He walked up to her, closed her wide open mouth with his finger, and kissed her with a passion that made her wish she didn't have a criminal to find.

He held her face in his hands.

"What are you doing here?" she asked.

"When Joe told me about Paul's discovery and that the FBI was flying back out here, I told him I was coming, whether he wanted me to or not. I snuck out the other side of the copter to surprise you."

"There is so much I have to tell you." Jacenda pulled him close. "I don't know where to start." She stared into his brown eyes—the soul of Tawa.

She looked into the basket after he opened it. There were three different kinds of cold salads, fresh bread, sandwiches and cold drinks.

"I know you still have work to do out here." Brandon kissed her on the lips. "But I've been worried sick knowing you didn't have very many supplies. Or even a damn jacket. I should have made you take mine when I saw you at Castle Rock. What was I thinking?"

"Brandon, Cody had threatened all of you. I didn't feel it safe. Not to mention, you were so shocked by seeing me appear the way I did."

"How did you survive out here?" Brandon opened a blanket and spread it out on the ground.

Jacenda sifted through the basket, pulled out macaroni salad and a sandwich, then sat down on the blanket. "I didn't need a jacket. Believe it or not, the ruins and perhaps the spirits themselves kept me warm at night. And the FBI left some coolers of food and water at the north and south trailheads."

Brandon watched her and smiled. "Actually, Joe and I brought some stuff back out."

Jacenda laughed. "I should have known. There's something I have to tell you. Something amazing."

Brandon moved closer to her. He took a wet wipe from the basket and gently washed her face.

She stopped him. "Honey, Cody and I were married."

"Jace, it's okay. Lorelei told me. You had no way of knowing until this journey."

"That's not all. You were also a part of my past life."

"What?"

She took his hands in hers. "Brandon, you were a Native American man named Tawa. My name was Tiponi, meaning 'child of importance.' We were lovers."

He stroked her face. "How can you know that?"

"When I first traveled into my past where Lowry Pueblo is, I saw Tawa. He had your eyes, your gentle nature. And there was something so familiar. I missed you so badly." Jacenda started to cry. Brandon took her sandwich and placed it on the blanket. He pulled her close.

She whispered in his ear, "And then Tawa showed up. He told me he you were his reincarnation."

"That's amazing." He placed his forehead against hers. "But if you were married to Cody…"

She nodded. "Cody's past self and a warrior friend of his killed Tawa. They saw us together. He, or you, wanted so desperately to get me away from him and show me how much you loved me."

She placed his hand over her beating heart. Passion overcame her while Brandon laid her down on the blanket. He moaned while she rubbed his chest. She wrapped her legs around him, wanting nothing more than to make love to him.

"Shit. Jace, no." Brandon pulled away. "God, I want you more than I've ever wanted you. We both know this isn't the place."

She sat up. "You're right. I can't believe I was about to be that disrespectful."

A low humming became louder, as if a massive hive of bees were heading their way. Brandon looked at Jacenda.

The ground began to vibrate. The ruins were calling her again. Would she find another of Cody's victims or more about her past?

He pulled her up on her feet and handed her the sandwich. "Take a few more bites because I think you're going to need strength for this next journey."

"I'm waiting for a very romantic dinner and night out."

"Baby, when this is all over, you're in for the time of your life."

She kissed him lightly on the lips. "I love you and I want to spend the rest of my life with you."

His eyes lit up. "Are you sure?"

She kissed him briefly, but passionately. "Does that answer your question?"

"I love you, too." He hugged her tightly. "You need to go. But I'll be here waiting for you. And when you return, you're going to be mine for quite awhile before I let you out of my sight."

The rectangular adobe walls surrounding Tiponi housed four rooms and twenty people. She was one of five people who had migrated from the Four Corners, including two friends, and a husband, wife and their baby—a long, arduous journey to a new place hundreds of miles away.

The farming people of the Phoenix desert had been highly reluctant to take the group of strangers in, but Tiponi had given them valuable gifts, including a black-on-red bowl, a bow and arrow, and a tool for removing the pulp from yucca leaves. She also proved her abilities as a healer when warriors from an outside village attacked and seriously wounded the son of a pottery maker. Her powers and medicine had healed the boy within days. They had told her and her friends then that she would have a home as long as she wanted it.

Tiponi had spent three hours grinding corn. The men were out hunting for game or tending to the cotton crops. A woman inside one of the four rooms weaved a mat; three other women were in the center of the plaza cooking beans and squash.

She went into the corner of an empty pueblo and carefully opened a deerskin cloth. Inside lay a necklace with fifteen smooth, cream-colored olive shells and turquoise beads. Tiponi had been working on it to show Tawa before he was killed. They had planned on running away together, but she hadn't expected him to come for her so soon. After Tawa's death, she didn't have the heart to finish it.

Tiponi opened a smaller cloth with a jade turtle pendant, the gift Tawa had placed in her hand right before he was attacked. She gently traced the head and feet of the turtle with her finger and smiled. After Tawa had died, so had she. But he continued to visit her even in death, both in her dreams and during waking hours. He wanted her to finish the necklace, and to leave Nukpana, her evil husband. But within a few months of Tawa's death, Nukpana became bored with Tiponi and moved on to other women.

The memories, hatred and resentment were too strong, so Tiponi had decided to migrate to Chaco Canyon with another shaman and his family. Many men attempted to take her hand, but Tiponi had no interest. Her one true love was gone. She couldn't imagine loving another.

Even as she sat cross-legged on a mat in the cool adobe room, a younger man named Shuman, considered an expert weaver among the village, stopped inside the doorway and watched her for a minute as she threaded the string with olive shells and square turquoise beads. Tall and lean with dark, shoulder length hair, Shuman opened his mouth as if to say something. Instead, he smiled shyly, then turned and walked away.

Within an hour, Tiponi had completed her work of art. She placed it on her neck as twilight descended upon the hundred villagers in the farming community. She left the four walls of her family unit; a risk, but worth the effort. Tiponi needed open spaces to breathe and commune with nature.

Five women in the village were focused on building a pit for roasting agave as she headed into the cotton fields. The intense heat of the day had dissipated. A cool breeze combined with soft mauves and violets welcomed her into the evening.

Tiponi entered among the rows of four-foot-high plants with white and pink blooms. It seemed ten degrees cooler among the crops. A pink dragonfly flew alongside her, flitting through the air, catching gnats and mosquitoes. Birds exploded from the Cottonwood trees surrounding the fields; feasting among the millions of insects.

Shouting and screaming emanated from somewhere within the cotton fields. Someone burst through the row of plants next to her.

"It's coming," Shuman screamed. He grabbed her hand, leading Tiponi back toward the village.

"What? What's coming?"

"A beast." Tiponi let go of her hand and leapt over an irrigation canal two feet across. "I've never seen anything like it." Shuman glanced around in terror. "Come on, we need to get back."

She wondered if Nukpana had followed her to get revenge for the curse she placed on him at Chaco. After she had transformed him into animal form with the ceremony, he hadn't been seen again, in human form or in enigmatic beast form. The curse had a stipulation that he couldn't get within fifty feet of another person or village without suffering. Had her malevolent ex-husband found a way around it years later?

Heavy breathing came from less than ten feet behind her. Footsteps thudded in pursuit, and low, deep-throated growling was occasionally interrupted by snarling. Though she couldn't see the beast, Tiponi knew they were leading it back to the village.

She made a split-second decision to lead the creature back through the fields. She pushed Shuman. "Get away from here." She ran alongside the canal and back into the cotton crops. It worked. Still in pursuit, she could hear what sounded like a deep, throaty voice.

"Get ready to die," it said.

She turned quickly to face her attacker. A six-foot-high creature that looked to be three hundred pounds stood before her. It had the body of a coyote with the *mouth and jaw of a javelina. Teeth were bared, dripping saliva, muscles taut and ready for attack, and claws out.*

Its shadow blocked out the moon.

Shuman called to her repeatedly from ten feet away. "Tiponi!"

The man-turned-beast glanced up at Shuman. It wanted both of them.

"No!" Tiponi screamed. "Not him."

It leapt at her.

Tawa's spirit waited. She could see him standing in the row of cotton next to her. Ironic. The day I finish the necklace, I am re-joined with the love of my life.

Tiponi placed her hand tightly around the chunk of petrified wood that had assisted Nukpana's punishment and kept the community in the Four Corners safe after his transformation.

The wood had been given to her by her father, passed down from generations of his family—a long ago relic from when deserts were swamps, marshes and forests and when much larger carnivores roamed the land.

The three-hundred-pound creature jumped on top of her. Tawa's spirit hand reached out for hers before the monster ripped her throat out with its two-inch fangs. Tawa's touch felt like a new beginning and his eyes welcomed her home.

Without a weapon to fight the monster, Shuman ran when the beast attacked her.

Tiponi's soul rose above her lifeless body. She looked down upon a feeding frenzy.

Nukpana raised his hairy head. His teeth dripped with her blood, his fur matted with her life. His body swayed from side-to-side and he emitted a horrifying howl before falling into a row of cotton plants.

Tawa took her hands in his. "Your strength. Your power. This is what killed Nukpana." He picked up the petrified object from Tiponi's inanimate form. "And this." He handed it back to her. "Not even you were aware when you mixed the recipe for transformation, your demise would be the death of Nukpana.

But Tiponi suddenly realized through a vision that Nukpana would eventually be brought back through a tall, beautiful woman with long black hair—Tiponi's future self. What form he would take, what powers he would possess, she didn't know. But after 1,000 years, Nukpana would be virtually unstoppable without the petrified wood.

49

Jacenda dropped on her knees, trying to catch her breath. Her whole body trembled. Seeing Nukpana's beast form had been a shock, and witnessing the death of Tiponi, her own past-life personality, would cause nightmares.

Jacenda had left Brandon at the Hovenweep Holly Group of ruins during the late afternoon. She wondered if he were still waiting. Her return to the present seemed to have left off from her past life, for the brilliant oranges and violet of twilight were rapidly being absorbed into the oncoming darkness.

A two-foot-long western diamondback rattlesnake slithered by in front of her and disappeared into a clump of grass. The words "Horseshoe House" kept coming into her mind, probably because of the unique ruin in front of her that had a square exterior with a circular inner masonry wall.

Scraping and moaning came from a small pueblo underneath a rock overhang within twenty feet of the Horseshoe House.

Jacenda stepped down into the once inhabited cave, littered with pottery sherds. A round mano and flat-surfaced metate, stone tools used for grinding corn, seeds and other foods, lay halfway between darkness and what remained of daylight. For a split second, she could see a woman spirit working vigorously, crushing corn with the mano.

Jacenda's hand tightened around the chunk of petrified wood in her jean pocket.

Cody sat completely still in the corner with a walking stick and a few empty bottles of water by his side. His eyes were closed. Jacenda slipped on some rocks but caught her footing. Cody hadn't moved.

Her breathing came in shallow spurts. Too terrified to move, Jacenda stared at him in shock, surprised to see him so defenseless. Could he be faking it to get her to come closer so he could attack her when she least expected it?

"He lied," Cody whispered.

Jacenda was surprised to hear him speak, while remaining so motionless and stoic.

"What do you mean?"

"Your lover. Tawa." Cody unfolded his hand and held up the jade pendant . "He lied about this." He had ripped apart the necklace. Turqoise and shell beads lay scattered over the ground.

She didn't understand how Cody could have such a close bond with his past—and with hers.

Anger and disgust overcame her fear when she saw the pendant. "He gave me that as a gift." Jacenda took two steps toward him. "Right before you and your friend murdered him."

Cody rolled his head back and forth against the cave wall. "This turtle was more than a gift. It supposedly has the ability to enhance one's talents. Tawa received it from another village."

Jacenda took a cautious step toward him. "Why would you need it to help your shapeshifting abilities? You've transformed into ravens, tarantulas and a giant eagle to try and take me."

Cody smiled. A malevolent grin that sent shivers down her spine. "For a while, I could stay in animal form. Or any other form I chose, for hours at a time. I started becoming weak right after you showed up." He attempted to stand up, but instead, slumped against the wall and slid to the ground.

"What, or who, made you into such a monster?"

Cody didn't reply. He closed his eyes and leaned his head back against the rock wall.

"If I had known the capabilities you held, and how they influenced my own, I would have killed you at Lowry Pueblo."

She looked around but didn't see any weapons Cody could use.

"How many women have you hidden out here in ruins and caves? Are there any still alive?"

He smiled. She realized Cody had no plans on telling her anything regarding his crime. He had lost his powers, but he still had the upper hand.

Something on Cody's lower ankle caught Jacenda's attention. She walked up to within a few feet of him and bent down.

"A snake bite," she whispered.

Cody didn't move or respond. And he barely breathed.

The wound was severely swollen and red. She winced and glanced away when pus oozed out of the necrotic tissue.

She would have to save Cody the way she rescued Stephanie. She grabbed the turtle pendant out of his hand and collected the loose beads from the necklace.

Staring at the small ruin in the middle of the twenty-foot-wide crevasse, Jacenda focused on the intensity of the energy to travel; on Joe, the helicopters and the agents who had been searching for Cody and the victims. But if they weren't in the vicinity of any ruins, Cody could die.

Part of her wanted him to perish in the middle of nowhere; to suffer like the women who were lucky enough to escape, the unlucky ones who died, and maybe the ones yet to be found.

But would that make her any better than Cody?

Energy emanated from the small pueblo in the cave, a reminder of her responsibilities.

"Okay, okay. I get it."

Jacenda stepped into the ruin, along with fear and trepidation. Tingling overtook her body and resplendent light preceded the journey.

Though she couldn't see Cody, she imagined him traveling with her. But could she trust him while trying to get him to safety? She hoped Joe would be at her final destination to take over. But without Cody's help, how were they going to find the other victims? And how would law enforcement be able to determine the number of women still out there?

Jacenda closed her eyes and took a deep breath, hoping and praying she would end up at a destination in the area—not stuck in some otherworldly portal, or with her body dispersed helplessly between sites. When she opened them, shapes roamed the ruins with flashlights. Joe wandered among the slickrock and into the ruins by Castle Rock. She was back at the trailhead.

A beam of light crossed past her. Then quickly came back.

"I found her," a woman's voice yelled.

Joe turned and ran toward Jacenda.

He gave her a hug. "Are you all right?"

Jacenda glanced around for Cody. "Yes. But Cody is supposed to be here. He was bit by a rattlesnake and is really sick. I tried to bring him with me, but I'm not sure it worked."

Two agents standing nearby went to look for Cody.

"Did he tell you if there were any other women out there?"

She shook her head no. "He's had to give up his shapeshifting abilities, so Cody's not about to give up the rest of his power. Maybe there aren't anymore victims."

"Shit. Joe, Brandon was waiting for me at the Holly House!"

Joe sighed. "I know." He wouldn't look at her.

"Joe, where is Brandon? You were the one who brought him to me at the Holly Group. He told me he would be waiting for me."

He placed his hands on her shoulders. "Brandon *was* waiting for you. I flew over the area after you left. He's gone. The basket and blanket were there. But we can't find him."

Jacenda collapsed on her knees. "Oh, no. I think Cody might have done this as a last stand. Brandon is the reincarnation of Tawa, my lover from the past during my marriage to Cody. This could be revenge. Cody knows I've weakened him."

He kneeled down to face her. "Relax. Go rest on the bench next to where Tony is standing." Joe waved to Tony, who came running over. "Let Jacenda here rest while we find her boyfriend and Cody."

"No," she said. "I have to go back to Holly." She stood up and jumped into the nearest ruin. Nothing happened.

"Your journey is over," Joe said.

Jacenda glanced around. She waited anxiously for news of Brandon and wondered if Cody would be found.

Joe's phone rang. He looked up at Jacenda as he listened.

"Great. I've got someone here who will be very happy to know you found him." He disconnected the call.

"Brandon's fine, though he has a slight sprain. He was wandering around the ruins while you were gone. Apparently, he slipped and fell into the canyon. He lost his cell phone, so couldn't contact anyone. The helicopter almost missed him, but they saw something rather unusual that caught their attention."

Jacenda stepped closer to Joe. "What do you mean?"

Joe handed his phone to Jacenda. The copter pilot thought he saw shadows moving around Brandon, so he took this photo.

Jacenda's jaw dropped. Hundreds of Native Americans seemed to be following Brandon. They were dressed exactly like those from her past life travels.

"Brandon may not have special abilities, but in this case, he had a whole bunch of guides to protect him."

They know who he is. They know he's Tawa.

"Jace!" Brandon ran to her, lifting her off the ground. "I just got here." He kissed her face repeatedly. "I got bored and wandered off. Found some loose rock and slipped."

Joe showed Brandon the photo the pilot had taken. "This might be part of the reason you keep hearing drums and chanting."

Jacenda pointed to the photo of the hundreds of ancient spirits. "The agents searching for you in the helicopter saw them surrounding you. They might have saved your life."

"I don't get it? I would think you'd be the one with such support."

"Brandon, I'm sure they know about your past as well and your ties to me. Speaking of which, we still haven't found Cody. What if he's played another trick on us? And how do we know there aren't other victims suffering alone out here?"

Joe removed a handkerchief from his back pocket and wiped his forehead. "There haven't been any additional reports of missing women."

Tony ran up to Joe. "We have agents scattered around the area to search for Cody, but we can't find him." Tony glanced at an officer scouring the ruins by Castle Rock. "We should keep a close eye on Jacenda, until we can find Cody—alive or dead."

"I have a feeling you're going to be extending your talents to other types of sacred sites," Joe said. "Mountain tops, sacred land. There are some pretty special places all over the world. Many are well-hidden or not yet revealed." Joe waved to two agents who were ten feet away. "Plus, the fact you were a shaman in your past life means there are skills, ceremonies, critical connections you have yet to remember."

Tony looked down at his cell phone. "The ruins near the farmhouse where Cody was hiding."

"What about it?" Joe asked. "We've had agents and law enforcement checking out there regularly, and the passage Cody's spider form came out of doesn't go very far in."

"We need to check again. I've had officers planted there continuously in case Cody showed back up. Activity has increased ten-fold, such as shadows, unintelligible conversations and strange light anomalies. The men are getting pretty freaked out."

"That doesn't sound like anything related to Cody. Have they noticed a pattern to all of the paranormal stuff?"

"Every time they go check the noises near the petroglyphs, there's another horizontal figure etched into the rock. We might have found a primary location for the race Lorelei's been so connected to."

Jacenda observed Joe and Brandon. They both stood with their mouths open, barely breathing.

Tony showed Joe something on his phone. "One of the agents took a picture. He noticed this in the middle of the back chamber where we saw the large spider, but he didn't see it until his last check during the height of the activity."

Jacenda leaned over to look at Tony's phone. It revealed the image of a large triangle.

"The triangle," Jacenda whispered. "I had a vision before I left Phoenix. Cody was sitting in the center of that cave, probably where the triangle is."

Joe stared intently at Tony's phone. "I wonder if this is really what Cody's been hiding. Not the ruins and not the chamber itself. Is he familiar with the powerful astral race?"

Jacenda slipped her jacket on. "Worse yet, could Cody be associated with the ancient race or with Galiena?"

50

J oe focused his flashlight on the rock art panel and traced his finger over one of the etched prone figures that had appeared mysteriously the evening before. There were at least ten more stick-like beings than he remembered. Someone, or something, had managed to incorporate additional symbols onto the cave wall under the close observation of the FBI.

Jacenda and Brandon stood next to him, staring at the ancient petroglyphs in awe.

The cavern had a much lighter atmosphere compared to when Joe infiltrated Cody's hideout only days before. They still hadn't found Cody's body. Joe hoped it wasn't another trick and that the torture and murder wouldn't continue.

Tony kneeled on the ground in the center of the dark chamber, swiping dirt away under the yellow caution tape to see if he could find the triangle. "Strange, I'm not seeing the shape from the photo, which appeared to be a solid, permanent shape. Not to mention, the lines between each point were exactly two feet long."

Brandon wandered the perimeter of the room, staring up at the ceiling. "From what I saw, the triangle looked more like a picture."

Joe turned to look at Tony, Jacenda and Brandon. "Have any of you seen or heard anything that would match up with what the officers were experiencing yesterday?"

"No," Jacenda and Brandon said at the same time.

Tony had stood up and circled the small section of ground where the triangle had been. "I haven't either, though I'm wondering if there's a link between all of the activity and the vanishing symbol."

Joe observed the small tunnel where Cody's tarantula form had come out of with trepidation. He could remember clearly the arachnid's eight eyes and the hissing that still sent shivers down his spine.

Tony noticed his discomfort. "Do you want me to go in first?"

"N– no." He glanced over at the young agent. "Let's see if we can find anything. And I hope it's not going to be a body of another victim. There are agents above us and in the ruins next door, so if we find a passage, I'll let them know so they can keep a close eye out."

Tony and Joe pointed their flashlights into the tight keyhole-shaped passage with the unusual round, bulbous formation.

Joe entered cautiously, working his way around the smooth, moisture-formed statue of time. He stopped and listened. The only sound was his own quick breathing.

Tony kept a watch on Jacenda and Brandon while Joe crept further in. The seven-foot-high entrance had gradually lowered so that he had to lean down. The passage seemed to end twenty feet in with two large boulders blocking the way.

"Are you okay?" Tony shouted.

"Yeah. I'm not that far in and there's nowhere else to go, but it looks like some rocks have collapsed. Maybe another passage got blocked."

Joe ran his hand along the cool rock for any sign of an object that might act as a switch. Various human shadows had been seen penetrating the tunnel, and with the discovery of the Caves of the Watchers near Wickenburg, Arizona and the caves and tunnels under the ranch in Southeast Arizona, Joe knew there could easily be more hidden clues in the Four Corners.

"Tony, stand where the triangle revealed itself," Joe called. "I want to see what happens."

"Just a sec."

Joe waited for Tony to position himself.

"I'm in the center of the marked-off area," Tony said.

"Damn it, nothing." Joe pounded his fist against the wall and glanced up in frustration to see what looked like a baseball-sized hole a foot above his head. His blood pumping, he spotlighted the opening. Something flew inside the hole—insect, bat or otherwise, he couldn't tell.

Could that be another chamber? If so, how the hell are we supposed to get up there?

Joe raced back to the entrance of the tunnel and waved to Jacenda, Brandon and Tony. "I found an access point to what seems to be another passage."

Jacenda and Brandon walked in first with Tony behind.

Joe pointed to the tunnel above. "Not sure how to get up there, but looks like something to investigate."

"Keep an eye on that opening. I'm going back to where the triangle was spotted." Tony hurried back out of the passage.

Joe held his breath, anxiously waiting for the revelation of a mysterious staircase or pathway. Perhaps it didn't lead anywhere, but Joe had a feeling something big awaited in the shaft above.

Footsteps echoed in the narrow space, preceding Tony's appearance.

"Did anything happen?" Tony asked.

"No," Jacenda stared into a dark, recessed corner next to where Joe stood.

He used his flashlight to see what she was focusing on. Joe saw her remove the turtle pendant from her jacket pocket, gripping it tightly in her palm. He noticed an alcove six feet above the ground. An indentation was in the center of the small niche— in the shape of a turtle.

"Unbelievable. Looks like your artistry from the prehistoric past might have something to do with the astral race Lorelei discovered." Joe moved aside so Jacenda could place the pendant into the niche.

He could see her handle tremble as she pushed it gently into the form.

It fit perfectly, yet nothing happened.

Joe's heart sank. "Maybe this isn't the key to the passage above, though it does appear to be some sort of altar."

Tony looked at Jacenda. "Can I have the pendant?"

She glanced at Brandon and Joe before giving Tony the piece of jewelry. Rumbling echoed throughout the tight chamber and rocks fell from the ceiling after he inserted it into its tiny alcove.

"Get out!" Joe started to push them all toward the main cave.

"Wait." Tony grabbed Joe's arm. A crevasse had begun to form, splitting the altar in half. The crack became a doorway three-feet-wide. Instead of another tunnel, a series of stone steps led up to the corridor above.

Joe observed Tony. He noticed Jacenda stared at the striking FBI agent as well. Due to her past bond with the necklace, she had thought she would be the way in.

Tony glanced at them both and shrugged.

Why was Tony able to use the pendant to access the unknown?

"Something must be back here." Tony started up the very narrow stairwell, the beam of his flashlight bouncing off the rock walls. This could be why Cody took the pendant from Jacenda."

Joe motioned for Jacenda and Brandon to follow Tony.

"Wait." Jacenda sifted through the remains of the altar. "Where's the pendant?"

Brandon took Joe's flashlight, using it to search for the valuable artifact, but the jade turtle was lost.

"Sorry, honey."

Joe placed his hand on her shoulder. "We'd better go. Not sure how safe it is to remain here after that shift in the cave wall."

Jacenda stared forlornly at the spot where Tony had placed the pendant.

Joe smiled at her. "I wouldn't be surprised if it turns up again."

Tony continued up the narrow stairwell, followed by Jacenda, Brandon and Joe.

Joe scanned the passage walls for petroglyphs similar to the rock art in Cody's hideout. The FBI continued to search for Cody, or his body.

Tony stopped, glancing back at Joe. "We've hit a tunnel, must be the one we saw from below. I'll go in a ways to check it out."

Jacenda and Brandon waited at the top while Joe made his way up the remaining stairs.

The hair on his arms and neck stood up and he could barely breathe. They weren't alone. He struggled between finding Tony or staying with Jacenda and Brandon.

Joe passed Brandon and Jacenda on the stairs and held up his gun, pointing it in the direction Tony went. "Let's go. I want to make sure Tony is okay. Stay close."

Brandon looked around nervously and put his arm around Jacenda. "Lore's going to be jealous she couldn't come with us."

The floor of the passage ascended gradually for approximately thirty feet before leveling off slightly and coming to an abrupt end. Joe nearly fell off the edge.

"Oh, no. Tony," Jacenda said.

He and Brandon scanned the darkness with their flashlights.

Joe breathed a sigh of relief. Tony stood below waving his arms.

"Get down here," Tony shouted. "You're not going to believe this." He pointed to the way down.

Joe leaned over the edge. A wooden ladder, set against the wall, descended about twenty feet to the bottom. He glanced at Brandon. "You and Jace might want to head back."

"No way," Jacenda said. "I'm anxious to see what's down there."

"It's safe," Tony said. "Didn't move when I climbed down."

Brandon placed his hands on her shoulders. "You're terrified of heights."

"Yes, but at least it's dark enough to where I can't see where I'm going."

"You both should go down first," Joe said. "I'll make sure it's safe up here."

Brandon stepped over the ledge and onto the first rung. "I'll go down a bit and wait for you."

He climbed down halfway before Jacenda took her turn. Joe could see her legs shaking as she descended, but she didn't stop. As they jumped off the last rung, Joe threw his leg over onto the first step. A white mist formed in the tunnel in front of him. Multi-colored flashes of blue, purple and yellow alternated throughout its shape.

He didn't feel threatened, but felt it was sizing him up. As he climbed down the ladder, the being moved closer to the edge and watched. The entity continued to observe Joe until he stepped off the ladder. Joe turned around to ask the others if they had seen the bizarre phantom, but the scene before him took his breath away.

A meandering river ran through the center of a giant, well-lit cavern, big enough for a semi to drive through. The temperature seemed to be a comfortable seventy-five degrees. Various trees and palm fronds lined either side of the water—species Joe had never seen before. He walked along the stream, touching the brilliant royal blue bud from the top of a plant that looked similar to a mini-palm tree. As he watched, the flower, silky to the touch, unfolded to reveal a collage of bright yellow stems with small round bulbs at the top.

Jacenda and Brandon roamed their way along the opposite side of the stream, gazing in awe upon a massive tree that looked similar to a redwood. A round hole went all the way through the ten-foot-thick trunk, where another form of plant life grew.

"Where did Tony go?" Joe asked.

Brandon kneeled down, peeking through the gap at the bottom of the tree. "Jace and I saw him wander further downstream."

"Try not to touch anything." Joe thought about the plant he had just come in contact with. He glanced at his hand nervously, which appeared to be unharmed. He hoped there would be no side effects from the brief contact with the radiant flower. "Looks harmless, but we have no idea what species we're dealing with. Not to mention Cody might have picked up his abilities from here."

Joe jumped across a narrow part of the stream to meet up with Jacenda and Brandon. "Let's stay together while we search for Tony."

"Such strange vegetation," Jacenda said. "I've never seen plants or trees like this before, let alone in the Four Corners."

Joe removed his phone from his pocket and attempted to call Tony, but there was no service.

Brandon lifted his head and stared downstream. "Do either of you hear that? Sounds like rushing water."

Joe did hear it. They were getting closer to the source. He looked ahead and noticed Tony standing amidst a clump of palm fronds with his back to Joe.

Tony whispered without turning around. "An underground paradise. This beats anything I've ever seen."

Brandon and Jacenda approached Tony on one side, while Joe stood on the other. They were standing on top of a waterfall about fifty feet high. The roaring water plunged into a clear, crystal blue lake surrounded by a series of stone monoliths—exactly like those the team had discovered in Southeast Arizona. Five spectacular obelisks lined either side of the lake, which looked to be the size of at least two football fields. A much bigger column of rock erupted from the center of the water.

Jacenda jumped away from the edge. "Whoa, that's pretty far down."

Brandon stared out at the picturesque landscape. "I can't believe this place. It's heaven on earth. I wouldn't be surprised if Cody did know about this underground utopia. Maybe he remembered this place from his past life."

A shiver went down Joe's spine. They had all thought the Caves of the Watchers, near Wickenburg, Arizona, was awe-inspiring with its labyrinth of passages, lifelike pictograph eyes and a tunnel representing the near-death experience. Joe sensed these caves were the mother lode. "The monument in the middle is nearly the height of this waterfall," Joe said. "The ones in Dragoon didn't come close to that."

Joe glanced around for a way to get to the lake and the sacred shrines of stone. He couldn't see a trail or way down.

Tony stared at the waterfall intently. He bent down and attempted to touch the raging water as it poured over the edge.

Joe's heart stopped, worried Tony would plunge to his death. He grabbed him and pulled him away from the falls.

Tony glanced from Joe to Brandon and Jacenda. "There is a way to the bottom, but we have to make it through the waterfall."

"What? That's insane. We'd be killed," Brandon said.

"No. You have to trust me. This isn't a true waterfall." Tony placed his hand into the stream. It shimmered in a rainbow of colors.

Joe dipped his fingers into the water. When he pulled them out, they were dry.

Joe placed his hand on Tony's shoulder. "Is there something you haven't been telling me? You were the only one who could open the doorway to this place. And now you know about a false waterfall?"

The young agent didn't seem to hear. He stared into the lake fifty feet below, as if seeing something Joe couldn't.

"Not again," Jacenda said. "I'm not sure I can climb down from this height."

"The worst part will be the first few steps. We will be walking down behind the falls, so you won't be able to see how high you are while you're descending."

"How do you know what it's like?" Brandon asked.

Tony glanced at Brandon before stepping into the faux waterfall. Joe couldn't see Tony for a few seconds, until he reached up through the water, which ceased flowing for a split second. Tony stood at one of the first stairs of a vertical descent.

"I saw how steep that was," Jacenda said. "If any of us falls…"

Brandon looked at Joe. "Maybe Jace and I should wait here."

"Not with the possibility that Cody might be alive." Joe took Jacenda's hand. Hers trembled so badly, he hoped she didn't feel his shaking. "We'll go together. Don't look down, just out at the top of the largest monolith."

"No," Tony shouted. "It's too narrow in here. You can't come together or one of you will fall."

Jacenda backed away from Joe and the cliff. "I can't do this. You all go ahead. I'll head back to the ruins and wait."

"There's no way you're going alone," Brandon said.

Joe watched the tallest of the stone structures intently. The atmosphere in the cavern of Eden had changed. The temperature became much cooler. The hairs on his arms stood on end and a sense of urgency overwhelmed him. "I'll go first. Tony and I will help you and Brandon." He took a deep breath and stepped down through the realistic-looking waterfall. He slipped but felt a hand grab his arm. The light from the cave penetrated the falls so he could see the narrow steps that led below at a sharp incline.

"We're going to have to take this very slow," Joe said. He stood up and started to reach through the faux fall when the water stopped. He could see out to the monoliths and lake below, only the once-brilliant blue lake held no water. Joe wondered if the cavern, and everything in it, really existed. If not, what would happen to the four of them if their environment ceased to exist?

Tony stumbled backwards and started to slide down the steep steps when the waterfall disappeared. He turned sideways and grabbed onto one of the stairs to avoid plummeting to his death. A deep sigh of relief escaped from his lips. Without the waterfall, the distance to the bottom felt much more intimidating.

"Are you okay?" Joe asked.

Tony slowly stood up and cautiously took two more steps down. "I'm fine. I don't feel any injuries."

"There's no way I can make it down those stairs," Jacenda said.

Tony knew Brandon wouldn't leave Jacenda. And he and Joe couldn't leave either of them alone in what used to be Cody's territory. Could the abductor have survived his ordeal with the snakebite and be hiding among the exotic, lush surroundings?

Tony wondered if he had he found the pendant for a reason. Was he as tied to its history as Jacenda?

He noticed Joe standing firmly on the stairs, his legs trembling. As Tony's mentor, Joe tried to seem brave and unaffected by the wide open view.

Joe stared at the dry lakebed. Tony realized it wasn't the now-waterless lake he observed, but the stairs that were rapidly disappearing from the bottom up.

Something didn't want them to find their way to the monoliths.

"Let's go," Joe shouted.

Tony attempted to leap up the few steps behind Joe to the top. He glanced back to see more than half the steps were gone. He thought he would have plenty of time to make it up the four small steps.

Are the stairs really missing or just invisible?

He only had two steps to go, which vanished in a split second from under his feet.

Joe reached for him, but too late.

"No!" Tony flailed his arms and legs as he fell. Halfway down, an unexpected calmness overcame him and his life flashed before his eyes—ceremonies, pow wows, his first love in high school, training in the Police Academy and acceptance into the FBI.

His heart stopped. The lakebed waited directly below. Would this be the end? He held his breath as the ground gazed up hungrily. He expected to feel the excruciating pain as fragile bone met hard earth, praying his death would be quick. Instead, Tony landed face first into a soft, spongy surface that absorbed the impact of the fall. His body sunk a short distance under the prodigious terrain before lifting him back up again.

He lay face down as he had landed, breathing in short spurts. Tony heard his name being called from far above. Could it be his guardian angels or angels from heaven to greet him? Afraid to move, he merely smelled the earthy scent under his nose. Should he attempt to get up? Was he really alive? Moving his hands cautiously from his sides, Tony placed them on the malleable landscape. He pushed up with his arms and pulled his legs forward. He slowly stood up among the lily-pad-like plants with long stems, his whole body trembling. He reached for something to hold onto when his feet started to sink. The earth covered his lower leg and stopped. Tony walked around in the strange muck for a minute and breathed a sigh of relief when he realized he had escaped with no injury.

Is this a miracle or a product of this remarkable cave system?

The voices he heard from above were those of his friends. They stared down at him in amazement.

"Are you okay?" Joe yelled.

Tony could only nod, still in shock. He glanced around at the ten, Stonehenge-like rock towers around the edge of the lake. He backed into a solid object and turned to see the fifty-foot-tall monument in the center. He walked the perimeter of the monolith, pushing his legs through the boggy-like substance.

Placing his hand against the smooth, slightly pitted surface of stone, a prominent vibration ran down his arm. His eyes scanned from the top to the bottom. A brilliant splash of color showed on the obelisk at the level of his lower leg. Tony pushed the soft material in the lakebed aside to reveal a set of blue eyes so lifelike he could see a glint of light in the irises. Joe had mentioned such paintings in the Caves of the Watchers. More than mere pictographs, the images turned out to be actual entities, watching everyone who entered the territory of the ancient race of astral travelers.

He felt the other rock structures, less than half the size of the main pillar, were watching him carefully. The temperature in the cave had increased from what seemed like a cooler seventy-five to at least ninety degrees. Tony wiped the sweat from his forehead with his arm. He backed away from the intimidating tower, but the heat continued to climb.

He glanced up to the top of the waterfall. Joe, Jacenda and Brandon were gone. He realized they would be looking for a way to get to him.

Brilliant emerald light beams appeared between each of the ten towers, creating a circle. He turned to see those same radiant beams emanating from the central tower and extending to each of the others. The circle transformed into the spoke of a wheel.

The monolith directly across from the center pillar had a powerful energy all its own. It looked no different than the others, but an air of familiarity stemmed from its surface.

Tony crept closer to the stone totem. There was something almost human about it. He touched the monument and experienced a shifting from within. Yet the exterior felt like solid rock.

For a few seconds, the human-like pillar in front of him became translucent. A face showed through of a man he hadn't seen in more than thirty years—his biological father.

51

Jacenda's heart leapt to her throat as she watched Tony fall the fifty feet to the bottom and land face down. Fear and panic overcame her when she remembered her own fall at Petrified Forest only days before.

Jacenda, Brandon and Joe had screamed Tony's name repeatedly. At first, he didn't respond. After thirty seconds, Tony started to move and slowly got up. He stared down at his body in shock.

She breathed a sigh of relief. Jacenda could have sworn she saw him sink into the ground and bounce back up. If so, what was in the lakebed?

Joe glanced around the tropical paradise of the massive cavern. "We have to find a way to get to him."

Jacenda looked out over the cliff. "All I see is a straight drop."

"The passages we came in on kept going past the entrance to this place. Maybe there's another way in," Brandon said.

"Let's go." Joe waved them back in the direction of the ladder.

Coming down the ladder was bad enough. Can I go back up?

Brandon grabbed her hand and squeezed it.

"Tony, we're coming," Joe yelled.

Tony didn't seem to hear. He walked around the central monolith in a daze.

Joe started to ascend the steps. He stopped and stared at something to the right.

Following his gaze, Jacenda noticed a small chamber about four-feet-tall.

Joe removed his flashlight from his pocket and infiltrated the darkness. "This passage is pretty small, but it's closer to Tony than the passage we came in. Not to mention, my intuition is telling me it's the right place." He stared at the opening in hesitation.

"I'll go in first to see if it leads anywhere. I'll be right back." Joe got on his knees and disappeared into the darkness.

Less than five minutes later, Joe crawled out of the tight space. "This looks like it could lead to the bottom. It gradually descends."

Jacenda sighed. She didn't like the idea of being enclosed much more than heights, but she didn't have a choice. She couldn't go back alone and wouldn't want to take Brandon and leave Joe. "Well, let's get going. We can't leave Tony by himself, especially after what he just went through."

Joe crawled into the passage first. The opening couldn't have been more than five-feet-wide.

She bent down inside the cool recess and realized she would have to creep along on her arms and knees. Joe's grunts indicated he was as uncomfortable. His bulk made it hard to maneuver, so he had to bend down lower than was natural for a human. She knew Brandon would have the same problem.

They had crawled twenty feet in when the ground began to slope down.

"I hope we don't have to do this for long."

"Damn!" Joe yelled.

"Joe, are you okay?" Jacenda saw Joe's hand go to his head.

"I hit my head on the ceiling, but I'm okay." Joe pointed his flashlight into the depths of the tunnel. "Looks like there's a bend up ahead."

The floor of the passage kept sloping down. They came to a sharp, rounded corner.

She heard Joe mutter a series of expletives as he attempted to manipulate his body past the corner.

"This place reminds me of ant tunnels," Brandon said breathlessly. "The confined, low ceilings and twists."

"This definitely is unlike any other tunnels associated with the ancients," Joe said.

They made their way further down and around three more bends. Jacenda had no idea where they were going.

She sweated from the effort of crawling, her back ached and her arms and knees felt scratched from the uneven surface. She couldn't even imagine the discomfort Joe and Brandon were feeling.

A few minutes later, Joe stopped suddenly and Jacenda's face ended up within inches of Joe's butt. She blushed and backed up quickly.

"What did you stop for?" she asked.

"This tiny pathway has ended." Joe used his flashlight to check out something to the side. "But there's a large room next to us."

Flashes of light came from a cavern to the left of the passage. Jacenda and Brandon crawled after Joe into the chamber. They stood up immediately and stretched.

The intermittent radiance in the room reminded Jacenda of heat lightning. The chamber wasn't nearly as big as the waterfall cavern. The ceiling was covered with what looked like thousands of shining stars and a distinct white streak that resembled the Milky Way. She also recognized the constellation Scorpius.

"Where the hell are those flashes coming from?" Brandon stared up at the ceiling."

Joe took a deep breath. "Have either of you noticed the smell? Like a thunderstorm."

"Not to mention the static electricity." Jacenda pointed to Brandon's dark hair, which stood straight up on his head. She patted the top of her own head. "I can feel mine doing the same thing."

"Interesting," Joe said. "We've discovered an underground utopia and a cavern that can recreate a thunderstorm. Except, where's the rain?"

As soon as Joe finished his sentence, a clap of thunder echoed so loudly throughout the cave, they had to cover their ears. Sizable drops of rain pounded Jacenda's head and arms.

Within seconds, the occasional drops turned to a downpour with pea-sized hail and gale-force winds. She attempted to cover herself with her arms.

That's not going to work.

The forceful winds whipped her long black hair across her face and threatened to blow her across the room. Barely able to breathe, she grabbed onto Brandon and they held each other tightly as the elements continued their persecution.

Jacenda, Brandon and Joe looked around for a place inside the cavern to hide.

Joe pointed to the direction of the passages they had crawled through. He leaned down to search for the exit. Jacenda knew it would be hard to find with the blinding rain.

Jacenda's jeans, top and jacket were soaked, sticking to her body and making movement harder. A frigid chill seeped through to her skin. She trembled uncontrollably, her muscles tightening.

Joe grabbed her and Brandon's arms and guided them to the other side of the cave.

She couldn't see any passages or way to escape the harsh weather.

Is it possible to be murdered by Mother Nature?

Just when she thought she couldn't take anymore, the storm stopped. Jacenda's teeth chattered and she wrapped her arms as tightly around herself as she could. Brandon pulled her close, rubbing her shoulders, but it didn't help the biting cold.

"Where did all that come from?" Joe walked over to a wall, running his finger down the surface. "There's no moisture."

The chill melted away as warmth began to spread through her arms and chest, down to her legs...like the intensity of the afternoon sun.

Relief washed over them as the temperature increased. Jacenda wondered if the same weather had occurred in the waterfall cave.

Brandon walked over to where they had entered the chamber. "It's not here. I can't find the opening to the passage."

Jacenda noticed a solid stone wall covered the section where the small gap had been. "So we're trapped?"

"Joe stared at something to the back of the cave. "Are you both seeing what I am?"

A rainbow appeared, arching over and highlighting another petroglyph panel. Light rays of pink, purple, blue and yellow gradually turned brilliant—much brighter than any rainbow she had ever seen. She inserted her hand into the lower arch of the rainbow. The sensation felt thick, similar to fog.

As she stood under the unnatural prism, Jacenda focused on the rock art; a carved image that looked like the constellation Orion. A triangle representing the shoulders of the mythical hunter were appended to an hourglass shape, which was the upper body. Miniature pueblos were painted at each of the points where the lines intersected.

Jacenda's eyes followed a crevasse next to the petroglyph panel to the ceiling. Her jaw dropped when she saw the same depiction. Only instead of pictures of ancient pueblos, there were brightly illustrated stars. She touched Joe's arm and pointed upward.

"Wait," Joe said. "There's a myth that the constellation Orion provides the template by which the ancestral Puebloan determined the locations of their villages. The "terrestrial Orion" supposedly mirrors its celestial counterpart, with prehistoric sites corresponding to all the major stars in the constellation."

"Are you saying the representation on the roof is the heavenly Orion and the panel in the center of the rainbow is the earthly version?" Brandon asked.

Joe observed the rock art in front of him, then the replica above. "Not sure, just a guess. But the map on the ceiling does show actual stars. Some of the ancient places that match to the heavenly Orion include the three Hopi mesas, which would be the belt of Orion, as well as Chaco Canyon, Walnut Canyon, Sunset Crater Wupatki National Monument and Canyon De Chelly."

Brandon used his flashlight to get a better view of the map on the ceiling. "Knowing this unusual race associated with Galiena, I wouldn't doubt if they can travel to these places through this map."

Jacenda watched the rainbow, which had started to fade. "I was thinking the same thing." She stared at the images of pueblos on the map of the earthly Orion and lightly touched one of the pictures on the shoulder of the great hunter.

"What the hell?"

She followed Brandon and Joe's gaze to the roof. An image overlay the pictograph stars and celestial version of Orion. Sharp volcanic rock, cinder cones and dramatic Indian ruins formed under a cloudy sky—a distinct picture of Sunset Crater Wupatki National Monument near Flagstaff.

Joe placed his finger on the small drawing at the top of the constellation. The roof switched images to reveal cliff dwellings among limestone alcoves.

"Walnut Canyon," Joe whispered.

"Why would such a race need this map to get to these sites?" Jacenda asked. "Especially if they are masters at astral travel?"

"I'm not sure they would." Joe observed the earthly version of Orion before looking back up at the surreal image of Walnut Canyon. "This could represent other subterranean locations associated with Galiena's race."

Jacenda couldn't stop staring at the stars on the ceiling. They seemed to twinkle. For a split second, she thought she saw a shooting star.

I must be seeing things.

"I wonder how much of this underground realm Cody knew about?" Brandon asked.

"That makes two reasons he'd want the pendant," Joe said. "To enhance his abilities and access another world."

"Cody mentioned the pendant wasn't helping him," Jacenda said. "Though that could be because I'm here weakening his powers."

Jacenda tried not to think about the reason for Cody's dramatic transition from a normal life to a malevolent shapeshifter. She wondered if her prehistoric curse had somehow initiated his rampage. She trembled thinking that her curse, which had stopped him from killing in a past life, led to the kidnapping and murder of innocent women in his present life.

Scraping and shuffling came from above. Whatever made the noise sounded large.

I hope whatever is up there can't make its way into this place.

She put her arm around Brandon and he pulled her close. All three of them looked nervously up toward the strange sounds. Could it be Cody? Had he turned himself into another large animal or beast, stalking and torturing them? Jacenda wished she were safe at home in Phoenix, curled up with a good book or with Brandon. She had had enough.

"How are we supposed to get out of here?" Brandon asked. "Don't tell me the Orion map is the key to our escape."

The scraping noise had moved to the other side of the wall from the petroglyph. The sound stopped for about thirty seconds. Joe slowly removed his gun from its holster.

Jacenda gasped when a tarantula a few inches across appeared at her feet. She couldn't tell whether it was her imagination or the effect of Joe's flashlight crossing the cave, but the arachnid seemed to be growing. Her focus on the tarantula caught the attention of Brandon and Joe. It had increased from the size of a baseball to a serving platter within seconds.

They stepped back as it continued to enlarge.

"Cody," Jacenda said. She glanced around for a way out.

Brandon pushed her behind him. "Joe, is this what you saw in Cody's hideout?"

"Yes, only it was already full height."

Multi-colored balls of light collected and surrounded the creature as it grew to within a few feet of the ceiling.

"I saw these same light anomalies with this thing a few days ago. I thought they were attempting to protect me and Tony from Cody."

"Maybe that's what's happening now," Brandon said. "This has to be Cody."

Jacenda stared over Brandon's shoulder. Something told her they had nothing to fear. The creature bent its hairy legs so that Jacenda, Brandon and Joe could look into its eight, dark beady spheres. An image of Joe and Tony in the cavern days before revealed itself in the giant spider's eyes. Within the arachnid's eyes, a thick, blob-like being eight-feet-tall towered over Tony and Joe from behind, which looked as if it could have absorbed both of them at the same time. The blob vanished into thin air when it saw the tarantula. Tony and Joe never knew of the threat.

"Holy crap." Jacenda was mesmerized by the scene playing out on the bizarre screen. "The tarantula wasn't Cody. This being *saved* you from Cody."

52

ony stepped closer to the obelisk, reaching out to the father who had abandoned him so long ago. Though his father looked helpless, locked inside the stone tower, he appeared calm and comfortable.

"Dad," he whispered. "Is it really you?"

Tony placed his hands on the granite monolith. He didn't know a way to get him out of his prison.

His father smiled. In that pleasant, caring smile, Tony suddenly understood why he had been able to access the series of passages with the jade pendant and why he had been drawn to dig in the spot at Lowry Pueblo. He created the pendant and had sensed his prized past beneath his feet.

Tony could feel someone, or something, standing behind him. He turned around to see a tarantula the size of a two-story home looking down from the top of the waterfall. He stumbled backward, falling into the network of entangling plants around him.

Tony hoped and prayed it didn't mean harm, for he had nowhere to run from something that large. Could it be the same creature that had threatened Joe and him?

Spheres of light danced around the tarantula. Purple, blue and yellow streaks bounced off the spider's back—similar to the scene at Cody's hideout. Only this time, the arachnid didn't seem as threatening.

He yanked his hands from the growth of greenery in the dry lakebed. His arms wore the foot long, thick stems like bracelets.

Tony glanced up to see the massive arachnid had disappeared. *Where the hell could it have gone?*

A shiver went down his spine. Afraid to move, Tony couldn't resist the urge to turn back in the direction of his father. The tarantula waited fifteen feet away, behind his father's obelisk.

The fifty-foot-tall pillar began to hum.

He glanced at the towering, imposing spider. He tried to look away, but couldn't. Its curved fangs made him want to run screaming. As if hearing Tony's thoughts, the tarantula somehow retracted the tool used to devour its prey.

The arachnid bent its hairy knees. Tony could see the symbol of the colorful eye from the obelisk within its eight orbs. Seconds later, another scene started from the depths of its cryptic gaze.

A nice-looking man with short dark brown hair ran his hand over a brilliant-colored pictograph. A smile began at the corner of the stranger's mouth. The reaction wasn't from excitement. Tony sensed malevolence. The scene drew back to reveal the man's whole body and part of the chamber. The person lifted a saw from the ground, placing it against the edge of a familiar image—a much larger version of the eye that he found on the central tower.

Tony's heart stopped when he understood the man;s intent to steal the enigmatic pictograph of the ancient astral race. The disturbing buzz of the saw made Tony cringe. The tarantula seemed to react in the same manner when it raised its front legs and backed away a few feet.

Sparks flew when the serrated blade hit the rock. The saw bounced off the cave wall and flew across the chamber. The man trying to steal the rock art had vanished into thin air.

Tony recalled the pictures of Cody before his transformation. The spider had showed him the recent past. The man who attempted to steal the mystical rock art of the highly spiritual ancient race was Cody.

Another movie played out in the tarantula's eyes, involving Cody in the midst of a spinning vortex. He struggled to remain upright while grabbing for something solid. A minute later, the dizzying movement stopped. Cody stood in a passage with a resplendent light at the end.

"Joe told me about a tunnel that recreated the near-death experience in the Caves of the Watchers," Tony whispered. "Lorelei, Ian and Shannon had an experience there."

The tarantula moved its head up and down slightly, as if confirming Tony's statement.

The scene continued to unfold, and Tony watched, mesmerized. He could only see Cody's back as he stared into the light, unmoving. When Cody turned around, he looked like the kidnapper and murderer they knew him to be, with burn scars, shaggy hair and a steely, penetrating gaze.

They had all wondered what had turned Cody into such a heartless human being. From what Tony had just seen, Cody already had the makings of an uncaring person. The unorthodox passage deep under the desert somehow brought his prehistoric past to the surface.

"Was that your intention?" Tony stepped closer to the tarantula. "Did you know imprisoning him in the tunnel would lead to the torture of innocent women?"

"No."

A voice behind Tony made him jump.

A young man who looked to be in his twenties stood in front of the tallest monolith. His thick, dark mane hung to the left. The right side of his head had been shaved and tinted a royal blue.

The gothic appearance gave the stranger away based on descriptions from Joe, Lorelei and Ian. "Dagon. I've been hearing so much about you, Galiena and the others."

Tony didn't know if it Dagon's unorthodox presence or the fact that, like the spider, he seemed to come out of nowhere, but Dagon had a formidable air. He may have been thin and of average height, but Tony got the impression this guardian of the caves could be a rather dangerous being if crossed.

"Cody should never have found such a sacred spot as the Caves of the Watchers," Dagon said. "He dug his way in, destroying part of the ceiling with the solar system as he rappelled into the cavern. That passage doesn't just recreate the near-death experience. We had hoped it would be a harmless way to teach him a lesson."

Dagon closed his eyes and took in a deep breath. Could he be feeling guilty for Cody's unexpected transformation?

Dagon glanced over at the arachnid. "Unfortunately, the tunnel brought his past to the surface. This event occurred days before the investigation of the house in Florence. Jacenda's connection with the haunted home could have helped strengthen Cody's murderous, shapeshifting side. She never turned him into a shapeshifter, but he somehow twisted those memories and became something more powerful and threatening."

"What is my father doing here? And where are Joe, Jacenda and Brandon."

Dagon's dark gaze penetrated through Tony, leaving him feeling exposed.

"Didn't you question why you were the one able to access such hallowed ground?"

Tony glanced behind him. The tarantula had left.

How can such a massive creature come and go so silently?

Tony did a 360-degree turn, watching the area around the pillars and the cavern above. When he faced Dagon again, the young man stood within a few inches of Tony's face.

Tony had almost forgotten about his father, who still stood serenely inside the pillar, his head bowed in prayer. Tony stared at him in disbelief.

"For some reason, when I first saw my father, a voice inside my head told me *I* made the jade pendant. That's when I realized why I was the one to find it at Lowry Pueblo."

Dagon walked over to the monument Tony's father stood in. He knelt on the ground and bowed his head before turning back to Tony.

"Tawa, or Brandon, gifted the pendant to Tiponi, Jacenda in a past life. A gift he bartered from you. You endowed that piece with the ability to enhance one's talents, especially for those who are only beginning to understand their skills. The pendant helps to open the third eye, which opens the mind to wisdom, insight and awareness. An exceptionally strong third eye can help with clairvoyance and telepathy."

"Jacenda, Joe, Mandy, Lorelei and Ian," Dagon continued. "They have certain abilities, but they also have strong ties to each other, relationships from the past and you are no exception."

Tony waited anxiously. *Joe, it has to be Joe.*

Dagon shook his head no, having heard Tony's wish.

"Jacenda, rather Tiponi, is your sister. You molded the turtle pendant and gave it your special touch, though you had no idea it would end up in the hands of your long lost sister."

"But she never mentioned a brother, only Cody and Tawa."

"Past memories can take years to surface. You and Jacenda were separated during a raid on your village when you were both very young. She hasn't accessed that part yet."

Tony remembered the encounter with Jacenda at Castle Rock. After she had vanished into the ruins, he had yelled 'where are you?' Dagon mentioned a tragic separation—the pieces were beginning to fit.

Dagon and his father both smiled.

"Why would I endow a piece of jewelry with such power only to barter it away?"

"Tawa requested it. He traveled many miles to the Painted Desert where you lived."

Tony felt overwhelmed. Cody, the new world they'd found, his father, Dagon and now his prehistoric link to Jacenda…he sensed the influx of shocking news wasn't over.

"You never answered my question about my father. And where are my friends?"

Tony could only stare at the man who had left him with total strangers when he was only five. He struggled with curiosity, anger, and resentment. He had so many questions, but the words wouldn't come out.

He tried to force the memories back, but they invaded his mind like a flood. His parents never mentioned where they were taking him. They drove him from Window Rock, Arizona to Gallup, New Mexico, to a small log cabin in the midst of a wide open desert landscape. His mother helped him out of the Buick. He could hear children playing in the backyard and noticed three turkey vultures circling over the cabin. As he walked by a tall saguaro with three thick arms, the voices started again, like they always did when he was surrounded by nature.

His mother kept sniffing and wiping her eyes as she walked him to the door. Tony glanced back to see his father sitting in the driver's seat of the Buick—staring straight at the road ahead.

Tony's voice choked while he watched his father. "Is it really you?"

He thought he saw a glint of a tear form in his father's eye.

"Your parents couldn't handle you because of your talents. Tony, you're a hybrid—part human, but a stronger part is star seed—sort of like Galiena. Your father was much like Galiena. Almost to her level, in fact. For some reason, he chose to come to earth when he was only twenty and like Galiena, forgot his true identity."

"So, I'm part alien?"

"No," Dagon said. "Galiena and her kind are unlike all others in that they are a part of space itself. They can be living beings with skin, tissue and organs, as was Shannon. But normally they are one with the stars, celestial bodies and the Milky Way, which is why Lorelei and Joe saw Galiena as a fiery entity sort of hanging in the heavens during their astral journeys."

Tony threw up his hands. "This is all too much. I haven't seen this man in thirty years and he shows up here." He looked at the tall pillars and up at the cavern above. "Now I'm being told I'm the son of someone who is similar to Galiena?"

Tony didn't think the man before him looked like a supreme being. He thought he looked like a coward.

Dagon gazed around at the tropical environment. "The underworld you've made your way back to has been waiting for your return. You were reborn here. They found you and brought you here to enhance your own abilities a few years after you were given up for adoption. Ironic, actually, since one of your past lives focused on helping others improve theirs."

Tony collapsed on his knees into the lily-pad-like plants in the lakebed. He held onto the central monolith for support. "There are so many questions, things I dreamt I would say to my father if I saw him again, but a conversation about other worlds wasn't one of them. And why wouldn't I remember any of this? I haven't had any dreams or memories of you or these caves."

"You've blocked it all out," Dagon said. "We worked with you for two years, until you were ten. The emotional turmoil of your abandonment, society's rejection of you because of your skills—it was too much. You didn't want to continue."

"How did I get here?" Tony asked. "I lived in Albuquerque with my adoptive parents at the time."

Dagon pointed to something behind Tony. He didn't have to look. He knew the giant spider waited. "Out-of-body travel. Mapiya guided you here. Unlike the earth arachnid, these are sentient souls. Her myriad of eyes watched you closely on your journeys, her eight limbs can touch into eight different dimensions at once and she can detect danger with the hairs on her legs. You and Mapiya had a very rare bond. She considered herself a mother figure to you."

Tony turned to look at Mapiya. He saw his eight-year-old-self clearly in her endless gaze. A sense of anguish and loss seemed to emanate from her body in waves. But there was something else. Mapiya glanced down at the ground and away from Tony.

Disappointment.

Tony glanced from Dagon and his father to Mapiya. "I'm sorry. I don't even know what abilities I have."

"Your connection to the universe is as strong as your father's. Your talents are endless."

"Mapiya—does she have anything to do with Cody's fascination between the tarantula hawk wasp and the tarantula?"

"It was his animal totem," Dagon said. "From his past life. Interesting, considering how terrified he is of Mapiya."

Mapiya stepped over Tony, her abdomen above his head. Her bulk blocked out the ceiling. Yet he didn't feel afraid. He got the sense she was trying to protect him from the shock to come.

"Why is my father in that stone tower? Why isn't he speaking?"

"His is but a memory," Dagon said. "You brought him here."

Dagon stroked the long hairs on her sturdy legs. "Unlike your father, your talents are surfacing again. And they can't be stopped. Like it or not, you are going to become another of Galiena's race—one of the Empyreans of the Milky Way.

Mapiya shrunk herself to half her size while Dagon turned to walk away.

"Wait. What about Joe, Brandon and Jacenda?"

Dagon didn't look back when he answered. "I believe you should be more worried about Jacenda."

53

A spectacular orange-red sunset took Jacenda's breath away. She could hear traffic from the freeway along with the roar of a jet plane overhead.

The re-creation of a round adobe pithouse stood on one side of a walkway. On the opposite side was a rectangular walled compound consisting of two small pueblos and a central community area. Jacenda glanced down the paved pathway to see a long, oval-shaped depression in the hard desert earth, which she recognized as a Hohokam ballcourt. In the distance was a platform mound with remains of ruins on top, along with a group of adobe structures at the base.

I'm at the Pueblo Grande Museum in Phoenix.

Shivers went down her spine and she glanced around in apprehension. She had been to the museum before. This time was different. The atmosphere changed and the city noises ceased. Normally grateful for silence and solitude among big city life, this quiet felt unnerving.

The cavern she was in with Joe and Brandon had no ruins. Yet she found herself transported from the enigmatic, underground setting among the Four Corners to Phoenix, 500 miles away.

Jacenda sensed someone watching. A man stood at the top of the platform mound, staring at her. The rapidly encroaching darkness hid his features, yet she knew it had to be Cody.

You bastard! How can you be here after being bitten by a rattlesnake? Why are you here?

As she asked the question in her mind, she knew the answer. This place, now in the midst of central Phoenix, was once her home among the Hohokam. Like Tiponi's showdown with the beast from Jacenda's prehistoric past, she realized there would be a final culmination of events between her and Cody.

He descended from the platform mound, and as he did, he began to change. She didn't understand how he could have the strength. He came closer and she could see the monstrosity he morphed into—a tall, bulky creature with the mass of a lion.

No, this is much bigger.

Her whole body began to quake and her legs felt like they would give way. This time, there was no place to hide. The confrontation had started.

A male voice within her mind started to scream. "Jacenda, where are you?" It wasn't Brandon.

She tried to focus, to let them know her location, but she couldn't concentrate with the half-coyote, half-javelina creature coming at her. She recognized the beast from her regression into her past life among the peaceful, desert-dwelling culture.

The voice continued to yell in her mind. He sounded so familiar.

Cody was only thirty feet away. Saliva swayed from his fierce jaws before dropping onto the pavement as he ran. She watched in terror while it snarled and grunted in an effort to get to her.

Jacenda turned and started to run. Tawa's voice from her recent vision reverberated throughout her head. "Not even you were aware when you mixed the recipe for transformation, your demise would be the death of Nukpana."

She hoped the present didn't follow the past. If so, she would have to die to stop Cody, and she wasn't willing to go that easy. She realized she had to stand her ground. Stopping to face him, she heard the male voice yelling in desperation inside her mind. "Jace, it's Tony. I hope you can hear me. Look in your pocket."

Jacenda felt the piece of petrified wood, but something else was in her pocket.

The coyote-javelina beast stopped five feet from Jacenda when she removed the jade pendant along with the wood.

How the hell did I end up with this?

It observed the petrified wood closely. She saw a glimmer of fear in the hellion's eyes. It backed up a few steps.

Jacenda felt a strong presence next to her, though she could see no one. She wondered if it was Lorelei.

A firm hand grabbed hers. She looked to see an opaque image of Tony next to her. His touch brought another memory of her prehistoric identity at about the age of ten, holding a boy's hand. It felt protective and safe.

She stared at him in disbelief. *You were my brother.*

Cody continued to back away from Jacenda. She didn't know if he retreated because of the petrified wood, the pendant, or both. The gift from Tiponi had led to the demise of Cody's past self. Jacenda understood Cody was remembering his own death among the ancient cotton fields.

Tony's voice came from next to her. "The pendant," he whispered.

She put the jade turtle in her right hand and Tony placed his hand over hers.

The beast cautiously stepped forward, watching Jacenda.

"He's going to kill me," Jacenda said. "And I'm not sensing the energy from this place to be able to escape."

Cody cocked his intimidating animal head to the right in curiosity. He didn't seem to know she had company.

He opened his jaws, bared his teeth and leaned back on his haunches—ready to attack. Jacenda thought of Tiponi, dying at the hands of Nukpana.

I'm about to be killed by my past.

The pendant still in her hand, she thought of the scene the giant tarantula had shown her, Joe and Brandon of Cody attempting to steal the rock art panel.

He leapt at her. She screamed and closed her eyes right before his massive bulk landed on top of her.

No oppressive weight or bone-crushing jaws descended upon her. She opened her eyes and looked around. Cody had vanished.

She glanced down and noticed a plate-sized tarantula at her feet. That's when she realized Tony had also disappeared.

54

Joe gazed up at the perfectly round hole in the ceiling of what Joe considered the "Cave of the Elements," due to the extreme weather changes within its chamber. The circumference seemed to be enough for him, Jacenda and Brandon to fit through.

Where does it go?

The opening had appeared suddenly, revealing the striking streaks of pink, purple and orange of sunset.

"There's no way. We came too far underground to be seeing sky." Brandon looked at his watch. "Yet it is almost six, which is the right time for sunset."

"Not sure how we get up there. Or if we're supposed to," Joe said.

Brandon glanced around at the inside of the cave to the terra and astra maps of Orion. "Where's Jace? She was here a minute ago."

Joe and Brandon searched the mysterious chamber.

"Not again." Brandon ran his hand threw his hair in frustration.

Joe wondered if the window to the world above was a deliberate distraction.

"Relax. We both know she'll turn up safely. Maybe she's in another part of the cave system."

"How are we supposed to escape this place? And we still have to find Tony as well as Jacenda."

Something blocked out the brilliant colors of twilight. Joe looked up to see a person staring down at him and Brandon—a proud, elderly

Native American man dressed in a long, elaborately beaded ceremonial robe, wearing moccasins and a coyote skin headdress. He held a wooden staff with a carved eagle head at the top.

A shiver traveled down Joe's spine.

Brandon stood next to Joe, staring up at the shaman. "Is he for real?"

Joe didn't take a breath. "He used to be. His name is Cheveyo and he was my father figure and mentor."

The shadow of another person approached Cheveyo's spirit and stood next to him.

"Oh, wow," Brandon said. "Joe, do you see what I see?"

Mattie held Cheveyo's hand. Her long grey hair cascaded forward as she observed Joe and Brandon.

Joe stumbled back a step. "He's one of you."

"Yesssss," she whispered.

Joe closed his eyes tightly and opened them again. Mattie and Cheveyo had vanished. Instead a wooden ladder led to the opening where he had seen his mentor.

Joe took one last look around the cave and at the Orion maps. He motioned for Brandon to go up first. After Brandon stepped off the ladder and into the last colors of twilight, Joe climbed up the rungs.

He ascended into the chilly night air. Brandon stared, mesmerized, at the new surroundings. He and Brandon weren't at the original entrance near the farmhouse. They weren't even near Lowry Pueblo or in the Four Corners. The two of them stood between the blowhole and ballcourt at Sunset Crater Wupatki National Monument, near Flagstaff, Arizona. The red sandstone remnants of the structures that the prehistoric Sinagua hunter-gatherers and farmers called home erupted from a spectacular landscape of mesas, buttes and desert grasslands.

The magnificent Wupatki pueblo, once four stories high, enticed visitors to explore its well-constructed walls, niches and rooms.

"I can't believe this," Brandon said.

Joe stared into the blowhole. "It's interesting that we not only ended up hundreds of miles south. We're also by a feature associated with a large system of underground fissures. This is supposedly one of several found in this area and they held a special significance for the people who lived here. There are also Navajo medicine men who use blowholes for curing ceremonies."

Brandon knelt down and gazed into the darkness of the hole. "The scientific part of me says this isn't possible to go from a cave system near Cortez, Colorado to ancient ruins hundreds of miles away. Yet the other part of me, which has been learning about teleportation, astral travel, and dream reality, somehow realizes these subterranean worlds are much more than physical reality."

Joe nodded and looked up at Brandon. The ladder was more than their escape. It represented emergence into a new realm of existence and understanding.

Joe heard footsteps. He glanced behind him to see Tony in the center of the ballcourt.

55

A *shaft of light descended between two boulders, landing in the middle of a cave. Black soot covered the ceiling and highlighted the hundreds of realistic stars painted in white and yellow. The cave wall revealed a massive pair of painted eyes, two feet tall by two feet wide and a foot apart. The iris and pupils seemed to be gazing toward the stars. While she watched, they turned from green to blue to orange-red.*

I'm in the Caves of the Watchers.

She detected something different about the stunning pictograph. The eyes seemed angry. Lorelei followed their gaze to the stars and realized they weren't nearly as bright as when she had first discovered them. Part of the ceiling had caved in and a rope hung from a hole at the top.

This chamber didn't cave in by accident. Someone smashed their way through.

Suddenly, her view changed. Lorelei observed from behind the wall—to see through the enigmatic eyes themselves. She shifted focus from the man-made heavens to a person at the bottom of the cave. A man with short dark hair laid face up, unconscious. At first, she thought he had fallen. She noticed a saw on the opposite side of the chamber. Sorrow overcame her when she understood the stranger had attempted to remove the panel with the unusual, living rock art.

But the man was no stranger. Without the facial scars, without the unkempt, scraggly hair, Cody looked completely different; attractive even.

While she watched the madman who had caused so much terror throughout the Four Corners, Lorelei caught a human shape forming next to Cody's lifeless body.

Paul, no! Stay away.

Cody began to stir. He opened his eyes and looked up at Paul. He sat up slowly and looked around the chamber in confusion.

56

Lorelei heard invisible fires crackling nearby, occasional footsteps resounding outside a room of the Wupatki Great House, and distant chanting accompanied by drums. Her psychic senses were picking up the past at Sunset Crater Wupatki National Monument, north of Flagstaff, Arizona. Only days before, Brandon, Joe and Tony had mysteriously traveled from the extensive cave system in the Four Corners to Wupatki. Before Brandon and Joe climbed to the surface, Joe had seen his beloved father figure from his childhood.

Did Cheveyo have something to do with their bizarre journey? Or did the magical Orion map send Brandon and Joe to one of its ancient sites associated with the stars?

Lorelei hadn't been able to explore the subterranean paradise near Lowry Pueblo with Joe, Tony, Brandon or Jacenda, but she hoped to find a clue tying ancient sites near Flagstaff, including Sunset Crater Wupatki, Walnut Canyon and Homolovi, to the maps of the Orion constellation.

She smiled watching Ian, Paul, Joe and Mandy wander through the ballcourt at the end of the path. Joe and Mandy kept saying they wanted to take things slow, but the way they looked at each other said the opposite. Mandy had her own home in Flagstaff, but Lorelei's psychic sense detected an upcoming move, probably within the next six months.

Lorelei couldn't understand why the skull had bestowed itself upon her at Cutthroat Castle, nor why she had thought it from a recent murder. She assumed the skull was that of a victim from Cody's prehistoric past—possibly a family member of the desperate phantom who had dragged her into the kiva to relive the horrendous tragedy of his wife and child. The skull continued to haunt her dreams. She understood the morbid object would reappear—perhaps as a clue to Galiena and her race.

Lorelei approached Brandon in a room marked "17" next door. The once two-story pueblo had served as living quarters for park rangers during the 1930s. He observed Tony and Jacenda as they walked down the paved trail along the main structure.

"You have no reason to be jealous."

Brandon smiled and pulled Lorelei close. "I know. Their brother sister bond from the past is definitely carrying forward, and with the murder mystery being solved, Tony and Jacenda have more time to renew that relationship. Tony confided in Jacenda and me that he's attracted to a woman who works for the FBI, though he did say he hasn't pursued a relationship." He looked at Lorelei. "You probably knew that already."

She watched Tony curiously. She recalled the way he stared at Julie with the Evidence Response Team at Lowry Pueblo and wondered if she were his crush. "No. Maybe I'll get a vision once I get to know him better."

Lorelei and Brandon walked toward the others, who were leaving the ballcourt and heading back in her direction. Joe stopped in his tracks, staring at his phone. Ian, Paul and Mandy also stopped to see what was happening. Joe looked up and motioned for Lorelei and Brandon to meet him.

She and Brandon glanced at each other and increased their walking pace to meet up with Joe. "Where are Tony and Jacenda?" Joe made a call on his cell. "I have some news. Come see me by the ballcourt."

A minute later, Lorelei glanced up to see Tony and Jacenda running toward them from the opposite side of the Wupatki pueblo.

Joe sighed. "I found out some news about Cody. We all know he was found in the Caves of the Watchers a few days ago, lying on the ground near the pictograph considered to be the watchers."

"Of course," Ian said. "Lore and Paul both saw him. He ended up there after Jacenda's encounter with Cody's beast form in Phoenix."

Tony glanced at Jacenda. "Maybe the end of his shapeshifting transformations were brought about by memories of his death in that same form from his past life."

Jacenda put her arm around Brandon. "I didn't *consciously* do anything to send him to those caves near Wickenburg. I've never been there myself."

"With this group of talent, there are always more questions than answers at times. Anyways, we found out Cody's been stealing rock art all over the Southwest," Joe said. "He's been removing sections of petroglyph panels in Utah, Nevada and Arizona. The crimes started soon after his layoff as a transportation inspector, probably in order to make money. When I interviewed him, he only remembered the thefts, but not the kidnappings and murders. He doesn't even recall being at the ruins in Hovenweep or Canyon of the Ancients."

"He's obviously going to have to do time for both crimes," Tony said. "Even though Dagon and the others were responsible for Cody being reborn as a rather horrible person."

Lorelei didn't understand how Galiena could have allowed such a tragedy—the loss of a life, the terror his victims endured and the fact that Cody would have to pay for a much worse sin than stolen rock art.

Joe stared up at the sky, as if he were wondering the same thing. "I think Galiena and the others, the Empyreans as Dagon referred to them, might be trying to atone for this mistake with Cody."

Tony took a step closer to Joe. "What did you find out?"

Joe held up his phone. "The FBI is only trying Cody for the rock art thefts. When I asked about murder charges, this was the response." He passed his phone around. The text message read, "what murder?"

"Amazing," Tony said. "I wonder if Galiena and her race wiped out the memories of the FBI."

Everyone watched Tony, including Lorelei. After all, Dagon had told Tony that he was one of the Empyreans, like Galiena. Did Tony know more than he was letting on?

"I know what you're all thinking. Give me a break. I'm still in shock from the news about my ties to their race. I'm not sure I believe it. Nor do I have any idea how I ended up at the Wupatki ruins with Joe and Brandon, or with Jacenda during her final confrontation with Cody."

"From what Jacenda told me, it sounds like the pendant and the petrified wood might have worked together to stop Cody." Brandon pulled Jacenda close. "And in the nick of time."

What if Cody reverts back to his past? Lorelei looked at each of her friends. She knew they were thinking the same thing. Especially Mandy.

"Wait," Mandy said. "What if he's lying about his memories of the past few weeks? I'm not sure I feel safe."

"We gave him a lie detector test, which he passed. He truly believes he was only responsible for the rock art thefts." He put his arm around Mandy. "Don't worry. Cody's under 24-hour surveillance because of his shapeshifting and for a suicide watch. With everything that's happened, he's been thrown into a major depression. " Joe stared into a pueblo as if seeing something. "There's no way to know if Cody wanted the pendant just for its ability to enhance and maintain his level of power, or if his prehistoric identity knew about the underground realm we found. Dagon never mentioned anything about it."

Ian shook his head. "Pretty sad. I can't imagine waking up and finding I've been accused of kidnapping and murder. I wonder if Galiena has plans on helping Cody through all this. Not that he's the perfect guy by any means…"

Lorelei's thoughts wandered to each of the ancient cities that mapped to the Orion constellation, including Wupatki. Did they each have distinct underground realms? Brandon and Dale had discovered a portion of a westward passage near the main Wupatki structure after their first investigation. Could that tunnel also be a small portion of an extensive and mysterious network of subterranean cities and tunnels all over the Southwest? What about the Caves of the Watchers and tunnels under the Texas Canyon Ranch in Dragoon, Arizona?

The final colors of twilight faded and darkness overcame the ruins rapidly. Lorelei noticed spectral figures walking toward them from the east under the full moon. "Is everyone else seeing what I am?" She turned to look at everyone. Their attention was focused on a group of at least a hundred men, women and children heading in the direction of Wupatki— what used to be a major convergence point for various cultures, goods and ideas. The weary travelers carried animal skins, drums, and food.

In the lead was a noble, elderly Native American man dressed in a long, elaborately beaded ceremonial robe, wearing moccasins and a coyote skin headdress. He carried a wooden staff and his thick, shoulder-length hair blew behind him.

According to Joe's description, that looks like Cheveyo, Joe's mentor. Why is he leading an influx of ancient spirits?

Joe stared in awe and took a few steps toward the crowd, only fifty feet away.

The stately man in front stopped, raising his staff in the air. The prehistoric phantoms ceased their march and Cheveyo waved for Tony to stand next to Joe.

Lorelei held her breath. Cheveyo had been Joe's mentor. She realized Joe was about to be officially anointed as Tony's.

Cheveyo motioned for the two of them to kneel on the ground. Within seconds, Tony and Joe turned into dark shadows, barely lit by the encroaching full moon. Cheveyo, Tony and Joe vanished, along with the gathering of primitive Puebloan ancestors.

Mandy ran over to the spot where Joe had been. She glanced around repeatedly.

No words could describe what had taken place. No one spoke. Lorelei looked up to the heavens. The Orion constellation revealed itself exactly as on the celestial map Joe described, including the lines connecting the stars—the brightest of which were at the top of Orion. In her mind, she saw the words *Sunset Crater Wupatki, Homolovi* and *Walnut Canyon*; the ancient sites Joe, Brandon and Jacenda had seen on the ceiling of the enigmatic cavern.

Somewhere, a ritual had begun to remind two Native American men about their roots and meaning in the universe.

Lorelei watched the bizarre map in the sky slowly fade. She wondered if the long-lost, rejected memories of Joe and Tony held the answers pertaining to the Empyreans, the Orion maps and a series of caves, passages and subterranean cities throughout the Southwest—and possibly, the world.

Made in the USA
Middletown, DE
30 December 2019